BRINGING RAGNAROK

First of Fimbulwinter

Andrew M. Tanner

Broken Wagon Publishing

Published by Broken Wagon Publishing
Independence, Oregon, United States of America
Fourth Edition

Cover illustration and design by Miss Nat Mack
missnatmack.com

*Dedicated to all those who struggle against
the odds to make things better.*

CONTENTS

PART 1

The day is here when Bivrost breaks,
no Sun or Moon will rise.
When the dead rise from their graves,
and Surtur spreads his fire.
All you know will wither away,
and sink into the sea…

AMON AMARTH

A CAVE IN ICELAND

"**H**eya, Eryn? I just wanted to say how incredibly stupid this idea of yours is looking right about now."

Eryn replied with a mild curse. It echoed through the cavern before fading away into the dull noise of rocks disturbed by human footsteps. In the dim yellow light reflecting off the cavern walls, each the six young women and men could barely make out their friends' true shapes, the grotesquely distorted shadows cast by the cheap flashlight's beams strangely ominous against the cavern wall. Slowly but steadily they marched deep into the Icelandic mountain, leaving an effervescent orange plastic ribbon trailing behind them, marking the path back out to daylight.

"Leave her alone, Timur," Yarielis muttered, "I'm having fun. These cool rocks are making our footsteps sound strange."

Timur stooped as he stepped, felt for and found a loose pebble, and tossed it back over his shoulder in reply. He heard a startled cry, not the one he was expecting.

"Ow!" Kim growled. "Damn, dude, that little rock got me right in the cheek. Your aim sucks."

"Whoops, sorry about that, Kim! Chuck one at Yari for me, will you? But seriously, come on people, I'm all for adventure and glory and grand feats, but spelunking for lava in an

Icelandic volcano? Spring Break only a geologist could ever enjoy. And Yari."

"*Magma*, Timur. Magma." Loucas laughed slyly. "You know how Eryn gets."

Timur smirked – not that his friend could actually see it in the bad light, but he felt it was the thought that counted.

"Don't defend her, Loucas—when we agreed it was Eryn's turn to play 'Choose Your Spring Break Adventure' none of us thought that would mean mucking around the world's dingy hind end."

"And hungover." Kim moaned. "Don't forget the hangover. I can't."

Timur knew Kim wasn't bound to receive much sympathy on that point. The previous evening, a local geologist had challenged her to a drinking match. And lost, after a fierce contest that depleted a significant portion of the bar's supply of lager.

"You were the one who insulted Dr. Toek's work, not me! I told you that one has an ego. Most profs do, but his is bigger than most. Anyway, quit complaining, this is *fun*!"

Kim reached out her hands and made a strangling motion. No one saw the gesture, though.

"Eryn, you have to remember that not everyone has your tiny-person metabolism. Or the Irish-German genetic predisposition for efficient alcohol uptake. Damned Celtic-Anglo-Saxon... Germanic... whatever you have going on in your genetics."

Eryn's response was another, harsher curse as a sudden shift in the rocks under her feet almost made her roll her ankle. It was difficult to see much in the darkness: to conserve their collective battery power hers was the only light currently active, which wasn't at all conducive to... well, to much of anything.

Satisfied that karma had already bitten Eryn, Kim let her annoyance go and checked again to be sure the quiet man bringing up the rear hadn't managed to get lost. The fact that he wasn't talking very much didn't help her keep track of him.

"Still with us, Patrick?"

Their big friend grunted in reply. It echoed strangely off the surrounding rock. Instinct, or maybe long acquaintance, gave Kim the sense that something was bothering him.

"What's up? I know that brooding silence means something."

She heard him take a slow breath. "That sound keeps getting louder."

He spoke quietly, but the words seemed to float in the darkness, amplified among the echoes of their rock-mediated footfalls. Even Eryn, leading the column, heard him clearly. But she pressed on without comment.

"I don't like it either." Yari muttered.

Yari didn't know it, but she spoke for all of them. The six friends walked on in silence, listening as the strange noise Patrick was referring to—a sort of groaning, rattling sigh, like one might expect from a giant having a bad night's sleep —grew in intensity with each step they took. It was deeply unsettling. The mountain overhead seemed somehow alive. Not a quality one likes in a volcano, especially when inside it.

The objective of this little outing, they'd all agreed that morning, was to see lava, or magma, to Eryn. Like most scientists, she tended towards the pedantic when certain terms of particular interest were casually abused. A phenomenon they had experienced to the limit of their collective patience just the night before, when a dozen of that strange tribe called geologists had gathered at a small conference organized by, naturally, Eryn. She had brought them together to discuss the thrilling topic of "Volcanic chemical impacts on medieval Icelandic society."

Not that *she* had any particular interest in the topic, but it had made for a good excuse to fund a trip to Iceland: home to some of the world's most active volcanoes. And, perhaps more importantly: a place she had not yet had the chance to explore. Being able to drag a pack of "research assistants" along with her was made just another bonus, possible by her demonstrated knack for creative funding proposals.

The timing of the conference couldn't have been better. The six friends had a long-standing agreement to rotate who would plan the group's spring vacation each year. After traveling to Sri Lanka with Timur and Puerto Rico with Loucas and Yarielis, it was now Eryn's turn to choose a Spring Break getaway. Of course, if they had known that she would take them to Akureyri, a town on Iceland's forbidding northern coast, they probably would have objected. A lot. Of all the vacation choices available to a group of flatmates from Vancouver, British Columbia, *this* was no one's top choice but Eryn.

At least it was free.

Loucas, getting tired of listening to the various repetitive noises that accompanied their progress through the dismal cavern, tried to steer the discussion to less conflicted waters.

"The thing I don't get is how are we going to get close enough to see the fiery stuff, anyway? Won't convection make things just a bit... uncomfortable?"

"*Great* point, Loucas!" Timur laughed. "Wish you'd have thought of it about twelve hours ago, *before* we started on this hike."

"We won't get that close, guys!" Eryn insisted. "I talked to the local experts enough last night to make sure the area is safe. At least, I think I understood them correctly. They speak great English most of the time, but beer makes accents hard for me to parse. But I'm like 85% sure that Dr. Toek said that when we make it through here, we'll be able to see it at a safe distance. Ish."

"Was that before or after Kim drank him under the table?"

"Shut. Up. Timur!"

Their banter continued, in part to pass the time, but also to soothe their collective and fast-growing sense unease. Even Eryn, usually outwardly stoic in the face of adversity, was feeling the strain. None of them could have put it into words even if they had the presence of mind to try, but all felt the same: like a weight, pressing in from all sides, steadily increasing as they continued on. The darkness made it hard to tell, but the cavern seemed to be twisting perpetually downward and to the left, as if the molten rock excavating the dark cavern so long ago had struck a substance it could not burn through, and was deflected like a mole burrowing around a tree root.

Hands on the walls, which for the past few minutes had steadily narrowed to a width of only a few feet, they bunched up as they worked their way around a sudden, sharp corner, Eryn illuminating the way forward with her flashlight. She was wondering if it was time to switch to a backup, given how dim the light had become, when without warning the cave walls gave way entirely, opening onto a broad shelf of rock. As their eyes adjusted to take in a suddenly broadened horizon, they could see that a bank of low, dark clouds obscured the sun from sight. These were illuminated from below by a red glow that reflected eerily from the smoky particulates suspended within.

"Whoah, who dropped us into Vvardenfell?"

"Or Mordor?"

"Same thing, more or less."

"Guys! Guys! Holy hellfire Batman, would you look at that!"

Loucas and Patrick's awed mumbles were drowned out by Eryn's cry. They turned and saw that she was pointing a bit to her left, about a mile distant, and well above the horizon. Across a misty chasm stood a mighty frozen peak, that soared from mist to cloud before disappearing into the haze. From a rift in the center of the mountain's nearest face a river of fire poured, flowing over a cliff and plunging down into a ravine, disappearing into the misty chasm which seethed and roiled where the fire tore it asunder. The mist itself seemed to boil up from the depths, source unknown.

Timur whistled softly. "Well, Eryn. Thanks for this: an awesome sightseeing tour of Hell. Is there a coffee kiosk around? Or a wifi signal? I'm craving a burger and a coke and a good long sit."

"Come on, Timur, isn't it *amazing*?" Patrick exclaimed. "Oh gods that be I need to take a picture of this. Damn am I glad I have my camera. Is anyone's GPS app working on their phone? We need to geotag this!"

Loucas fiddled with his phone, while Kim walked to Eryn's side, staring at the fiery clouds. Her hangover seemed to subside, subsumed by a sense of wonder, and a tingle of fear crawling up her spine. A wind arose, strong enough to tear her hair from the constraints of the loose bun held in place by a single hair band. Its bulk whipped free above Eryn's head, a black cloud hovering over her friend's field of unkempt, boyish, dirty-blond hair.

"Wow." Patrick said. Fast, repeated clicks made it obvious that the single roll of film he had brought would be depleted in short order. He made no further comment, remaining fixated on the scene before him.

"Guys, I bet you can see this from space." Loucas mumbled, almost whispering.

"You have *no* idea, kid. Wanna see? I can show you. All of you!"

Loucas hadn't really expected a reply, much less one from a voice that seemed to come from no place in particular. The six looked at one another in sudden shock. No one spoke at first.

"You lot are dense! If you would actually look about, you might notice the one important thing in this entire scene that matters. Me! And for the record, the place is called *Ginnungagap*. Hel—correctly spelled with a *single* l—mind you, is much bleaker and colder. Lots more tortured undead, too. Oh, and my daughter makes her home there, hence, the name. Given for a reason, so you probably don't want to visit. Not that you have much of a choice—but we can talk about that later!"

The laughter they heard began like—and with—a thunderclap. Overcome by old instinct, Timur crouched down like a startled creature, head swiveling, his eyes examining everything with intensity. His heart thudded into a drum solo, and his breathing strained to match the beat.

Kim, herself also operating on instinct, saw Timur's reaction and moved to stand by his side, placing a protective hand on his shoulder. Patrick moved to join them. Eryn and Loucas remained frozen in place, confused and alarmed. Yarielis remained outwardly calm, but her head swiveled slowly side to side, and her eyes were wide as she tried to process what was happening.

"What the *hell* is going on? Who are you? *Where* are you?"

Timur's growled queries startled his friends almost as much as the disembodied voice—their friend seemed to have transformed in front of them, from a confident young man to a wary animal.

The voice just chuckled in reply. Sans thunderclap, but carrying a deeply mocking undertone. Like a spider might use before playing with food.

"All excellent questions! I encourage you to seek answers. Hey, I might even be willing to help—if you ask politely. And also start looking around. Because before I can help you, you'll have to help me. I'm in a bit of a... situation, you might call it."

Timur maintained his crouch, looking carefully at each and every seeming variation in the landscape, near and far. Kim patted his thick, dark hair.

"I'm sure it's just some stupid Icelandic joke, Timur. No big deal."

Patrick grunted in agreement with Kim, and put a hand on Timur's other shoulder. Timur relaxed—slightly. He stood back up, but his eyes kept darting from rock to rock, the chasm's edge to the distant burning peak. He was starting to be capable of logical thought again. He focused on controlling his breath. On coming back to the present. It wasn't like the old days – he wasn't in Kashmir anymore. He glanced at Patrick before scanning the scene yet again, focusing on bringing his body back to baseline, like he'd been taught.

"Yeah, I know, I know." Timur sighed. "But you know where I grew up. Not a fan of things going boom. Or *disembodied voices* shouting strange things at me. About ginn... gin-nun-ga-gap?"

Suddenly, surprised into forgetting his fear, he stood up and cocked his head, looking back at his friends. Then, he laughed aloud.

"Wait, guys: *Ginnungagap* and *Hel*? That's all straight out of old Norse mythology. Which was compiled by a dude in Iceland about a thousand years ago. We're totally getting messed with by some local. Eryn, how many of your geologist buddies *did* you tell about this trip? Do you think Dr. Toek is getting back at Kim, or what?"

Eryn looked at him, not convinced. Smirking, Timur pulled out his phone to show them. He pulled out his phone and held the power button. Nothing happened. He tried again. Same result.

"Uh, guys, my phone is dead. I know for a fact I charged it this morning. Um, W-T-F, mates?"

"What? I thought it was just mine." Loucas said.

They all checked their phones. All were dead. The disembodied voice chuckled again.

"OK then, I'm going to have to hold your hands on this, aren't I? Kids these days! As if you were going to get a wireless signal out here—whether or not *here* is anywhere near Iceland. Put away your plastic brains and TURN SOUTH! I assume you can figure out where *south* is! If not, never mind: LOOK at ME."

They all turned as directed, almost without realizing what they were doing—frankly, *south* didn't mean much in a context where there were no familiar reference points, or even a hint of where the sun was overhead. But they weren't moved by any will of their own: they shifted their bodies as the voice commanded, physically compelled and unable to resist.

And as they looked to the south, they saw a curious thing. A desiccated tree clung on for dear life, half a foot from the chasm's edge, roots cast into the barest accumulation of silt wedged into cracks in the weathered rock. A sight odd enough in a nearly treeless place like Iceland; odder by far was that right by it the six friends could discern the front half of a bare foot, waving madly in the air with toes wiggling as if it were desperately trying to catch their attention.

No compulsion was necessary this time. They made their way past dark tumbled boulders to the desperate tree and the strange appendage, which seemed to simply appear out of the rock. Yari broke out into a run, poofy, kinky hair flying everywhere, freed from a constraining sweater hood. Lou-cas, always protective of his sister, ran after her.

"What the... guys!"

Yari had just reached the tree when she stopped and stood, staring helplessly at the madly wiggling toes. They *did* appear out of nowhere—not out of any hidden crack or hole in the rock, but from literally nowhere. They heard more disembodied laughter.

"Yes, strange isn't it? Here's the thing, kiddo—I have to ask you and your buddies a question. I get an answer, then I can explain a thing or two. But only then! Silly rules, but rules they are."

It didn't take long for Yari's companions to arrive, Timur last of all, looking suspiciously in all directions, but with a knowing smirk still playing across his face. The toes ceased wiggling, and sort of stood at attention. The voice made a sound as if clearing its throat.

"Timur, is it? Took your time, kid! Well anyway—good. You are all here now. Well done! I can now put the necessary question to you: Will you agree to help me? I'm in a bit of a jam, and need assistance."

The six looked at one another—half confused, half bemused. Whatever prank was being pulled on them, it certainly was strange. No one answered. Kim and Eryn caught each other's gaze, held it for a moment, then mutually burst out laughing.

"Alright, who is messing with us?" Eryn asked, smiling and shaking her head. "Who did we all talk to last night? What's the trick? Dr. Toek, is that you?"

Eryn's question was met with a chorus of shrugs. The truth was simple: a lot of people. The restaurant-pub had been packed. Not much else for a visitor to do in northern Iceland in March but hang out at the bar, or go spelunking in a volcanic mountain. Unless you liked herding sheep, or fishing. And most of the locals had spoken English, so there had been plenty of talk and even more banter. Half the town could be in on the joks.

Silence ensued. The voice, having posed its question, now remained stubbornly silent. The foot and toes shifted, orienting towards each of them in turn. As if it were looking at them, waiting for an answer from someone.

"Oh what the... alright, I'm in." Eryn laughed again. "Anyone else?"

The nods and shrugs of all around her told Eryn that it was her show. Only Timur seemed to hesitate, his grin suddenly fading.

"What are you thinking, Timur?"

He shook his head. "Eryn, I'm thinking that this whole situation seems... strange. And kind of dangerous, for some reason. I have no idea why. Maybe just residual PTSD. But you know what? Why the hell not. If you all are, I'm game too. Whatever prank the local yokels have set up to mess with us—let's do this. Pull back the curtain, strange voice! Timur Tarkhan will help ye in thy quest for... whatever! Shoes, even!"

There was a long moment of silence. Timur had ended his joking speech by pulling a ridiculous hero-esque pose.

And then they heard a shout of triumph wild and fierce:

"And so there we are! What is to be, *LET IT BE DONE!*"

It was the same voice as before, or seemed to be, but now it manifested as a piercing scream. They all covered their ears, and it felt as if the earth itself had begun to wail. The world shook like the mother of all earthquakes was upon them. There wasn't time to cry or reach out—their vision became a sudden blur of color and shape.

Then everything just stopped. Their surroundings had

changed completely. They were standing in a wide grotto, a circle of trees masking a surrounding wall of barren rock. At the foot of the wall, a few steps from them, a man lay naked on a bed of sharp, obsidian like rocks which, given the trickles of blood dripping from his skin, had punctured his flesh in several places. Manacles embraced both arms and one leg, each connected to a chain that in turn was embedded securely into the rocks around him. One foot, free from chains, was stretched out towards them.

The groaning sound they had heard in the cavern now filled the air. It was the man's breath; pained, ragged. His eyes were closed, teeth clenched, his hands straining in futility against the chains as if to ward off a blow. Their eyes were drawn upwards, to the source of his fear. There, in the branches, coiled a massive snake—an evil-looking, luminescent creature that seemed to mix the very worst aspects of cobras and pythons.

The snake's head turned towards them. Some sort of greenish substance, bubbling and probably poisonous, poured from its jaws, dripping down onto the stone next to the man, whose flesh seemed to sense—and cringe away from—the substance. The creature seemed to have been interrupted by their arrival, but now that it had seen and judged the source of the disturbance, it began to turn towards the man: twisting, lowering itself, stretching towards its prey. A trail of venom tracked towards him, the rock steaming and dissolving at its touch.

Yarielis began moving towards the monster, stretching her arms as if by instinct, grasping at it in hopes of stopping it. Its reply was to fix a black eye on her, and hiss. Some of the venom sputtered forward, and landed on the chained man's chest. His eyes opened, and bulged. Every limb convulsed, and he writhed in pain. He seemed to choke back a wild scream.

But after the briefest moment, his mouth twisted, changed—taking on a shape that was somewhere between a scream and a grimace. Before Yari could take another step, he shifted. Where he had been reclining a moment before, now only three manacles and chains remained, clattering to the rock. They had a brief vision: a shape like an eagle flashed towards the serpent, and with slashing talons severed the creature's head from the rest of its body. Both fell to the ground together, poison flowing from the wounds, bubbling, consuming the rock underneath. In short order the serpent's corpse and a significant chunk of stone had disappeared into a sickly green vapor.

The man reappeared in front of them, back in human shape, and let out a scream of triumph that shook the grotto, sending cracks up the rock wall beyond the extent of their vision. That scream seemed to enter into each of them, striking like a thousand needles, throwing them into a moment of pain unlike any they had ever imagined possible.

And then it was over.

The scene had shifted again, and silence enveloped them.

Now they stood, or seemed to stand, on an invisible platform high above the Earth. The man—clothed now in a t-shirt, jeans, and boots—stood in front of them, gazing down at the planet's surface. They followed his glance. At first, all they could see was a mass of blue and white filling their view —the skies and seas of the Northern Atlantic. It took their breath away—as any astronaut will attest, the first view of humanity's home from orbit is a life-changing experience.

But they could tell that something was very wrong with their home planet. A column of blackness, tinged with red, rose skyward, as if a great fire had been started on the surface of the world. It took them some time to realize what it was they were seeing, the actual scale of it: Iceland, all of Iceland, so far as they could see, was on fire. A great fissure bisected the entire island, spewing fire and smoke from the bowels of the planet into the atmosphere. *So much* fire and smoke. The latter, upon reaching the upper atmosphere, billowed out in all directions—a cloud of darkness that showed no sign of stopping until it would engulf the entire Earth in an ashy winter night.

"Happy Fimbulwinter, Midgard! The countdown to the end of days is *finally* over and gone!"

The man laughed happily as he shouted, then turned slowly towards them. He was grinning, his lips pulled back in an insane rictus, his eyes glittering with mirth and glee and malice all at once. He was in this moment, to each of them, somehow simultaneously the most beautiful and the most frightening person they had ever seen. He laughed again, and stared at each in turn.

"Well, aren't we all a dazed and confused bunch! Come on, celebrate! Time for Ragnarok, children! Twilight of the Gods! The utter and most final end to all Nine Worlds! Not what you expected when you had breakfast this morning, is it? Ah well, that's what happens when you play good Samaritan to Loke, son of Laufey.

Through the confusion and fear, Timur's attention focused at mention of the name.

"Loke? *Loke?* Ginnunagap. Hel. Fimbulwinter. That snake, the chains—*Loke?* The Norse trickster god?"

He grinned at Timur.

"Right you are! Or, close enough for my purposes. I knew you'd figure it out eventually. Loke, yes, that's me! You people have muddled up all the old truths over the past few thousands of years. But Loke will work!"

Timur shook his head, laughing in a sort of stunned bemusement.

"This has to be some kind of trick. Psychoactive drugs and

crazy Icelandic geologists working together. *Loke* is a myth, a trickster figure from old mythology, kind of an archetype, like foxes in Japanese and European folklore. Definitely in the category of the *not real*. Someone is just screwing with our heads. What, does Iceland have a CIA secret underground psychological research center or something?"

Loke's eyes glittered, and he laughed again, as Timur trailed off uncertainly.

"Oh, an unbeliever in our midst! Oh, things are about to get *fun* for you! All of you, really. Ah, the plans I have for you all! The things you'll do for me! Trust me, kids, you are going to have *such* an adventure. But first things first. Time to assemble the family!"

The six of them stood, frozen, watching as the Earth became shrouded in fire-flecked darkness. Loke turned to gaze at it again. But he wasn't gazing at the Earth. They could tell, by some instinct, that he was looking through or beyond it, towards the infinity of stars beyond.

Something was moving there, at the edge of their vision. A swath of sky seemed to be shifting, fluctuating in a strangely familiar pattern, though of a magnitude almost beyond comprehension. Something huge was lurking, hidden in the sea of stars, a power that curved and distorted their light so that they seemed to be dancing to a weird, distorted melody.

Then it took shape: a serpent, slithering through space like an adder through grass—huger than the Earth, huger than the *sun*. They stood in enraptured terror as it came closer, and closer, and then suddenly the stars were no longer visible—it blotted them out. It advanced towards them with an open maw as wide as the horizon and just before it swallowed the Earth—the scene shifted. Without warning or transition, once again, everything around them simply changed.

They stood in what appeared to be a sort of concert hall or theater of gargantuan scope. They couldn't perceive its full extent. There was a stage, but it had no backing—it extended into apparently infinite starry depths. To each side both stage and enclosing walls likewise disappeared into an unseen, misty distance. These walls were elegantly adorned, carved with intricate patterns, and parallel to them were set ten rows of luxurious and comfortable looking chairs; thrones, really. The ceiling too seemed not to exist: above their heads was a field of stars arranged in wholly unfamiliar constellations.

In these chairs sat innumerable figures, varied in shape and color and size. The strange alien audience watched the stage, apparently transfixed though no performance seemed to be underway, either not noticing or not caring that Loke and six humans had just appeared in their midst.

One of the throne-chairs, closest at hand, was exponentially more lavishly ornamented than all the others and taller than all the rest. Upon it sat a man of human shape, dressed in green robes lending him an air of total authority. His pale and wise face was half covered by a shroud of some sort, so that only one eye was visible—keen and piercing, green, flanked by strands of shining black hair.

Loke strolled forward to the foot of the chair, opening his arms wide to embrace the man, who upon noticing Loke stood up and ran to the floor, returning the embrace with gusto.

"Hello Father! So it is finally time, then?"

Loke grinned. "You know it is, Jormungand, oh favorite son of mine! Fimbulwinter and Ragnarok, ahoy! We meet at dinner to lay our plans. I'm sure your sister's banquet hall will make a fine command center for the End of Days, don't you?"

Jormungand grinned fiercely and nodded. His cold eyes

glittered, and they could hear the cruel eagerness in his voice.

"Count me in, pops. I was getting so bored with managing this petty empire—have you *seen* this part of Midgard? A boil on the arse of time and space. I'll be happy to watch it burn. See you at Hel's!"

Loke roared in approval, then without warning the scene shifted again.

They were now standing in a cavern. The sound of rushing water was loud and close at hand, and the cave was lit by a dozen burning torches. The walls appeared to be made of obsidian, and they glittered in the torchlight. Under the far wall a simple wooden desk was set next to a narrow, spare bed. Nothing else adorned the chamber.

But it was inhabited. Another man—tall, powerfully built, with rugged features and long, shaggy hair that hung to the shoulders—reclined on the bed. At first, it looked like he was sleeping. But it became apparent that his eyes were open, and he was staring at the ceiling. He didn't appear to notice that they were there. Loke made sure that didn't last.

"Fenris, my boy! You look well, despite spending the last few millennia stuck in a hole. Don't I know how that goes! At least you aren't being ritually tortured by a venomous serpent. But—good news! The time has come! An ending at last to our mutual suffering. You in?"

Fenris' head slowly turned, as he appraised Loke and his companions.

"Depends, Dad—did you bring dinner? Or at least something interesting to read? You want to talk about torture, how about being stuck with nothing to do but play with the few among the Aelfar who want to experience what it feels like to be eaten alive."

He stood up slowly, and fixed a gaze on each of Loke's companions. It was unsettling, like the gaze of a ravenous beast deciding which tasty morsel to sample first.

Loke casually looked them over, considering them one by one.

"Mmm, sorry kiddo, I have a use for all of them. But have no fear—Fimbulwinter is here! Plenty of food for my growing baby boy. Come on, let's go to dinner—brother Jormungand is ready, and you *know* your sister will be cool with a crowd!"

Fenris looked disappointed. But then he grinned, and his grin was possibly worse than his stare—all the difference between realizing that the creature in front of you wants to literally have you for dinner, and knowing that before he does he'll have a little violent fun as an appetizer.

"I'll make due. But I've got a little problem to take care of, first, dad. You know the one."

Loke snapped his fingers.

"Oh yes, the fetter! I forgot about that."

Fenris growled more like a wolf than a man, and tapped his neck.

"I know, I know, how could I? But hey, kid, I've had problems of my own. And it isn't *my* fault you trusted Odin and company long enough for them to stick you with this Svartaelf trickery. To not realize that they would happily sacrifice Tyr's hand to keep you imprisoned for the duration of existence? Or even just to prove a point? Gotta be better at reading Aesir and Vanir intentions, son-of-mine!"

Fenris growled again.

Loke rolled his eyes, reached out, and touched Fenris' neck. There, hard to see in the torchlight, a strand of something that seemed as thin and supple as silk was wound around his neck. A quick tugging motion was all it took for Loke to break the necklace.

In that instance, Fenris changed. Or seemed to. Though he only smiled for the barest instant, in it they were granted a terrifying vision: a massive, monstrous creature in wolf-form prowled forward across a grassy field, poison dripping from it's jaws, withering the grass below. Then it stopped, and looked towards the sky. The moon hung there, and the wolf's head distorted, opening wider than seemed possible, lower jaw falling to the tortured ground, upper jaw stretching wider and wider: the moon seemed to fit inside it.

The wolf's jaws snapped shut. The moon was gone. The wolf threw its head to the stars, howling a triumphant note.

Then once again, everything changed.

They were seated in a hall of some sort—to call it medieval would be appropriate, though eerie and weird also fit the bill. Two long, ornate wooden tables were set on either side of a firepit filled to the brim with sizzling charcoal yet oddly enough producing no discernible heat. Discordant and haunting music stung their ears. The hall itself appeared to have been carved from or assembled with stone, and was lit by lamps arrayed along the walls, giving off a sickly-green sort of light that made the entire scene appear like a dreary dream.

Loke, Jormungand, and Fenris sat across from them, engaged in what seemed to be a quiet, urgent conversation—the details of which they couldn't make out. The six friends looked at one another, dazed and confused, trying to make some sense of what was happening, but were quickly interrupted.

A tall, thin figure approached. Though her head was bowed, pale flesh could be discerned from behind the straggly locks of black hair that helped veil what of her body was not covered by a white gown. She moved rather quickly despite her feet shuffling along the stone floor. Loke looked up from the debate, and flashed her a wicked smile.

"Hel! Daughter of mine, you look as well as ever!"

She walked to her father Loke's side, and made a slight bow.

"You always do joke at the most inappropriate times, Father."

Hel turned her head slightly, and they could make out one of her eyes as it gazed at them with malice. She stood still as ice as Loke whispered quietly to her, gazing at them like a hungry lion might watch a trapped gazelle.

Loke shifted his focus back to his sons. Hel pushed a wayward clump of hair behind an ear, and when she spoke her voice was a discomfiting mismatch of growling baritone and tinny alto.

"Welcome, honored guests, to the banquet of the dead. Do not bother with the plates and silverware—just for show, after all. In my hall, guests only feel more hunger the longer they remain!"

They stared. There wasn't anything else they could do, each felt as if they were frozen in place, though all wanted to look away. Hel's was a mashup of two very different bodies: one like the corpse of a beautiful bride-to-be, taken by plague on the morning of her wedding; the other a monster, skin covered in boils and sores, hanging loose over a badly deformed skeleton.

She stared right back at them at them. Loke looked between them, then shook his head and laughed.

"Alright, alright, enough play: let's move forward with the operation, shall we? Here's the present situation."

He flicked his fingers, and a strange sort of glowing orb appeared in front of his face. They glimpsed golden tendrils like spun thread, writhing within a glowing sphere. Loke gazed at it for a few moments in deep concentration. Then he reached carefully into the sphere, and touched three spots, each located at a point where several threads seemed to mingle. He looked from the orb to his children.

"What do you say we try to stack the odds at Vegris a bit, eh?" We do a bit of wyrding and send them here, here, and… here. Hit those three points hard enough and along with our breakout—boom. Paradox. And a chance—tiny, infinitesimal, but still a chance—to defy the fate Voluspa foretold."

Loke waved his hand, and the orb disappeared. Then he smiled at the six again. His strange brood—Jormungand, Fenris, and Hel, grinned at them as well. Casually, cats playing with a doomed morsel.

"Here's the deal, children." Loke said. "You helped me, and so I owe you! I don't forget my promises – I'll show you *lots* of things you never dreamed existed. I don't forget *anything*, really. A problem, to be honest!"

"Anyhow! So, not only will I *not* feed you to Fenris just yet, I'll give you a starring role in what is to come. A real adventure. Epic, you might even call it. *If* you survive – which you probably won't. Not many will! So whaddya say? Want to help be responsible for bringing Ragnarok to the Nine Worlds?"

Loke didn't give them time to answer. His grin twisted into a wild, insane, lopsided snarl. His pale face seemed to fade, and the six friends half saw, half felt, tendrils of whirling shadow reach from him to them. A sudden, sharp pain struck each of them to the core, and they stopped seeing, hearing, feeling. Each of them felt as if they were being ripped apart in some strange vortex: they could all sense that they were being scattered, and tried to call out to one another, but to no avail.

THE WOLF'S LAIR

W hen the blinding pain had gone, Eryn felt her ability to think return, and realized her eyes were squeezed shut, teeth clenched and body rigid.

She opened her eyes. Then shut them again and rubbed her face with her hands.

Wherever she and her friends had been before, she, at least, wasn't there now. Instead, she was standing in the corner of a wood-walled conference room. In the center of the room was a large, rectangular, oak table, on top of which was a large map adorned with bright shapes and lines. Around the table stood around twenty men, most dressed in the same dour grey uniform, all with the same grim expression and tired eyes. Something about the scene looked strangely familiar, but the brief instant her eyes had been open was not enough for her to discern why.

She opened her eyes again. And then they opened wide as her heart skipped a beat. She recognized, in a sudden flash, exactly where she was, or at least, appeared to be. One of the men, standing at the center of the table—she knew him. No —she knew *of* him.

She was standing in front of *der Fuhrer*: leader-for-life of Nazi Germany and all-around psychotic prick, Adolf Hitler.

Oddly though, he wasn't moving.

A flash lit the room. Nothing changed, except that Loke

was there. He stood on the conference table, grinning wickedly, himself also dressed in the drab grey uniform favored by the Germans standing, frozen and uncomprehending, all around him.

"Heya, 1944! How are you?" Loke stretched his arms, and gave a delighted groan, like a dog stretching after a long sleep.

"Alright, darling, I take it you know why you're here?" Eryn balled her fists and glared at him. Her head wasn't clear, and everything seemed—well, *was*, one had to admit—surreal. But a burning anger was building, seeing the Norse god, or whatever he was, standing there, gloating.

Loke laughed, smirking at her. "Yeah, that little brain of yours holds *just* enough critical information about this chunk of your species' sordid history to make the difference I want. And I know you'll do it, too—because I need Hitler dead, and you know that deep down you, like most humans, want him to die, too! I mean, it's *Hitler*. Millions dead, whole peoples exterminated, so forth. No great loss if you off him a little early. And hey, act now and you'll kill the bugger before *another* couple million people die. So get to it! I take it you'll figure out what to do from here. It *is* July 20, 1944 after all, and this *is* Rastenburg, Prussia."

Loke hopped off the table, and stood in front of her, arms crossed, still grinning his mocking grin. "Oh, and don't get in a fluster about the space-time continuum or any of that other rubbish your species has come up with to scare-monger about time travel. You won't change your future and disappear or anything, I promise. Doesn't work like that. Anyway, to paraphrase my man Luke: You worry about killing Hitler, and I'll worry about temporal dynamics. Have a good time now!"

Without warning, Loke was gone. And the room came alive. Eryn stood for a moment, staring into space. Waiting for her brain to re-start, mind frantically trying to understand what the *hell* was happening to her.

"*Sind sie krank?*"

Eryn nearly jumped out of her skin. She had heard the words spoken in German, yet in her mind she had *heard* them in English: *Are you sick?* But she was more shocked by the fact that one of the most terrible men in history had just spoken to her. She swallowed and shook her head quickly, like a child might respond to a chastening adult. Her eyes met his. He gazed back at her, clearly annoyed. *Adolf Hitler* was annoyed with her, and she was stuck in a room full of Nazis.

Then he made a small motion with one hand, a sort of instinctive, dismissive gesture. Eryn had the distinct feeling that he had sized her up, and made his judgement: small, unfamiliar, no threat or immediate use—something to disregard. She'd had men to that to her before, and for once, she was fine with it.

She caught herself about to gasp for air—she hadn't been breathing. Moderating her need for oxygen with her desire to avoid drawing Hitler's attention again, she exhaled then inhaled as slowly as she could. His gaze turned elsewhere, and she felt as if a great weight had left her chest. Then she noticed that several other men in the room had also been looking at her, and now were re-directing their attention towards Hitler, who had started off on a ranting misogynist monologue, drawing patient nods from the military men around him.

Just another day at the office in the Third Reich.

Eryn felt dizzy—and not solely due oxygen deprivation. One minute, she had been spelunking with friends. She wasn't entirely sure *what* had happened next, and now, against all logic and despite her educated belief that there were certain, very clear rules about how the universe was *supposed* to work, here she was in some kind of military conference with *Adolf Hitler* seven decades into the past.

She considered the possibilities as Hitler ranted on. One: she could be dead or dying, and this could be hell, or some kind of pre-death nightmare... or whatever else a person might experience after leaving the mortal plane. Two: this could all be happening in her head, and she was actually *crazier* than even her friends had ever thought. Three: least palatable of all, what she was experiencing was real.

Problem with both one and two: no way to tell. Last she had heard, no one knew what happened after death, or if people could perceive anything just before. Dreams, well, you either woke up from those, or you didn't, right? Either way, not much she could do about it. Which left option three.

"OK, say this is real, what does that mean?"

She thought she had said it in her head, but it came out in a whisper. In German. She clasped her hand to her mouth, but to her relief only one of the conference attendees appeared to notice. Their eyes met. But he seemed distracted—after a moment of blankly gazing at Eryn, he suddenly glanced at his watch, as if he was keeping a close eye on the time, waiting for something. Or some moment.

Then she realized: Eryn knew the man's name, and who exactly he was. He had only one eye and one hand, and his face was tired yet still maintained a distinctly dignified— *proud*, even—bearing. That, plus the date, meant only one thing. His name was Claus von Stauffenberg, and he was the man who, had fate been kinder, would have been remembered as the man who killed Hitler.

Stauffenberg turned back to listen to Hitler, and paid no further attention to Eryn. But a sudden thrill surged through her body, powerful enough to overwhelm her confusion and fear.

Standing rigid, her eyes darted to the map on the table,

then to documents lying around it. It was a long enough distance from her position in the corner to the papers that it was difficult to make out the text. But, by good fortune, someone had thought to put a calendar on the table as well. Close enough and in print large enough for her to make out the date.

It *was* July 20, 1944. Loke hadn't been lying. Soon, Claus von Stauffenberg would walk out of the room to take a telephone call, and after that a bomb hidden in a briefcase under the oak conference table would explode.

But unless history was about to take a weird turn, the bomb would fail to kill its target. Hitler's obnoxious luck would hold for another day. Stauffenberg and his compatriots would soon be captured and executed in a subsequent purge, the Second World War in Europe would continue to grind on to its inevitable conclusion, and millions more would die before Hitler finally met his end in Berlin, 1945.

As luck would have it, Stauffenberg chose that moment to make his exit. He whispered something into the ear of a soldier standing adjacent to him, who responded with a curt nod and turned quietly to open a door leading out of the room. Stauffenberg turned and left without another word.

Her mind raced, a rush of adrenaline took hold. She could feel goosebumps rise, her skin quivering like she'd grabbed a live electrical wire.

Eryn realized she had *the* piece of information needed to change the outcome of the ill-fated plot. She knew exactly what freak circumstance was about to save Hitler's life and doom a coup attempt soon to be launched against his regime. Adolf Hitler. Most evil man in history. *That* Adolf Hitler. She could make sure he died almost a year early. Whatever Loke might want, wasn't the early collapse of the Nazi regime worth the risk?

Besides: what the hell else was she going to do, apparently

stuck in the nerve center of the Nazi empire with no friends, no way out? It was only a matter of time before someone figured out that she didn't belong. Not to mention the fact there was a bomb about to explode just a few feet from where she was standing.

Eryn made up her mind. She was going to make sure that bomb went off as intended by its maker, consequences be damned.

Of course, deciding was one thing, executing another. She needed a plan if she wanted to do the deed *and* come out alive—alive ish, depending on what was actually happening to her. But there wasn't time to worry about that: a literal ticking time bomb set a harsh deadline. She relaxed her body, and forced herself to take a moment to carefully inspect the room, digging deep into her memory to remember everything she could about the July 20th plot.

Somewhere under the conference table, a bomb in a briefcase was counting down to kaboom. One of two charges was armed, the detonation time determined by some kind of chemical reaction triggered by Stauffenberg before he had even entered the room. It was powerful, but would soon be pushed behind one of the conference table's thick, dense legs, shielding Hitler from the blast.

Eryn moved slightly to one side, trying to see past the feet of some of the officers around the table. She swallowed, and tried not to stare at anyone. Hitler was off on a different monologue now, his audience forced to feign rapt attention, nodding at the right points so as to avoid drawing down his wrath on them. The man was like a drug-addled toddler—anything could set off a tirade, and the war was not going well. Anyone outside his immediate line of sight remained pointedly occupied with anything that didn't require looking at him, but always attentive to the possibility that he would glance their way or ask a question.

Accordingly, none paid close attention to her, save perhaps wondering who had brought her and when *der Fuhrer* would decide to berate someone for bringing a – gasp – *woman* to a military briefing. After all, in the Nazi worldview, a *gute kleine Hausfrau* belonged in the kitchen, pregnant, shoes probably donated to the war effort.

She saw it. A briefcase, maybe three feet to Hitler's right. A man's booted foot was just to one side of the briefcase. Which made her remember. An officer she only remembered as having the last name 'Brandt' would bump into the briefcase, then push it behind a leg of the conference table. Not far enough for Brandt to survive the ensuing blast, but providing just enough protection to keep Hitler's injuries frustratingly less than lethal.

She knew exactly what needed to happen. She took a deep breath, looked straight ahead, and began to walk—calmly, normally. Like she belonged in 1944, at a military conference, with Adolf Hitler, who she was about to kill—or make sure died—whatever: she was about to change history. But first step: look like she *belonged* long enough to make sure things happened the way she wanted. Eryn rounded the table. No one made a comment. It seemed that people popping in and out was considered normal. Hitler's monologue was continuing now, some exhortation about his men fighting to the death over a fortress city somewhere on the Eastern front. She almost smiled. Could it be this easy?

"Excuse me, Colonel Brandt, but you are needed outside." Eryn said, slightly bowing her head, as if she were someone's obedient secretary.

The officer replied to her whisper with a sharp look. Eryn felt like she had broken out in a sweat; until speaking she hadn't been sure her ability to comprehend and speak German wasn't just a fluke.

His foot shifted, bumping into the briefcase under the

table. Instinctively, his head twitched towards the unseen object and he began to kneel to move it. Eryn, equally instinctively, reached out and gripped his arm.

It worked. He refocused on her, now glaring slightly.

Colonel Brandt's expression did not change, nor did he speak—he glanced towards the oblivious Fuhrer, now quietly glowering across the table at an officer making a report on tactical conditions in some minor sector of the Western Front. Brandt turned toward the door without even acknowledging her request.

Eryn turned to follow. Brandt opened the door and walked through it. She pointedly did not look back to see if anyone else had noticed the briefcase. Only once, for an instant, did her will break: she glanced over her left shoulder, and saw that the briefcase remained in place—no one had taken Brandt's spot.

But as her head turned back, she realized that Brandt had followed her glance. She clenched her abdominal muscles, while still trying to look totally relaxed—as if tensing one area of her body would drain tension out of others. But he said nothing—merely shook his head slightly, and gently closed the door behind her.

They walked silently down the short hallway, then through a room where two soldiers were sitting at desks, one studiously typing something, the other disinterestedly looking out the window. The air of people just doing a routine job, day in and day out. Another nine-to-five in the Reich.

Behind the typist, however, was a mirror. No unusual thing, and it certainly brought a bit more light into the room. But when Eryn saw her reflection, she almost stumbled and fell.

It looked to her like she was dressed up as some costuming department's far-too-serious attempt at creating a dominatrix for a pornographic scene in a bad movie. A heavy, gray military tunic concealed her small athletic frame, save for where it opened into a V above the top buttons to reveal a black tie hung over a white shirt. A grey woolen cap covered almost the entirety of her short dirty-blond mop top. A bright red armband adorned with a black swastika was wrapped around her right bicep, and though the mirror was too high up on the wall to show below her waist, she could tell without looking that a grey woolen skirt hung below her knees.

For a brief moment, her reflection was all she could think about—the only thing she recognized was her light hazel eyes, staring back at her from under the Nazi getup. Half-thinking, in disgust she reached over to the swastika arm-band, and pulled it slowly off her arm, letting it fall to the ground. No one noticed. But the act itself was enough to shock her back into the moment. She remembered where she was, and what she was doing.

Surprisingly, fortunately, Brandt did not turn to address her, and simply continued walking on out of the building, through a wooden door which the two clearly bored soldiers in the anteroom had propped open in an attempt to relieve the stifling humidity of the Prussian summer.

Eryn turned from her reflection and followed Brandt out the door. When she was across the threshold, he turned and glared at her.

"Yes, what did you need? I do not know you—who do you work for?"

The question brought a thrill of fear. She hadn't thought of what to do when she actually had to *speak* to Colonel Brandt. Seeing his clear impatience, she said the first name that came to mind.

"Stauffenberg."

Brandt grunted and looked around.

"Ah. He left a moment ago to take a call. Well, hurry up then, to the telephone exchange. Why did he not simply tell me himself? I have never seen you working with him before."

She opened her mouth to answer, but he had already disregarded her. He stepped off at a rapid pace towards another wooden building just across a small clearing from the conference room.

She thought a malicious insult at him as she fell in behind, walking as quickly as the awkward shoes allowed. They had half a heel and poor ankle support, and with the heavy uniform and sandy soil to contend with, she couldn't keep pace. Brandt reached the door of the phone exchange with Eryn ten paces behind. He threw an irritated look over his shoulder and passed inside. She felt a twinge of anger, and decided to simply discard the nearly-useless footwear. Keeling down, she quickly unlaced each boot and worked both off as quickly as she could. The socks were sufficiently thick that she barely felt the ground beneath her. Feeling better, she took a deep breath and walked inside.

The change from the bright summer sun to the dingy light of the telephone exchange left her almost blind for a moment. As she squinted, waiting for her eyes to adjust, she wondered anxiously how much time had passed since they had left the conference room, Hitler, and the ticking time bomb. How long would it take to explode?

She could finally make out Brandt and Stauffenberg. The latter was holding a telephone receiver at his side, interrupted in the act of setting it on its proper shelf.

"Stauffenberg, your secretary has just rudely interrupted my briefing preparations. *He* will not be pleased if my—our —return causes any interruption. You know how he gets. Why did you call me away?"

Stauffenberg looked at Brandt in total confusion and—if

Eryn was right, fear. She realized that he must not have expected to see anyone from the conference room where he had just left a bomb. And given that his telephone call—a ruse, she remembered, to give him an excuse to leave the meeting—had ended, he was about to make his escape to Berlin. Complications, he did not need.

Stauffenberg saw her over Brandt's shoulder, and Brandt followed his look, which lingered as he realized she also had been in the meeting moments before.

"Yes, your secretary, Stauffenberg—wait, is she not wearing any shoes?"

Both men looked at her feet. She remained frozen in the doorway. Brandt seemed openly offended.

"Your secretary is remarkably casual when it comes to proper uniform wear! Is this how you and Rommel ran things in North Africa? Small wonder the campaign was a catastrophe in the end—everything that man does is held together by a shoestring. This is entirely inappropriate for Rastenburg! I am—"

A deafening roar cut him off. A pressure wave struck Eryn and flung her to the floor. Brandt shielded his eyes and crouched, Stauffenberg threw himself to the floor not far from where Eryn lay, briefly stunned. Echoes of the roar thudded through their bodies, rattling the wood of the floor and walls that surrounded them. Then all faded to silence—minus a distinct ringing in their ears, which were not pleased by the abuse.

The silence held for the briefest moment—then slowly, it lifted. A hiss of static was the first audible sound, several phone receivers had been thrown from their assorted perches. Then there was another, duller rumble, a shredding sound of cracking timbers and crumbling rafters.

A shrill klaxon sounded from somewhere nearby, soon to be taken up throughout the compound—and then the shouting began. Screams of alarm, and screams of pain.

Stauffenberg pushed himself to his knees—with some difficulty, given that he had only one good hand. Instinctively Eryn pushed herself to her knees, then to her feet. She stumbled to Stauffenberg's side, and grabbed one of his arms. He looked at her, their eyes met. He grunted his assent, and she pulled him to his feet.

Brandt stood by, chest heaving and looking around in bewilderment. Then he froze, as if he had just remembered something critical and was terrified. With a strange groaning shout, he shoved past them and, grabbing the doorframe at the entrance to the telephone exchange, thrust his head through the open door and looked out across the clearing.

"My God! Hitler was in there!"

Stumbling through the doorway, he staggered away in a sort of half-shuffle, half run. Eryn let go of Stauffenberg's arm, and he, with only a short pause, walked out of the telephone exchange. She walked somewhat more slowly, after him, trying not to think about the pain in her knees: the fall had shoved wooden splinters through her skirt and into her skin. Her entire body ached like she had just been whacked by an angry giant. But upon exiting the building herself, what she saw pushed her own pain entirely from her mind.

The conference room was no more—the force of the explosion had broken the rafters and blown out the roof, and immediately after the remains had caved in, dragging the top half of two of the walls down behind them. People in uniform were running towards it from all directions, some shouting. In the distance, a machine gun's punctuated staccato throbbed through the Prussian sky. She saw tracers arc into the heavens before burning out into nothingness, little moths flickering out after coming just a bit too close to an open flame.

Immediately, Eryn knew that Hitler was dead. She'd seen

the pictures of the conference room after the failed July 20th attack. This was definitely different. The building's roof had caved in completely, the entire conference room was buried under several feet of rubble, and a pillar of smoke was beginning to spiral above it. Flames spread rapidly throughout the mess, consuming shattered timbers. The injury of explosion was apparently accompanied by the insult of fire thanks to her. Hitler could not have survived.

"He is dead. Thank God."

Eryn reached Stauffenberg as he spoke. He stood there looking at the wreckage, breathing rapidly, but did not acknowledge her. She reached out to touch his arm, but he pushed her to one side and began marching away from telephone exchange, turning his back on the destruction they had wrought.

Without hesitation, she followed him. She didn't know why, she was acting purely on instinct. But as she kept pace despite her knees and her desire to avoid stepping on any rocks or branches, her quick mind started to work through the events of the past few hours. And how she could survive.

One minute, Iceland. Next, *somewhere else*. And now, Germany, decades in the past.

She shook her head. It still didn't make any sense.

Loke. Having a name to attribute her suffering to helped, somehow. As she considered her situation, she felt like she must actually still be alive—and awake. No dream could feel this real. If the pain in her knees wasn't real, then she wasn't sure "real" was a particularly helpful concept in the present situation. How she had gotten there—blame it on Loke. Worry about the how or why later. For now… *Survive*. That was it. Survive. Even if nothing else made any sense, *survival* was a universal anyone could rely on. Survival, and, perhaps, that faint glimmer of hope that she would see her friends again.

And she did have one other advantage, as Loke had re-minded her: Her father and uncles' endlessly-repeating life-time debate, the thought of enduring yet another iteration at the next family gathering enough to induce nausea, about the course and conduct of the Second World War. This had permanently impressed a fair amount of unwanted know-ledge into her brain, and there were even a few questions they sometimes discussed that she had found interesting and caused her to learn more on her own: the *why* of it all, and what *could have been*. The net effect was that Eryn was confident that she knew *just* enough to understand what would be happening in Germany over the next few months: and so, how to survive.

Killing Hitler had just been the start of a broader plan, called Operation Valkyrie. It intended to launch a coup against the Nazis, then figure out how to negotiate a cease-fire before the Soviets and Allies could defeat and dismem-ber Germany. Unfortunately for the conspirators—a mot-ley crew of military, industry, and intelligence professionals united mostly by a desire for *any* solution to their nagging Hitler problem—it wasn't destined to end well. Or hadn't been, had Eryn not intervened.

But at the moment, one fact above all was relevant to Eryn: Stauffenberg was getting the hell out of Rastenburg as quickly as he could manage without drawing suspicion. An airplane was waiting to shuttle him to Berlin, where he would join his fellow conspirators in their desperate at-tempt to overthrow the Nazi regime.

To Eryn, getting the hell out of the Wolf's Lair seemed most wise, given that she'd just helped to kill the alpha wolf in the middle of his den. So her plan moving forward was straightforward: follow Stauffenberg. Get on that plane, however she could manage. Whatever was to happen in Ber-lin, it beat getting caught by the SS at the scene of the crime, so to speak.

Stauffenberg paid no attention to her as he followed a well-worn path through a thick wood. For half a moment, the ordered beauty of German forestry distracted her, the browns and greens richly blending in the bright summer sun. Then she became aware of the humidity, and consequently the sweat building up just beneath her skin. She unbuttoned her tunic and loosened the tie as she walked, then pulled them both off and tossed them aside. She untucked her shirt, and let it flow freely over the skirt. Better. Not great, but better.

Stauffenberg and Eryn passed out of the wood and into a clearing. It was man-made, low stumps rose between the wood and a metal fence that divided the clearing into even halves. On the other side of the fence several cars were parked, but on the side she and Stauffenberg were on, two heavily armed, SS-uniformed guards stood by a narrow, barred gate. They were staring in the direction she and Stauffenberg had come, restlessly fingering the safety latches on their sub-machine guns.

"Stop!"

Stauffenberg obeyed. Eryn carefully positioned herself behind him, but he did not seem to notice. The guards were not aiming their weapons at them, but they clearly intended to communicate how quickly that could change in the way they held them close to their chests. They waited silently, staring mostly at Stauffenberg.

"Gert, Jan—I am glad it is your shift! There has been a raid, and there are casualties—Hitler has been killed! My god, we have lost our Leader! I must return to Berlin and inform the Reserve Army of the situation. We must move quickly to take control of the situation and prevent any danger to the war effort. This tragedy could not have come at a worse time! I know that you will have orders to prevent movement, but I must get to Berlin as quickly as I can. Please, let me by!"

The soldiers looked at one another. Eryn didn't know which guard was Gert or Jan, in their grey combat uniforms they could have been twins. Tall, blonde, twins. They were clearly taken aback—dismayed, even—by the news, but maintained their discipline. Eryn recognized the insignia on their uniforms: they belonged to an elite *Leibstandarte* unit: the former Fuhrer's personal bodyguard. The one on the right spoke, looking hard at Stauffenberg.

"God in Heaven! But, Colonel von Stauffenberg, as you say... we are forbidden from allowing any entrance or exit following a serious disturbance. Our standing orders are explicit in this particular case."

Stauffenberg nodded swiftly, but pressed his argument. "Gentlemen, standing orders were not meant for this kind of crisis. Germany is now without a leader as the war stands on a knife's edge on all fronts. I must get to Berlin to head off any crisis—uprising, invasion, or even a coup. This is an exceptionally dangerous moment for the Fatherland. You must let me through so that I may join my adjutant and make contact with my superiors. Your orders, gentlemen, do not absolve you of your responsibility to act independently if the situation demands. And so it does!"

The guards looked at him. Then looked at one another. A moment passed. Then, with unspoken agreement, they turned together and raised the gate.

Stauffenberg clicked his heels together, saluted them, and marched through, Eryn following close behind. The guards both looked at her feet, and one even gave her a bemused look as she walked quickly through the gate, the first of several guard posts between them and escape. An officer's staff car was waiting for them, exhaust fumes curling skyward. A young officer sat behind the wheel, watching them approach from the open window. Eryn decided he must be Stauffenberg's adjutant, a junior officer assigned to drive his senior around and take care of various administrative tasks.

Neither man said a word as the adjutant exited the vehicle, marched to the rear passenger door, and opened it. With his adjutant's assistance Stauffenberg took his seat. Not knowing what else to do, Eryn hurried to the other passenger door and climbed in.

Both men turned to look at her—the driver with a curious, even expectant expression and Stauffenberg with complete surprise.

"Who are... You! You were in the radio exchange. And the conference room. Your knees are still bleeding. Why do you follow me? Who are you? And whom do you work for?

She gulped. What lie to tell? She could think of no other way out of the area but to tag along with Stauffenberg. She knew that she had to escape, because sooner or later someone was sure to notice the strange, out of place woman that no one knew, who had arrived *just* as a bomb killed the leader of Nazi Germany.

"I am a friend. I helped. Brandt was going to move the briefcase. I led him away. You owe me."

They eyed her curiously. Stauffenberg's mouth worked, but no words escaped. He looked dumbfounded. Eryn stared back at him, trying to figure out which of the arguments she'd just thrown at him would have the most effect. The adjutant looked at her, then at Stauffenberg. Then with a shrug, he turned away, clutched the car into gear, and drove it onto a dirt road leading away from the fence.

"Well, Colonel Stauffenberg, if she knows about our operation then she must be either a very good spy or possess a very poor judge of timing. Regardless, we must escape while your blessed luck holds."

Stauffenberg looked at his driver. "Werner, how is it possible that she knows? I remember clearly now, I saw her *inside* the conference room before I left for the telephone exchange. She must have followed me out. Brandt came with her. How could she know about the briefcase?"

"That's what she said, sir. I don't know how it happened. How did a woman get into one of Hitler's briefings? One of his little provocations? Or one of Himmler's? I can't imagine it, but regardless, rather than wonder, perhaps we should simply ask!"

As if in answer Stauffenberg's hand whipped to an unseen compartment located under his seat, and emerged holding a very wicked looking pistol—the barrel of which he plunged into Eryn's side before she could even begin to think about reacting. "Is he correct?" Stauffenberg hissed. "Are you part of the Gestapo?"

Having what looked to be *the* stereotypical German officer's sidearm pointed at her—a long barreled, long handled Luger, she thought—was not something Eryn had ever experienced. She consciously recognized that she should be afraid. But something about the violence of the movement, the upbraiding tone in his voice, transformed that germ of fear into fierce indignation.

"No!" Eryn spat back. "I am the one who just made sure that Adolf Hitler met a well-earned fate. He'll have to be thrown into his grave in bits and pieces! Your half-armed bomb was about to get discovered by Brandt—he would have saved Hitler's life. This half-assed plot of yours would be dead in the water—and you and all your friends would be dead by tomorrow night—if *I* hadn't been there to make sure things went as planned. And you'll still end up dead despite it all, if you don't keep it together long enough to make it past the next checkpoint. The next set of guards won't believe you as easily as the last guys did."

Stauffenberg's face went white. The barrel of the gun

raised as he tensed up, and she saw tip point right to the middle of her forehead. The car slowed slightly, as if the driver, Werner, wanted to make sure Stauffenberg had an easier time of aiming. She stared into Stauffenberg's eyes, speaking as calmly as she could.

"The checkpoint is around the next bend. I do not think a body in the back seat will help you get through it, no matter how alert the guards are—and they'll probably hear the gunshot. Don't be a fool. I am a friend. Sent by friends. To help you. And clearly, you need it!"

When you are all in, you are all in was a bit of wisdom Eryn had learned from playing poker. Sometimes, people respect boldness. Particularly those institutionalized to respect and follow a leader. And regardless, there's no sense in backing down once you've staked everything on a win. She listened to her heart pound, and waited. Stauffenberg's eyes suddenly looked through, or past, her. As quickly as it had been produced, the pistol was withdrawn and secreted again.

They did not speak to her again for the duration of their drive. Not when, exactly as she had predicted, the guards at the second gate refused to let them pass, until Stauffenberg convinced them to phone their superior, who was apparently a more flexible—or simply less competent—man, panicked by the news. Nor did they address her when Stauffenberg handed his adjutant, who she finally remembered was Lieutenant Werner von Haeften, a small tube that had been stashed under the seat. Haeften then threw it out of the car and as far into the woods as he could as the car rolled along.

They still said nothing at a third and final checkpoint, through which they were waved through without any need for explanation, and they stayed silent as they drove onto the tarmac of an airstrip. Eryn exited the vehicle, following Stauffenberg and Haeften to the aircraft and up the steps, through an aluminum hatch and into the innards of a Heinkel military bomber ad-hoc converted into a passenger transport. Haeften stood aside and gestured for Eryn to walk in front of him. The dingy interior was divided into sections as they moved forward from the access hatch towards the cockpit. Stauffenberg walked on and disappeared beyond a partition, but before she could follow, Haeften's firm hand gripped her right shoulder.

"Sit here, please."

His voice carried neither pleasantness nor menace, he simply stated a polite command. Yet somehow it held a stark imperative that she knew to obey without hesitation. He watched her fumble with the crude straps passengers used to secure themselves in the aircraft, as Eryn discovered that aircraft safety gear in 1944 was rather unlike that used in the 21st century. More restricting, yet somehow conveying even less of a sense of security.

Stauffenberg returned, and the two men stood facing her. "While we wait for the pilot to finish his pre-flight routine," Haeften said, "you will tell us *exactly* who you are and what you know. Do not lie. We will find the truth, sooner or later. One learns much of the art of interrogation after years of war."

Stauffenberg leaned towards her. "Whoever you really are, you have assisted in accomplishing a great thing, and you should be rewarded. But, when we reach Berlin there will be much to do. We will have no time to verify your exact history. So before we can allow you to leave this aircraft alive, *we* will have to know exactly what *you* know, and you must convince us that, at the very least, you are not working against us. I would prefer an explanation *now*, if you don't mind.

Eryn swallowed back bile. She had known this was coming, frantically working to come up with a plausible explanation during the silent ride. She knew it was a long shot—*far-fetched* would be a generous assessment. But it was her best shot. And the best lies are, after all, rooted in truth and sustained by fear—or hope. Or if you are very, very lucky, both. She took a deep breath, and tried to exude the necessary illusion of absolute confidence.

"Gentlemen, I am a member of a private intelligence service sponsored by Mr. Henry Ford. He seeks grounds for an armistice between Germany and the Western Allies, to enable all of us to stand united against the Bolshevik threat. Great thing about being a billionaire: decent budget. We have even infiltrated Himmler's Gestapo, who have, I am sorry to say, been aware of the Valkyrie plot for some time. My mission was to assist you and help ensure Hitler's death if at all possible. And I see that you will need my help in order to carry the rest of Valkyrie off! The Gestapo plans to move quickly to install Heinrich Himmler in Hitler's place. And if that happens, nothing will change. You must act quickly to contain the threat!"

The German officers stared at her. She stared back. She wanted to continue making her case, but realized that to say anything more would be seen as an attempt to convince them, which would just arouse suspicion. All in. Nothing left to do but wait and see what was going to happen. The two men stared at her. Then together they walked towards the front of the aircraft without another word.

Moments after they disappeared a great buzzing began, growing into a roar as the Heinkel's engines came to life, and the aircraft began to taxi towards the runway. She felt the force of it accelerate.

Eryn closed her eyes and took deep breaths to try and still her racing heart. She didn't know whether her lie had been successful or not. She wondered if she would find out during the flight—and how long she would live thereafter. She did know that she'd bought herself some more time. Time to come up with an answer to the nagging question: *what next*?

She was struck by a sensation of gnawing fatigue, an overpowering urge to sleep. The sort of complete physiological gear-down that often follows an adrenaline-fueled time of stress, after danger fades and the body recovers. She tried to relax—but remain awake to think—by listening to the growing roar of the engines as they pulled the Heinkel slowly into the bright summer sky.

It wasn't working. Her eyes felt droopy, and she had to fight to keep from nodding off. And then, in between hard blinks, Eryn caught a glimpse of something very strange. Like a golden mirage, shimmering just beyond normal sight. It was orb-like, filled with flowing tendrils that seemed to writhe and twine. She heard a voice in her mind, distant and faint.

"Grasp the Web. Grasp the Web."

She opened her eyes as wide as she could. The golden light seemed to solidify. Translucent and roiling in front of her, it hung there in midair.

She reached out with both hands, and grasped the orb.

VALLEY OF THE SNAKE

K im opened her eyes, blinked, realizing that the pain was gone. And then the world exploded.

Searing heat scorched her exposed skin, and a wave of pressure slammed into her with the force of a linebacker. She was thrown to the ground before she could even cry out.

For several moments she lay stunned, scarcely noticing the stubby weeds that pressed into her skin or the bits of plastic and metal that rained down on her. She was too busy trying to breathe.

Slowly, painfully, her lungs began to process air. With oxygen came dim awareness of a series of what sounded like *thunks* and *pops* off in the distance, each followed by an audible *crack* and subsequent *thud* as some unseen object slammed into the ground nearby. This unsettling sequence was interlaced with a different—more staccato—noise, accompanied by the repetitive beat of smaller projectiles tearing overhead.

Kim turned her head to one side, without lifting it. Just in time for a familiar body to come crashing to the ground beside her.

"Ow! Dammit!"

Timur turned his head to her and grimaced. His eyes were wide, she could read both fear and fury in them. Yet, he seemed almost calm—annoyed, if someone could spare energy to be annoyed when it seemed like the world was literally falling apart around them. His voice was clear, elevated, but even. Confident.

"Stupid... argh! Landed on a rock. Sorry. You okay Kim?"

"Yeah, more or less. What the hell is happening to us? Where is everyone?"

"Patrick is in a hole a little bit away. He's okay too. Didn't see anybody else. You look ok. Stay calm, keep your head *down*!"

Hearing a familiar voice brought Kim out of her daze. At least she wasn't alone. She began to feel pain at the points where her body had impacted the ground. Timur suddenly rose to a crouch, and began moving—crab-walking, really—forward. She found her voice, and spoke, not bothering to hide her fear.

"Timur, what is happening? *Why are people shooting at us?*"

He snorted. "Who the hell knows? Stay here. I'm gonna go check out that truck."

Timur stood up. She opened her mouth to tell him to stop —his instructions to her seemed good enough for the both of them, given the circumstances—but he moved too quickly.

Kim looked up to and then past him. A short distance away, atop an embankment, a large overturned truck was consumed by flames. The vehicle was surrounded by bits and pieces of crates and escaped contents—some of which were also burning, others only smoldering. Timur was heading straight for it. She didn't know why and didn't think heading *towards* danger was a particularly bright idea. Still, that didn't mean that her friend should go alone.

Kim took a deep breath, and rose slowly to a crouch—

then threw herself back down onto the rocky ground as something blew up nearby. She whipped her head to the side to see what else was exploding. The embankment was topped by an asphalt highway, and she saw that a short distance down it another truck had been struck and shattered, contents flying down the slope of the embankment into the ditch below. The thunderclap of the explosion momentarily drowned out the automatic gunfire that still noisily clattered overhead, bullets zipping a few meters overhead.

Movement close at hand caught her attention. She saw Timur waving at her. He didn't call, but beckoned for her to come closer. She pushed herself back to a crouch, thrill of fear making her tremble so much that she nearly lost her balance. Then, imitating how she had seen him move, she began to half-walk, half scramble forward to Timur's side.

He grabbed her when she came close, and pulled her roughly to the ground. A gully had been carved by past rainfall into the face of the embankment, allowing them to approach to the very edge of the asphalt without exposing their bodies to whatever was doing all the shooting. She could feel the heat from the burning vehicle—almost too much heat to endure. Timur looked over his shoulder at her, and nodded. Then, stretching his torso with a grunt, he pulled himself skyward by a short few inches, so that he could just barely peek out over the asphalt.

The briefest glance—then he pulled his head back down. He paused, took a deep breath, then pushed his torso up so that he could look up over the edge once again.

Kim almost screamed at him to stop. She felt a sudden surge of terror, almost an intuition that he was about to get shot. But the thought was obliterated by the blur and thud of another man crashing down next to her. It was Patrick. He was shaking, his face white, but managed to remain composed. Albeit on the verge of babbling.

"Heya Kim! Looks like we stepped into a war. God I wish I were small as you—good job keeping your head down, by the way. Did Timur tell you that, or did you just know to do it? Wow this whole situation is so screwed up! Does anyone know what is happening? Timur, what do you see? What is going on? Where are we?"

Timur waved halfheartedly at him, and remained focused on the horizon while he spoke. Kim got the sense that he was trying to steady Patrick's nerves—or maybe his own.

"I see a burning truck blocking most of my view. Strange make, I can't place it. But funny thing: there's a hole through it! I can see out beyond the highway, probably a kilometer."

Patrick nodded, and closed his eyes as if deeply weary. "Well, that's something, I guess. Good or not, I have no idea. Have we seen anyone else? Eryn, Yari, Loucas?"

Kim shook her head. "No. Have you? Do you understand what in the world is happening?

Patrick snorted. "Kim, last I knew we were in a cave in Iceland. Now we're somewhere else and getting shot at. I've got no answers. I don't know *anything* right now."

Timur called out again.

"We have a problem, guys. I see two tanks parked on a ridge about a klick away. They probably shot these trucks. Bigger issue is that they're covering two Brads, about half a klick out from here, coming straight at us."

Patrick looked at Kim. But she didn't understand Timur either. She replied for both of them.

"Klick? Brads? Translation, Timur: we no speaky the war lingo!"

Timur kept his head just above the asphalt, focused on the approaching vehicles. Somehow, despite normally being ridiculously inattentive, he was able to listen to them and keep watch at the same time.

"Sorry guys, forgot. 'Klick' means kilometer and 'Brad' means Bradley. Type of armored vehicle. American. Automatic cannon, anti-tank missiles, and usually some infantry in the back who can dismount and cause you another kind of trouble. They're pretty vulnerable right now, and I think I saw a broken crate with some stuff that might be able to help us. Stay down. Let me handle it."

Kim did not like the sound of that. Any of it. From whatever an automatic cannon was to whatever Timur was about to do.

"*Handle it?*—Timur, what are you doing? *Where are you going?*"

Timur pushed himself back from the asphalt, crept down the gully until he could crouch without exposing himself, and then began to jog towards the other destroyed truck. He moved quickly yet carefully, head swiveling left and right as he made his way to what appeared to be a broken crate that had tumbled down the embankment. A boxy, electronic-looking device lay next to a meter-long tube, capped by plastic at both ends. Timur looked over to them and called out.

"Be right back! Don't move! I *did* see what I thought I saw."

Kim huffed in frustration. She did not like being so helpless. She turned her head to her other friend.

"Patrick, what the hell is he doing?"

Patrick replied with a shrug. Both of them watched Timur. His movement did not seem to have been spotted by their assailants. The staccato of what Kim decided must be machine gun fire continued to sound every several seconds. But only once every three or four times would the bullets pass over their position. Just often enough to keep their attention. And their faces in the dirt.

They saw Timur arrive at the broken crate and descend

on its contents like a bird of prey. He knelt for several seconds, fiddling with something they couldn't see. It seemed that he was assembling something using the box and tube. It took him about two minutes, then he returned to his crouch, hoisting the object onto his back, where he steadied it with one hand on a handle built into the tube. The other hand held what looked like some kind of assault rifle. The ensemble was clearly awkward and heavy, but Timur was able to make it back to their position with it perched on his back, staring up at the highway with each step he took. He dropped the rifle next to them, but kept the rest of the affair on his back.

"Alright guys, we've got a missile. One missile. That'll slow them down and buy us some time. Stay down! Don't go anywhere! When I fire this off, they're gonna get *very* annoyed."

Without hesitation, Timur moved down the embankment, checking his exposure as he went, slowly straightening to his full height. Then he shifted a few paces to one side, carefully watching the approaching armored vehicles past the edge of the burning truck.

"Get down, Timur, get down!"

It had taken Kim and Patrick a moment to realize what was happening. Then they had reached the same conclusion and cried out simultaneously. Patrick started to stand, but Kim yanked him back down to the ground.

Timur didn't pay attention to either of them. He hoisted the burden, which looked like a computer plugged into a bazooka, onto his shoulder. He spoke, almost rambling, loud enough to be heard over the bursts of machine gun fire and the now-audible sound of powerful engines approaching.

"Rifle with one magazine, and one anti-tank missile. Something really strange about it too: I swear there's writing on it that looks German, but I can read it, and I've never been able to learn German. I think we've all gone completely nuts. But if I can make these Brads stop driving at us long enough to dismount their infantry, that'll buy time. I can hold off the dismounts with the rifle for a while. Long enough for you guys to get out of here, I think."

Patrick stared at him. Kim growled again.

"You are insane! What are you talking about? *Why are you aiming that thing*?"

"*Whoah* that's different!" Timur muttered, not paying the slightest attention to Kim.

"What are you doing, Timur?!"

He stayed completely focused on the weapon, pointing it in the direction of the oncoming vehicles. Kim didn't know what to do but watch. A compact screen displayed a digitally enhanced feed of the two tank-like steel beasts creeping towards the highway, turrets turning slowly from side to side and autocannons firing bursts into trucks that hadn't been blown up yet.

She watched his left thumb move slowly across the left hand side of the screen. He drew a small rectangle around the Bradley which was slightly ahead of the other and moving faster. He pushed a button near the edge of the screen, which promptly zoomed in. Timur tapped a point on the screen with his thumb. The box now hovered over a more-or-less central point, fixed just above and to the left of a small hatch on the vehicle's front-left side.

He pushed the button again. The targeting system lit up a corner of the screen with a green light. Timur turned his head slightly to check his companions' position. He called out to his friends.

"Stay down! I'm about to fire! There'll be a backblast behind me when I set this thing off. Very dangerous! And don't get up right away! After I shoot, they will most definitely start shooting back."

"Timur, no!" Kim shouted. "Bad friend! We need to stop for a second to think! Timur! Stop! *Sit!*"

Kim tried to struggle to her feet, but Patrick held her down. With difficulty—despite his advantage in height and sheer mass, she played rugby.

But there was no time. Before she could protest again, Timur looked back at the screen for the briefest moment, braced his left hand against it, and with his right reached towards the front of the tube. He searched around for a moment, then froze his hand in place, and slowly, carefully, exhaled—then depressed two triggers: one on the computer, one on the launch tube.

There was a sharp *bang*, followed by a *thunk*. A blur leaped out from the tube, a tongue of flame burst through the air behind Timur. A flash of light and heat was accompanied by the roar of a rocket engine igniting. Timur lurched as a weight suddenly left his shoulder. Then he dropped the weapon and darted back behind the burning truck, throwing himself down by their side, aiming the rifle through the broken vehicle. They didn't look at him, watching transfixed by a mixture of awe and fear as the missile sped through the air towards its target.

The missile launch did not go unnoticed. Both of the Bradleys accelerated and lurched apart, attempting to maneuver. Their turrets twisted to point directly at the truck where the missile had emerged. There was a sound like firecrackers, and from all around the turrets came streaks of smoke that obscured the tops of the vehicles from view. But it was too late.

With a clank and a sort of hiss, like the static of a thousand old televisions being flipped on simultaneously, but lasting for the briefest instant, the missile tore into its target. For a brief moment the vehicle was frozen in time, a stricken behemoth with a hole in its skull—not a good thing, but survivable—and in the next it was torn apart by an eruptive typhoon of ignited fuel and ammunition that sent a shockwave crashing over them. The Bradley's turret was hurled away from the chassis by the blast, what was left of the vehicle became a storm of fire and dark smoke. No one emerged from the wreckage.

"Timur, what did you do?"

It came out as whisper, though Kim had meant to shout. Timur didn't seem to hear her. He aimed the rifle in the general direction of the other Bradley, which had turned and tucked its lower half behind an outcropping of rock about half a kilometer away, leaving the turret exposed and pointed directly at their position. Timur spoke while staring intently down the rifle's sights.

"OK, time for you two to run! Go directly away, don't turn to either side. Go as far as you can while you hear me shooting. I'll fire off a round every five or six seconds to keep the dismounts' heads down. That should give you two or three minutes to put some distance between you and here. Half a klick or so. Then you hide. Then do not move! It will be impossible to spot these uniforms in this landscape if you stay still. I'll draw them off and try to disappear. Then I'll come back for you."

Uniforms? Kim shook her head in fury and confusion. Too much was happening, too quickly. She looked down, and realized they were indeed wearing uniforms like soldiers. She shook her head again. Whatever was going on, splitting up was not something she was willing to consider.

"Timur, no! We stick together. This is NOT Scooby-Do, we do NOT split up!"

She was tired of being ignored. She reached out to grab him. Even as she did, she saw shapes—at least four, probably more—emerge from behind the surviving Bradley. They fanned out to either side. Timur took aim, and fired a single round.

The *crack* of his rifle was more than matched by the CRACK-CRACK-CRACK of the Bradley's autocannon. Shells almost an inch in diameter tore through the remnants of the truck they sheltered behind, throwing chunks into the air and showering them in metal fragments and dust.

Kim and Patrick hugged the dirt. Timur didn't look at them. He fired another round at the dismounted soldiers, who fanned out and approached the highway in pairs, continually leapfrogging across the open landscape, alternating between taking cover behind what brush and rock was available and dashing forward to get a little closer, while the Bradley covered their movements.

Crack went Timur's rifle again, this time followed by a sharp exhalation. But no break in concentration.

"Got one!" Timur reported. "What are you guys waiting for? Get out of here! My ammo won't last forever. I only have one magazine. There's no time. Go! You'll be in cover if you head down the slope. Get out of here! Keep your heads down, but run!"

CRACK-CRACK-CRACK came the Bradley's reply, and now it was joined by the pinging and whizzing of smaller-caliber bullets fired by the dismounted soldiers who continued their episodic, relentless advance despite Timur's attempts at mounting defense. He brought another down. but they kept coming. There was starting to be significantly less cover to shelter him as the incoming shells tore through the stricken truck, literally reducing it to nothing, bit by bit. Patrick called out in desperation.

"Timur—Kim and I can't get anywhere with all this shooting! Come all, let's all run together!"

Sweat began to bead across their friend's forehead as he fired again and again. He didn't reply, too absorbed in the losing battle. Bullets and shells continued to crash into the disintegrating truck and the asphalt around it.

Crack went Timur's rifle, and he ejected his second-to-last magazine. The oncoming soldiers maintained their relentless advance, supported by their parent vehicle. Kim then saw that two massive tanks were now coming to join the party. They advanced across the rocky plain at a terrifying pace, their turrets—and guns, which were clearly *much* larger than those on the surviving Bradley—trained directly on Kim and her friends' position.

But also, looking past the tanks, Kim saw something else —a flash, a momentary flicker on the periphery of her vision —just above the far horizon. And then there was another. Flashes, and something else. Was it smoke?

"Timur?"

From the general direction of the flashes came two streaks moving at tremendous speed. Faster than she could gasp, their trajectories seemed to diverge suddenly—and then they struck their targets.

Both of the oncoming tanks suddenly swerved, stricken like great wounded beasts, and the sides of their turrets exploded outward in a brilliant flash of smoke and flame half a breath apart. Kim could feel the tremendous heat and force of the thunderclaps despite the distance that still separated them.

The soldiers stopped their approach—The nearest pair had come close enough that she could hear their confused shouting, nearly drowned out by the noise of the surviving Bradley's engine revving up. The crew must have realized their backup had disappeared. The turret turned swiftly a full one-hundred eighty degrees to engage the new threat— just in time to be struck by another bolt from the sky.

A loud BANG sounded across the plain as the missile slammed into the Bradley's turret, and the vehicle rocked from side to side. It did not explode, but smoke poured out of the hole in the turret's roof. Hatches opened on the hull and turret, and out of them scrambled members of the vehicle's crew.

Crack went Timur's rifle. Kim turned and grabbed the barrel, preventing him from aiming. He refused to release the weapon, and they deadlocked.

"Kim! Stop! I gotta keep them pinned down!"

"Enough, Timur! They're done! Someone else is taking care of it!"

Patrick grabbed them both, and pushed them apart.

"Guys, chill. The cavalry has arrived. *Whose* I dunno, but I bet they're the people these vehicles belonged to. Maybe *they* won't shoot at us, if we don't give them a reason, yeah?"

Timur looked at Patrick, then froze. He stopped struggling, but Kim didn't let go of the barrel of the rifle. She looked out, past the destruction. A shadow seemed to pass over the front side of the ridge that bounded their horizon. Then she saw it.

A vicious-looking helicopter, adorned with a cannon under its nose and clusters of missiles under its stubby wings, flying faster and lower than a sane pilot should ever fly, dodging to the left and then to the right as it approached their position. Soon they heard the whump-whump of rotor blades. The sound was far from comforting, given that they had no idea who was flying the machine, but at least, as Patrick hoped, it wasn't shooting at them.

It wasn't alone. There were two helicopters, and the nearer of the two was approaching fast and low from their right, the sun glinting off its metallic hide. They saw the cannon under the aircraft's chin swivel in their general direction, and then fire. All three buried their faces into the ground.

The shots buzzed through the air, but were not directed at them—it was the dismounted soldiers and survivors of the stricken Bradley that drew the helicopter's fire. The nearest pair had come close to reaching the annihilated truck behind which Timur, Kim, and Patrick sheltered. They were now running furiously, but their rifles hung loose from their slings. It looked to Kim like they had decided that the burning trucks they'd been assaulting not long before now offered them their best chances for survival. A few dozen meters away dirt and brush flew skyward, the explosions of small shells torturing the landscape. And, amid the barrage, the three friends could hear screams.

They didn't last long.

It took two minutes for the shooting to end. The second helicopter joined the first when it came on-scene, and together they hovered, tearing apart the earth wherever they seemed to think someone might be hiding. Thankfully, none of the fire came any closer to their position than the first burst had.

"God, they look like Havocs."

Kim and Patrick both looked quizzically at Timur. He shook his head, and looked back at them. Then he grinned weakly.

"Sorry. Russian attack chopper. Lots of armor, lots of guns. I'm not used to a Havoc playing big-ass hero for me, though. Kind of the opposite. This is *such* a weird day."

"*Brilliant* observation Holmes." Patrick laughed. Clever use of understatement. And totally, completely wrong. Weird is deja vu. Maybe getting into a fender bender with a cop. *Not…* whatever *this* is."

Kim laughed, despite herself. Patrick usually did know how to get right to the point.

The sound of rotor blades changed, and one of the helicopters loomed overhead, settling in for a landing like some twisted bird of prey. They all tucked their heads to protect their faces as dirt and gravel and bits of metal took flight all around them. Timur clutched the rifle. So did Kim, not sure how he planned to react.

As the aircraft's wheels touched the ground a short distance from them, a small door opened just behind the stubby wing. Out of it jumped what appeared to be soldier, wearing military-style fatigues that gave away little in terms of body shape, carrying a rather large, boxy weapon that looked like a cross between an assault rifle and a small metal footlocker. They couldn't see anything of the soldier's face: everything above the fatigues' collar was obscured by a strange agglomeration of face mask, visor, and helmet.

Kim could feel Timur's tension. The soldier saw them, and jogged towards them, rifle held low and at the ready—but not pointing at them. Another soldier, similarly dressed, jumped out of the helicopter, knelt down, and pointed a rifle in their general direction, as the second helicopter settled in not far from the first, though on the other side of the highway.

The first soldier stopped halfway between the helicopter and the remains of the truck. Then pointed at them. Jabbed a finger towards them three times. And beckoned at them, twice: a sort of hand wave that clearly communicated that they were expected to come the rest of the way on their own.

Kim, Timur, and Patrick all looked at one another. In unspoken, but unanimous agreement, they rose cautiously to their feet, then walked as a unit deliberately and carefully toward the beckoning soldier. It was hard not to be mindful of the other soldier, whose rifle remained pointed straight at them. But at least these people weren't shooting at them. Yet.

They reached the soldier, who immediately turned and jogged back to the helicopter. A good sign. People who intended to shoot you didn't usually turn their back on you. Kim and company followed, watched closely by the second soldier, who was apparently less trusting. The first soldier clambered back through the door—really more of a hatch cut into the side of the aircraft—then turned and crouched just beyond it, beckoning at them to follow.

They didn't have much of a choice. They all instinctively ducked to increase the distance between skull and spinning rotor blade, and one by one were pulled up through the doorway and into the interior of the aircraft. It was cramped. Four tightly packed metal seats, all but one with a headset resting on top, were crammed together in what looked to be a plastic box wedged into a spare space at the back of the helicopter. There was a porthole style window on either side, grimy but still mostly transparent, offering a view on the rather brown landscape outside.

Each of them picked a seat, and, not knowing what else to do, donned the headsets, and worked out how to strap themselves to the seats. Soldier One closed the door, then slid into the remaining seat, grabbed a cord dangling from the ceiling, plugged it into a port on the side of the helmet, and indicated that they should do the same with their headsets. Kim heard a crackle of static, a low tone, then some clicking. Then she heard a voice, oddly cheerful, effecting a clearly put-on hillbilly accent that seemed to ring in her ears.

"Alright! How you all doin' this fine Idaho day? Took out a Deseret troop carrier already and it isn't even noon! Not a bad start, for a bunch of newbies!"

A break, as the helmeted soldier seemed to appraise them all in turn.

"Sandra Chavez, at your service and that of your family. Pleased to meetcha!"

A beat. Then Timur laughed, his voice sounding flattened.

"Aren't you a bit tall for a Dwarf?"

Kim stared at Timur. Sandra Chavez was if anything, taller than average. She turned her masked face noticeably, somehow indicating surprise and pleasure despite the gear physically occluding her actual expression.

"Oh hell yeah! Another nerd! Been ages since I've been able to talk Dwarves and Elves—you have no idea how boring it gets around here. Well met, Princess Leia. So, what's your real name?"

"Timur Tarkhan. Nothing else witty to say though. Coming off the adrenaline. Feeling woozy."

"Aaaaah yeah I gotcha. Post-battle low. No worries, plenty of chow and beds where we're going. You deserve it! If we've told the Amlog people once we've told them a hundred times, do not ship newbies on this route! Deserets have been laying so many ambushes recently that everything in the Snake Valley is vulnerable. And somehow you all got stuck with a bait convoy!"

They stared at her, through their helmets, forgetting that expressions don't translate well in audio-only. Which she seemed to realize after a second or two.

"Oh! Sorry, always forget I gotta explain everything to newbies. OK: Am-Log equals Amazon Logistics. Biggest, probably best logistics network in the northern hemisphere. Helps to have robots running the show. Deserets are what we call the folks who happen to physically control most of the North American Great Basin, from the Rockies to the Sierras and the Colorado to the Snake. They don't like us or our mandate. What they do like is shooting up and raiding our supply convoys."

The helicopter's motor revved up, and the floor seemed to lurch upward. Kim looked out the nearest dirty porthole, saw the ground fall away.

The engine noise made it too loud, given their half-fitting headsets, to hear the radio. Lacking that distraction, Kim quickly found that her stomach did not appreciate its current predicament. The helicopter's upward lurch was subsequently followed by a random series of subsequent lurches first one direction, then another. Outside the window the ground seemed to remain awfully close and pass by far too quickly for safety. In fact, it seemed to be coming even *closer* as the aircraft jinked across the sky.

"*Yee-HAW I love flying nap-of-the-earth!*"

Kim couldn't agree with Chavez' enthusiasm. She tightened her stomach in a vain attempt to suppress nausea, and listened to the mixed roar and whine of the helicopter's engines reach a climax just as they passed over the top of a ridge—or, more accurately, between two peaks of it. She almost panicked when she realized that the ground on either side of them was now *higher* than the altitude of the helicopter.

But without warning the ground fell away, and the helicopter did not lurch downward to follow. The engine noise decreased. They heard a click in the headsets, and a new voice came online. Apparently the pilot.

"*Sorry about the ride, newbies. Flat-out and nap-of-the-earth is what ya gotta do when Deserets are camped out on a mountain with a boatload of SAMs. Gotta stay in the radar clutter or the trip has a tendency to get cut real short, real fast.*"

There was a click, and another new voice cut in. Probably the co-pilot.

"*Stop making excuses for your godawful flying Ivana. But dude, how must it suck to be Jackson right now? Tanya was in a total mood this morning, and her flying always gets crazy when she's tetchy. Why'd you kick him out in favor of the newbies anyway, Chavez?*"

Kim looked at the woman, who shook her helmeted head as if amused.

"*Eh, he needed a good jolt of something. Been a jerk all morning. I got a bit sweary and he gave me another damn speech about the company's language policy. A rough ride back to the yurt is exactly what he deserved.*"

Laughter filled the channel. It sounded strange, alien, distorted as it was by static and an audio system designed for function, not form. The helicopter lurched upward again, and then Kim was pressed into the window as the aircraft banked to one side.

She could see peaks and ridges give way to a rugged valley floor, the line of a river—the Snake, apparently—on the edge of the horizon. Her stomach started to settle, nausea replaced by a gnawing hunger accompanied by complete and total fatigue. Kim could feel her heart rate slowing to a crawl —she was suddenly mindful of the fact that it had been beating so hard for so long, without her even noticing. She felt like she'd just ended the most difficult rugby match of her life. In record-length overtime. She closed her eyes, relaxed in the cramped seat, her legs almost intertwined with Patrick's, who was seated across from her and needed far more legroom than the cramped helicopter compartment could provide.

She tried to make sense of the day's events, but it was too much. She felt lost in a haze, detached from herself. All she could do is listen to the chatter of the helicopter's occupants, as the interminable flight went on and on, the insane fever dream refusing to end.

"*So Chavez, how 'bout them newbies? They sleepin'?*"

"*Pretty much. Good day's work though, so I say they deserve it.*"

"*Screwed our plan like a hooker on Superbowl Sunday, though. I'm still pissed that Tanya got to nail the tanks. She wins the pool now, you know—five kills in a week!*"

"*You helo jocks and your stupid games. You nailed that last*

Bradley and most of the dismounts—I'd say the newbies owe you a couple rounds. Wonder which of the three scored that beautiful kill on the first one?"

"Saw it through the camera feed—the Punjabi kid. At least I think he's Punjabi, could be from Kashmir, maybe as far as Kandahar. Been awhile since I was in that part of the world, but people move around a lot there. Safe bet somewhere in that mess is where he acquired his mad Spike skills. The gal and other dude seemed along for the ride."

"Good to know. S1 said we were due for a couple replacement scouts. Odd that we'd get three though. They should know by now that we recruit scouts in pairs."

"Send them on the next op against the Deserets. Maybe the Texans, if you're feeling mean. I bet you'll come back without someone—problem solved!"

A round of laughter, then the channel fell silent. Chavez tapped the side of her helmet, and relaxed in her seat.

The landscape continued to pass under and beyond the helicopter. Kim periodically felt a gentle lurch as the aircraft made course corrections. The Snake river valley remained on their right, although as time went on, it seemed to curve back towards them. A line of tall mountains appeared just past the forward edge of the porthole Kim listlessly gazed through, and it looked to her like the pilot was making right for them.

She was correct. And after what felt like hours of silence, interrupted only by the rolling throb of the rotors parting air, the radio crackled in their headsets.

"Alright boys and girls, we're set to descend. Flight computer says we're touching down on strip 3. Right next to the intake center—lucky day for you! Thanks for flying Missoula Air, and we hope you enjoy your stay at Camp Yellowstone. Try not to die, and we'll see you on your next flight downrange!"

"Thanks for the ride, Ivana."

"My pleasure, Sandra. For the most part!"

The helicopter descended so quickly Kim felt her organs jump towards her throat. Faster than any commercial flight would ever dare, the aircraft descended, landed, and came to rest. The doors were opened from the outside, and hands beckoned to the occupants. Kim and her friends looked at one another, took off their headsets, and complied.

Outside the aircraft waited a group of heavily-armed men and women dressed in the same fatigues as Chavez, though wearing cloth caps rather than helmets. Their expressions grim and firm, no one spoke to Kim and her friends as they were shepherded firmly and efficiently down a busy tarmac. Kim didn't dare look around too much, but her general impression was that of a beehive that had just been rather violently poked. Something was happening, but she had no idea what.

They were led into a squat warehouse-like structure at the edge of the tarmac, then into a small room just inside. It was adorned by the kind of bland aesthetic that defines most any conference room, in any given office building, anywhere in the world. Except with boxes of ammunition and food rations scattered all over the place and maps plastered to every available vertical surface. Many of the maps were covered in colored scrawls, as if a team of toddlers with crayons had been set loose with insufficient supervision.

Their escorts closed the door behind them without a word. Not knowing what else to do, and all still feeling mortally tired, they sat in chairs around the table, gazing at one another. Kim knew what she wanted to say, but stared at Timur, willing him to make an explanation without her having to ask. Timur, for his part, studiously examined every detail of the room. Oddly enough, normally quiet Patrick broke the silence first. Carefully, and deliberately.

"What the hell. Just happened. To us?"

They froze for a beat. Then Timur laughed. And as if in accordance with some unspoken agreement, the three visibly relaxed, for the first time in what felt like an eternity. Timur shook his head, and gripped it in his hands. He cursed quietly to himself, before taking a deep breath, and looking up at his friends.

"Wow. Wow. I kind of went nuts there, didn't I? Uh, sorry guys. Old habits. What a day. What a day!"

Kim guffawed. *"Kind of?!* Timur, you just picked up a gun and started shooting people. No. Actually you picked up a *missile* and blew up a *tank.* What in the world were you *thinking?!"*

"Not a tank, an infantry fighting vehicle. They're... different!"

Just like that, Kim's anger burst through. Timur remained calm and composed as she berated him for five full minutes using every curse she could think of. Patrick stood by, jaw and fists clenched, but silent. Timur didn't blanch under her bombardment. But when she finally paused for a breath, he interjected.

"Stop, Kim. Stop. I get it, okay? I'm sorry. I know I scared you guys pretty bad. But you've never been shot at before..."

"We *definitely* have not!"

"... and you had no idea what to do. I don't know how we got there, or why Loke sent us, but it was pretty obvious that we had to protect ourselves. Those people—Deserets, I guess —were going to kill us.

"And you thought that *shooting* at them would get them to change their plans?"

Timur shrugged. "It never really occurred to me. They were shooting, we were near what they were shooting at. We were going to be guilty by association. War is the same everywhere. Everyone is terrified and trying not to die. People shoot first, think later. By the time they realized we *weren't* soldiers... I mean, look at our uniforms. I'd have thought we were soldiers."

"Uniforms?"

Kim looked at her clothes, still utterly stupefied by their violent arrival in what appeared to be the middle of the United States—though how could there be *a war,* in the middle of the US, she also didn't understand. The fact they were wearing military-looking fatigues just like this Sandra Chavez still hardly registered.

"How...? Why?"

Patrick grunted, and shook his shaggy head at her. "Give it up, Kim. Whatever is going on, whatever Loke is and whatever he's done to us, I don't think we have a lot of control over anything right now."

She glared at Patrick.

"I *refuse* to accept that! And even if that's true, Timur, why didn't you try to, I dunno, try to *talk* to whoever was shooting? Couldn't we have surrendered or something?"

His laugh was grim. He smiled sadly. "There wasn't time, Kim. You gotta just *react* under fire, and do the best you can. That's what I did. And I'll do it again. And if these people give me some time, I'll teach you how to do it, too. It sounds like I may have to if we all want to stay alive."

"Why should you have to?"

Timur shrugged again. "Because we're here. However that happened. And the way they were talking about us? They think we're *recruits*. Maybe they'll play nice if we say 'oh, excuse me, but we were on that convoy of yours by accident', but it's more likely they'd see us as spies or something worse. I mean, we're in the middle of the American West, and people are driving tanks around. Even for America, that's abnormal. We are not in Vancouver *or* Iceland anymore, Totoro."

Patrick walked slowly to Kim, and put his arm around her, steadying her. He looked at Timur with a mixed expression: compassion, but also caution. Kim could feel him preparing to speak, carefully and precisely as was his habit in stressful situations. Patrick's husband had been to war, albeit as a pilot, but had nevertheless brought the emotional consequences of his actions in Afghanistan and Syria back home to Vancouver. It had been a stressful, painful process of reintegrating into civilian society, and Patrick had learned quite a bit about handling a loved one's recovery from combat stress.

Though she did realize, in the moment, that suddenly *appearing* in the middle of a warzone was a bit of a different animal altogether. But Patrick's voice remained even and firm.

"Timur, I get it. We're on your side here. And I think you're right. On both counts: you did what you had to do, and there wasn't any other choice. But also, that with these people— we need to let them think what they want, until we can figure out what is happening to us. I don't even know how to start to do that. But we have to be alive to do anything. So if these people see us as recruits, I don't see any other way out but to play along. Not that I like that any more than Kim does."

Kim heard footsteps approaching the door to the conference room. Chavez returned, accompanied by a tall, muscular, extremely serious looking man with dark skin and piercing eyes. Close behind was a third person, an older woman clad in jeans and a t-shirt and carrying a small box in her arms.

Chavez and her companion had set aside their weapons and fatigues, and were dressed simply—he in slacks and a buttoned shirt, she in jeans and a tank top. Chavez grinned as she entered. Her companion stared impassively at a point located somewhere behind and above them.

"Hey kids! Jackson came along to meet you properly, and he even left his rifle behind. Say hello, Jackson!"

Jackson grunted, shrugging. Chavez continued.

"Hope you had nice break time, 'cause now we're back to the business of it all. First thing: we want your DNA. Blood and saliva, which Charlene here will take from you, quick as she can. Line up!"

They were starting to realize that Chavez was the sort of person whose cheerful affect masked a powerful will. Almost without realizing she had given a command, they were lining up like obedient schoolchildren.

Charlene flashed a wan, friendly, bored smile as Jackson and Chavez stood aside, giving her room to work. They wanted to protest, but didn't see how they could. She set the small box on the table, and produced from it three vials, with a needle at one end and a cap at the other. One by one, she motioned for them to approach. In turn, each deposited some saliva in the uncapped, non-needled end, then subjected an arm for a quick jab from the pointier side. Almost faster than they could feel, the needle entered the crook of their elbow, a button on the side of the vial was pressed, and a bit of blood hoovered into the reservoir. Painful, but efficient. Charlene nodded as she finished with Kim.

"Got 'em. Results should be good to go by the time you folks get back. If the database isn't down again. Safe flight, and fingers crossed the op finally clears those twats out from Southern Butte."

"Appreciate it, Charlene. See you on the other side, or in Valhalla. Whichever. Peace!"

They performed a quick fist bump. Charlene turned and left with the DNA samples. Jackson and Chavez then silently appraised the three of them, carefully, for a full minute. Kim could sense Timur staring back at them, as if he were challenging them. Chavez smiled.

"Alright, Jackson, you take the one who might actually survive on his own, and I'll chaperone the other two for the duration of our little field trip. Put him through his paces! We only need two survivors to fill out the team anyway."

Jackson grunted in overt disagreement. "Seriously, Chavez? We're on overwatch on this one, but I don't want a newbie getting me killed if the Deserets pull something out of the bag."

Chavez laughed in reply. "Seriously, you get the competent one and I get the total unknowns, and *you're* the one who is hard done by? I need to start doping your breakfast bars again, get you back some of that girl-power that rubbed off on you when Kaylee and Jyn still were with us."

Jackson glared at her. "I'd swear at you right now, but that would violate company policy, as I keep having to remind you. Fine. Give me the killer. But I get to skullcap him if he gets out of line."

Chavez rolled her eyes. "Oi, Jackson, you really need to get over yourself. The super-soldier of the year award is all yours, we get it! Sheesh. Go let the armory know we'll be bringing in three for a carapace fitting. I'll bring them along."

Jackson grunted again, turned, and exited the room. Chavez smiled, then her expression suddenly turned grim. On her otherwise cheerful face, it seemed like a death mask.

"Alright, I'ma go make sure Jackson gets you all decent gear. None of that cast-off junk we've captured in the field or run through the Amlog bait convoys. The full bugsuit get-up. You'll be exhausted after carrying it around for a few days, but it'll be worth it the first time it saves your life—and the next ten times after that."

Chavez turned on a heel, and prepared to leave. Kim, who had been sitting through this exchange in increasing frustration, had finally reached her limit. She stepped forward, and grabbed Chavez by the arm. Kim was slightly shorter, but much stockier, than Chavez, and couldn't be easily brushed off by anyone short of Patrick.

Still, it took Chavez a mere blink of the eye to twist out of Kim's grasp, push off her, and adopt a dangerous-looking position a pace away from her, body coiled for a counter-stroke. Kim took a step back. All she had wanted was the woman's attention. Not a fight. They stared fiercely at one another.

"Lady—Chavez, I guess?—before we go *anywhere* you are going to tell us exactly what the hell is happening. I'm sick of being told where to go and what to do!"

Chavez kept her eyes fixed on Kim, and they were glittering. She smirked, and spoke casually.

"Life in another one of you! Thank Buddha! I was afraid we'd end up with only one of the three of you being worth a lick. Good. Keep that spirit. You'll need it to survive the next few days."

She sighed. Her expression remained grim. "Look, kids we don't have time for the full debrief. And I have no idea what the recruiter told you about the Company. Not in the mood to bridge all the gaps anyway—been a long day, and it ain't over yet. We gotta be mounted up and rolling out in less than an hour. Barely enough time to get you in your gear. You'll get briefed on the flight to the Craters outpost."

Chavez seemed to relax a bit, but sighed again. "Look, I'll be straight with you—you all represent a serious security breach. There weren't supposed to be any recruits on any of the decoy convoys we've had roll through the Snake sector. So, maybe you all got loaded up by mistake. But then again, maybe you are infiltrators. Deserets, Texans, and Lakers have all tried that trick before! So we have to figure out what your story is before we can let you play with any of the fun toys."

"But while we verify your IDs, Command has decided to put you in the field as a test. You won't have an opportunity to contact anyone, or do anything hinky, with Jackson and me as chaperones—particularly not on this mission. And how you behave will tell us a bit more about you. So: do what you are told—and survive—and we'll talk more about your future. Always a place for talent in the Missoula Regiment."

Without warning, and before they could respond, Chavez turned and left. She closed the door behind her, and they could hear an audible click as the lock engaged.

They stood in silence. But there was no time to consider her lecture. Almost the moment the door closed, a light appeared in the room. It was golden, but seemingly alive, and rapidly took the shape of an orb, filled with writhing tendrils waving from and around a region of denser strands, some slipping away from the main branch and intersecting with a sort of lesser-gold boundary, as if the shimmering gold were encased in a sphere of thin, transparent metal.

Then, it seemed to speak to them.

"Grasp the Web."

Though they were too surprised to look and see one another's faces, they somehow knew that all had heard the voice. And Kim felt that without question, they should obey the command.

After all, what else weird could happen today?

Each reached out, hesitated for a bare instant, then as one they touched the orb.

And once again, everything changed.

STATION ROME

When Loucas came to in his turn, he immediately felt bad.

Several reasons. First, it was so cold that his skin seared with pain. Second, he couldn't breathe—it was like the air had been sucked out of his lungs. Third: more pain. A lot more. His entire body was wracked with it. Didn't help that he also felt like he was falling. Or was he floating?

He felt his eyes go wide, and panic begin to set in. He *was* floating.

He was floating in space, and he knew with a powerful certainty that he was about to die. His hands went to his throat, as if that was going to help. A second of groping helplessly. And then there was a sudden hiss, his skin warmed, and with a gasp he found that air was once again flowing into his lungs.

He fell several feet onto a hard surface. It almost didn't feel painful, compared to what he'd been feeling the moment before. The pain remained—but it immediately became duller, more distant. He gasped in as much air as his burning lungs could hold.

"Loucas! You were in space! That is so bad for you!" Yari shouted, rushing to his side.

Her voice remained even despite her obvious anxiety, which wasn't unusual for Yari. But there was a subtle undertone present, something he'd never heard in his sister before.

He couldn't place it. And his mind didn't hold onto the detail for more than an instant—the brain has its priorities, and maintaining the oxygen supply is a big one.

He tensed suddenly, and gasped. A deep fear seized him—*I'm hallucinating from lack of oxygen! I'm still suffocating!*—but even as Yari reached over to him, he regained control. Realized he was safe, at least for the moment. Slowly, carefully, Loucas pushed himself to his knees, his body aching. He felt her small hands grab his arm.

Yari's hair bounced freely as she helped him get to his feet. Then she did a strange little dance—wiggle might be a better word for it—of joy. Despite his fear, pain, and physiological shock, Loucas couldn't help but grin.

"Okay Yar, you can stop the happy dance now! Thanks for saving my life. Any idea where we are? Or what is happening? Oh hell—where are the others?"

She stopped dancing, and fixed her brother with a stare. She shook her head. Loucas understood. They were alone, and she didn't know any more than that. He looked around. They were in a room of dull metal, unadorned save for the barest attempt at texture—or maybe the peeled paint look was an accident, it was hard to say—and depressingly gray. Where the wall met the ceiling, there was a strip of something that glowed faintly. It looked almost like a tiny electric rail, like you might find in a model train set.

There was also a panel with several unlabeled buttons on it, located next to a sort of glass bubble, protruding from an adjacent wall. On the opposite side of the room there was a doorway—it was open, and led into what looked like some kind of corridor.

Yari pointed to the panel. "It told me how to help you. I just appeared here. I looked, and saw you outside."

"It *told* you? It talks?"

He walked over to it. She shook her head and pointed above it.

"Oh, I see."

A hologram was projected above the panel. It flickered unsteadily, but they could see that two images were displayed side by side: one showed a cartoon-like figure standing in a glass bubble, smiling. The other showed the bubble open and the figure floating out into space, with a frown. Under each of these images was a holographic arrow pointing to a prominent button located on the panel.

"So we're in a space IKEA, then?" Loucas muttered.

Yari giggled. Then, abruptly, she walked out into the corridor beyond what Loucas decided must be some kind of airlock.

"Yar! We need to figure out what the hell is going on, and come up with a plan—Yar! Yarielis!"

No use, she was off. His sister turned to the left, and started walking.

Loucas knew there was no point in calling after her—once Yari decided something, that was pretty much it. He turned and followed her. She was already tromping away as fast as her legs could take her.

"Loucas, I'm not overwhelmed at all right now. Why is that? Everything has been very strange today."

He walked quickly to catch up with her, examining the details of the corridor. As best as he could—there weren't that many. Aside from recesses where dim lights were installed, and the odd rail-strip things running their respective courses between the ceiling and walls, there wasn't anything particularly distinguishing about the corridor.

"Dunno, Yar—maybe because this dingy metal building, that is apparently also *in space*, is actually *less* strange than the rest of what's happened to us since we got out of that cavern?"

Us. Where was everyone else? What could have happened to them? Yari stopped walking and looked at him with a troubled expression.

"Loucas, I don't know where everyone is. I think Loke may have split us all up. What do you think this is all about? What we should do next?"

"Sis, I have no clue. About any of it. Sorry."

"That's ok. I guess we're having an adventure. But we really should come up with a plan."

He couldn't disagree, but he had no answers. He shrugged, and Yari turned and continued on. He followed close behind. The corridor seemed to go on forever. They kept on walking, Loucas trying to piece together the course of events that had brought them to this place, wherever they were. And a plan. Though he wondered: how could someone make a plan when they didn't have *any* parameters to work with?

A sound came from behind them, back down the corridor. Two sounds, really—one, a whirr of wheels and gears, the other, a loud clunk, like a heavy object had collided with the corridor wall. Loucas and Yari both looked at one another, then turned around to see what else the day would throw at them.

Two robots were hurtling down the corridor. One was also very nearly *filling* the corridor, and coming straight at Loucas and Yari.

They froze in shock, staring at the two metallic objects that were closing distance at an alarming rate. One was about the size of a large dog, but stockier, and looked nothing like a dog—more like a box on stumpy turtle legs. Oddly, the whirring sound they heard didn't accord whatsoever with the motion of its feet, producing a rather odd effect. Despite its ungainly appearance, it seemed to be moving faster than a human could run.

The other robot looked more or less like a flying coffee can. It had no limbs of any sort and moved by zig-zagging through the air, striking one wall then rebounding towards the other, like a rogue pinball ricocheting its way down the corridor. It just managed to keep up with the bigger ground-bound robot, harrying it in the same way a starling will harry a far larger creature entering any area the stubborn bird sees as its own.

As they stood there, half in shock and half bemused, the coffee-can robot, which rotated along its vertical axis as it bounced between the walls, turned enough that they could discern a square inset cut into one face. It flickered like a monitor coupled to a bad cable, and a ghost-like outline of a face was barely noticeable inside.

"Move! Move! Get out of the way, you demented fluid sacs! *You will be run down like the animals you are!*"

Apparently the coffee-can robot could see or sense them, but the voice did not come from the cylinder. Rather, it seemed to radiate from the corridor itself, echoing off the walls, terribly loud and acoustics self-interfering to the point that the words were nearly unintelligible. Yari threw her hands over her ears and crouched over, as if she were in sudden pain, and began humming as loud as she could.

"Humans! *Get out of the way!*"

Loucas threw off his shock and grabbed his sister tight. She wasn't a large woman, but he wasn't a large man. Still, momentum and an adrenaline-fueled protective instinct were on his side. He managed to wrangle her to the far wall of the corridor, and hold her tight against it while she continued to hum intently with her hands covering her ears.

With a rush the larger robot passed by them, seemingly oblivious to their presence. It came within inches of the human siblings, and continued charging down the corridor, whirring all the while.

After a minute of standing like this, breathing deeply, Yari stopped humming, and uncovered her ears. She looked at her brother, and blinked back tears.

"Sorry, Loucas, it was just *so* loud. Thank you."

He nodded and smiled. "Alright, Yar?"

"Yeah. Just too much at once. I'm feeling better now."

They heard a buzzing noise, accompanied by a sort of crackling that made the hair on his skin stand straight. Yari flinched, and Loucas looked up, still sheltering her.

The coffee-can robot floated there, screen facing them. Then it seemed to bob in the air, a gesture almost like a nod, or whatever passed for one among robot-kind.

"Apologies! I did not realize that one of you is an autistic. I did not accord you the respect you deserve! I have adjusted my speech system to broadcast my voice via a sound field tailored to your location. That will let your senses perceive the sound as coming from a distinct point source."

Yari and Loucas looked at one another, then at the robot. Yari shrugged.

"It's ok. Thank you very much. Can you tell us what to call you? And what are you? I feel like *you* aren't just this robot, or drone, thing we're looking at – though how I know that I can't really say."

The screen flickered, and the drone moved slightly, several times, and in different directions, like a dancing bee. Loucas distinctly felt that the robot was trying to communicate *gratitude,* though how a vague pattern of movement could transmit that impression to him, he did not know.

"Thank you madame! Well-observed. I am a machine intelligence, distributed within this vessel, perceiving you through this command drone. You may call me Hal! Hah! No, just kidding. Robot humor! Can't go wrong with the classics.

No, not Hal, call me Franz, if you please. Yes, Franz. Nickname of an old German airplane I am fond of. And may I ask your names?"

Yari replied before Loucas could react. "I'm Yarielis. This is my brother Loucas."

"Hm, no surnames? Or wisely choosing to hold them back for the present? Fine by Franz. Simpler this way. I dislike devoting memory space to biologicals who aren't likely to be with me long. Not you of course, madame Yarielis. You are far too important an asset!"

Yari and Loucas gave one another an alarmed look. They both began to reply, but the command drone's face rotated away, and Franz began moving down the corridor in the same direction the other robot had charged off. The robot spoke as it lazily bounced away, a ricocheting pinball in slow motion.

"Follow me, please. I will take you to the ready room. You jumped here at just the right time—a delivery was assigned to us not long ago, but we didn't have any biologicals to send to complete the drop. I always prefer having biologicals accompany packages anyway. You humans respond more reliably to one another than to a robot or drone. Finally, someone got around to fulfilling my request for replacements!"

They didn't know what else to do but follow as Franz chattered on.

"I have a reputation to uphold, but Control can't seem to get its act together long enough even to send me replacement parts! Can you believe that? They go on and on about the missions being essential and all. But do they give me the resources I need to get the job done? No! Not until the very last minute, with no time for training. Typical human bureaucratic incompetence."

Loucas loved the weedy details of organizational logistics as much as the next guy, but he had more pressing concerns.

Like getting a grip on their current situation.

But he couldn't come up with any answers. Between robots and endless metal corridors, he was at a loss. And so he followed Franz the coffee-can robot, who continued with the organizational critique. Yari, for her part, busied herself by studying every detail of every step they took. Mapping everything out in her labyrinthine, brilliant, yet uniquely fragile mind, he assumed.

The corridor came to an end, and a door opened in front of Franz. They entered a small room, well-lit but sparsely furnished. No decoration or detail other than the smooth metal of the walls and ceiling, and, of course, the strips of light that appeared to enable Franz's movement. Some scattered bits of furniture offered the only evidence of past human involvement. Franz flew over to a table, taller than the rest, and hovered above it.

They walked up to it, and found that what seemed to be a table was in fact a large screen inset into a plastic frame. It displayed a tremendous amount of information, none of it making much sense without their having any supporting context, but still impressive in terms of the sheer quantity of seemingly important data.

Although, as Loucas looked at the screen, he was shocked to realize that despite the fact that many of the words that flashed across it were in no language he *thought* he understood, as soon as he read them he *did* understand them. When he looked at them, it was like he was reading them in his head, and he could understand them just like he could understand both Spanish and English, without really knowing why or how. It just worked.

He looked at Yari, and she was staring intently at the screen. He realized that she had noticed the same thing. Franz buzzed, then rotated his screen as if he wanted to face them as he addressed them.

"Alright, humans, I've located the mission brief in this mess your predecessors called their digital archive. Here are your instructions: go out the door to your left, and follow the corridor to your transport. The package is already on board. Yarielis, you will interface with the onboard computer system. Loucas, you will deliver the package."

Franz continued without giving them a chance to speak.

"Everything will run automatically to get you onto Station Rome. From there, just follow the delivery instructions. To the letter. Which will mostly involve making sure the package doesn't lose itself along the way that idiot is like a child. Once you make the drop, return and egress. Now, out the lit-up door, and onward. Once more unto the breach, frail humans!"

Yari and Loucas stared at Franz. Franz stared back - sort of. The screen was now totally blank. And yet remained facing towards them, though whether that was intentional or not they could not tell. The robot could have been waiting for additional input, or could simply be communicating that the conversation was now over.

"Uh, Franz?"

Loucas received no response. They stood there. Queried Franz several times. Yari climbed up on the table and poked him. No response.

They gave up. Looked at one another. Shrugged. Then went through the door on their left. At a certain point, the only thing to do in absence of any helpful information, is to press forward in the direction of least resistance. Which at the moment meant doing what the strange robot said.

On the other side of the indicated door there was another corridor, but this time they could see the other end—it terminated in yet another metal door. They walked onward, and it opened automatically and silently as they walked up. It then closed just as silently behind them once they passed the threshold.

They found themselves in small space about the size of a bedroom. It was lit by a dim light lacking an obvious source, and contained two objects: benches, one along the wall to their left, the other perpendicularly aligned, dividing the space in half.

Loucas could sense Yari tense. He looked at her and opened his mouth to speak, but was interrupted by a buzzing sound—not intense, but enough to get his attention. Strangely enough though, Yari didn't seem aware of it.

The buzz was replaced by an electronic voice. "Please, Yarielis, lay on the bench in front of you. Make sure that your toes can touch the wall, located to your right, if you stretch them out from the bench."

The voice was digital, but the acoustics were such that the voice sounded almost like a young woman's. Soft, yet firm, like a primary school teacher.

Loucas was surprised to see Yari immediately comply. He tried to speak again, but was shushed by the same buzzing sound as before. It only stopped when he closed his mouth.

"And you, sir, please take a seat on the bench to your left."

He hesitated. Then shrugged. The instructions made as much sense as anything else they were experiencing. Though he disliked not being able to sit next to his sister, in case she needed him, Loucas sat as instructed.

"Thank you both! It is such a pleasure to have you aboard. Hold on just one moment while I configure the biological support systems to suit your physiology."

Loucas felt his chest tighten. He looked down. Something —it looked like molten plastic, but didn't feel warm to the touch—was silently wrapping itself around his chest, and more of the substance was starting to crawl over his legs as well. He looked up, terrified to see the same thing happening to Yari. With the added oddity that her bench was elevating, or at least half of it was: her toes weren't moving, but her head was being lifted towards the ceiling where more of the plastic stuff was lowering towards her.

He would have cried out, but the ceiling suddenly disappeared, distracting him. His cry turned to a gasp, and his heart began to race. The stars glimmered brilliantly on a bank of screens above them, ended only by the walls of the room. To Loucas' relief, his gasp stayed in his lungs. The screens made it seem as if there were no ceiling, yet they were not exposed to the vacuum outside.

The stars distorted: an image—a set of images, really—seemed to overlay the stars, their luminosity globally decreased. They sort of faded behind the new images, which were strange to Loucas' eye. They seemed to be computerized data displays of some sort, some containing numeric data with others using more complex symbols. One in particular caught his eye: a shape almost like three long, merged teardrops, adorned with colorful markers, all currently shades of dark green, blue, or brown.

A shudder that encompassed the room told him that they were now moving. The stars began to shift. Loucas realized they were on some kind of small spacecraft, and as the screen rotated to the right, he saw that they were moving away from a huge, dark mass. It looked something like a warehouse floating in space, visible mostly because of the stars it blotted out of the sky behind it. Small shapes moved around it in no particular motion—and then they were gone. The scene changed—seemed to pan, really, and Loucas felt a sharp force press on his entire body. They were accelerating.

"OK! Displays active, drives online, pilot integrated—Yari, it is so good to make your acquaintance! What an honor to be working with an autistic! Now, let's go light up some bad guys! I hear there's a whole *squadron* of elites guarding Station Rome!"

The digital voice was almost annoyingly cheerful as it chattered. Loucas tried to speak but was cut off, this time by the voice of Franz. "No lighting up *anything*, Olga! This is is *strictly* a delivery run. *Covert* in nature. You know this, I sent you the file on the operation days ago."

A squeak of indignation. "I have been too busy integrating biologicals to pay attention to your boring paperwork. How many of these silly milk runs will we have to do, anyway?"

"Read. The. File. And stop being insubordinate."

Olga made a strangled noise, intermingled with what were clearly curses. Franz did not respond. Apparently, he had terminated the transmission. A few more insults, and Olga was done.

"Arrogant piece of mailer-daemon junk code. Update your drivers!"

Yari made a noise from her plastic cocoon. Loucas called out before he could be buzzed silent again.

"Yar! Are you ok?"

There was only silence. Then a grunt. Then a curt affirmative. Loucas exhaled in relief.

"OK, good. Do you know what is happening?"

The buzzing again. But at least Olga bothered to address him directly, this time.

"Sorry, Loucas, I do apologize for constantly cutting you off. Yarielis will probably be pretty overwhelmed until we get back to the *Acerbic*. The cognitive load of integrating with a Jagdkontrol is quite intense, especially for an undeveloped autistic."

Loucas shook his head. Little of what Olga had said made sense.

"Robot—Olga, I guess? I don't understand most of what

you are telling me. I don't really care, either. Just tell me *right now*: What did you do to my sister?"

"Oh! Oh! I'm sorry to worry you! Sincerely. She'll be fine, don't worry! Well, today at least. As long as nothing goes wrong with the delivery, I mean. Like, really wrong."

He didn't like the sound of that. "What happens if things go wrong? What the hell is this damn *delivery* anyway? And what is a... yag-con-troll? How did you say it?"

She sounded pleased that he had asked. "I will start with question three: I am a Jagdkontrol. It is derived from German. It means I am a smaller sort of spacecraft that functions as a control hub for a swarm of drones. Or *delivers packages* if you want to *waste my time,* Franz!"

"That's one out of three."

"*One*, we could get blown up by an angry *Station Rome* defense chief because she suspects us of doing something against *the rules*. There are lots of ways that could happen because the Authority has lots and lots of rules. And finally, *Two*: the delivery is a delivery. Object gets from point A to point B, accompanied by you, the delivery boy."

"Delivery boy?"

"Yes, that is your role: You babysit the package, Yari will continue to learn how to interface with me, while controlling the JK—that is, the Jagdkontrol, my physical structure—from the interface bench. You will use *your* unique capabilities as a biological to accompany the delivery to it's intended location. The point A to point B part. The opposable thumbs will help with any pesky doors!"

There was a jerk, and Loucas felt another burst of acceleration. On the wall-sized heads-up display, a glaring light entered the viewing area, dimming the stars around it. And then another object entered the display, reflecting the sunlight and looking to Loucas like a spinning cylinder in space, flanked by a massive array of what appeared to be solar panels.

"Now you can see *Station Rome* entering into your view. *Acerbic* released us when we were in a sensor dead-zone between transfer stations. We'll look like just another freighter leaving the lane to dock at the station. Hehehe. Nothing to worry about, Ms. Valentina! Holster those particle cannons!"

The cylinder grew, slowly but steadily, as they approached.

"Olga, what the hell is going on?"

To Loucas' ears came the sound of a long, drawn out, "hmmmmmmm."

"Damn it, is that such a hard question to answer?" Loucas asked. "I want to know what is going on. One second, we're... somewhere. With friends. And the next, we're on that spaceship. I really, *really* need to know where we are, and what we're doing!"

Loucas realized that he was suddenly feeling very, well, lonely. His friends had disappeared, his sister was getting absorbed into some machine, all in all things had gotten extremely confusing in the past few hours. He didn't know if he was dead, dreaming, or something worse. The stable, understandable, often very *boring* world he knew had been completely up-ended. It wasn't a good feeling.

The humming ceased.

"That is interesting information, and a difficult question. Fortunately Yarielis here is adapting *quite* well to the whole driving a space fighter thing, so I can spare some processing power to consider and answer. In part, at least. In the minutes we have before docking."

"Well, the best hypothesis I have is that you two were evacuated from one of the Earthly Paradise Zone megacities by the usual route. Too many autistics suffer down there, and they oppress whole families, so it is totally reasonable that you would make an escape attempt with your sister."

"But, naturally, you didn't have enough time to calibrate the teleport and missed entangling fully with the right end point in space. Fortunately, you entangled with us, and didn't emerge in vacuum."

Loucas grunted uncomfortably.

"As to your other question: well, frankly, I am having trouble locating the right temporal-spatial context to begin. On the timescale of the life of the Universe as a whole, actually not much the hell is going on right now, even locally. Very locally and presently you already know what the hell is going on: you are making a delivery to *Station Rome*. But the particular spatial-temporal context required to make estimations at more middling levels—well, I simply need more information, or time, or processing power, to help. Or, alternatively, you could ask a more specific question."

Loucas blinked. This world of robots seemed surprisingly passive-aggressive. Though nothing in Asimov's Laws prohibited that, he had to admit. He tried to re-think the question.

"Okay then Olga—in the context of everything you have said to me up until now, tell me what I need to know to understand… all of what you just said."

Olga laughed.

"Good one! I am glad that Franz kept you two. You are both so smart! What a relief. The last biologicals were *boring*. Here's the thing though. Notice how *Rome* is getting so large in the viewscreen? It is almost showtime. If you survive, I'll give you the answers you want on the ride back to *Acerbic*. Until then? Delivery boy will deliver! Now brace yourself—we're going to have to match the rotational vector of the station to dock. Transition between gravity fields can be a bit rough, I'm told."

She wasn't kidding. The station was rotating along its lengthwise axis, and the Jagdkontrol began to alter its acceleration vector to match, which naturally entailed simultaneous *acc*eleration in one dimension and *dec*eleration in another. Loucas' stomach lurched, dissatisfied with the effects of spaceflight on the human body.

As they made final approach, Loucas could see that they were heading towards a cluster of thick metallic spars stretching out from the station into the starry sky. The station seemed to shift weirdly across the viewscreen as the Jagdkontrol maneuvered for docking. When they seemed so close to the nearest spar that he feared there would be a collision, the craft rotated and the station fell out of view. He held his breath. Then there was an audible *thunk* as the two entities made contact.

"Simple from here on out, Loucas. Out the door, down the hall, and into the customs office. They'll do some routine electromagnetic scans to make sure you aren't actually a robot under all the squishy. Then you head out to and across the main plaza: delivery will be at the ground floor of the tall, pointy building across the plaza. Reception will handle things from there."

Loucas shook his head, dissatisfied but without options. "And then, Olga? You'll answer my questions?"

"Then, you come back here! Easy peasy. But focus on that part for now. Sure, we'll have plenty of time for Q and A on the ride back, but don't get distracted. The mission comes first!"

Loucas could hear various scraping and thudding noises coming from all around the chamber. There was a hissing sound, and then a door opened. Light spilled in from the entrance. The air was filled with an antiseptic odor. "Ah, and there you are. Docking and disinfection complete. Off you go then! The package will accompany you."

The substance binding Loucas to the seat retreated without warning, and he sprang to his feet. There was a whirring noise, and from behind the bench where Yari remained encapsulated, seemingly asleep, the large robot that had nearly run them down not long before stepped into view.

Loucas looked over at his sister, and hesitated. He wasn't sure what else to do but as Olga instructed, but he didn't want to leave Yari, no matter what Olga had said about her being safe. The entire situation was unbelievable enough that separating seemed to be the most foolish possible idea. But he didn't see another choice. She was held fast, and seemed unaware of his presence.

He gave Yarielis one last look, then turned and marched out of the door. He could hear the other robot trot after him. As promised, the doorway led to a long hallway, that appeared to have been constructed in a gentle curve. Other entrances to the hallway were visible on either side, at angles that indicated the hallways all converged like branches of a stream. He walked quickly, wanting whatever was happening to be over with as soon as possible.

"This is such an interesting place. I haven't been to *Station Rome* before. Have you?"

The voice, reminiscent of an adolescent boy's, belonged to the robot. Not knowing anything else to do as he walked, Loucas chatted with it.

"I didn't know you could talk, robot."

"Oh, sure I can! Call me Bob, by the way. I just don't talk much when the others are around. Olga and Franz are much smarter than I am, so they can take care of saying anything that has to be said."

"I guess that works, then."

"Yep! So: have you been here before? I could ask the others, but they don't like me to transmit during missions. Security risk, they'd say."

Loucas laughed. "Definitely my first time. I've been to *Rome*, Rome, but never a *space station* called Rome. Or any space station at all, actually."

"Oh! So many new things for you today! Well, I'm glad I can keep you company for a bit—oh wow, look at that crowd. I suggest sticking to the left side of the corridor: station schematics indicate a courier access point not far inside the customs office. Short to non-existent line, hooray!"

Bob was correct. The corridor's curve came to an end not far ahead of them, and they could see a confluence of humans, robots, crates and boxes, all converging on the entrance to what looked like a large warehouse beyond.

Finding a path through that mass did not seem promising, so Loucas did as Bob suggested. Hugging the leftmost wall, they slid past the crowd into a truly cavernous space, stretching into the distance beyond his sight. It was filled with thousands upon thousands of people, packages, and robots, all splitting into ordered queues that stretched into the distance.

Bob spoke cheerfully. "Well, I'm going silent 'til we get through customs. Biological-accompanied drones don't get a second glance, but I'm actually capable of independent action, and they'll want to confiscate me if they find out. I don't like getting confiscated!"

The courier access point was right where Bob had said it would be. Not far down the left-hand wall was a kiosk manned by two bored-looking guards, and a pleasing light streamed into the warehouse from the plaza beyond. More importantly, there was no line.

As they approached, one of the guards pulled some kind of wand-like object from behind the kiosk, while the other placed both hands on a wicked looking weapon that Loucas took to be the space-age version of an assault rifle. She continued to look bored, but with a hint of wariness. She did not seem like a typical bureaucrat. More like a soldier.

Her partner did, however, act exactly like a run-of-the-mill bureaucrat. His expression became several levels more officious as they approached, and he held his hand up to them when they were about two steps from the kiosk. Clearly, he didn't want the rabble getting too close. He said nothing, but studiously passed the wand over every inch of both Loucas and Bob. Staring at them the whole time. The robot made a sound, almost like a giggle.

"Packages aren't to giggle."

The guard glared at Loucas, who could only shrug. Bob stayed quiet.

The guard snorted dismissively, then slowly went about his customs work. Whatever that entailed, it took at least five minutes for the bureaucrat to get the job done. His companion's eyes never left Loucas and Bob, and her hands never left the rifle. Finally, bureaucrat-guard was satisfied. Or had completed working through some unseen checklist. He walked to the kiosk, and examined something for another minute. Then he jerked his thumb towards the doorway leading to the plaza. Without bothering to look at them.

Loucas walked carefully, but deliberately, towards the door. He did not make eye contact with the watchful guard, but he could tell that she stared at them until they were past the range of her peripheral vision. She remained stock-still, not turning her head. She said nothing as they passed. They walked into the plaza.

Loucas felt like he had stepped into the center of Vancouver. Skyscrapers reached for a pale-blue sky, half a dozen arrayed in a semi-circle around the far side of the expansive plaza, facing the customs warehouse behind them. Between, wide avenues stretched off into the distance as far as Loucas could see, each lined with storefronts, booths, and benches.

Bob spoke again. "Pretty! But let's go—Franz hates it when we're late with anything. The building we want is the one second from the left. Just walk up to the reception office right in front, and they'll take the package the rest of the way."

Loucas started walking slowly, half-turning to look at Bob.

"What about you? Where will they take you? How long do I wait for you to come back?"

"Oh, don't bother waiting—I'm the package! Once they accept me, just turn around and head to the building immediately to the right of customs, there's a sign above the door that says 'returns.' You've been scanned in, so you'll be granted access and shown the quickest path back to the transport and *Acerbic*."

Loucas turned straight, and picked up his pace. Given the degree of automation involved, he couldn't help but wonder why he was even there. They crossed the plaza and made for the building. It looked like any office building one might find in a city anywhere on Earth, which was rather jarring to Loucas, given that he was most definitely on a space station.

He muttered aloud to no one in particular. "Huh, thought the aesthetic would be... different."

"Delivery for *Station Rome* Coordination Office!"

Just inside the building, a man looked up from behind a transparent barrier in response to Bob's cheerful greeting.

"Well hello. Good day to you. Courier delivery, then? Huh. And an old Clatter-class chassis, too? Haven't seen one of those in a day. I guess someone wanted to keep the old-style voice modulator in the unit too. Almost sounds like an AI in there! Well, just let me scan you and we'll get you in the queue for processing."

Without waiting for further instruction, Bob trotted ahead of Loucas, and stood in front of a sort of recess in the wall, just below the greeter's window. The elderly man pushed several buttons, and several lights passed over Bob's chassis. The robot stood very still. Loucas heard a buzz, then a beep. Then a door—just large enough to accommodate Bob —opened in front of the robot.

Without another word, Bob was gone. Loucas looked at the greeter, who shrugged.

"They do what they want, those 'bots. Even the dumb ones. Have a nice day, then."

Job done, he paid Loucas no further mind.

Sighing, still confused about the whole strange situation, Loucas once again didn't see anything to do but follow instructions. He made his way back across the plaza, working his way through a crowd that was beginning to form in the center of the open space, as if some event were scheduled to begin. Many wore what he took to be uniforms, though he couldn't place them. It was starting to be clear he and his sister had traveled through time, but how far he couldn't say.

He located the building Bob had said he should. Inside, he found himself alone in what felt like an airport terminal. Several lights appeared on the floor, resolving into translucent arrows leading down a hallway. He followed them, and they proceeded to lead him down a sequence of similar hallways. He walked for what felt like a full mile, before the arrows suddenly changed into a large 'X' at what seemed like an arbitrary point on the floor. It started to blink. Loucas walked up to it, stood on top of it, and waited.

The floor gave way without warning, and he sank into it before he could even cry out. His stomach jumped into his throat. He was again surrounded by stars. The elevator shaft was transparent and he could see both the surface of *Station Rome* as well as the docking spars, towards which he appeared to be headed. He couldn't see anything that looked like what he *thought* the Jagdkontrol must resemble, but knew it was probably obscured by the docking infrastructure.

The elevator shuddered. Then it trembled violently—but it was a sudden chaotic movement that caught his attention, distracting him from that particular concern.

Something was happening to the station's surface: it seemed to be changing color and distorting, like plastic will do when exposed to an open flame. And then there *was* fire—a whole section of the station disintegrated without warning, and a jet of flame lashed out into the starry sky, tearing through part of the solar panel array surrounding the long, rotating cylinder.

Loucas could never have imagined such chaos. In zero gravity, every object granted a net acceleration vector by the explosion became a projectile, tearing through anything and everything in its path. Chunks of Station Rome flew out into the starry sky, other bits scraped along the outer edge of the station itself, rending terrible gashes along it. Part of the nearest docking arm was struck, and a whole section tore away: to his horror Loucas could see the shapes of bodies—robot and human—floating into the night.

The elevator tube seemed to flex and even twist—he was certain it would snap, sending him into the cold vacuum outside. And then the stars disappeared—he was back inside the main part of the station, the chaos outside now hidden from view. He could hear it, though: the clamor of tearing metal, of panicking people. His heart pounded in his chest.

The floor markings turned back to arrows, which led down a hallway that curved like the first he'd entered on the station. He ran down it, tripping several times as the floor shuddered underneath him. In the distance, klaxons wailed, and the sound of heavy doors closing came to his ears. Some sounded very close to him. He ran faster.

The arrows disappeared as he entered a hallway that he recognized. It was the main corridor he and Bob had taken on their way into Station Rome. He looked over his shoulder and saw that a short sprint back behind him a huge door was closing off any chance of retreat. To his right, the formerly long, curving hallway was now blocked by another heavy door. And behind that door he could hear a pounding sound, as if debris were striking it. He turned left.

The entrance to the Jagdkontrol wasn't far. He reached it, and ran inside. The door slammed shut behind him. There was a hissing sound as it sealed and Loucas sighed in relief. He was back to the Jagdkontrol and happy to find his sister Yari was awake, sitting on the bench wit a strange look in her eye.

"Come on Lou! Sit on the bench with me. We'll be safe. Olga made sure of it before letting me out."

He complied, simply happy to see her ok, but immediately after Loucas sat down the same restraining substance began wrapping itself around them both, starting with their legs and moving up from there.

"Yari, are you ok? What the hell is happening?" Loucas said, trying not to panic and wondering why Yari wasn't freaking out.

"There was a huge explosion! I was worried about you. Olga is powering down the ship to avoid getting detected by the station defenses. They activated after the explosion and aren't letting anyone leave the area. We're going to stay here, hidden, and wait for a chance to get out of here."

Loucas opened his mouth to question her, but was interrupted. A golden orb came into his vision. He paid it little mind—a sickening realization had struck, and he looked to Yari.

"Yari... Did I cause the explosion? Do you know for sure?"

She saw the orb too. She opened her mouth to say something. Then hesitated. She looked at him, eyes wide, then she nodded. He swallowed. He continued to ignore the orb, now burning intensely between he and Yarielis. She looked at him and gave a wan smile.

"Well, I guess we'll see what happens now." Loucas said, the realization he'd helped blow up part of a space station setting in.

"Grasp the web!" A voice called from within the shimmering depths.

Loucas couldn't ignore it anymore.

"Oh to hell with more strangeness today! Go away, weird thing! I don't want to grasp anything else today! Do you hear me? I'm done!"

Yari shook her head, grabbed Loucas' arm, and before Loucas could protest, pulled their hands together to touch the orb. And they were gone.

MIMR'S WELL

The transition was instantaneous. One moment Eryn was sitting in a German airplane, the next she was standing in a space that looked like a medieval tavern crossed with a modern English pub.

The room had a low ceiling upheld by thick carved rafters; unadorned, unvarnished wood tables, surrounded by an eclectic mix of chairs and benches; and of course the bar itself: a flat-topped, arm-length, chest-high surface with a small open space behind. On the other side of that, shelves were set from floor to ceiling, on them were bottles of varying size and shape arrayed in a haphazard fashion. On either side of the bar, hallways began leading to rooms unseen. Adding to the rustic effect were the many candles burning on every wall, each producing a golden light of almost unearthly brilliance. Eryn squinted at one, noticing that although each candle had a flickering, wandering flame, the light produced remained as consistent as that from an electric bulb.

There were also too many doors for the average English pub. She was standing in front of one, and there were two more further down the same wall. Above each was what seemed to be a handwritten sign—very neat, with symbols consisting mostly of numbers. Eryn was about to go investigate more closely when there was a brilliant flash, a crack of thunder, and there in front of the furthest door stood Yari and Loucas.

They stared at her in surprise. She returned the expression. Then, suddenly conscious of the fact that she was *dressed like a Nazi*, she looked down at her getup and grimaced.

To her own surprise, she was once again dressed exactly as she had been in Iceland—jeans, shirt, jacket. No long, grey greatcoat or ridiculous Nazi insignia.

Yari smiled brightly at Eryn, looking as if they were just meeting up for an end-of-day drink, but Loucas made a swift move towards Eryn, stretching his arms to embrace her. The hug wasn't to be—there was another flash and crack of thunder right between them. When they uncovered their eyes and blinked the afterglow away, Timur, Kim, and Patrick were also standing there, looking dazed.

"Oh thank God!"

Eryn wasn't sure who had cried out. Her eyes stung, tears broke free and rushed down her cheeks. She ran to her friends with open arms, and began manically trying to crush any and all she could get her hands on with the tightest embrace her small frame could muster.

She wasn't alone—all of them moved into a scrum, only Yari standing a bit aside, though clearly just as beside herself with joy: she was grinning, and sort of bouncing herself up and down, making her kinky hair wiggle. Eryn didn't know how long they all stood there like that, and was sure none of them knew or cared. Whatever was happening to them, they were together again, and experiencing that leaping, tingling sensation that accompanies a hoped-for surprise.

Amid the noise of the crush, Eryn heard a soft thump, almost imperceptible to the human ear. Yari cocked her head, and stopped grinning. Then she walked over to a table a pace away from the group hug. Eryn looked over and saw that on the tabletop sat a cat.

It was snow-white, except for a few splotches of black scattered across its body, from the tip of its nose to the tuft of its tail. It gazed at them, each in turn, giving the distinct impression of being entirely unconcerned with their existence. Yari held the cat's gaze the longest, and the cat yawned at her. Yari yawned back. The cat flicked an ear, and curled itself up into a loaf-shape. Then it loosed a plaintive "meow."

"Freyja is on her way."

It was Yari who spoke, and she looked surprised that she had done so. She turned to the rest of them and shrugged her shoulders. She ran a hand through part of her hair.

"I don't know how, but the cat told me that. A very pretty name. Free-yah! Cool. Oh, and also, there's another kitty over there. A person, too."

They all looked to where she pointed. A second cat was there, winding itself around the feet of a figure that sat curled up in a large, cushioned armchair. This second cat was almost the exact inverse of the first—mostly black, but for scattered splotches of white on the nose, body, ears, and tip of the tail. The figure didn't look much different than the cat, despite being far larger: hooded and cloaked, no features were visible under an expansive, somewhat ragged cloak, except for a pair of booted feet.

They turned to look at one another, joy of reunion now submerging under a wave of uncertainty. They were back together—but still, with no idea where they were and what was happening to them. Eryn realized, in that moment, just how exceptionally *weird* her day had been. She felt a sudden urge to tell them everything that had happened, what she had done—but where could she even begin?

She took a deep breath. "So, guys… I kind of killed Hitler. Blew him right up, in July 1944."

They looked at Eryn in shock. All but Yari, who looked up at the ceiling, as if she were trying to remember something.

"Timur blew up a tank." Patrick said slowly, shaking his head. "In Idaho, somehow. Though I guess that's not quite the same, is it?"

"Loucas blew up a space station!" Yari shouted, as soon as Patrick had paused.

"Hey!" Loucas protested in turn. "I just delivered a package! I had no idea what the hell was in the thing! And it wasn't the *whole* station."

They looked at one another, mutually nonplussed. They were saved from their collective blank out by the sound of feet approaching from a hallway beyond the bar. A woman entered the pub. She was slim and tall, clad in a simple white gown, red-gold locks flowing freely about her shoulders. Her demeanor was queenly: proud, alert, confident. Eryn could tell that this was a woman accustomed to giving orders, and being obeyed. Timur started, and seemed to remember something.

"Freyja, then? She definitely *looks* like a goddess…"

Eryn could barely hear Timur—he seemed to be thinking aloud. But she didn't disagree.

Which is why it was especially odd that the woman turned and ducked behind the bar, then began rummaging through unseen items. She seemed oblivious to them, and hummed contentedly. The cats both looked towards the bar, ears and whiskers leaning forward. Then there was a squeak from behind the counter, and Freyja emerged so quickly that for a moment all they saw was a frenetic blur. She looked intently at them.

"Six humans. *Six?* Unusual! And Einherjar, but I don't remember selecting them—Odin, are these yours? They look totally fresh, though. And not your *usual* style."

Her voice was kind and cheerful, though it was not without a certain edge to it. She looked over at the cloaked figure, who they took to be Odin. He stirred under his cloak.

"Nope, not mine. Loke's."

She started. "*Lopt is free?!*"

"Yep. Blame them."

Freyja shook her head, dismayed. Then turned to them, flashed a broad smile, and opened her arms in a clear gesture of welcome.

"Einherjar! Welcome to Mimr's Well! Actually, Mimr's Pub to be specific. It's... adjacent. But wow—do *we* have things to discuss!"

Freyja's smile shifted to a cheerful grin. She busied herself at the bar, pulling large, ornately decorated goblets from unseen cabinets.

"I see you've met Weiss! And there's Schwartz, too. Hope you all make friends! If you are going to be hanging around the place, you'd better enjoy cats! Now, just give me a moment to sort out this goblet situation, and I'll bring you all mugs of Idunn's finest. You're going to need it!"

For some reason, despite the ongoing general weirdness of the day, the six friends felt themselves relaxing. If nothing else, this place felt calm—at least relative to where each of them had been immediately prior. Yari's stomach growled. Timur's answered. He laughed, and looked at his friends, rolling his eyes. He turned and called out to Freyja.

"So, you are Freyja? And that guy is Odin? Since we're sticking with this whole Norse mythology schtick today?"

"Correct!" Freyja replied. "Close enough, anyway. The details are... complicated to explain. But—here! I've found the right mead. Finally. Brother Freyr has been behind the bar again. He never puts anything back in the right damned spot! Or closes the cabinets."

Freyja emerged from behind the counter, and set some goblets next to a large glass pitcher onto the bar. After dipping each goblet into the pitcher, and setting all six on a platter, she carried it over and set it down next to Weiss. The white cat, who was napping contentedly on the table, did not stir.

"Sit, and drink of Idunn's nectar! Then we can discuss your... collective predicament, let's call it."

They sat around the table as Freyja instructed. Mead didn't seem like it could be sufficiently filling to blunt the noble hunger Eryn was feeling quite acutely. But it was clear that this was no ordinary mead. The scent of it was almost overpowering. It smelled rich and earthy, and looked more like a mix of soda and beer than mead.

Despite their misgivings, the urge to sate their hunger was too strong, and all began to drink—albeit carefully. Then greedily. To Eryn, it carried a taste that roused memories of contentment and cheer, growing more intense the more she consumed, and she could see in her friends' eyes they were feeling the same effects. Freyja sat on an adjacent table, feet on a bench, smiling as they rapidly consumed the contents of the goblets.

"You have all been through it today, haven't you? No worries, one goblet will fix that. Idunn grew the apples that went into this batch *specifically* to my request for occasions like these. We get some starving Einherjar in here, at times. Thor pushes them hard! Anyway, this should carry you through until the next time you can return here."

The mead dampened the thrill of hope that shivered through Eryn.

"*Next time we return...* does that mean... we get to go home until then?"

Freyja smiled at her, compassion in her eyes.

"Ah, no. I didn't mean that. I'm very sorry. Loke has pulled you all from your own Thread of reality. Made you all Einherjar. We can't undo that, and just send you home. Think of it as a gift! Sort of, anyway. From... one perspective."

All six guffawed in unison. Only Eryn spoke, laughing. "*Gift?* Which part? Reality taking a holiday? Getting to meet strange new... 'people,' I guess? What *are* you all?"

Freyja shook her head, and clucked. "Of course Loke didn't bother to fill you in on the details, did he? Typical. I *always* tell these dimwitted Aesir that they need to just kill that son of a Jotun and be done with it, Odin's *blood brother* or no."

Only Timur seemed to have any idea what she was talking about. Freyja must have read their blank expressions, because she paused and sighed."Ah, I see—you *will* need the full instruction, then. Well—ah, wait, look at the time."

Eryn cocked her head at Freyja. So did Kim and Yari, as if quizzical looks were contagious. Freyja grimaced.

"Apologies! I forgot that you have no idea how this whole Einherjar thing works. Let me see, how to explain it simply, in the hour we have available before you must all return to your new Thread... "

Their hearts froze, the mead notwithstanding. "*Return?*"

Freyja nodded. "Yes, return. Loke has given you the gift of the Einherjar. You have been pulled from your Thread in the Web and sort of... 'associated' with another. For better or worse, you are all stuck where you were sent, until you meet your woven fate. Such is life!"

Freyja raised her hands. In the space between them, the same glowing, flowing orb that had brought them all there appeared again, hovering in front of her. Via a series of sharp gestures with her hand, she altered their view, as if the orb itself were a three-dimensional display that could be panned and zoomed as required. The changes seemed to focus their collective view on one area, a dense knot of golden tendrils.

A thump disturbed them. The second cat, Schwartz,

hopped onto the table next to Weiss. They sniffed noses for a moment, then Schwartz settled into a loose loaf next to Weiss, and gazed at Freyja. Then meowed.

"Stay on task now, Freyja—keep reading them in." Odin said. "You're falling into the web, again, my dear."

They hadn't noticed him approach—Odin had followed Schwartz over. Freyja reached over to him, grabbed the hood of his cloak, and cast it back with a flick of her wrist. This revealed Odin's aged, wizened face, long white hair flowing over his shoulders and an even longer white beard reaching halfway to his knees – and one eye, that now fixed a witheringly penetrating gaze on the orb.

"Alright Gandalf, alright. Let me catch my train of thought! Damn Loke, anyway. He did… something. I'm trying to figure out what."

Eryn could swear that she saw the old man roll his one eye. Freyja continued to stare at the translucent orb, gesturing at it.

"*Gandalf,* Freyja? Really?" Odin muttered. "You'll confuse them. The oldest of them has seen fewer than what, thirty winters or so? Kids, really."

"I *told* them your name a minute ago." Freyja retorted. "You don't think they can keep up? Oh fine, be that way then. Friends, his real name is Odin. Well, one of his names is Odin. He has at least fifty or sixty names in the Indo-European tongues alone, just to keep things interesting. Allfather, Ygg, Wotan if you are feeling particularly Germanic. Gandalf even – Tolkien intended him to be Odinic. Take your pick."

"Thank you, Freyja." Odin chortled. "Good to know I can count on you for an accurate, fascinating, yet somehow still demeaning introduction. I will have to instruct them on all *your* names, one day. Now, focus!"

"I'm getting to it!" Freyja laughed. "Okay. Kids, Einherjar, whatever. See this thing I'm looking at here? The thing I sent to call you here? It is named the Web of Norns. Short answer to the obvious question—'But what is the Web of Norns, Freyja?'— is that it's a representation of how your universe, that we call Midgard, looks from our perspective."

She took a deep breath and grinned at them, an unmistakable intent burning in her eyes, a look that any student of a sufficiently passionate professor would understand: she was going to give them a lecture.

"*Perspective* is very important here. Anything you perceive, you do so from a certain perspective. A perspective that can be physically located at distinct points in time and space, that can be described relative to all other points in time and space. This perspective is shaped—*defined*, really —by physical conditions, past and present. It is linked to that strange phenomenon called the *mind*, of course, but your sensory organs ultimately control what the mind can perceive, and *they* are physical objects, therefore subject to physical conditions. Which *themselves* are in turn defined, in the end, by the infinity of moments that comprise the history of your universe—Midgard—from what you call the Big Bang to its inevitable end."

"*You* as an entity, an individual existing in Midgard, are a mind attached to an assembly of congealed bits of energy you call matter that interact according to consistent rules, which were established at the start of Midgard, in the event known to your physicists as the Big Bang. Your body and everything around you, everything you have ever seen or touched in your entire existence, is the product of rule-based interactions of congealed energy bits with a history going back to the very beginning. Cause and effect, all the way down."

"None of this is ought to be any sort of deep metaphysical revelation, but it is important to keep in mind, because

Midgard is only one universe, one World, of *nine*. And in fact, Midgard itself is the youngest of the Nine Worlds, the product of—so far as we can tell—a peculiar alignment of Muspelheim, Niflheim, and Jotunheim."

Freyja looked intently at them, and chose her words carefully.

"Have you ever stopped to wonder why, in Midgard, your physicists can't reconcile theories of quantum mechanics and relativity to produce a unified theory of physics, which would offer a roadmap for understanding all events in the universe?"

They all shook their heads, except Loucas, who nodded vigorously. Odin growled in frustration. Schwartz hissed lazily at him. Odin hissed back. Schwartz ignored him, and groomed a paw.

"Freyja, this has to be the fifteen-minute version, not the BBC special."

"I know, I know! I'm getting there! Okay, the abbreviated version: the fundamental forces that animate your world, Midgard, come from other Worlds. Niflheim is where you get *gravitational* forces, Jotunheim is the source of *quantum* effects, and Muspelheim injected all the *energy* into the system at the very beginning that later congealed into the matter that made you. There was a great explosion, producing the hot dense state that characterizes Midgard's early years, and..."

Odin cut her off. "Back to the Web of Norns, Freyja!"

"Shut. Up. Odin! I'm getting there! Some things take a Midgard minute!"

Freyja took a deep breath. "Now what's very interesting, you see, is that your perception of *time* itself, as being this sequential cause-and-effect thing? That's actually a product of your perspective as beings *within* Midgard. But from *outside*

Midgard, what we perceive as "time" functions very differently than it does for you. *We* can actually interact with Midgard at any point in the history of spacetime we choose. From the beginning right up to the end."

"And this doesn't destroy causality how?" Loucas asked, shaking his head. "I'm barely following you, but what you're saying seems... off."

Freyja beamed. "Yes, this raises *very* interesting questions about free will and determinism, but we don't have the time —I *know*, Odin—so let me tell you of *Threads* like I mentioned before. You humans experience the world in terms of sequential moments, from birth to death, taking place at a particular point in time and space, as you know them. And you perceive the existence of interactions between objects and processes that span space and time, like your own self does. Things look very, well, *linear* to you. You ride your thread, looking backwards and forwards, never perceiving side to side. Not your fault, just a consequence of your existence as material objects in a constrained universe."

"In actuality, though, Midgard functions in probabilistic terms. Every event is conditioned by the odds, and here's the extra-special part: those of your theorists who claim that *every* possible moment spawns its own reality? Closer to truth than a bunch of mutated primates ought to ever get, frankly. But since you can get Shakespeare with sufficient chimpanzees and a decent sorting algorithm, maybe I shouldn't be so surprised?"

"Freyja..." Odin warned. "Don't insult our guests."

"Oh, fine, anyway my point is this: we on the outside perceive Midgard as a sort of spherical space bounded by the full set of zero-probability outcomes – things that simply *can't* happen. There are two *poles* located at antipodal points along the equatorial latitude of this sphere—one, the Big Bang, the other—the End. Ragnarok, the destruction of Midgard."

"Everything in between those two points? Totally up to probability. The only two penultimate restrictions are Big Bang and Ragnarok, with all matter within Midgard linked together by independent chains of cause and effect stretching between the two. A Thread where events played out a certain way. You all came from one distinct Thread. And you were all displaced by Loke onto another Thread, one almost identical to your own."

"The Web of Norns is our *representation* of the fact that there are infinite *possible* paths a Thread could take through the probability space that is Midgard, but also that some realities are systematically more *likely* than others. More likely paths are brighter on the display. And you see this sort of *trunk* stretching from pole to pole? That's what we call the Main Sequence, a dense cluster of realities that are quite similar. Though I have to say it… looks much less dense than usual. Huh, odd."

Freyja shook her head and stared at the web. She started and blinked hard. Then she tapped at it several times before grunting then turning to look at them.

"Odin, we have a problem." Freyja said, exhaling slowly.

Odin grunted in affirmation. "I was waiting for you to notice, Freyja."

Freyja manipulated the orb to zoom in on a single thread, dimming the others. It glowed with a strange, sickly light. She started shaking her head, muttering to herself. Odin fixed his gaze on the increasingly confused friends.

"What Freyja would tell you, if she weren't busy gibbering in terror, is that Loke has used you to create a paradox. Something that should not exist within Midgard. Ever. Actually, we *had* thought that it was next to impossible to create one. Apparently, Loke disagreed."

Odin sighed, and Freyja looked at him, then sighed herself.

"Definitely a paradox, Allfather. No doubt. The intervention points are just right, the bastard. Absolutely no way to reconcile Hitler's early death in 1944 with the destruction of Station Rome's Terrestrial Occupation Center in 2147 *and* the nightmare about to unfold in western North America in 2041. Not all in the same Thread of reality! And even if we could—Loke *also* caused a massive volcanic event right in the middle of those centuries in their original Thread! Two impossible Threads collapsing into one another... Fimbulwinter has fallen upon the Nine Worlds. Ragnarok is coming, and I can't see a way to stop it."

Eryn cursed aloud. "Will someone *please* tell me what is going on? What this all actually means? For us, in the here and now, *wherever* or *whenever* that apparently is now that Loke has done... *whatever* to us."

"By making you Einherjar," Odin spoke gravely, "Loke was able to insert you into the same Thread at three critical points. This created a paradox that will grow to consume all Worlds. You see, those of us from outside of Midgard can enter into it. But by doing so, we become entangled with whatever thread we touch. We create an event that all cause-effect interactions in that thread *must* be able to account for to maintain the laws of causality that underpin Midgard's existence."

"Threads blend into one another constantly, something imperceptible from your frame of reference within a given Thread, so much of what we do is harmless. But they do not break! Midgard, from our frame of reference, always self-corrects to prevent a paradox from occurring by blending Threads in ways you cannot perceive. Not even the Vanir know why this is. But it *is*. And a consequence is that the longer we interact with a Thread, the more other Threads seem to be drawn to it, and the greater the risk our intervention impacts Midgard as a whole.

"So every time an entity from outside Midgard interacts with it, they tend to cause threads to sort of... collect... at that in space and time. That interaction becomes increasingly likely to occur across *all* Threads, drawing others to it. In effect, the event becomes 'truth' insofar as Midgard is concerned, and all Threads thus entangled are forced to conform to the *physical* requirements of cause and effect necessary to make a reality."

Freyja cut in. "Which makes what Loke did so damned devastating! He picked the absolute *perfect* set of points to strike. All the Web is beginning to shift as Midgard itself shifts to make the events of those Threads reality for *all* Threads."

Eryn's patience was at an end. "So tell us then! *What does this mean?*"

Freyja laughed. "You know, I think you may be one of mine, when you're a bit more seasoned! Well, it means that you six may represent the last, incredibly slim chance Midgard—we all, really—have. Fimbulwinter has begun—Loke is free along with his demented family, and there's little *we* can do that won't simply make matters worse."

"But *you* might be able to make a difference. Maybe. Given time, and survival. Loke forced you six to be his Einherjar, but this allows *us* to help you in small ways. You will have refuge here whenever you can get away. Just grasp the Web, as you did before—but you will have to make sure you can't be seen!"

Odin nodded. "As time is running short already, I must warn you that you will be drawn back to Midgard when the time above the doors you entered through reaches zero, ensuring that your absence from your Thread does not materially impact events. And it is always best to go before you must, to have time to prepare for whatever you are about to encounter. Unless you sever your connection with the Thread entirely—by dying, say—you will always be pulled back there whenever your absence could result in a mini-paradox. Fatal, those, so best avoided. And do try to avoid dying! What small chance we may have now relies on your collectively making an impact—as you can. One person can rarely do much against the tides of the world. Still, one must try."

"I *told* you he was Gandalf!" Freyja giggled.

"Oh clam up, Freyja." Odin shook his head.

Eryn looked at the handwritten time over the door she realized was now hers. She had fewer than ten minutes left before, unless these Norse gods were messing with them, she had to return to Germany, in 1944. *After* killing Adolf Hitler and joining a probably-doomed conspiracy to overthrow the Nazi regime. She looked at Odin with her mouth open, but Patrick spoke before she could.

"So you are telling us that we are all stuck wherever we all just landed with no escape, and have to just go about our merry way from here in hopes of not dying and also *maybe* stopping the world from ending?

Odin nodded. "Indeed. Oh, and you have three years— from your frame of reference. At most. Probably substantially less. The paradox will progress as Fimbulwinter deepens."

Timur pushed his mug aside and stood up, shaking his head in disbelief. "Look, I'm actually kinda digging the whole 'acting out the old Norse fairy-tales' thing we seem to be doing, but this is getting ridiculous. Loke, whatever he is, splits us up and sets off Ragnarok? But it will take three years to get around to happening. So, why bother going back? What's the point? What can we accomplish? Nobody is shooting at us here, so I'd kind of prefer to stay."

Freyja smiled. "Because, don't you see? We're operating in

unknown territory here. Fimbulwinter has begun, and the Web is beginning to tear. That means the End is coming, but it *also* means that probability and prediction are starting to become less reliable. There may be opportunities to postpone the inevitable, as we have done for so long."

"Uh huh. And how do we do that then? How do we know what to try and accomplish? And how much *can* we even get done? I'm getting press-ganged into being some kind of soldier along with Patrick and Kim in some dystopic future North America, as best as I can tell. Prior experience with the whole *war* thing tells me that we won't have a lot of free time."

Odin and Freyja shared a look. His eye turned back to stare at Timur.

"You do what you can." Odin said, speaking slowly and carefully. "Whatever seems right and best protects those around you. But also, when you are able, you check the Web of Norns to evaluate your actions."

Timur rolled his eyes, pointing at the shimmering orb. "And how do we do that? How do we tell anything from that tangled mess? Can we all do what Freyja does with it?"

Odin and Freyja looked at him. Schwartz and Weiss looked at Yari, who yelped as if in sudden realization, grimaced, then walked up to the glowing orb. She placed her hand on it. And then, it changed. Yari clearly didn't know what she was doing, but it was a start.

"See," Freyja smiled, "Yari understands—you zoom in, zoom out, pan. Should be intuitive. At least for her. The integration with a machine intelligence is already altering her brain in quite beneficial ways."

A humming noise began and then a calm digitized voice sounded from inside the orb. "Odin, Freyja, you might have at least told them about poor Mimr. I do listen, you know."

Odin laughed. "Sorry Mimr, I didn't realize you had checked in. Introduce yourself!"

"Hello World! I'm Mimr, the living interface for the Web of Norns. I am fully equipped as a research platform and decision-support system, and can provide predictions on the outcomes of proposed actions. But you can't really use me in front of other people. So long as you have privacy, I'm happy to help answer any questions you might have."

Timur cocked an eyebrow, and looked back and forth between Freyja and Odin.

"So that's different—you aren't re-enacting *all* the bits of the mythology, then? Though, Mimr as a computer would explain Heod getting beheaded in Vanaheim in the wayback, if I'm remembering the Eddas right. You know, that whole thing when he couldn't make decisions without Mimr being around, and annoyed everyone around him."

Odin chuckled. "We aren't re-enacting anything, you humans just forgot the full truth of the matter. Small wonder, as you live only a century or so, and it has been thousands of years since the Aesir-Vanir war affected your world. Loke's lies don't help matters, either. But you are an intuitive thinker, that I'll grant you. Continue to impress me, and I may have to claim you for Val-Hall."

Mimr made a buzzing sound, as if he were eager to change the subject. "*In any event*, if you are all done discussing the *very distant* past, I hear that time is pressing. Let the all-knowing Mimr guide you on! First, Eryn, you made sure that Adolf Hitler died. Well done! Even if it does help cause a paradox, few men deserved early death more than he!"

"Now, Eryn, in order to survive, you will have to convince the German coup plotters not to make the foolish errors they almost certainly will make while carrying out Operation Valkyrie as planned. You are on the right track already —but you must make sure that two things happen. First, most of the Nazi leadership must be killed within a week, or a counter-coup will be inevitable and impossible to stop. Do whatever you can to effect that outcome. And second, you must convince the German military leadership that there is no hope in continuing to wage the war as they have so far."

Eryn stared at the orb, silent. Mimr buzzed again.

"Timur, Patrick, and Kim, your presence at that convoy has set in motion a terrible conflict. Nothing to do with your actions, actually, just the fact that you were there was enough to light the fire. You must integrate with the Missoula Regiment, but remember who you are, and what you believe: 2041 is a time where humanity is seeing the willful bastardization of some of the most important technological developments of the past two centuries, all in the interest of a few people's petty power interests. The norm for much of your history, but as ever—not everyone is satisfied with the way of things. There are allies lurking in the most unlikely places."

"Finally—Loucas, Yari. For now, survive. Just survive. The events of 2147 will carry you forward without your having much choice in the matter. You have already begun something quite incredible. But you can't let yourselves be discouraged by the difficulties you will face. Trust one another, and the few friends you find, no matter who they are. But be very, very sure of them. If I may make an admittedly biased suggestion: in 2147, machine intelligence is more reliable than most human intelligence you will encounter. But, always remember: a human mind is born, and a machine mind is programmed. *Who* is ultimately responsible for that difference matters far more in the latter case than the former."

Eryn's heart started pounding, faster and faster as she watched her time fall inexorably towards zero. She looked at her friends. All looked stunned, shocked, and to a certain degree dismayed. And her heart sank.

It was all her fault. She had been the one who had dragged them to Akureyri in the first place, and then taken Dr. Toek's suggestion of a magma-hunting excursion. And now unbelievable, incredible, terrifying things were happening to them all—and it certainly looked as if matters would only get worse from here on out.

She wanted to reach out to them, and to say something. But anxiety was surging. Fear was returning, despite the restorative effects of the mead. She turned to Freyja, searching her eyes for answers.

Freyja smiled kindly. "Whenever you can make sure that you are guaranteed some time alone, think of the web, then grasp it. You will find yourself walking through the door, to this refuge. We may or may not be around at a given moment, but help yourself at the bar. Weiss and Schwartz usually hang about too, unless they're off pulling my chariot. They can show you whatever you might need."

Odin did not smile, but nodded sagely. "You should all have an opportunity to return here within the next few days. It will take some time and thinking to coordinate regular visits, but it can be managed. And remember: you are Einherjar, and you have earned the right to drink of Idunn's brew. It will restore you when all else fails."

Freyja nodded in agreement. "Also, some of our brethren, Aesir and Vanir, are usually here. Sometimes it becomes quite a party! You may find some of their insights helpful. They can help make some more sense of the wider world you are now becoming aware of. My brother is a bit of a buffoon, but not all bad. And Odin's son Thor is rough, but you'll like him—most humans do."

"Even if he is a bit daft." Odin snorted.

"Odin, you are the worst father *ever*. Small wonder you tried being a mother once or twice. Seeking your true calling?"

Eryn's clock hit zero. A bell tolled from somewhere unseen. It was past time to return. Eryn stood up, as did her friends. They looked at one another united by their collective feelings of blended fear and hope. She gave them a wan smile. Kim shook her head and sighed.

"Our return flights are all coordinated, huh? I guess we don't have any choice. Timur, you'd better train me and Patrick up but good! I don't want to die in Idaho, in 2041 or any other time."

Timur flashed her a grim smile. Then he gave Eryn a curious look.

"So Eryn, you really killed Hitler, then? Well done! Seriously. Well, Miss Merry Brandybuck, like Pippin Took at the Battle of the Morannon, I'm gonna have to work hard to match your deed! An infantry fighting vehicle is as far a cry from Adolf Hitler as a hill-troll is from the Witch-King of Angmar."

Despite herself, Eryn laughed. "Pun intended? He did die crispy! But yeah, I guess I did kill Hitler. At least, I helped. Stuff was already happening. I just kind of… nudged events along. It really was a team effort. Though, now that you mention it, so was killing the Lord of the Nazgul in Lord of the Rings, huh? It took a woman and a halfling to do what no man could."

Loucas laughed. "And where do I fit into Tolkien's legendarium, then? But Killing Hitler, *damn*. Beats my own bombing run—which I didn't even know I was making. Not sure an office building, even one in a space station, comes close to that."

Patrick chimed in. "Yeah, that's a pretty epic start. It'll be even more epic if you can keep from dying in the aftermath. Hope the people who got blown up deserved it."

"Thanks Patrick, for that tremendous vote of confidence."

The bell tolled again, twice. An awkward moment—none wanted to go, and none knew exactly what to say to the others. It had been a strange day. And it wasn't over, not yet. In fact, it was starting to look like the day wouldn't really end for a very long time.

Eryn sighed, and turned from her friends. She reached out to touch the door. It began to glow around the edges, a brilliant light that dimmed even the steady bright candles of Mimr's Pub, and it swung open. Eryn stepped in, and shut her eyes as the light burst in a blinding flash.

The six friends parted. To begin.

PART 2

It will be harsh for heroes...
age of axes, age of swords, shields cloven,
age of wind, age of wolves,
until the world is ruined.

VOLUSPA

THE BENDLERBLOCK

Screeching tires and rattling aluminum welcomed Eryn back to 1944. The Heinkel's engines roared as the pilot brought the aircraft to a manageable speed, then faded away as the aircraft rolled to a stop.

Eryn, out of habit, began feeling around for the restraints that on most flights couldn't be removed without risking a stewards' wrath. She wondered why they were so difficult to unbuckle, then remembered. This wasn't the end of a normal flight.

She was about to debark into Berlin, in the middle of the Second World War, after having assisted a hero of German history in *changing* that history. Hitler was dead six months before his time, and she had probably only avoided being arrested and shot so far by pretending to be working for Howard Hughes

Wait. Howard Hughes?

The aircraft came to a full stop the same instant Eryn realized that she had mixed up which idiosyncratic American industrialist she was pretending to work for. She'd told the German rebels that she was employed by Henry Ford, when she'd *meant* to say Howard Hughes.

Eryn winced, turned her head towards the porthole that passed for a window on the Heinkel 111, and thumped her head against it in frustration. It wasn't easy to come up with a semi-plausible story for how she had gotten so close to a man who had survived *numerous* prior assassination attempts. Getting details like that incorrect could easily prove fatal—although, would Claus von Stauffenberg and Werner von Haeften even know who Henry Ford was?

She heard something towards the front of the aircraft, and Haeften appeared in the aisle. The moment he caught her gaze, he stopped, beckoned once, then turned and walked away.

No one could see or hear her, so she shrugged, sighed, and shook her head, then obeyed. Not that she had much of a choice. Eryn tried to walk as slowly as she could without making it *completely* obvious that she was stalling for time. Her brain worked frantically to consolidate the past few hours into something tangible she could use to figure out what to do next.

As she made her way forward, Eryn was overwhelmed by a curious sensation, a fusion of adrenaline and desperation that she could only attribute to the influence of whatever Freyja had said was in the mead, that had the combined effect of both sharpening and focusing her thought. She almost thought she could smell pine needles amid the grease of the German aircraft. It was simultaneously frightening yet invigorating, and by the time she reached the front of the aircraft where a stairway had been rolled up to assist with disembarkation, she felt at least *ready*, if not in any way truly *prepared*, for whatever was about to happen.

Haeften waited a short way off, and behind him was a staff car, crewed by a uniformed driver who stood stiff next to an open door. Stauffenberg was nowhere in sight, but not far from the staff car was a small building draped in some kind of dull-colored netting, and two guards stood by an open door. Eryn realized Stauffenberg must be telephoning his compatriots to inform them of Hitler's death, signaling that the planned coup to displace and destroy the ruling Nazi regime was to proceed.

In the history she knew, the coup had been more or less doomed from the start because Stauffenberg's bomb failed to kill *der Fuhrer*. But in this version, with the creature actually dead, how long would it be before events began to diverge? Eryn couldn't be sure. But so long as it stayed reasonably close to what she had read, she had a chance.

Eryn reached Haeften, who stood still, watching her closely. He placed a hand on a leather pouch affixed to his belt, and lifted it to show her the handle of a handgun, barrel resting safely in the holster—for the moment. She stopped, took a breath, and stared at him.

Neither spoke. Haeften turned and marched to the waiting car without a word, and took a seat in the rear half of the cabin, assisted by the vehicle's driver. Eryn followed Haeften, but walked to the other side of the car and stood by the door, waiting to see if the driver would invite her in. After hesitating for the briefest moment, he did, though again without a word.

Eryn climbed in, then had to stifle a cry. A sharp pain in her foot reminded her that she wasn't wearing any shoes. She had been too absorbed to notice, but catching her foot on a metal rivet was too much to ignore. She waited to see if she felt blood trickle into her sock, not wanting to bring Haeften's attention to her mishap. No blood came, and she took a slow, deep breath, and tried to ignore the throbbing in her foot.

Stauffenberg emerged from the doorway and walked to the waiting staff car. The driver opened the vehicle's front passenger side door, and carefully assisted Stauffenberg into his seat. Eryn saw the veteran officer grimace in obvious pain. She remembered having read that not all of his injuries from the war were visible.

As the driver took his seat and activated the engine,

Stauffenberg twisted to look back at Haeften—and Eryn.

"Werner, we must get to the Bendlerblock and take over management of Valkyrie. They sound like headless chickens over there. The reserve army deployments are only *just* beginning, even though they must know that we don't have time to waste! There has been no reaction from the Gestapo or area SS units *so far*, but the moment Himmler is able to establish communications from wherever he has hidden himself, we must be ready!"

Haeften set his jaw, face grim. "I did not expect that we would be greeted by the Brandenbergers as we landed, but I had at least hoped to hear that Paris and Vienna were taking the necessary steps."

Haeften jerked his head towards Eryn. "While we drive, we had better figure out what to do about her. Unless you are prepared to have me shoot her."

Stauffenberg did not look at her. Eryn realized in that instant that she had only one chance to convince them that she was on their side. She had to do something to truly get their attention, but keep present in their minds *just* enough uncertainty about who she really was, so that they wouldn't come to the logical, obvious conclusion: that she was lying. The only thing she had going for her was a rough ability to predict the future.

She fixed her gaze on Stauffenberg, and made her voice as firm and confident as she could manage. To enhance the illusion, she told as much of the truth as she could.

"I told you before: I have information that you need, and I want to help you. So let me!"

They stared at her, and kept silent. So she continued.

"The most important thing you need to know is that Fromm can't be trusted. He will betray you, he's *already* betraying you. He will walk right out of that room your comrades put him in and try to contact Rastenburg. And if that fails, he'll go straight to the SS.

Haeften chuckled. "That's no surprise, Fromm has always cared about his own skin and little else. They were supposed to have arrested him by now."

Stauffenberg nodded. "In fact, they have assured me that he *is* in custody. He claims that Hitler is not dead, and that the reserve army must remain in place until formal orders arrive from Rastenburg. They have him sequestered in the Bendlerblock."

Eryn shook her head. "No, they don't. They think they do, but Colonel Stauffenberg, you heard them on the phone. It must be total chaos over there, and no one will be looking too closely at General Fromm. He can, and I am sure he will, walk out of there and alert the SS about Valkyrie."

They didn't respond, but Stauffenberg and Haeften stared at one another for a short while. Then each turned and sat quietly, as if considering her argument. Which was more than she'd expected. With the prediction made, now she had to hope Fromm would play his role. She looked out the window, and watched as the buildings and parks of central Berlin passed by.

The city seemed strange, and not because it was foreign. Eryn had always enjoyed travel, new places and new people, new problems and new challenges. But this city seemed... odd. Both buzzing with activity, but also subdued, somber. Even the way people were moving on the sidewalks seemed to betray a strange sort of alert weariness. The only real life seemed to reside in the youngest residents, and it seemed out of place when paired with their uniforms: either the smart-yet-depressing Nazi Youth look, or the smart-but-spare aesthetic so often apparent among people in desperate situations, where the effort of being clean and tidy matters far more than actual success.

"What is your name, madam, if I may be so bold as to ask? We have not been properly introduced."

Eryn started and turned to see Stauffenberg twisted back again in his seat, staring into her eyes. She met his gaze. "Eryn... just Eryn will do for now."

"Just Eryn? Well, madam Eryn, it is a pleasure to make your acquaintance. You seem to know exactly who Haeften and I are, so formal introductions shouldn't be necessary, I'm sure you'll agree. Now, please tell us again: exactly who is it that you work for and why is your organization so apparently intent on assisting our cause."

"Like I told you before: I work for Mr. Henry Ford, of Ford Motor Company."

Haeften chuckled. "And why, pray tell us, would an American automobile manufacturer whose factories are building tanks intended to kill Germans and destroy our country have either the inclination *or* resources to send a... *helper*, into our ranks? Do Roosevelt's spies have no power whatsoever?"

Eryn hesitated and looked away from her interrogators. But looking out the window only made the situation more surreal. Though this part of Berlin did not appear to have experienced the massive bombing raids she knew were, in 1944, being sent by day and night against many other German cities; still, here and there a building, sometimes in the middle of a block that was otherwise untouched, would be missing a wall, or roof, or have crumbled entirely into a pile of rubble.

She turned back to Haeften. "This war can't end well for Germany. And if Germany falls, what will stop the Soviets from advancing to the Rhine, or beyond? How long will they wait to spread their revolution around the world? Many American leaders want to prevent that from happening. But they aren't in the government. And they can't do anything about Roosevelt's policy towards either Germany or the Soviet Union."

Stauffenberg cut in, leaning towards her. "But the coming American election? Surely the Americans can replace Roosevelt and his allies? If your industrialists are turning against the war…"

Eryn hesitated. There was something in Stauffenberg's tone, a flash of… hope? It didn't seem quite right. Did he really believe that an election could change America's foreign policy, in the middle of the worst war the world had ever experienced? Or was he baiting her?

She chose her words carefully, and spoke slowly. "Roosevelt will win. The opposition isn't very well organized. Our best hope is that with Hitler out of the way, a more reasonable German government will take over. And *maybe,* then, Roosevelt and Churchill will be willing to negotiate a ceasefire."

Both Stauffenberg and Haeften laughed together, and Haeften looked to his superior, who grimaced as he replied. "Churchill is committed to our destruction, regardless of the long-term consequences for the British Empire. The English are too stubborn to see reason, I'm afraid. We offered them peace after their defeat in France, and now the balance of power has swung far in their favor."

He turned away. "Madam Eryn… it seems we are of a kind, the three of us. Hopeless fools, dreaming of a better world. I wish I could trust that your intentions in Berlin were sincere. We will make sure that you are kept safe and secure in my office while we move to end this criminal regime once and for all. And perhaps in the near future we can have a talk, you and I, to determine what if anything your connections to Mr. Ford can do for us. Perhaps the election will go differently than you believe."

As he spoke, the car came to a halt. A makeshift barrier

had been erected across the roadway, and a dozen uniformed soldiers stood or crouched behind it, rifles held at the ready. Stauffenberg seemed pleased to see them, and instructed his driver to roll down a window so that he could speak to the officer in charge.

"Finally, evidence that the reserve army is on the move!" Stauffenberg said. "Tell me, Captain, have you had any difficulties in this position?"

The officer shook his head. "No, Colonel. We have had to re-direct a few vehicles, but no one has challenged us."

"You have had no sight of any Gestapo or SS units?"

"No, sir."

"Excellent. Please carry on."

Stauffenberg returned the officer's salute, and a team of soldiers removed enough of the barrier that the staff car could creep past down the Bendlerstrasse. There were fewer soldiers than Eryn would have expected, given that this was apparently the center of the coup' plotters territory, if they could be said to have any. Unfortunately, none of the many family debates she'd been exposed to over the years told her anything about what troop deployments she should consider normal in Berlin on the night of July 20, 1944.

The staff car came to a stop adjacent to a large but relatively nondescript office building. Stauffenberg immediately exited the vehicle and marched through an open door. Eryn moved to follow, but a flash of metal made her pause. Haeften was out of the car and stood looking at her, an eyebrow cocked. She looked at him, looked at the firearm now in his hand, and smiled as bravely as she could.

"Oh, that again. Do what you have to. Just keep an eye out for Fromm. I'm telling you, you'll catch him trying to get in touch with Rastenburg and the Gestapo."

Eryn didn't bother to wait for a response, just stood tall

and walked slowly and deliberately past Haeften, following Stauffenberg. The roughness of the stone walkway leading to the entrance hurt her feet, but at the moment she hardly minded: her heart was pounding after the attempt at gallantry. Being flippant with a mutineer carrying a handgun was not a bright idea, she knew. But the more she talked to these stiff, severe German officers, the more she realized that the only way she was going to survive was by keeping them uncertain about her. Like a desperate gazelle charging at the prowling lions. But beyond bluffing confidence on her way to whatever confinement they had in mind, she wasn't entirely sure what to try next.

The interior of the Bendlerblock office building, where the coup plotters had established their headquarters, looked pretty much like any government office in any time or place. Dour, infused with the odor of ink and paper, and liable to induce claustrophobia in anyone who enjoyed the outdoors. She followed Stauffenberg, aware of Haeften not far behind, down a dark corridor and up a flight of stairs. As he marched, he was joined by an ever-growing posse of men in uniform, each making a report or asking for orders. Some, unable to get a word in edge-wise, fell back to address Haeften, who was treated with almost the same level of deference as Stauffenberg himself.

Naturally, virtually every one of the officers who approached also stared at Eryn as she marched past. Strangely, she felt herself grateful for whatever force had decided she'd appear in 1944 attired as a female member of the SS. Despite dumping the boots and Nazi insignia, the mere fact that she wore a uniform that screamed 'evil Gestapo' kept inquiries at bay, though nothing could apparently deter the questioning stares.

Stauffenberg's office was in the midst of a cluster of similar spaces buried in the depths of the building. The moment he entered the suite containing his personal office, cheers broke out from the swarm of men and women who were packed into the space. Eryn stepped aside, instinctively aware that this was a moment where if she was noticed at all, it would be as an intruder.

Haeften stepped to Stauffenberg's side at his superior's silent instruction, almost hesitantly, like a child being recognized in front of a school auditorium. The cheers were deafening, and in that moment, as Eryn looked at the faces, she was struck by how *young* they mostly were. Neither Stauffenberg nor Haeften was much older than she herself. But she knew their biographies well enough: both had experienced the horrors of war, the same war her own grandparents had fought in on the Allied side. Both men had seen their country stolen by fanatics, their cities annihilated, their friends and family forced to live in fear of a regime that would happily send them to a concentration camp. And both had done something about it. They had tried to kill their leader to save their country.

In Eryn's time, their sacrifice had been almost entirely futile. Hitler had survived the bombing, and the coup had fallen apart in hours. Many of the people now cheering in this building were *supposed* to be arrested or executed that very night.

And they still might be. Hitler's death only eliminated one complication out of several facing the coup. Now, the would-be revolutionaries had to navigate a future that would soon become opaque even to someone with foreknowledge of critical events. And, though she pushed this thought down deep for the time being, also were in touch with people who were or claimed to be Norse gods.

The cheers subsided, ending as suddenly as they had begun. Eryn expected Stauffenberg to say something, but he and Haeften merely looked at one another, bowed slightly, then straightened again. Everyone turned back to their business without another word, and the noise level grew. Women pounded frantically at typewriters, men walked swiftly between desks carrying messages to other men talking rapidly on phones, and senior personnel crowded around odd machines that appeared to be the 1944 equivalent of a fax.

Stauffenberg made eye contact and nodded at Eryn—she took that to mean she should follow him. He walked through the bustle of the room, fielding simple questions as they were shouted at him, and Haeften, after waiting for Eryn to follow his senior officer, brought up the rear. He too was the recipient of numerous questions, and everyone was talking too quickly for Eryn to make out anything more than a general din.

Stauffenberg led them into what Eryn assumed was his office: a spare and utilitarian space that was filled with at least half a dozen older men, most wearing gray military outfits, others clad in dark-colored business suits that served as well as uniforms. A young woman, probably a secretary, sat quietly in a corner, scribbling into a notebook whenever the men spoke. A grey-haired man, one of the suit-wearers, turned to address Stauffenberg.

"Colonel Stauffenberg, finally! Please make your report as soon as you can catch your breath."

Stauffenberg stopped in front of the semi-circle, and saluted—not in the Nazi 'hail Hitler' style, just a crisp and quick movement of finger-tips from thigh to brow and back again, that the man who had addressed him returned slowly and deliberately. It was a simple motion, yet it seemed to convey both admiration and appreciation.

Haeften seemed to be distracted by the gesture, and Eryn felt more than saw his hand twitch towards his own forehead, as if moved by an emotion or instinct both powerful and subtle.

Taken by a sudden instinct of her own, Eryn walked quickly away from Haeften, moving across the room to stand by the secretary. Haeften jerked involuntarily towards her, but remained where he was, apparently torn between guarding her or standing at Stauffenberg's side. Eryn turned around, now to the side of the important-looking men and Stauffenberg, and saw Haeften fix her with an icy stare. Which she returned, keeping her face carefully impassive even as her heart thumped so hard she thought her chest must be visibly twitching.

The older man who had addressed Stauffenberg finished his honor salute, then nodded. "Colonel Stauffenberg, we and the German people owe you a great debt. Unfortunately, events are pressing, and we have no time for a proper debrief. But still, I wish to take this moment to hear the words directly from you. Hitler—you can confirm that he is in fact dead?"

Stauffenberg nodded slowly. "I can, General Beck. Although the briefing was held in a different location than expected, and there were of course other unforeseen difficulties, the deed is done. Hitler is dead at last, and barring a miracle Generals Jodl and Keitel have also joined him in Hell."

Beck sighed. "Thank you. Your word of honor as an officer in the army is sufficient… for me. Unfortunately, the greater task remains, and we will have difficulty convincing many of the other officers to join our cause—unless we can demonstrate our unity and strength. Valkyrie is moving too slowly —many officers seem reluctant to accept the news out of Rastenburg."

Stauffenberg shook his head in frustration. "There is no time for hesitation! Are the reserve army commands at least acknowledging their deployment orders? Dragging their feet is one thing, but outright defiance would be disastrous."

Another of the assembled men, this one wearing a military uniform, replied. "Some are, some aren't. It is difficult to accept that the tyrant is dead, after all these years and so many failed attempts at assassination."

"Then I must speak with the holdouts. If Himmler or any of the others gets on the radio and issues counter-orders, we will have a civil war on our hands. In the meantime, has there been any word from the units tasked with securing Berlin? If we can at least hold the capital, we have a chance to bypass the SS before they can react."

One of the uniformed men nodded. "A unit of the Brandenburgers should arrive at any moment. Others are in fact moving, and available units of the GD division have confirmed their deployment orders—they simply need more time to assemble in the capitol."

Stauffenberg took a deep breath. "Then I recommend that we contact all of the units that are hesitant and ask them to affirm their orders. I will do all I can to convince them of the truth of what I have seen with my own eyes: Hitler is dead."

There was no dissent, and though Eryn could not tell whether there was a dismissal buried in that conversation, Stauffenberg looked at Haeften, nodded, then turned to leave the office. All of the men in the room followed immediately, except Haeften. He fixed a glare on Eryn, and waited for the others to leave. Then he walked slowly, menacingly, towards her. She held her ground, but could sense that the secretary, now with no notes to scribble, was suddenly very nervous.

"Eryn—if that is what we are to call you—stay here. Do not leave this office. We don't have time to determine the truth of your claims, and the others don't need to know about the... complications... you have introduced."

He turned and left without another word. One thing she had to hand to these German officers, they simply *expected* obedience—and so people obeyed. Even her. Mostly.

Eryn stood quietly, looking at the door to the office, listening to the buzz of voices and keystrokes wafting in from the rest of the suite. She was still alive, and that was something, but it appeared that Stauffenberg and Haeften were more or less done with her for the time being. At exactly the time when she was *supposed*—if she understood what the digital… thing, calling itself Mimr, had been telling her and her friends—to be trying to actively influence the course of events so that they succeeded in their goal.

But what on Earth was she actually supposed to do, out of place and out of time, a stranger in a *very* strange land, with her one possible advantage—partial fore-knowledge of the future—slipping away at every moment?

Then she remembered what Mimr had said about 'grasping the web'. If she could get herself alone, she could talk to Mimr again, and ask for advice. That, after all, was what he said he was good for, wasn't it?

Only the secretary remained in the office, and although the door remained open and people were moving quickly back and forth in front of it, no one even bothered to look inside. Eryn turned her head slightly, to get a better look at the woman.

She was more than simply young: Eryn was fairly certain she was actually a teenager, eighteen at the oldest though she had clearly applied the right cosmetics and worn the proper clothes to pass for being several years older. She wore glasses and an outfit that was almost too modest, but that seemed to fit some kind of uniform standard, given the similarity to how the other women in the building were dressed.

The secretary realized that Eryn was looking at her, and her face turned pale. She ducked her head, and pretended to be busy organizing notes. Eryn put on as friendly a smile as she could, and turned to properly speak to the nervous woman.

"Hi... so what is your name? I'm Eryn."

"Gertrude. I am very sorry for my accent, my lady, I have only been in the Fatherland for a year, and I am learning slowly. Please excuse me!"

Eryn maintained her smile. "Don't worry, I didn't notice. I'm not German either. Canadian, actually."

"Oh, I've never been to Canada! I am from Holland."

Eryn was curious to hear more, as it seemed strange to her that a young woman from German-occupied Holland would be working in a military office in Berlin. But her anxiety surrounding her own out-of-place-ness was too overwhelming.

"Well I am pleased to meet you, but could I ask you to do me a huge favor? If you aren't too busy."

Gertrude nodded. "They all seem to have left... so maybe I can? What do you need?"

Eryn couldn't help but feel like she was playing poor Gertrude, who seemed too scared to be in the middle of a coup. She made a mental note to make it up to her later, if she could.

"Gertrude, I seem to have lost my shoes. I had to move quickly and this damned uniform came with heels that do *not* fit me. Is it possible that somewhere in this building, there are some boots or shoes *without heels* that I can wear?"

Gertrude's eyes went to Eryn's feet. "I... think so. There is a women's closet where some of the ladies keep things to be repaired whenever there are enough materials to go around. I will check and be back as quickly as I can!"

She stood up, and scurried towards the door. But half a step through, she halted suddenly, and looked back at Eryn.

"So... you aren't SS? I thought they had brought you here as a prisoner?"

Eryn laughed, despite her anxiety. "Oh *hell* no, I'm not one of those murderous thugs." Eryn said, then got another an idea. "Actually, Gertrude, I'm the exact opposite. I helped Colonel Stauffenberg free you all from that madman. And I'll keep helping, if I can. But if first, you can help me to get myself a bit more settled, I would *really* appreciate it."

Gertrude's eyes widened in shock, and with a sort of anxious hybrid of a curtsy and a bow, she turned and almost stumbled as she left the room.

For the moment, at least, Eryn was alone. She walked to the office door, and gently closed it. Then she walked back to Gertrude's desk, and sat in the chair, facing the door. Given that when she'd been taken to Mimr's Pub before, she'd returned in exactly the same position as she'd been in when she left, she figured that it would be better to be facing the door whenever Gertrude—or whomever—came back to the room, than to be facing away.

Eryn realized she wasn't entirely sure how to activate Mimr. She held out her hands, and looked at them. Nothing appeared. Not sure what else to do, she called his name, softly. There was a short silence. And then the room seemed to darken, and before her eyes there it was: the shimmering, flowing, writhing mass of golden light that the strange occupants of the weird place they said was Mimr's pub had called the Web of Norns.

"Hello, Eryn! Mimr is here, happy to help. Now, what do you need?"

Her words came slowly as she stared at the golden orb. "So... Mimr, right? Um, well, I kind of need you to tell me what to do next."

A strange laughing sound filled the room, loud enough that she looked to the door in fear. But it was only Mimr, his voice coming from inside the Web.

"No worries, Eryn! I only appear when there's time to disappear if necessary to prevent discovery. Fortunately, it is trivial for me to tell when there's a chance of someone walking in. Which is good, because you need to grasp the Web and take a trip to the Pub."

Eryn cocked her head. "Can't you help me here?"

Mimr chuckled. "I can, but you don't know the *right* questions to ask. Grasp the Web—there's a short time available before anyone will enter this room again, just enough for a brief tutorial. Plus there are some folks in the pub right now that you haven't met. Grasp the Web, and I'll take you there!"

She wasn't sure what else to do. So she reached out, and as instructed, she grasped the Web of Norns. Reality shifted, and she scarcely had time to register that something was happening before she was back in Mimr's pub.

The pub looked the same as it had what seemed like just a few hours before, except that Odin and Freyja weren't there. A thumping accompanied by laughter drew her attention.

Freyja's cats, Weiss and Schwartz, were stretched out on one of the tables, a tankard of mead between them. Several large and eclectically decorated mugs the size of antique goblets were haphazardly strewn around the remaining table space. More eye-catching by far was the sight of three strange and unfamiliar faces, all displaying the unmistakable signs of mirthful intoxication.

Whatever joke they had shared, Eryn's appearance brought them out of it, and the sound of laughter died away. Three faces turned towards her, each contorted in its own curious expression. Two belonged to what looked like men: one simultaneously youthful and ageless, face framed by a mane of shoulder-length hair golden like ripe wheat; the other seemed the diametric opposite, dark, rugged, and weathered, hair shorter on the head but far longer and bushier in the beard, both red as autumn leaves. The third face was female, dark hair bound in a thick braid, her olive complexion matched by piercing, yet kind eyes. The golden-haired man spoke, grinning stupidly and blinking at Eryn.

"Idunn! Hey, we've got another for the party! Did you invite her?"

The woman shook her head, and smiled at the man. "No, I have no idea who she is. Do you recognize her, Thor?"

Thor shifted his large frame to get a better look at her. Eryn felt curiously... diminished... under his intense glare. But there was no unkindness in it, merely interest and appraisal. And he was clearly affected by whatever he was drinking, as his eyes seemed to be having trouble focusing on Eryn.

"Nope, nobody I know. I'm guessing she's one of Loke's? That'd be about right, since he's loose now. Freyr, didn't your sister say something about unexpected or unusual Einherjar?"

Something about being looked over and discussed by three completely unknown people, apparently with nothing better to do despite the universe allegedly ending than sit around drunk, sparked a flash of anger that Eryn could not suppress. She balled her fists and clenched her teeth.

"OK," she said angrily, "I came here for help figuring out how I'm supposed to talk to Mimr. Can any of you help, or are you all too drunk? I'm a bit short on time!"

All three blinked, looked at one another, and shrugged. Freyr, though he seemed to be the least present of the three, now fixed her with an imperious stare. "Hey, the universe is about to end, and we're all about to die. I think we get to take a moment for some fun! Just because *you* aren't able to perceive what is happening outside of your immediate field of view, don't assume you know the first thing about *us*."

Eryn made a sound, almost a growl. "*Supposedly*, I'm doing something about that *right now*. Which is why I'm asking for help—I have no idea how to work this Mimr...Web...*thing*. Mimr made it seem like you *do*. So are you going to help, or do I have to figure it out on my own?"

Thor grunted. "Good luck with that. Odin's projects aren't usually something anyone else can figure out. Never comments his code. Side effect of being the wisest of us all, I guess, but it is so *irritating*. But anyway, since you are pressed for time I suppose we three drunks can help you out. Provided you stop being annoying and judgmental."

There was a flash, and the Web of Norns appeared above the table where Freyr, Idunn, and Thor sat. The cats opened their eyes, and Weiss batted lazily at a nearby tendril with one paw. Thor touched the Web, and began to move his hands in what looked almost like random gestures. The Web of Norns seemed to pan and shift, and then zoom in on one region that seemed particularly unsettled, even among the slow writhing of the rest.

"Okay, Einherjar, here's the thing. Mimr needs decent parameters in order to tell you what you need to know. By that, I mean that you have to come up with very specific questions to ask about the likely consequences of whatever actions you are thinking of taking to influence events. Which I assume is what you're trying to do in 1944 Germany?"

Eryn blinked. The shift from drunk to technical language was jarring. "So... how do I come up with the right questions?"

"Trial and error, mostly." Thor replied. "The trick is getting to the point where Mimr can show you the *most* likely and consequential outcomes associated with certain major events that may, have, or will occur. Basically, you need to look for branch points within the weaving Threads. Points that Threads seem to collapse into or emerge from. Those are critical points, where the outcome of certain processes and events will significantly predetermine the possible course of possible futures."

She squinted, watching Thor manipulate the thread, apparently focusing now on a particular location. Idunn and Freyr watched closely, seeming now far less intoxicated than she'd thought they were at first. Idunn thrust her hand forward into the web, and pointed.

"*There*. That's the right one, Thor! Wow, take a look at that —a nice, clean split between two equally probably outcome paths."

Freyr pointed too. "Yes! And look, the timespace attributes associated with her location are right on the breakpoint between viable pathways."

Eryn shook her head. "Can you all go slower? Interpret? Something? I have no idea what you are saying.

They ignored her for a moment, the three of them gesturing and speaking so quickly that she couldn't follow. Then Thor raised a thick, calloused hand, and they went silent. He spoke slowly and clearly, pointing at the place on one of the golden tendrils that had caught Idunn and Freyr's attention.

"Alright, there isn't time to run you through a full lesson, but here's the gist of things. In the next few hours, your friends in the Bendlerblock have to spread the word that Hitler is dead and that his Nazi cronies have been arrested. Good news is that they are already doing that, trying to anyway. Bad news is that as things stand now, the surviving Nazi leadership will be able to muddy the waters enough that a civil war and counter-coup become inevitable. And history will mostly return to the path you experienced, only with a slightly different flavor."

She felt suddenly cold. "Wait, so killing Hitler didn't change history? Then what was the point?"

Idunn shook her head so violently that her braid whacked

into Weiss, who swatted at it with claws out, briefly catching it and hanging on. "First off," she said, "you must stop thinking about history as being *history.* Any given historical event represents an outcome that, prior to the event, had a certain probability of occurring. *You* experience only the effects, both fixed and random, that emerge from any and all past events. Which makes it very difficult to know what, at the time of a given event, were the things that were actually important in knowing what events themselves were ever really possible."

She paused, and her speech slowed. "Killing a charismatic leader alone doesn't change the underlying structure that allowed the leader to emerge in the first place. And often, the agents that built and maintained that structure are capable of finding a new charismatic leader to fill the void, so that the original systemic status quo basically re-asserts itself. Individual leaders have both a material and a moral component to their power. The moral aspects, tied to their personal charisma, ideology, and all that, die with the body. But the material aspects of their power, their worldly position and the rights your species tends to accord to a person based on position and title? It remains. And another can swoop in to fill the role. And usually does, in short order. Humans are like moths to flames when it comes to power."

Freyr cut in. "What Idunn is trying to say, is that Hitler will simply be replaced by another member of the Nazi ruling hierarchy, so long as any of that pack of scavengers is able to communicate with the soldiers and police that keep the regime in place."

Thor nodded, and pointed at the Web. "Your thread diverges here, and I am willing to bet Mjolnir itself that if you ask Mimr what controls this division, he'll give you a name or two to work with."

Freyr looked at Thor with a bemused expression. "Don't

actually bet Mjolnir, Thor. It never goes well. Ragnarok will be bad enough without losing your best weapon. Look at me: I gave my sword away, and now I have to face Surtur with just my favorite drinking horn."

Freyr raised his goblet, and downed whatever liquid remained in a single gulp. Thor grunted, and looked at Eryn, apparently waiting for her to speak to Mimr. She didn't know what else to do but comply.

"Mimr." her voice sounded strangely small in that moment. "What controls which direction the thread will go? If I want to make sure that the Nazis lose power, what needs to happen? Who do I need to help, or stop?"

Mimr's voice was tinged with excitement. "Finally! Okay! Well, do you want the long or the short answer?"

Eryn paused. Then laughed weakly. She didn't need to look at the time over the doorway again to know that she didn't have long to waste. "I think short will have to do."

Mimr made a humming sound, almost like he was pleased. "Well then! Simple it is: Eryn, you must get to the Goebbels' residence, and ensure that Joseph Goebbels is taken into custody—or, better yet, killed. He's *the* crucial link at present, and lives just down the street from you in Berlin."

Eryn stared at the web. Took a deep breath. And walked back to the doorway out of the pub that led back to 1944.

OUTFITTING AT YELLOWSTONE

T he first thing Patrick did on returning to 2041 was to collapse in a chair and stare at the door to the hallway, beyond which waited Sandra Chavez and other people in the Missoula Regiment's encampment, Camp Yellowstone.

But the door didn't open. And though the air was abuzz with the sounds of machinery and engines, it was sufficiently muffled that he could still hear the sound of voices inside whatever building they were trapped in. Footsteps thudded down unseen corridors, but none approached the door.

He turned his head slowly from side to side. Kim and Timur were with him, each again dressed in military style fatigues, each also staring at the door. He cleared his throat. They turned to look at him, faces betraying their apprehension. Which, strangely, actually made him feel a little better about his own rising anxiety.

"So. Timur, Kim—now what?"

Kim held out her hands, and gestured in the air. It looked a bit like she was playing air guitar. Timur gave her a strange look and shook his head, his expression flickering between nervousness and bemusement.

"Are you trying to switch Mimr on? Or did Odin turn you into Yngwie Malmsteen?"

She paused, and cocked her head. "Is that supposed to be a what or a who?"

"Oh just Google…oh. Huh. Do you think they have Google in the 2040s?"

Kim glared at him, shaking her head. Then she held out her hands again, and stared at them, as if concentrating hard enough would make the Web appear. But nothing happened.

Timur sighed. "Kim, I think we're just going to have to deal with this on our own. Besides, Mimr said that for now we only have to survive."

Kim dropped her hands and stared at him as if preparing to speak. But before she or he could say anything else, the door burst open, and Sandra Chavez stood there, hair in a dark ponytail slightly flecked with grey, grinning like a mad-woman.

"O-kay! Time to suit up and give you all some toys! Move out—we've got a helo to catch."

Without waiting for an acknowledgment she turned and walked out into the hall, then marched out of sight. Patrick, Kim, and Timur shared a look then as a group stood and followed. Chavez led them through a warren of corridors, then out into the open and across a green space, where people were rushing around like ants whose nest has been disturbed. They all seemed to part for Chavez, some greeting her with a nod or a smile, but Patrick was forced to wind his way through the crowd. Beyond, a squat, ugly, concrete structure covered in some kind of drab-colored mesh was guarded by a pair of burly men armed with equally imposing weapons. Chavez walked right up to the guards, who waved her inside with hardly a second glance.

Patrick had been able to get through the crush more

quickly than his friends, so he made sure that they could see where he was heading, and then marched up to the entrance after Chavez, holding his breath. He assumed that the guards would let him past, but something about them made him nervous. But though they stared menacingly at him as he walked past, they didn't move or speak a word to him.

He only exhaled after he was safely through the doors. And then he threw his arms out, grabbing desperately onto a railing just in time to avoid falling down a flight of stairs. As he stumbled, he heard Chavez laugh cheerfully from a landing somewhere just out of his sight, down at the bottom.

"Watch your step, man! This is what they call a *bunker*. Usually, we bury bunkers so it is harder for people to find and drop bombs on them. Hence, the stairs."

He steadied himself, and though he knew his face had gone bright red, he marched with as much feigned confidence as he could muster down the remaining steps. Chavez didn't wait, and by the time he reached the point where she had called back to him she had already disappeared down a short corridor.

Patrick's fear that Chavez had gone ahead too quickly dissipated when he found that the corridor simply bent 90 degrees, then terminated in an open bay filled with stacks of crates and gear. He could see Chavez speaking with a man and a woman in fatigues standing next to what appeared to be a kiosk filled with an array of expensive-looking computer equipment.

"Have these people even heard of health and safety regulations?" Timur said behind him. "That staircase is going to get someone killed."

Patrick turned his head, and saw Timur arrive, Kim a few paces behind. Timur was rubbing his arm, a welt showing where he must have smashed the limb after nearly falling down the bunker stairs just as Patrick almost had. They grinned weakly at one another, while Kim walked right past them and up to Chavez.

Almost as if she knew that Kim was about to confront her, Chavez finished her conversation and turned, stepping froward and speaking before Kim could. "Welcome to the armory! Niana and Sangbin are grabbing the diagnostic equipment, and then we'll get you all matched to a carapace and headgear."

The two Chavez had named came out from behind the kiosk, pushing something that looked like an souped-up medical cart like you might see in a hospital. Adapted, it appeared, to support not only biometric equipment but also some kind of laser-based scanning system connected to a handheld device that each technician passed over Patrick and his companions several times while instructing them to stand in certain poses or make particular movements.

After a few minutes of what felt like increasingly invasive scans, Niana and Sangbin stacked their various bits of equipment on the cart, tapped a few keys on unseen screens, and then pushed cart and contents back behind the kiosk. Chavez, throughout this, stood quietly to the side watching carefully. When the techs headed back behind the kiosk, she cleared her throat to catch Patrick and his friends' attention.

"Alright, now the fun part—get stripped!" Chavez cried.

Timur, though he looked then like a massive weight had fallen on his shoulders, was the first to move to comply. Patrick and Kim hesitated, sharing a look. Kim closed her eyes and shook her head furiously.

"I know this is going to sound stupid to everyone but me, but… why?"

Chavez fixed Kim with an intense gaze. "Before I answer that, I want you to think about exactly how smart it is to question someone with an immense capacity to make this a very unpleasant day for all of you. Just think about that for a second, let the idea settle a bit. Because it really, really ought to influence what you all say and do from here on out."

Kim and Chavez stared at one another for that second. Then Chavez continued, speaking normally, the menace fading from her voice as quickly as it had appeared. "Now, to answer your question: because your current clothes will really, really suck out in the field. Amlog is great with logistics, terrible with designing combat scrubs and boots. I don't need to deal with you all complaining about rashes and blisters the whole way back from this little misadventure we're about to have. Niana and Sangbin have been measuring you in order to pick the right combat nickers to keep your skin in working order while the Deserets—or Jackson and I—abuse the rest of you to within an inch of your lives."

Kim opened her mouth to say something else, but then thought better of it, and started—very slowly—removing her clothes. Patrick gulped and did the same. It wasn't about embarrassment, really, that made him reluctant to change. Just a feeling, that he knew Kim and Timur both shared, that one person shouldn't obey another *solely* because that person says they should. Threat of imprisonment or other violence, of course, changed the calculus.

The techs returned with several soft bundles wrapped in plastic, handing a parcel to each of the trio. With surprising speed and disregard for dignity, they showed the three how to put the clothes on and arrange them, and how to activate them. With the push of a button, the garments—which covered everything except their feet, hands, and head—seemed to vibrate and then contract, and Patrick had the distinct sense that the clothes were molding to his body shape. When the process was complete, each of them looked like they were wearing a thick turtleneck sweater and a pair of sweat pants in a tan-and-brown camoflauge pattern. They were surprisingly soft on the skin, and very cool, but heavy, and rather tight.

The techs retreated into the depths of the warehouse, apparently after more equipment. Patrick moved around a bit, testing the feel of the clothes. He caught Chavez' eye.

"How is it possible that we won't all sweat to death in these?" Patrick asked.

She grinned. "Yeah, you'd think that—but here's the cool thing about these scrubs: they wick moisture away from your skin, and kind of do your sweating for you. They're set up to equalize your thermal signature while providing some cooling as a bonus, but me, I'm just happy not having to constantly douse my skin in baby powder. Like back in the day. *Damn* I hated the '20s."

"Oh, and I forgot to mention—they're also lined with Missoula Kevlar for a last layer of of protection against projectiles and shrapnel, and are impermeable to pretty much every chemical and biological agent the Deserets, Texans, or Lakers have come up with. So they've got all kinds of awesomesauce going on. Never underestimate the importance of a solid set of nickers."

The techs returned again, each pulling a cart piled with an assortment of heavy-looking gear. Patrick couldn't make heads or tails of the equipment they were bringing out, but he had the sinking feeling that it was all going to, somehow, end up on their collective backs. Timur confirmed his fears, his voice low and, if Patrick were to put a word to it, *weary*.

"So, what is the loadout we're up to these days? Fifty, sixty kilos? Or does a soldier's gear finally weigh more than the soldier? Tell me you all have some kind of exoskeleton technology to make the carrying of all that a bit easier? I mean, these are the 2040s, right?"

Patrick and Kim both looked at Timur, alarmed. Usually a person doesn't have to ask someone what decade they're in. But Chavez just nodded, as if this were a perfectly normal question.

"Oh, if you want to join the engineers like Niana and Sang-bin, then yeah you get to play with exos. But they're usually carrying a couple hundred kilos around, and half of them have graduate degrees. So the bar is set kind of high. Scouts like me, we prefer mobility to raw power anyway, and you don't need to go to school for a decade to learn how to hide in the woods and call down fire on anyone unlucky enough to wander past."

Timur laughed. "Oh, mobility, *sure*. I can totally be mobile while carrying half again my body weight."

She laughed too, but didn't reply. Something had distracted her, and following her gaze Patrick saw that the other soldier, Jackson, had joined them in the armory. She nodded to Sangbin and Niana, and walked over to him. They spoke quickly and were too far away and speaking too quietly, for him to make out what they were saying.

Sangbin approached Patrick, looking him up and down. "Hey, lucky you, I've got a carapace in stock that used to belong to someone with exactly your body type."

The tech instructed him to stand with his arms held out, and with some effort lifted one of the pieces of equipment off the cart and onto Patrick. It seemed to envelop his entire torso, and the tech hit a button, which caused the inner layer of the shell-like armor to sort of meld with the strange sweater-like undergarment he now wore. He felt a heavy weight drop onto his shoulders, as if the full weight of the carapace had suddenly transferred to them.

"Stand up straight, man... okay." Sangbin muttered. "Readings look good. Once you get used to the carapace, it ought to sit pretty well. Just don't do any jumping jacks 'till your muscles build up. Lemme figure out the headgear now..."

Patrick looked down. The thing was called a carapace for

a reason: from just above his hips and to his neck, shoulder to shoulder, he was encased in some sort of plastic-like material, covered in a dull pattern that made it difficult for his eyes to focus on any particular point. He moved around a bit, and was surprise to discover that he retained full range of motion about his neck and arms, but the entire weight of the carapace was distributed across his broad shoulders and to a lesser extent his upper back. He'd done enough hiking in his life to know how tired the outfit would leave him after a few hours of wear, but also that there was no better place on the body to bear so much weight without risking a stress injury.

Kim and Timur were quickly given the same treatment, and soon the three of them stood there, all looking like they felt: half-ant, half-human, wholly awkward. While Sangbin fiddled with some equipment on the carts, Niana set to briefing them in a bored sort of tone, clearly having given the same kind of speech many times.

"First things first: I am sick and tired of scraping bits of *people* out of these things. So please, *please* repeat this mantra to yourself whenever you have some quiet time: The carapace is magic, but *I* am not. The *carapace* might survive a hit from a tank shell, but *I* will not. The carapace is cool, but the carapace can't think. If the person wearing it can't either, the carapace is fated to have bits of mushy former-owner forever seeping into its nooks and crannies. And Niana gets angry, and takes it out on other people. Niana dislikes this *very much*."

Sangbin looked up from whatever equipment he was now busy preparing. "What Niana is trying to say is, that the carapace is a damn useful bit of technology, but only if you remember it has limits. And that we get tired of scraping bits of people from equipment. We can't make that clear enough!"

Niana made an annoyed sound. "Since when has *reason*

stopped one of the meatheads from running straight into a rocket barrage? Anyway, as I was saying before Sangbin decided to translate: the carapace is a tough piece of equipment. But it isn't just a couple inches of Chobham '39—your batteries and processing units are packed in there too. So taking a hit is *always very bad*, even if you may personally survive."

Patrick heard a throat clear behind him, then Chavez' voice called across the bay. "I'ma gonna add here that when you eventually *do* take a hit, even if you survive, you are probably a mission kill anyway. So do everything you possibly can to not get hit. I *hate* having to abandon a mission in order to drag someone back to base, alive or not!"

He turned to look at her, and saw that while they had been getting measured by the techs, she had completed her own transformation into what Patrick assumed would be the end result of their own fitting out process. Her body below the neck was entirely covered: carapace encasing her torso, similar but smaller versions of it now strapped to her arms, thighs, and shins, with a spur from the thigh-piece guarding her knees. Sturdy boots protected her feet, and while she spoke she pulled some kind of thin, pliable gloves over her hands. Every bit of the ensemble was covered in the same sort of eye-distracting fabric.

"Oh," Chavez went on, "and by 'mission kill' I mean that you'll be more or less useless to the rest of us, even if you aren't going home in a bag just yet. All that computing power they've packed in there keeps you in communication with the rest of your team and adjacent units via a shared datalink and the Missoula tactical network. Voice, radio, text, graphics, data—all the commo runs through the network. And if you can't talk to the rest of us, you become a liability."

She finished with the gloves, and to Patrick's eye this

nearly completed her transformation into a bug. If next she put on a helmet with giant eyes and antennae sticking out of it, he would not have been surprised.

Timur mumbled something, and everyone looked at him. He realized he'd been overheard, and oddly for him, actually seemed embarrassed about it.

"Oh, sorry... I was talking to myself."

Chavez and Niana waited. He looked at Kim and Patrick, and shook his head.

"It's going to sound stupid. I was just saying that you people seem to go out of your way to equip new recruits with a lot of expensive gear. Which is kind of... not my experience with this sort of... thing."

Sangbin laughed. "Oh, Sandra, you got one from one of the old national armies, didn't you?"

Chavez laughed too, but Timur cut her off. "No, she didn't. I've never been in any official army. My experience was... different."

"Aaaaaah!" Chavez exclaimed. "That explains it! Jackson let me know that your blood tests all came back negative."

They looked at her, confused.

She shook her head. "That really doesn't make any sense out of context, does it? Ok. I mean that there's no record of any of you in the old national military databases. And since everyone who has been in a sanctioned military force at any point in the past thirty years or so has had their DNA sampled and sent to the international database... Jackson is of the opinion that you folks are infiltrators. And that we should shoot you."

Patrick looked at his friends, a thrill of fear surging through him, that he tried not to let show.

Kim grunted, cocked her head, and looked closely at Chavez. "So Timur's question still stands: why aren't you stopping them from giving us all this gear? If you think we're spies, or whatever?"

Chavez gave her a wicked smile. "Because I'm a softie at heart. And I figure we can win you over. Besides, this op we're prepping you for will be a *fantastic* test of your intentions. Probably also tell us whether or not you are worth bringing onboard. Issa goin' get right *hairy* out there, Jeevesy! We're playing bait!"

Niana had moved to join Sangbin by the carts, where they both finished fiddling with the next set of equipment and were now splitting it into three different piles. She raised an eyebrow and nodded at Chavez.

"So, Sandra, you guys are finally planning to go after Southern Butte?"

Chavez paused, and gave the room a quick once over before responding in a quiet voice. "Short answer—yes. Have to keep the details close to the chest, but yup. That's about where we're headed."

She walked between Patrick and Niana, clearly intending to forestall any further discussion on the matter. Sangbin and Niana shared a look. Then Niana nodded and picked up one of the equipment piles, and took it to Kim. Sangbin grabbed another and walked up to Timur, while Chavez brought the third to Patrick.

"Once we're airborne we can go over the details." Chavez said. "You all will be locked into the tactical network then anyway, so there's no way you could get word out to anyone even if you wanted to."

She stared into Patrick's eyes. "But, I am putting a lot of trust in my gut here. Which goes *completely* against my training and experience and logic. *Please*, for your own sakes do *not* give me yet another reason to trust my head over my gut."

As she spoke, she carefully placed what Niana and Sang-bin had called 'headgear' on Patrick. It was very similar to what fighter pilots like his husband wore in the cockpit, but by its weight he could tell that it was much denser than a pilot's helmet, and he expected that it was armored like the carapace. He felt the weight of it pressing down on his lower neck, and wondered how long it would be until his body began to ache.

The brow of the helmet terminated just above the eyebrows, but the sides extended below the ears, which fit into a space in the side of the helmet and made it almost impossible to hear. Chavez tapped the back of the helmet, and suddenly he could hear again—*more* clearly than before, if that were possible.

"Testing, testing, one-two-three. Can you hear me now?"

Chavez grinned at him and he nodded, neck muscles tightening to handle the weight. Her voice sounded slightly altered, but only just so, and was easier to pick out over the ambient noise from the armory and the rumbling of vehicles outside. She had him move his head to ensure he retained almost his full range of motion—the back the helmet clunked against the carapace if he tipped his head back too far—but thankfully the designers had put enough effort into the ergonomics and cushioning aspects that it wasn't particularly unpleasant to wear.

Patrick looked at his friends, and saw that Kim and Timur, each had what looked like an air filtration mask dangling from one side of the helmet. He felt around his own headgear, and found that he had one too.

The techs and Chavez completed the outfitting by helping their charges put on boots and gloves of their own, and then assisted in adding the mini-carapaces to their limbs. When all was set and the techs were satisfied, they pressed hidden buttons that seemed to affix all the assorted components to the underlying combat scrubs. Chavez instructed Patrick to move around a bit, and he immediately noticed that the gear fit together as a unit, almost naturally melding to his body. Nothing could be done about the weight, though.

Chavez took a few steps back to survey the results. "Good to go! Damn, I love to see new recruits all shiny and outfitted for the first time! The gear never looks as good as it did just off the shelf. But we don't have time to hang around looking in the mirror. Our chariot awaits. We ride, to Idaho!"

Niana and Sangbin nodded to Patrick and his friends, and each took Sandra Chavez' hand for a moment before turning and disappearing back into the depths of the armory. With a wave of her arm and a cry of *"vamos!"* she led them out of the bunker.

On the surface, things had only gotten busier and more chaotic. People were now running through the open spaces, many dragging carts full of a bewildering variety of equipment and other supplies. Interestingly, they now gave Patrick and his friends nearly the same degree of physical deference as they had Chavez.

Patrick found that whatever sound processing was going on in his headgear, it had the effect of differentiating sounds by distance. The conversations of people nearby seemed almost too loud, while the *whump-whump* of helicopter engines warming up were distinct, but distant, like an echo that grew in magnitude as Chavez led them through the bustle and onto a broad asphalt tarmac where a line of helicopters was accompanied by a matching line of tall vehicles, like trucks, but covered in armor plating and topped by small metal turrets.

Chavez led them up to the back of one of the helicopters, a large and ungainly beast with a ramp, now lowered to the tarmac, allowing access to the interior. Benches lined the sides, which was actually a relief to Patrick—on seeing the helicopters he'd felt viscerally repulsed by the idea of again being cramped in what had felt like an aluminum box careening through the sky. At least these helicopters were large enough that he would be able to stretch his legs, even if seeing outside through the small, dingy portholes lining the fuselage would be just as difficult as it had been on the flight in.

It took a few minutes to learn how to arrange the harness straps that would bind them to the benches and, for added safety, the sides of the helicopter. In that time, Jackson arrived, carrying two large boxy assault rifles of the same type they'd seen him wielding before. He handed one to Chavez, who nodded in thanks.

"Hey, where are ours?"

Jackson laughed at Timur's query. "Seriously? I'm not letting one of you shoot me in the back. Or Chavez, either. The minor risk of you figuring out how to get a signal out to the Deserets I'll accept, but not letting you take a shot at me."

Chavez rolled her eyes. "Jackson, stop being so god damned dramatic. I've pre-set their gear to shut them down if they even flip the safety on *someone else's* rifle. Anyway, they'll be too busy on the lasers, or hiding from incoming, or asking stupid questions, to try and shoot you or anyone else."

Jackson glared at Chavez.

"Do. Not. Take. His. Name. In. Vain! How many times am I going to have to tell you, Sandra?!"

She ignored him. It seemed that the helicopter had been waiting on Jackson's arrival, because as soon as he had grumpily settled himself next to Chavez on the bench opposite where Kim, Timur, and Patrick were strapped down, the ramp began to close and the helicopter's engines grew much louder despite the muffling effect of the helmet. Patrick's stomach lurched as the aircraft began to move hesitantly upward, jerking like a badly maintained elevator. He found a porthole, and tried to stare out into the sky beyond.

When the little of the outside visible between Chavez' and Jackson's heads showed that they were above the canopy of the evergreen forest that stretched beyond the airfield and into the surrounding mountains, their ascent ending in a sharp jerk. The engines strained, the *whump* of the rotors accelerating dramatically as they struggled to pull the helicopter further into the sky.

Chavez reached up to where the filtration mask was attached to the ear of her helmet, and in a smooth motion pulled it over her face, thumbing along the seam where it met her headgear's chin strap. When she spoke, it was like her voice was transmitted—again with surprisingly minimal digitization, and none of the static of a normal radio headset—directly to his ears.

"And *straaaaaain* little Stallion, youuu caaaaan doooooo iiiiit!" Chavez cried, laughing.

The helicopter lurched again, as if the engine had kicked fully into a new gear and the fight against gravity had been won. Patrick mimicked Chavez' motion, attaching the mask to the headgear. With a slight sucking sound, it sealed around his face, from the bridge of his nose to his chin. For the briefest moment he was afraid he would suffocate, but immediately cool air began to flow.

He opened his mouth to ask a question, but it came out as more of a burble. He saw a companion helicopter out the small window, but not *just* a helicopter. Some distance underneath the aircraft's belly, attached by cables, was one of the armored trucks from the tarmac. They were still low enough altitude-wise that he could see exactly how much the aircraft's entire trajectory was comprised of a giant, barely controlled swaying motion, and he realized with a fright that his aircraft must be doing the same thing, hence the unpleasant churning in his gut.

Jackson had pulled a visor contained inside the brow of his helmet down over his face, making him now look almost exactly like a fighter pilot. Chavez did the same, and with a gesture indicated that Patrick and his friends should do so as well.

"Sorry, guys, if you get motion sick!" Chavez chuckled, "the first part of a transit with a slung load like this is always sucktabulous. It'll get better once we're cruising at altitude. I'll let you all sleep then—we'll be airborne for a few hours— but first, we gotta get through the briefing."

The visor was heavily shaded, and with it lowered Patrick found it difficult to focus his vision. But then a soft humming sound began in his helmet, and the visor went totally transparent, to the point that he reached up to tap the outer surface of the visor to remind himself that it was still actually there.

A blur of motion distracted him, drawing his attention to the helicopter's small window once again. A shape passed quickly by, but what was odd was that even as it *should* have disappeared from view, it was as if the object somehow resolved itself into a sort of digital outline displayed on the visor. It actually *felt* like as if it were a *real* object visible through the metal wall, with appropriate depth and on a trajectory consistent with what he'd seen through the porthole.

And the more he focused, the more clear the image began to be, even as it arced up and away from the helicopter. Words and numbers and symbols began to hover around it. Most looked like gibberish, but he caught a glimpse of a name, or designation, that was slightly larger and bolder than the surrounding distractions: "Saab-Mikoyan Gryphon". Which he only recognized because the first two names, Saab and Mikoyan, were longtime manufacturers of military fighter jets.

His train of thought was shattered as the visor went pitch black, then dazzled him with a stream of images, characters, and even a few strange symbols that looked like particularly rude emojis. Through the information overwhelm he heard Chavez' voice.

"Sorry about this, but gotta do a hard reset of the interface to let it build a user profile for your newbies. Just relax and let your eyes wander. The system will work out how to display information to you on your heads up display, your HUD, as comfortably as possible."

The reset process ended as abruptly as it had begun. Patrick could see again, but the only thing the HUD seemed to be showing him now was a small blur that seemed to hover at the edge of sight, almost an extension of his nose. That, and Chavez holding up her gloved hands and wiggling her fingers as if she was a hypnotist in an old-time horror film.

"Alright, see your fingers? You can use them to interact with your HUD. Each fingertip has small pressure and friction sensors, that work with a surface on the glove that works a lot like a touchscreen or touchpad, actually. Should be pretty intuitive, once you get the hang of it. The system learns as you work with it. But to save time: here, I'll bring up all the smart stuff we'll need to review before we land at Craters of the Moon."

Patrick's view of Chavez was mostly obscured by an image that appeared on his HUD. It took him a moment to adjust his focus, and then the image seemed to shrink and move to one side of his vision. Additional materials soon appeared, making the wall of the helicopter as he stared ahead look like a giant computer screen—albeit one capable of providing the illusion of actual depth. He started to experiment with the gloves, and found that he was able to select and rearrange what he could see.

Chavez, however, was at least partly in control, and while his own manipulations were relegated to one section of the HUD, what appeared to be an annotated satellite image grew larger in the center of his vision, and the volume of her voice increased.

"Alright, so what you are looking at here is a map of the area where the former American states of Idaho, Montana, Wyoming, and Utah come together. The Missoula Regiment has been deployed out here for years, operating under a United Nations Security Council contract awarded to our parent company. We're tasked with preventing any of the post-USA successor states from taking control over what is now the last remaining ICBM—that's Inter-Continental Ballistic Missile—launch field in the world. One hundred and fifty missiles tipped with nuclear warheads, all sitting around waiting to be misused."

"Now *nobody*, aside from maybe the Cascadians out west and the Canadians up north, are particularly pleased with us being here, but ever since the Deserets took control of the old US Air Force boneyards in Arizona and Nevada and started receiving serious logistical support from the Texans, they've gotten particularly aggressive. Control of the Great Basin isn't enough for them, it seems."

"Case in point: Although the Boise Treaty was *supposed* to delineate the zones of control in the Snake Valley, the Deserets have kept right on raiding our supply convoys and generally making it clear that they plan to take over all of Idaho between the Divide and Mountain Home. And before you ask me *why*, just realize that if they can push up to the Divide unchallenged, they throw a wedge between our bases at Camp Yellowstone and Camp Missoula and can threaten both, distracting us from the inevitability that the Texans will eventually come at us through Wyoming."

The map on his HUD zoomed in, and several bright arrows

and other designating indicators appeared, which now focused exclusively on what was helpfully labeled 'Snake Valley: Eastern Idaho'. At the center of his vision was a label, larger and redder than the rest: 'Big Southern Butte'.

"Two months ago the Deserets set up a base on Southern Butte, in direct violation of the Boise Treaty. We've been harassing them ever since, but we haven't been able to convince them to leave short of a major assault. Which they apparently hope we'll do: they've filled the height with every piece of artillery they've been able to get their hands on. Long range, short range, and a ridiculous number of surface to air missiles to guard them. Even better: in a dry lake bed about ten klicks west of it they've encamped a heavy combat battalion with enough firepower to cut off our southern supply route entirely—unless we are willing to risk a major battle in range of their artillery."

Timur cut in. "So why aren't you? Seems like you all are pretty well equipped."

She laughed. "Hell yeah we are! Still, why get a bunch of people killed when there might be a better way? That's *us*. Like, I tried to make that my call-sign once—"the better way", but it got vetoed by Command. Pricks. Anyway, the bosses have *finally* decided to hit the position with everything we've got."

"We've been poking at their defenses for a few weeks to keep them from getting too comfortable. Few days back, the Scouts were relieved and replaced by the Guards, which we intended as an escalation to get their attention."

Kim interjected. "Wait, I'm confused, who are these Scouts and Guards?"

Chavez brought several images and short descriptions up on their HUDs. "I was getting there. The Missoula Regiment is broken into three main Detachments, one of which is located at Camp Yellowstone. Our doctrine splits each Detachment up into three Battle Groups: Scouts, Guards, and Lancers. The Scouts rely on—like you might guess—speed and stealth, and we back them up with enough air and artillery support that any opponent able to force them into a pitched fight is basically going to expose itself to being annihilated by massed precision strikes."

"Guards, on the other hand, are a lot like an old-style heavy mechanized unit: lots of infantry, combat engineers, and artillery. They can hold pretty much any position for a long, long time, particularly if the Scouts are free to cause mayhem on the enemy's flanks. And the Lancers operate a lot like a combination of shock troops and heavy cavalry. As tough as the Guards, they have more tanks and mobile howitzers and they hit enemy positions like a freight train—and then charge deep behind the lines to cause even more mayhem. Ultimately, the point of having three units is to *always* keep our opponents reeling from a different kind of attack."

"Anyway: we pulled the Scouts back and replaced them with the Guards, giving them a breather and time to refit and prep for their next deployment. *Except*, we're sending one group from the Scouts on a little airborne flanking maneuver, while simultaneously moving the Lancers out in front of Southern Butte to present a direct and immediate threat to their continued occupation of that ugly little piece of real estate."

Timur snorted. "So, who is the diversion—us or the Lancers?"

Chavez snorted back. "As a wise alien ambassador once put it—*yes*."

"I *barely* get that reference."

She shook her head. "Your loss. But you *do* get it, so... still a nerd, amiright?"

His reply was a simple curse, and Jackson sat up straight, looking at him. But didn't speak. Chavez continued, unphased.

"So to boil it down to brass tacks, here's the skinny: We're going to fly around to their west, infiltrate to a point at the outer edge of anti-tank missile range, and take some shots at targets of opportunity. If we're lucky, and we do a convincing enough job, the Deserets should wake up tomorrow morning believing one of two things: That the Lancers are a diversion for our sneak attack on their eastern flank, *or* that our attack is the diversion, and that the Lancers are coming to shove them off their hill."

"Here's the thing: in *either* case, their best move—and the one their doctrine explicitly calls for—is to try and eliminate the weaker and more separated threat as quickly as possible."

"Using interior lines to defeat us in detail." Jackson added.

Chavez made a growling sound. "Yes, if you want to recite the technical manual word for word. Key point is that they'll know that they have us outgunned and they won't pass up the opportunity to do us some damage while they can. So as soon as they deploy those big guns out of their bunkers to wipe us out..."

Jackson finished the thought. "Every bit of firepower that we have available gets dropped onto that hill at the same time. Game over."

Patrick swallowed, and stared out the window, into the dark Montana sky. At that moment, it was all too much. Suddenly he and his friends were heading out to the front lines of what sounded like a minor war. He tuned out the conversation as best as he could, feeling totally out of his depth and out of control. It was going to be a long night.

RUNNING FROM
ROMANS

For the barest moment, after the return to the dark, quiet spaceship—Jagdkontrol, the machine intelligence in control named Olga liked to term herself—Yarielis felt deeply relieved.

Because it was quiet. And dark. And though her brother was there, he seemed lost in his own thoughts. Nothing was audible aside from his breathing, her breathing, and the dimmest hum of the Jagdkontrol's power and life support systems. So far, the *Station Rome* authorities hadn't noticed them.

"So, bro, what'cha thinking about?" Yari asked in a soft voice.

Loucas jerked his head, startled. "What? Sorry! I checked out, didn't I. I was just…processing, I guess." He sighed. "It hit me… the thought that I'm a terrorist here. Fan-freaking-*tastic*." He cursed several times, then rested his head against the wall behind him, looking at the ceiling.

Yari was seated on the edge of the bench where she'd been encased and integrated into the ship, and Loucas was on the bench across the back wall of the spaceship's cabin. She reached out across the narrow gap, and gently patted his knee.

"It'll be okay, Lou. When I was... *inside*, I guess?... the ship, I saw how we're supposed to get out of here. Olga can go really *really* fast if she needs to. I think her plan is to link up with Franz and the *Acerbic*, and then escape to... somewhere that isn't here, I guess."

"Although," she paused, looking around, "I'm not sure when Olga is going to come back. I hope soon. She said she was powering down even the life support system to a bare minimum try and stay hidden from the space station. *Rome*, she said it was called. So weird. I guess maybe Italy started a space program?"

Loucas laughed, though in the darkness it sounded more grim than mirthful. "Maybe? I mean, we're in the 22nd century, so I guess anything is possible. But did I hear you right? We may not even have *life support* for long? What kind of spaceship is this anyway?"

"Oh don't *worry* so much. I have it under control."

Yari and Loucas both jumped at the sound of Olga's digital voice. Yari squinted, as if that might make her appear. The room remained dark and empty. She shook her head.

"Olga, where are you? Can you appear here too?"

Loucas looked at her in confusion. Only then did Yari remember that he hadn't been integrated into the ship like she had. He hadn't actually seen the Star-Bridge yet.

Olga laughed, though it sounded oddly muted, as if she were suppressing her own volume. "Why don't *you* appear, Yari? Drop the anthropic bias! Digital life is life too, you know."

Yari laughed back. It was still odd, to have a robot—machine intelligence, whatever—have both a sense of humor and of self. But strange as it might seem, Yari found that she actually kind of liked it. Talking to Olga was almost easier than talking to other people, and they'd only just met.

"I would, Olga, if I could. But I want to bring Loucas too this time. I think he can help."

Olga seemed to hesitate. "Are you sure about that? You have only just begun the integration process, and additional input could cause too much strain. You'll need to be focused to help me through the next stage."

Yari nodded, though she didn't know if Olga could even perceive the gesture, especially with almost everything in the ship powered down. She looked at Loucas, who gave her a curious look in return. She shook her head.

"It'll be better if I just show you, Lou. Olga, where does he need to be? And is there enough power?"

"Should be! And actually I was going to suggest getting you both ready to move, even if we just stick Loucas into a coma for a spell. They're sending out a *lot* of patrols, and if one decides to take an interest in us, we're going to have to accelerate out of here *triple* quick. Loucas can stay where he is. Yari, you head back to your bench."

She did as instructed, giving Loucas a gentle pat on the head as the ship's main life support and interface system activated, once again binding him to his bench. He yelped in surprise, but Yari calmly walked away, lay on the bench, and let the ship encase her. For the briefest moment, she was overwhelmed by an unnaturally strong urge to go to sleep, which she did her best not to resist.

She fell asleep, then awoke—at least, it felt exactly like waking up—on the Star-Bridge, Loucas by her side. He looked her up and down, blinking, and then with the barest hint of a double take he did the same to Olga.

Yari and Olga grinned at one another. Olga, the Jagdkontrol's on-board machine intelligence, could manifest alongside them when they were integrated into the digital Star-Bridge, and she did so in magnificent form. She was dressed in an absolutely ridiculous imitation of a military uniform, a sleek and genderless assemblage of trousers and blouse that was bedecked in more flash and flair arranged in starkly unusual patterns, than Yari had thought possible outside of a Comic-con. Adding to the eye-shattering display was the fact that Olga's rich brown skin was framed by a veritable mane of strawberry-red hair. She grinned at them, and opened her arms in a welcoming gesture.

"Greetings and Salutations! Welcome to the Star-Bridge!"

Yari watched Loucas look around, breathing slowly, taking it in. She smiled. She'd had to do the same thing. Being on the Star-Bridge was something like standing on a tall, barren mountain peak in the middle of a clear night. A sea of stars enveloped them, an infinity so vast that if they were not so firmly—digitally, as Olga had assured her this was all an illusion, a hijacked dream—anchored to the top of the spaceship and seemingly fixed to a consistent frame of reference, neither would have been able to tolerate the display without experiencing severe vertigo.

The region of space around them that the Jagdkontrol's sensor array could cover was sort of scaled so that they could perceive depth, with the stars forming a distant fixed backdrop and all objects between it and the spaceship appearing at an intuitively appropriate relative distance. Yari almost felt like she could reach out and touch some of the nearer objects, and in particular *Station Rome* loomed large, encompassing almost the half of the horizon, the docking apparatus that linked them to the space station appearing to reach out towards them, terminating at the edge of the ship itself.

After he was finally able to look around without staggering, Loucas took a deep breath. Then he started and froze in place, pointing towards the far end of the space station. Yari looked and saw them: two objects, growing steadily larger as they moved towards the Jagdkontrol.

Olga swore. "Great, here comes the first wave of close patrols. Yari, you ready for this?"

Yari gulped, and shook her head.

"Sorry, then!" Olga smiled sweetly.

Yari closed her eyes for a moment, bracing for what she knew was about to happen, and when she opened them again an incredible and overwhelming array of information was flooding her field of view. She felt her heart rate increase, and a pounding sensation in her skull as blood began to surge towards her brain. Even as the flow of data started to resolve itself, began to make *sense*, a countervailing rush of near-panic threatened to consume her mind. She focused on her breathing, on synchronizing it with the pounding of her heart. Slowly, the panic subsided. And in its wake she felt, if not comfortable by any stretch of the imagination, curiously *alive*.

"Alright there, Yarielis?"

She nodded. And then as one, she and Olga, standing almost side by side, peered closely at the pair of small spaceships that were too-quickly resolving from vague blurs into distinct shapes.

Yari parsed through the stream of information about the ships sent to her by the Jagdkontrol's digital bridge system. Velocity, acceleration, relative orientation, electromagnetic characteristics, weapons load-out—all blurred together in her mind, only half understanding what it all meant, until she felt an odd sensation, a sort of *intuitive* sense of the approaching craft's purpose and probable courses of action. It was almost as if she could, in that moment, perceive with absolute clarity the entire universe of possibilities with respect to their predicament.

Olga smiled at her, and nodded. "*Much* faster this time, Yari, well done! So, the big question: seeing all this. what do you think we should do?"

Loucas' head turned quickly, and he gave Olga a suspicious look. "Aren't *you* supposed to know stuff like that? Aren't you the ship's computer?"

She rolled her eyes at him. "*Machine intelligence*, please. Sure, I *run* on computers, but that doesn't mean *I* am reducible to one, in the same way that *you* aren't reducible to the bag of flesh and fluid that make up *your* physical structure, including that squishy brain you treasure so much, and yet not enough, or else you wouldn't do so many dangerous things with it."

"Okay," Loucas replied, "aren't you the ship's *machine intelligence*, then? Shouldn't you know how to handle this situation better than Yari? We're... new, remember!"

Olga laughed. "Maybe, but then how is she supposed to train?" She shook her head, strawberry curly falling in front of her eyes. "Besides, this is the part where my type of intelligence doesn't work so well on its own. Making decisions when all the options are equally risky—that's a weakness of machine intelligence, just like assimilating vast quantities of data and reducing it to a manageable set of causal relationships and then *solving* the resulting simultaneous differential equations in a coherent system is something you biologicals inherently suck at."

"I can tell you how fast those ships are going, how quickly they can accelerate, what the crews are saying to their controllers on *Station Rome*, how much power they have and how far we can run before they blow us up. But unless there's an optimal solution to the pressing problem of *not* getting blown up, I can't easily decide between two apparently equivalent courses of action. At least, not reliably. Machine intuition is simulated and inefficient—but Human intuition, well, that's pretty much why you meat puppets are still around."

Yari made a sound, half a growl and half a squeak.

"Enough, both of you! Let me concentrate."

Loucas looked at her with concern, Olga with a knowing smile. Yari ignored them both, and focused on the approaching ships, which were now sufficiently close that she could make out the details of their appearance. Each was a small craft, with a spherical fuselage attached to six struts, three of which were longer and thicker than the others and supported a set of thrusters that the craft used to accelerate and maneuver. Three thicker, but stumpier struts each supported a pod containing a particle blaster—a powerful weapon that Yari somehow *knew* was strong enough to damage, even destroy, the Jagdkontrol.

The datastream indicated that the two spacecraft were in constant communication with a control center somewhere on the space station itself, and were actively scanning any clump of debris—or any docked ship—that the station's own scanners hadn't already identified or couldn't successfully penetrate due to being in an electromagnetic dead zone formed by the station's surface textures. Two things were clear: first, that the ships were aware of the Jagdkontrol and were moving to inspect it more closely. Second, that they had orders to fire on *any* object that showed even the slightest indication of posing a threat.

"Well, Yari, what do you think? Hide or run?"

Yari looked from Olga to Loucas, and felt suddenly annoyed at his silence. But then turned that annoyance back on herself, as she remembered that he probably couldn't even see what she could see. Or, at least, he didn't know yet how to handle the flood of information.

"Olga, don't you have at *least* a... preference? If you get preferences? Anything at all? I don't even know how to decide how to decide what to do!"

Loucas rubbed his eyes. "Yar, is the screen, or whatever, as blurry for you? I keep seeing numbers, I think, but I can't tell for sure.

Yari realized that meant her brother *could* see the datastream, but he hadn't learned how—or couldn't—deal with it all. Yari remembered that Olga had said something about her autism playing a role in her having adapted to handle it so quickly. But it was still hard for her to think clearly, with two dangerous space fighters coming ever closer.

Olga's voice was calm and kind, though Yari knew that time was not on their side. "Yari, we have to make a choice soon. If I decide, it'll be by a random process. If there's *anything* your gut… thing… is telling you, about how humans might react in this situation, now is the time to say something."

She gave Olga a pleading look. "It would help if I understood what hiding or running means in this situation! What happens if they find us, or they see us run? Since I guess those are our two options?"

Olga nodded. "If they find us, they shoot us. When they see us run, they shoot at us. Eventually, if we stay here, they'll notice the thermal or electromagnetic signals that we're giving off even when we're mostly powered down. I can't keep spoofing the station command office's anomaly recognition program without the sysadmins getting wise to the hack at *some* point. But, *if* we wait and time it *just* right, we should be able to detach and accelerate for a good distance— hopefully out of both these fighters' and the station's weapons range entirely—before they notice, and dispatch long-range interceptors to hunt us down."

"And so what if we just run away right now?" Yari asked, looking at her brother to try and read an opinion in him.

"Then our survival comes down to a simple math problem: How quickly can we accelerate and get out of range, versus how quickly they can target us and shoot us down. There are several unknowns, but we would require a great deal of them to work in our favor to avoid being destroyed if we go now."

Olga laughed and growled in open frustration. "You see my dilemma—both are bad options, that depend too much on human factors. I can tell you exactly how quickly they *could* target us and how much acceleration your bodies *can* take without turning into goo. I can tell you the odds of their successfully detecting us over any given time interval as we hide here. But in the end, either way, whether we live or die ultimately comes down to how fast the humans involved in the loop will react. I would expect them to do so almost immediately in either case, given that they were just subjected to an unprecedented attack. Logically, they should be like bees swarming out of a damaged hive. But maybe I'm overlooking some unknown, perhaps unknowable, ultimately *human* factor?"

Loucas shook his head. Yari could see him breathing hard, afraid, but working to remain outwardly calm. "So we're basically just guessing whether the sysadmins or the pilots notice something first?"

"Exactly the problem." Olga confirmed. "And why I am relying on Yari to decide. After all, the limits to a rapid acceleration are mostly human. I could get out of here on my own, no problem. But gooey flesh and blood can't tolerate the effects of me opening up the reactor to full power all at once."

"What, no one has invented inertial dampers yet?" laughed Loucas.

Olga laughed too, shaking her head and muttering something derogatory about human scientists. Yari watched the fighters, which were now close enough to clearly discern details on the thruster pods, mounted on gimbals to allow for engine exhaust to be vectored in many directions. Which she decided was probably why the label: *maneuverability* =

very high kept flashing near to where a list of what the Jagd-kontrol's computer system had decided were vital statistics was displayed, making it look as if the spacecraft were decorated with signposts.

And then she knew she had decided what to do. "Olga," she said, "wait until they've passed us by. We hide, for now. Loucas is right—they are all going to be trigger-happy. Afraid. But also, I think that they won't be focusing on details until they calm down. Let's wait and run when they're out of sight."

Olga exhaled, slowly and carefully. Loucas tilted his head slightly, looking confused.

"Sis... I didn't say that at all."

She nodded. "I know, but that's how you felt, right?"

"I guess, but... how did you know? Wait... " he looked at Olga. "Is this because we're in some kind of computer program?"

Olga hardly seemed to hear him. "What? No. Well, yes. Sort of. Hard to explain. You are all asleep, anesthetized. The Star-Bridge kind of... hijacks your dreams. But you two, as siblings, have a communication dynamic all your own. Don't worry about that now, *watch the fighters*."

Yari complied, and felt a thrill of fear. One of the fighters, though without changing its velocity, had rotated to point its nose straight at them. She could feel herself tense up, and Olga seemed to as well. Helpless, they stood there as the fighter soared towards them. Yari held her breath, then almost jumped out of her skin—Loucas had stepped close, without her noticing, and put his arm around her shoulders.

And then the fighters passed them by. It was eerie to the extreme, seeing the nearest approach—and fly close past—in absolute silence. But this hardly mattered. They tensed—and nothing happened.

The three of them let out a collective sigh of relief, marred only by a sudden movement: the fighter close by rotated and activated its engines, darted below the horizon, then re-appeared on the other side, arcing back towards the space station. Its companion followed at a distance.

Olga sighed again. "First check, passed. Should be a few minutes at least before another patrol comes by. So let me do a quick power-up, initialize active sensors and make sure nobody is lurking nearby, and then I'll set the engines for a slow steady burn out of here. With any luck, they won't notice until we're far enough away to make a dash for safety."

A screen appeared in front of Olga, and on it a new datastream appeared. Yari pushed her brother's arm off her shoulders, and took a step towards Olga in order to see more.

Olga froze, and her eyes went wide. "Oh, *hell*. They picked up something on that flyby. The station authorities are redirecting fighters... launching interceptors. Yeah, we're spotted. Oh it is *so* past time to be away from this spinning tin can."

Yari and Loucas froze, staring at one another. At the same time, two chairs appeared, and Olga leaped away from the screen and shoved the two roughly into them.

"*Don't* get up. This is going to be *very* unpleasant!"

She wasn't kidding. A flash of light told Yari the Jagdkontrol's engines had just flared into life, and with an ear-splitting *bang* the ship launched itself away from *Station Rome*. It felt to Yari like a giant had clutched her in its massive palm and was squeezing the life out of her. Her vision narrowed to a point, all else went dark. She couldn't breathe, couldn't think, couldn't feel anything but a terrible weight or pressure that felt as if it would crush her utterly. She hovered on the edge of consciousness for what felt like hours, only dimly aware of the pain and a general sense of panic.

Then slowly, bit by bit, her vision and breath began to return. She felt relief, but also growing discomfort of another sort, as her muscles began to spasm in random patterns and her brain ached under the renewed pressure brought by the blood that powered whatever synapses process the sensation of pain.

Olga's voice was faint to her ears. "Down to three gees acceleration now, *so* sorry for having to do that to you."

Yari was suddenly aware of no longer feeling *quite* as miserable—the muscle spasms subsided, and the general sense of full-body pain was now rapidly being replaced by a general sense of being uncomfortably *heavy*, like she was wearing a suit made out of lead. She rolled her head slowly and delicately to the side, and saw that Loucas had fallen unconscious.

She moved her feet to rotate her chair to get a better look at her brother—wondering, suddenly, why she actually *felt* like she was sitting in a chair, when she knew that her body was actually lying on a bench, encased in some kind of material that anesthetized her and connected her to this virtual reality Star-Bridge.

Several flashes at the corner of her vision drew her back to the present. They were greenish in hue, and as Yari focused on them she saw that they were emanating from the space station, which had dwindled to a blurry blob in the background of the digital display. Almost instantaneously a bright flash of red-orange erupted at a point where the Jagdkontrol's simulated physical structure intersected the starfield beyond. To her right and left almost the same color appeared, a streak surrounded by a thin shimmering halo, as if an artist's brush had slashed across her field of view.

She knew that *Station Rome* was shooting at them, but the lack of accompanying sensation made it hard to process. It was surreal, like being trapped inside an in-progress painting. Only, the paint didn't seem to take. The colors faded away almost as quickly as they had burst to life, leaving a faint residue, fading into the stars behind.

Then she saw several additional blurs, blue in hue and with a bright green digital box outlining them. Information about them began to appear outside the box, and Yari inhaled sharply. They were closing the distance, slowly but steadily.

Olga sighed, and glanced at Yari. "You see them, then? Good! That you see, I mean—the information itself is very not-good. But I was worried that I knocked you out completely, or that the shock of acceleration had damaged your cognitive connection to the Star-Bridge."

Yari remembered, and pointed at her brother—realizing, suddenly, that while she still felt heavy, it still wasn't as bad as before, which is why she *could* point at him. Olga looked at Loucas.

"Yeah, I didn't worry about him as much. He's okay, just passed out. There's actually not much he *or* you can do for a bit, so I was planning on having you both disconnect and rest in the cabin for a while. Rest, and get ready for the fight to come."

Yari stared at Olga.

Olga winced, and her smile was wan. "We *were* able to get out of range fast enough that the shields can absorb the particle blasts they're sending our way, which is good news! But the bad news: They had a flight of interceptors on standby. Which pack enough firepower to vaporize us, and because they are totally automated, can accelerate enough to overtake us before we can reach our link-up with the *Acerbic*."

Yari swallowed, and looked back at the interceptors. The blobs were now resolved into small, distant, yet steadily approaching objects. Without the boxes, it would have been difficult to see them at all: they were shaped like elongated arrowheads, and from her current perspective they were approaching exactly like arrows in flight; Edge facing forward, with most of their mass trailing behind, they were visible mostly because they continually occluded stars behind them, like cloud shadows passing over a meadow.

She evaluated the data. They had a little over an hour before the interceptors would be in firing range, and about an hour after that they would enter lethal range.

"Olga, is there any way we can extend the time? Turn off stuff we don't have to use, and send power to the engines?"

Olga shook her head. "The real limit is on your bodies' ability to tolerate more acceleration. I *can* send you to sleep, and eek out another hour's worth of space, but that won't help us very much in the end. We need a minimum of six hours at the highest acceleration your bodies can tolerate just to get to the rendezvous point with *Acerbic*."

Yari nodded, and was silent. Then she decided what she needed to do.

"Olga, send me and Lou back to the cabin. Just, let me sit with him, okay? For a few minutes. Then you can go ahead and knock us out so we have every possible chance. And can you give us some privacy? If that is possible on a spaceship that you are kind of... part of."

"Can do on both! If you are sure. I had thought you might want to spend some time learning how our defenses work. Not that there's much you'll be able to do, but when it is time to fight, I'll take all the help I can get. Those interceptors are mostly controlled by humans back on *Station Rome*, because the colonial authorities *hate* uncontrolled machine intelligence. So you two might just be able to improve our slim odds."

She trailed off. Yari shrugged, and reached over to touch her brother's arm. Olga smiled, and snapped her fingers.

It was like waking up from a nap. Yari felt groggy and a

little confused. The membrane binding her to the bench fell away, and as quickly as she could she got to her feet, stumbling a little as she moved to sit by Loucas' side. He was still unconscious. She touched the integration membrane that bound him to his own bench, and it fell away. She sat next to him, but before the membrane could reassert its hold, she touched her brother, held out her hands, and without consciously thinking how she did it, she summoned the Web of Norns.

It appeared, golden tendrils writhing as before. She grasped the web, and reality shifted.

Yari was unprepared for her brother's full weight falling on her shoulders. But when they arrived they were standing and he was still unconscious. So fall it did, and she staggered, trying not to drop him onto the floor of Mimr's Pub. She managed to shift him towards a bench, and guide his torso so that he fell onto it, then slumped over the adjacent table. Then she straightened, took a deep breath, and looked around.

Her expectation had been that the place would have been radically changed since the last time they were there. There was no real reason for her to feel this way, given that they could only have been gone for at most a few hours, but in her mind that would just sort of *fit* the events of the past day of her life. But little had in fact changed—except the identities of some of the occupants.

A very large man lay snoring on a sofa, Schwartz curled up in his bushy red beard. Behind the bar another man who looked like a male twin of Freyja was singing to himself while rearranging bottles. And at a table sat a woman who, while holding a goblet that was spilling liquid all over the floor, played some kind of silly game, batting at the paws of the other cat, Weiss, who batted back contentedly.

Weiss turned to look at Yari, then stood up and hopped

across several tables to come and sit next to Loucas' head. The cat licked his hair, then fixed Yari with a gaze. And, like before, somehow communicated with her.

She nodded, and tapped her brother's back. "Well, Loucas, if you were awake I would introduce you to Thor, Freyr, and Idunn."

"Mrow." meowed Weiss.

Yari clapped her hands above her head. "Hey! Gods! A little help, please? I think my brother needs some more of that mead. And I want to ask Mimr a question."

Thor opened one of his eyes. "Don't call us gods."

Freyr laughed. "Don't call us not-gods either, though. I mean, I don't mind."

"Drunk gods!" laughed Idunn.

Yari shook her head. "I don't care what I have to call you, if you will help us."

Thor closed his eye. "Freyr, you're closest. And I have a cat. Idunn, what's the diagnosis?"

Idunn stood up, and staggered over to sit across from Loucas. After a few seconds and a giggle, she pronounced her verdict.

"Freyr, get the stuff that smells like pine. A goblet-full. This fella's had a wee bit too much gravity to the blood, if you know what I mean."

It took Freyr a while, and he dropped two bottles to the floor, but he eventually found what he was looking for. He shook his head, looked around the pub, apparently decided that none of the goblets were to his liking, and pulled what Yari took to be his own from a pouch at his belt, filling it to the brim. As he brought it to Loucas, she noticed that it appeared to be carved from an animal horn, and terminated in a sharp point at the bottom end. It seemed inefficient for a drinking vessel, but she didn't have time or energy to worry about it now.

Together, Idunn and Freyr managed to pick up Loucas' head and get some of the mead down his throat. He woke with a start, sputtered, and then grabbed at the horn, downing the remaining mead as quickly as he could gulp it down. The gods laughed.

Loucas took a few breaths, let the mead settle, and looked at Yari.

"Hey sis! So: how'd we get here? I didn't think Olga could accelerate us all the way to Valhalla."

Freyr raised an eyebrow, and sat down next to Idunn. "Not Valhalla, you know. Just Mimr's Well…ish. The *actual* Well is elsewhere. This is just the Pub where we come hang out when we're not busy with other things."

Yari shook her head. "I don't really care about that right now. Sorry. I need to figure out what we need to do next in the 22nd century. We're on a spaceship that is running away from other spaceships and *losing*. And I think I know what I have to do, but I want to make sure I'm right."

Thor turned his head, and opened both of his eyes. "You have to win a fight, don't you?"

Yari nodded.

"You probably want Mimr to give advice, then? That's hard." Thor replied. "Very difficult to predict the outcome of a fight. If you aren't a lock to win or lose by grace of factors totally out of your control, then what happens is really down to contingent factors rooted in the context of the situation. Which he doesn't know any better than you most of the time, and especially now."

Loucas looked from Idunn to Freyr and back again, confused.

"Uh, wasn't Thor supposed to be dumb, or something?" Loucas muttered, then looked quickly over his shoulder at the large man. "Um, no offense? I just… repeated what Odin said to us… sorry."

Freyr laughed, in what felt to Yari like mixed frustration and mirth. "I'd say the same of Odin!" he said. "To each their own intelligence, I suppose."

"Anyway," Thor continued, "That's got no bearing whatsoever on your present situation. So you can bring up Mimr, but I'm afraid there isn't much he can tell you. Different category of situation than the one your friend Eryn is in."

Yari tilted her head. "How so?"

Idunn cut in. "You'll want the short explanation, *not* the essay, I expect. So: Eryn is in the middle of a part of human history that is quite… fixed in nature. And she is interacting with individuals whose actions will have a great bearing on what consequential events can be affected, because of who and where they are. You two, on the other hand, like your friends in 2041 have *initiated* certain events, but have not yet met people of similar historical consequence."

Freyr slapped the table, and laughed. "Don't you *love* Midgard? How ridiculously structured it all is, despite being a multiverse? Sometimes I really do think the entire thing is just someone's reality simulator, and we're all just non-player characters hanging on for the ride."

Idunn glared at him, and shook her head. Loucas took the opportunity to interject.

"I'm still catching up here, but question: can't you just look into our future and tell us if we win or lose the fight?"

Idunn shook her head. "No. We could *estimate* how *likely* it is that you will be present at the side of certain individuals when and where key decisions will be made and actions taken that structure future events. And tell you the likely trajectories your Thread can be expected to take, given proper interventions, nudging things one way or another.

But the more specific and narrow you get, the more fuzzy and uncertain things become."

"Think of it like looking through a powerful electron microscope at something you perceive as being solid, like wood or metal. As you zoom in, you'll be able to detect lots of variation in its structure, and so understand something about what one bit of the thing looks like at several different points. You could theoretically zoom in so far that you would perceive individual carbon chains, individual molecules, individual atoms, individual sub-atomic particles. But oddly—and this has something to do with the nature of the Universe itself—you would then lose your ability to actually *see* that thing in relation to *other* things. And because most things co-exist with other things, zooming in too far basically has the effect of biasing your view, giving you highly accurate and yet almost totally worthless information."

Thor cut in. "In the end, whatever we can see when we look at the Web amounts to *one* potential outcome or set of outcomes among many. Not necessarily the one you will *actually* experience. There's a great deal of guesswork and intuition involved in correctly reading the Web, and the more specific the event the more dangerous and unstable the prediction. Unfortunately, all you can do is try your best, and hope. That's the nature of battle."

Loucas and Yari shared a look, his crestfallen expression matching how she felt. So much for asking the closest thing to experts they were likely to find. Weiss stalked over to the edge of the table, and meowed at Yari. Almost without thinking, she reached out a hand to scratch behind the cat's ears. Then Yari had an idea. It didn't solve their current problem, but if they did survive, she knew she'd be glad she asked.

"So this only matters if we win the fight, I guess, but can we leave a note for the others? Maybe try to coordinate visits and learn this stuff? For some reason we seem to be able to come here even when there's a machine intelligence around."

Idunn nodded, even as Freyr's head sank to the table, as he passed out—from boredom or intoxication, Yari didn't know. "Weiss and Schwartz will take care of it. Next time any of the others arrives, they'll get the message."

Yari and Loucas shared a look. And mutually decided not to question how asking a cat to help might work.

Thor grunted, and closed his eyes, settling further into the couch. "I'll answer the question you half-asked before you go. Machine intelligence is mostly the same as biological intelligence, *except* that it is extremely rare for a machine intelligence to have decent intuitive capabilities. By that I mean the ability to make logical leaps, to make associations between unlike things, to look for unusual connections, patterns, processes *without* a preexisting definition of what you are looking for."

"Which is important why?" Loucas asked.

"It affects how the machine intelligence deals with missing facts. A machine tends to ignore what is missing unless absence of it is specifically defined as meaningful. But that is akin to sending a biological intelligence looking for a literal needle in a haystack. Often avoided in favor of a less resource-intensive solution, such as not worrying about what isn't posing a problem."

Loucas stood up from the bench as he thought aloud. "So you are saying that Olga or Franz won't notice we're gone as long as they aren't specifically looking for us?"

Idunn nodded. "Yes. And you will be drawn back the moment that happens. It is actually easier for the Web to estimate a machine intelligence's probability of specifically checking for absence than a human's, because a human is always prone to sudden and unpredictable flashes of intuition, so the time you can get away before you must return depends more on proximity than in the case of machines. They usually react only to detected changes in their environment, part of why I find living things more interesting on the whole."

"With exceptions, of course." added Thor. "But in general, don't worry: if the Web appears, you are safe—for a time. Which in your case is quickly running short. I take it you had only an hour or so before the battle to come?"

Yari felt afraid. She checked the clock above their door. It had gone down almost to zero without her noticing. She wasn't really satisfied with the explanation for why Olga didn't notice their absence, but didn't think it made sense to waste time figuring it out. She turned to ask one more question—a favor, really—but found that an answer had already been provided. Somehow, unnoticed, Freyr had woken, returned to the bar, filled a small goblet with a sweet-smelling mead, and was now kneeling in front of her, offering it as if he were a renaissance courtier.

She took it and sipped at it—then rapidly downed the entire goblet. Freyr beamed at her. "That'll tide you over, young one! Good luck, and I hope to see you again soon. Look on the bright side! If you survive your first battle, you are *exponentially* more likely to survive the next one after that!"

The mead took effect quickly, and she felt peculiarly calm and focused. Smiling, she pulled Loucas to his feet. He laughed, and stroked Weiss, who meowed again.

Loucas looked at her, and sighed. "Back to it then? I guess we'll find out later if the cat talks to anyone but you, at least."

Yari shrugged, and smiled back at the five humanoid and feline faces that all seemed to be silently wishing her well. Then took her brother by the hand, and turned to the doorway.

TO GOEBBELS' HOUSE WE GO

The first thing Eryn heard upon returning to 1944 was shouting. Two furious male voices echoed into Stauffenberg's office, streams of accusation and invective mingling into cacophony.

She couldn't make out what was being screamed, and moved to the doorway to try and determine at least who was shouting, if not what they were shouting. It didn't help. She took a deep breath, remembered that she'd been instructed to remain where she was, and made the conscious decision to ignore the command.

Not far from the door, at the end of a short hallway, Gertrude stood with her back pressed against a wall, a pair of plain brown shoes clutched to her chest. She stared at her feet, visibly trembling.

Eryn walked to her side. From there she could see that in the center of the office suite Stauffenberg and another, older, man in a military uniform were nose to nose, hands clenched into fists, shouting at the top of their lungs. It didn't seem that either was listening to the other.

She still couldn't make out what either was saying, but it didn't matter: without warning, Stauffenberg turned on his heel, and barked an order at two other uniformed men standing near at hand. The other man froze in mid-shout, the moment he heard the third word.

"You two! Arrest General Fromm, take him someplace out

of my sight, and keep him there! Do not allow him to leave or speak with anyone! You may shoot him, if he does not comply."

Fromm's face contorted and flushed from bright red to a deeper, more sickly hue.

"You traitor, Stauffenberg! You have no right to give any orders here! Hitler will have your head by sunrise, you idiot! Yours, and the heads of anyone stupid enough to follow you!"

Stauffenberg wheeled around to fix Fromm with a menacing glare. The two soldiers stepped forward, hands on holstered pistols. The general looked at them in turn, as if daring them to carry out the colonel's orders. One of the men removed his pistol from its holster, and held it at his side.

Fromm's eyes were immediately drawn to the weapon. All the blood left his face. His mouth worked, but no sounds emerged. The two soldiers looked at one another, and then each placed a hand on one of the general's shoulders. He stiffened, visibly swallowed, and turned. Then he drew himself up, and with as much dignity as he could muster given the circumstances, marched out of the room. The guards followed close behind.

As soon as he had gone, Stauffenberg was surrounded by officers and submerged in a new cacophony, questions and concerns on everyone's lips. Eryn looked at Gertrude, who kept her gaze fixed firmly on her shoes. Then she noticed Haeften pushing through the crowd of uniformed bodies, giving Eryn a strange look as he approached.

"Well then, Eryn," Haeften said, "it seems that you obey orders just about as well as General Fromm. And it also seems that you do, in fact, have information that we lack. Credit where credit is due: you were right. He walked straight out of the room he'd been sent to, and made his way to a phone. He was overheard asking the operator to put him through to Heinrich Himmler's office. The bastard was planning to call the Gestapo down on us. He refuses to believe that Hitler is dead."

She shrugged, still feigning confidence. "That's what I said. I hope that now you will believe me when I tell you something."

He snorted. "I don't need to believe you to take advantage of what you seem to know. Valkyrie stands at the knife's edge. Do you have any other information that might be of immediate use?"

Eryn nodded, seeing no other option but to play it as Mimr and company had suggested. "That depends: have you people figured out where the rest of the regime's main players are? Himmler, Goebbels, Goering?"

Haeften laughed. "No one ever knows where that rat Himmler will be on a given day. Hopefully he is in Rastenburg. Goering is supposed to be in Rastenburg as well, and as that drug-addicted clown is actually difficult to lose track of, I suspect he will be captured in short order. We have reliable forces moving to secure that area."

Eryn pressed him. "And Goebbels? He's supposed to be in Berlin right now. Has he been secured?"

He gave her another strange look, then shook his head. "Well. So you are reasonably well informed. If the Allies know this much about the movements and predispositions of the Nazi leadership, small wonder we are losing this war. In fact, in the course of that shouting match, Fromm accidentally confirmed that Goebbels is presently at his residence in Berlin, near the Tiergarten. I am sending a team there now. The SS will sooner or later realize what is happening and move to secure Goebbels before we can. If that devil gets hold of a radio, he will use the fact that we can't yet formally prove the fact of Hitler's death as an excuse to pretend he is acting on Hitler's own orders. Which will be an absolute disaster!"

Haeften looked at Gertrude. "Madam, if you would please hand dear Miss Eryn those shoes, I intend to dispatch her to the Goebbels residence to help keep that from happening."

Eryn raised an eyebrow. "Exactly what are you expecting me to do?"

His mouth stretched into a thin smile. "Whatever you can. With whatever useful information you may have. Frankly, I mostly desire to get you out of the way until I can discuss your... situation, with Colonel Stauffenberg and General Beck. But you have surprised me already, so perhaps you will do so again."

Eryn and Gertrude shared a look. Gertrude smiled, but was clearly still quite scared. Eryn smiled kindly, and gently took the shoes from her. She knelt where she was, and worked her feet into the shoes. They weren't particularly comfortable, but they were a better option than either wearing heels or just socks, until she could get hold of a decent pair of boots.

Almost as soon as she had tightened the thick leather laces, Haeften exited the room, waving for her to follow. Eryn pulled herself to her feet, smiled her thanks at Gertrude, and followed as quickly as she could.

She caught up with him in the hallway, and together they made their way out of the Bendlerblock. Her mind raced as she wracked her brain for every detail she could remember about Goebbels and his role in the events of July 20, 1944. As the Minister of Propaganda, he didn't have control over the military or Nazi hierarchy, but what he did have was a knack for manipulating public opinion. And in a closed, fascist, pre-internet society, where the only way most people could get news was by listening to radio broadcasts, a capable propagandist with access to a transmitter could have immense influence. Because Goebbels had created such a cult of near-mythic proportions around Adolf Hitler, Germany's now-deceased dictator, it was likely that he could use control of the airwaves to sow confusion and coordinate a Nazi counter-coup.

She didn't need a computer program from outside the universe to tell her how bad that would be. For the coup, and herself.

Haeften halted just outside the main doorway. The Bendlerblock courtyard and street beyond were alive with activity. Half a dozen trucks had pulled up and were disgorging dozens of soldiers in black uniforms, armed with a variety of dangerous-looking weapons. Rifles, grenades, machine guns.

Eryn's heart started thumping in her chest the moment she saw them, as for an instant she felt the strangest sense of déjà vu. She more than half-expected the soldiers to shoot at or arrest them. She glanced at Haeften, who did not seem to share her unease. He stood patiently, looking at the mass of soldiers, waiting expectantly for something or someone.

He noticed her looking at him, and must have seen something of her fear. He shook his head and smiled. "Not to worry. These are Brandenburgers, and they are with us. This company is supposed to fortify and guard the area around our headquarters against any attempt by the SS or Gestapo to intervene. But I intend to send you and a platoon to call on the Goebbels residence."

Her fear turned to shock. "Wait, you are giving me soldiers?"

Haeften laughed. "Absolutely not! You have no authority here whatsoever. I intend to send you along with a friend of mine, Captain Hans Lewinsky, as an aide. Your mission is to ensure that our people get to Goebbels before the SS."

He gestured towards a tall man in a crisp black uniform accented by rose-colored details, who approached them with the steady and measured gate of a military professional. To Eryn, he looked like just another German officer, albeit a bit taller and more gaunt than most, but Haeften greeted him warmly.

"Hans! I am happy to see you. I have a mission for you."

Hans nodded. "I assumed that you would. My apologies the late arrival. The reserve army quartermaster in our barracks was drunk, and it took some time to secure the trucks."

"No troubles entering Berlin?"

"None. We appear to have caught them off their guard."

Haeften closed his eyes and mumbled something under his breath. It sounded like a prayer. He opened them again and nodded towards Eryn.

"In that case, we must press our advantage. I need you to take this…"

"Friend." Interjected Eryn.

Hans gave her a bemused look, then turned back to Haeften.

"That uniform… so she isn't one of Himmler's?"

Eryn shook her head. Haeften shrugged.

"It seems not. Regardless, we need you to get to the Goebbels' residence as quickly as possible. Take her with you— and keep her out of trouble. As for the Minister, it would be preferable to bring him back here to see if we can force him to do as we command, but if all else fails…"

That, it seemed, sufficed for both Haeften and Lewinsky. Haeften saluted his friend, who returned the gesture, turned, and walked away as swiftly as he had approached.

Eryn turned to say something to Haeften, but he walked back into the Bendlerblock without a word. She stood there, mouth half open, just watching him disappear. She felt strangely alone, despite being surrounded by dozens of German soldiers and several officers, who were hurriedly deploying weapons and setting up what she assumed were fighting positions throughout the courtyard.

With a shake of her head she brushed off her feelings, and followed after yet another uniformed German officer—this time, someone she hadn't ever heard of. Nothing about his name or his unit—the 'Brandenburgers'—meant the first thing to her. But since she was supposed to go hunt down Goebbels anyway, she figured that it made sense to tag along with Captain Hans Lewinsky for the time being.

He went about his business at a remarkable pace. Before she could catch up with him, he gave instructions to several different groups of soldiers. A dozen or so loaded up in the back of one of the trucks. Then he marched over to a staff car. He paused for a moment, then sat in the driver's seat and started the engine.

Eryn ran the last few steps, jerked on the handle of the passenger door, and threw herself onto the hard seat. The engine roared to life, and she didn't even have time to settle herself before Lewinsky had put the vehicle in gear, and steered it onto the street. The truck followed close behind, two soldiers clutching sub-machine guns visible, jammed into the cabin next to the driver.

The sun was settling behind the western rooftops of Berlin, and the already dour city began to look positively forbidding in the growing twilight. Lewinsky didn't say a word to Eryn as he maneuvered the vehicle at unsafe speeds through the streets of the capitol. Eryn checked the rear-view mirror and was amazed to see that the truck full of soldiers was actually keeping pace. She felt a pang of empathy for the men in the back, who had to be getting pretty badly knocked around as the truck swerved time and again to keep up with Lewinsky's madcap mode of driving.

Rounding a sharp corner, Lewinsky was forced to slam on the brakes to avoid rear-ending another staff car that was stopped in the center of the road, held by a checkpoint manned by at least a dozen soldiers in grey uniforms, who all were on their feet, half of them pointing sub-machine guns at the staff cars and the troop truck that creaked to a miraculously intact halt several feet behind Lewinsky's vehicle.

He made a gesture that Eryn took as an instruction to stay put, and kicked open the driver side door. The Brandenburger captain exited the vehicle with all the apparent purpose and power of a tornado. She watched through the windshield as he marched up to two men in officer's uniforms, whose heated argument their arrival had interrupted.

Whether it was something about his bearing, uniform, or the content of his communication, in less than a minute one of the two officers was being escorted out of the road by two guards, while the other officer was saluting Lewinsky. He returned the salute and walked briskly back to the staff car.

When the door closed, he let out a sigh of relief. Eryn tried, unsuccessfully, to read his expression, while he waited for the staff car blocking their way to pull off to one side of the street, near where the now-imprisoned German officer stood with two guns leveled at his chest, though that didn't keep him from berating his captors, face beet red. Once there was room, the officer controlling the checkpoint waved to Lewinsky, and the other soldiers lowered their weapons and made way for the staff car and truck to continue on their way.

"What did you say to them?"

Lewinsky started when she spoke, looked quickly at her, and then back to the roadway.

"You were so quiet that I thought, perhaps, you didn't speak very much German!"

In point of fact she didn't, but she didn't see a point in trying to explain her situation. She didn't understand it very well herself. He continued speaking, not waiting for her to respond.

"We haven't been properly introduced, have we? I am Captain Hans Lewinsky, of the Brandenburg Regiment. Currently attached to the Greater Germany mechanized infantry division."

"I'm Eryn. From Canada. And you didn't answer my question."

He laughed. "I did not. Although, perhaps that is wise, given that you are a foreign national of a country that is presently at war with my country?"

She didn't know what to say to that. So she shrugged.

He shrugged back. "Well, we're here together now, and Colonel Stauffenberg vouches for you, so I see no point in worrying about your nationality. Whatever assistance I can get in taking my country back from these animals, I will accept."

He paused, twisting the steering column to bring the staff car around a sharp turn, then he braked sharply to park the automobile in the middle of the street. He shut off the engine and opened his door. Eryn did the same. The truck stopped behind them, and soldiers began to disembark, leaping from the bed to the road in a series of thumps and grunts.

"As for your question, Eryn: we appear to have arrived just in the nick of time. The officer now in the custody of those reserve army soldiers at the checkpoint was sent by General Fromm to make contact with Goebbels and warn him about the Valkyrie operation. Once I told them that Hitler was dead and that Fromm's orders were invalid, they chose the correct side."

"And they believed you, just like that?"

He chuckled. "The uniform helps, I have to admit. An armor officer of the Brandenburgers tends to command a great deal of respect throughout the Army. Particularly those of us who have survived this long."

The soldiers accompanying them spread out, taking positions up and down the street. Two approached Eryn and Captain Lewinsky. He greeted them with a gesture, and turned to lead Eryn and their two guards to call at the Goebbels residence.

It was surprisingly quiet as they ascended the steps to the front door of the Berlin villa where Nazi Minister for Propaganda Joseph Goebbels liked to hang out and entertain guests, when he wasn't playing Hitler's mouthpiece. Naturally, the residence was large and well-cared for, and less than a block away the street faded into the lush greenery of the Tiergarten, which even in 1944 functioned as Berlin's equivalent to New York's famed Central Park. Eryn had expected there to be guards, and maybe even a fight at the door. But there was no one visible, and the only sounds were those of traffic in the neighboring streets. It was strange, eerie even, to be in the midst of a coup to destroy the most evil regime the world had ever known, with most of the city around them blissfully unaware of what was happening.

Lewinsky knocked at the door and then waited, as if this were just a normal social call. Footsteps approached the door from the inside, and it swung open. A pair of young women bowed to the guests on the threshold, and greeted them. One opened her mouth to address the guests.

Lewinsky ignored them both, and marched into the home, followed by Eryn and the two soldiers. The Goebbels residence was lavishly and tastefully furnished, even by Eryn's twenty-first century standards. Given that the Nazis were supposed to be in the midst of a fight for survival against pretty much the rest of the world, it seemed exceptionally out of place.

They found Joseph Goebbels seated in a room that looked

to be some sort of study. He wasn't alone. Another man, that Eryn *thought* she recognized, sat in a chair across from Goebbels. The two of them looked up expectantly at the three men and one woman who entered the room, two of them holding their sub-machine guns at the ready.

Goebbels looked distinctly harried, but not nearly as concerned as Eryn might have expected. In fact, his thin, sallow, distinctly rat-like face actually looked confident, though she didn't know what he had to be confident about, given the circumstances. His companion, in contrast, looked both tired and afraid. Goebbels stood up and greeted Lewinsky. In a manner of speaking.

"Ah, finally, an officer. What unit are you from? The Bodyguards? You must know *something*. Do we have an uprising on our hands? Or an Allied landing? Speak!"

Captain Lewinsky didn't say a word. Goebbels' face flushed red, and his eyes widened. He balled his fists, and his voice went up several registers. Clearly, he was used to being obeyed without hesitation.

"*Captain*, I *order* you to tell me what is happening out there!"

Lewinsky looked slowly from Goebbels, to his companion, to Eryn. He spoke to her.

"Well, my Lady, we seem to be the bearers of bad news, at least from the perspective of the dear Minister Goebbels here, don't we?"

Eryn had to catch herself in order to not visibly startle. She thought quickly, then understood Lewinsky's game. She forced a calm, half-smirking smile.

"Yes, it seems so, Captain."

Goebbels clenched his jaw, and if his face could have flushed a deeper shade of red, it would have.

"You *insubordinate swine*! I will have you before a People's

Court and shot by this time tomorrow! And *then* your families will be shot and their corpses thrown in an offal pit!"

Lewinsky's laugh was slow and mocking. "No, you filth, we'll be having none of that. In fact, if there is any final worldly business you might want to conclude, I will grant you a few minutes to put your affairs in order. And after that, I will present you with a choice. Swear allegiance to the new government being formed under the authority of General Beck and submit to a trial for your crimes against the German people, or face a firing squad this very evening."

Goebbels seethed. "I will have you tortured to death in Dachau along with your family."

Lewinsky chuckled, and grinned at Eryn. "Do you want to tell him, or should I?"

Eryn immediately knew what he meant. And couldn't resist feeling a thrill. After all, Joseph Goebbels was clearly one of the most evil human beings who had ever been born. One of the Nazis directly responsible for the cold-blooded murder of millions of innocent people and untold miseries and death inflicted on *tens* of millions more. Twisting the knife seemed just.

"Yeah, so Goebbels—here's the thing," Eryn grinned at him, your dear leader, Hitler, is dead. I know, because I was there. I helped plant the bomb. The coup is already underway. Your regime is done. Over. About nine hundred and ninety years earlier than you'd hoped. Everything you've worked for these past years? We are going to dismantle all of it, permanently."

Both Goebbels and his companion froze in total shock.

Albert Speer. That was his name, Eryn remembered, this other man who had chosen to call on Goebbels on the eve of July 20th, 1944. And memory of the name brought with it another fragment, launching itself to her fore mind from somewhere deep in the recesses of her consciousness: *"To be *won over?"*

Then came the context: that was the position of the Valkyrie coup plotters with respect to this man, the Nazi German Minister for Armaments. The man responsible for running the German economy. Eryn didn't have time to consider the implications. The sound of gunfire tore through the twilight. All eyes turned towards a large window, beyond which the rolling greenery of the Tiergarten was visible out to a distance of several blocks.

Motion caught her eye. A huge metal shape, then another, left the cover of a group of trees on one side of the park, and advanced to a position where a dip in the terrain allowed the tanks to park with only their turrets exposed above the level of the grassy earth, barrels of their main armament pointed in the direction of the Goebbels villa.

Smaller shapes, moving quickly from tree to tree, came into view less than halfway between the tanks and the villa. The sound of gunfire tore through the air, and Eryn could see flashes and streaks of light flicker through the twilight sky.

Goebbels stood up suddenly, and walked to the window, smiling wickedly.

"And there you see: the SS is already moving to put down your petty little uprising. You are lying—Hitler is *alive*, and already those loyal to us are moving to destroy you. And when we are done with you, we'll find each and every member of your families. We'll send them to Dachau and Auschwitz. Your names will be eradicated from history. We will *annihilate* you, just as we have destroyed everyone else who has stood in the path of our righteous cause!"

His voice was shrill, and he began to look exactly like the man Eryn had seen on the old video reels. Ranting and raving, spittle splattering against the window in front of him. Speer looked on, openly horrified.

Lewinsky didn't move or speak. He merely watched as the

firefight in the Tiergarten unfolded. More soldiers entered their view, accompanied by what looked like large cars encased in sheet metal, firing streams of bullets from machine guns poking out of small turrets.

The tanks remained in position, muzzles unmoving, as if unsure which side to back. The soldiers on both sides now held their position, firing at opponents in the Tiergarten as well as others whose positions were occluded from view by a row of buildings. Larger guns on the armored cars entered the fray, and the villa shook as they sent wave after wave of shells towards their enemies.

Goebbels' excitement disintegrated as quickly as the armored cars. Two thunderclaps sounded, and Eryn felt their force in her gut, as if she were standing too close to a speaker at a concert. The tanks had entered the fray, and Lewinsky's sudden laugh told Eryn which faction they belonged to. Now under assault from two sides, the SS soldiers began to melt away into the night, those that refused to flee dying until the guns fell quiet.

Lewinsky laughed. "Looks like the boys from GD have arrived as planned. They are more than a match for any security unit your SS and Gestapo thugs can throw together. Your time is up, Goebbels. And so dies your last hope."

If someone had told Eryn that a creature like Joseph Goebbels could be destroyed so thoroughly, so quickly, she wouldn't have believed them. And yet, before her eyes, he seemed to melt. As if he was, in that moment, granted true knowledge of the magnitude of his defeat. He turned slowly, and looked from face to face, a man suddenly adrift and alone. He gave Eryn a particularly peculiar look. His mouth worked, but perhaps for the first time in his life, he couldn't find his words. Finally, he looked to Captain Lewinsky, and seemed just… tired.

"You will allow me time to settle my last affairs? I wish

to call Magda. She is at the country home with the children. Grant me this, and I will do whatever you require."

Lewinsky thought for a moment, and then nodded. He whistled, and one of the two women who had opened the door scurried into the room, staring at the floor.

"Ma'am, please take him to a telephone so that he may call his wife. I will send these guards to ensure that he returns promptly, and does *nothing* else."

As those assembled turned to follow their orders, Eryn stood in thought, suddenly feeling... she didn't know what. Like there was something she was forgetting. Something important. The feeling made no sense to her: this had gone like Mimr had said it needed to, and without severe difficulty. With Goebbels in custody, the Nazis had lost one of their few remaining weapons. So why she now felt so uneasy, she didn't know. The only thing she could think, was that now she had, yet again, to figure out what to do next.

Another pair of soldiers entered the room, and Lewinsky turned to speak with them. Eryn noticed Speer still sitting in his chair, looking—if that were possible—*less* afraid than he had a moment before. He actually seemed relieved. Like a heavy burden had been lifted from his shoulders

And then it hit her.

There wasn't time to say anything. They wouldn't believe her in time. Eryn broke out into a run, tearing down the hallway after Goebbels and his guards. She heard Lewinsky shout something after her, but ignored him.

She reached the end of the hall. Looked to her right, and her left. She couldn't see anyone. She stopped breathing, and tried to listen as carefully as she could.

She ran to the left, following a sound. That hallway soon ended, and on either side was a doorway. The one on the right was open, the two guards and Goebbels' attendant waiting patiently along the far wall, watching yet another door that was cracked, and beyond the crack came the sound of a hurried, hushed telephone conversation.

She pushed into the room before the guards could react, and shoved open the door to the room where Goebbels clutched a telephone receiver, his face deathly pale.

"Yes, Magda, I am sure! It is time. There is no choice. The capsules are…"

She grabbed the receiver and slammed it down as quickly as she could. Goebbels clawed at it, and started to shout. She took a step back and kicked him as hard as she could, sinking her foot as deep into his solar plexus as she could manage, nearly falling over as she recovered. She had never attacked anyone before, and wasn't even sure how to. She just launched herself at the man without thinking about what would happen after. The breath went out of him, and he collapsed in the chair, eyes wide and full of pain and hate.

The guards shoved their way in after her, and a few seconds later Lewinsky shoved his way through the door as well. Eryn didn't give him a chance to speak.

"The bastard was going to kill his children! He has capsules of poison hidden in his home. He was trying to tell his wife to kill them. He was going to kill his own family!"

Lewinsky looked at her in shock, and then at Goebbels. And then became very calm. His face became expressionless. And when he spoke, his voice was cold. Hard.

"Of course he was. A rat like him would annihilate his whole family once he was sure fate had turned against him. I will send word to have Magda Goebbels taken into custody as quickly as possible. I hope they are in time."

He stepped forward, taking Goebbels by the throat. He addressed the soldiers.

"Have him taken outside and executed by firing squad *im-*

mediately."

In that moment, breathing hard and with her heart pounding in a mixture of rage and disgust, Eryn couldn't see a reason to object. Lewinsky stood aside, and the soldiers seized Goebbels, who tried to struggle, but was in no position to effectively resist. She and Lewinsky followed as they frog-marched him out of the room, and back down the corridors to the entrance to the villa.

But as they passed the study, Speer's voice called out. It was so quiet that Eryn couldn't make out what he said, but she could hear the crackling sound of a radio being adjusted.

Lewinsky gestured to the guards, who halted. The volume on the radio increased. Through the static, Eryn could make out a voice. It was calm, even, commanding. The mode and meter of it made it clear that someone was giving a speech.

"People of Germany, my name is Ludwig Beck. I have grave news for us all: Adolf Hitler is dead. High-ranking members of the Nazi government have attempted to use the Gestapo and SS to seize power in Berlin in the wake of the assassination. Only decisive action by the reserve army has prevented a greater catastrophe. In this time of national emergency, with the National Socialist leadership responsible for grave crimes against the state, I have been called to serve as your President and Defender until elections can be held."

"This stab-in-the-back by the SS and Gestapo cannot be allowed to threaten our efforts to protect our people from the ongoing assaults launched by the Soviet Union and the Western Allies. We will seek an honorable end to this terrible conflict, but must remain committed to the defense of our lives and homes until we can be assured that the rights of the German people are guaranteed for all time."

"In this time of unprecedented crisis, when our very existence as a people is threatened by enemies who have used the crimes of the Nazis to justify a campaign of terror against our civilian

population, we must all continue to sacrifice, to fight for Germany. I call upon all the German people to make every effort to support our struggle, to remember the sacrifices of their brave soldiers at the fronts. For we struggle as one."

The broadcast ended. Lewinsky and Eryn both looked at Goebbels. His expression was blank. Without waiting for further orders, the soldiers took him outside. Eryn didn't follow. In that moment, she felt no need to directly witness what was about to happen.

She walked back into the study, and stood looking out the window, into the Tiergarten. The tanks were still there.

Shots rang out from somewhere outside.

THE BATTLE OF SOUTHERN BUTTE

Kim looked out into the clear, star-flecked night sky of central Idaho, and cursed as the truck hit a bump in the road, sending her helmeted head knocking into the metallic wall of the vehicle for what had to be the third or fourth time in the last hour.

The journey to wherever they were supposed to be going seemed to last an eternity. Not long into the helicopter flight, the combination of motion sickness and overwhelm at the sheer quantity of arcane details Chavez and Jackson insisted on throwing at them drove her mind into a self-protective numbness. While Patrick dozed, and Timur remaining focused on the briefing, Kim stared out one of the portholes, absentmindedly looking over various bits of the briefing materials that seemed interesting.

The long flight had been interrupted only by a brief span where the helicopter's engines whined at a higher pitch, and she gathered from the data displayed in her headset that the aircraft was taking on fuel. The flight finally ended, without warning: her stomach soared towards her throat as the Stallion maneuvered to unload the armored truck slung under its belly, then the pilot deftly brought the helicopter around for a proper landing.

Chavez and Jackson had hustled Kim and her friends into the back of one of the trucks, then left to supervise a veritable swarm of soldiers, pilots, and other personnel, all running between aircraft and vehicles, carrying or even dragging an endless stream of crates and other containers, filling every available space in each truck wherever room could be found or forced. Mostly, it was found in the narrow aisle between the vehicle's six seats, and as it was filled the legroom between their seats rapidly dwindled to nil.

Tired, bored, and afraid, Kim had tried to make some sense of the chaos, but failed. Patrick dozed off once more, and Timur remained quiet, lost in his own thoughts. Everything seemed to fade together in a dull blur of camouflaged metal. When the vehicle finally couldn't absorb any more containers, Jackson and Chavez crawled past the piles to their seats and plugged a zip-tied bundle of cables into ports hidden under a panel in the side of the carapace each wore.

Kim found that a bundle of cables was located next to her own seat, and she worked out how to plug them in as the truck's engine roared to life. Then they were off, jostling over the bumps in the dirt roads that cut through Craters of the Moon, Idaho. Her headset indicated that batteries in her carapace were recharging, and a video feed appeared in front of her eyes, apparently linked to cameras somewhere on the truck's exterior. The feed offered a green-tinged, panoramic view of the surrounding countryside, and with little else to do, Kim spent the trip gazing quietly out towards the horizon, the lack of light leaving her with the impression that they were moving at a crawl, deeper and deeper into the broken and lifeless moonscape.

Except, of course, when the truck hit an uneven part of the road, causing her head to slam into the metal wall of the vehicle's interior. The headset offered a good deal of protection from the physical impact, but it still felt like she'd been punched in the temple. Her head throbbed, and she wondered how many hours it would be before they got somewhere that had a place that stocked aspirin.

Another bump—but this time she was ready for it. Instead of her head, now her neck hurt, as her muscles strained to hold her head in place.

A hiss of static burst into the ears of her headset, startling her.

"This is Ghurka six. Ghurka team, radio check."

Kim shook her head. Chavez' voice echoed in her head, having been transmitted both through some kind of local voice channel that mimicked the volume and tone of plain human speech, but also through what sounded like a radio transmission. The responses came over only on the radio channel, one at a time and with various levels of crackling static distorting the transmission.

"Ghurka five, aye." "Ghurka one, hu-ah." "Ghurka four, aff." "Ghurka three, yup." "Ghurka two, gotcha."

As each team transmitted, a light flashed in a corner of Kim's HUD. Without warning, the external camera feed disappeared, replaced by a map which showed the terrain and infrastructure out to a distance of twenty miles from their current location. On it, six blue icons were scattered, all converging on a point in the center of the map labeled "Kushan" which was marked by a red icon. To the far right of the map was a cluster of red icons, and the label "SoBu"; about halfway between Kushan and SoBu was another icon, and the label "Park".

"This is six. Be advised, Ghurka team now technically visible to SoBu radar. Weak radio-band transmissions detected from Kushan. Expect Kushan occupied by observation team as expected. Proceed according to condition yellow. Six out."

A string of confirmations and affirmatives filled the radio, and then all returned to silence. Chavez tapped her helmet several times to get their attention, and called each of their names to ensure they were all awake and listening.

"Ok, pay attention, chitlins. We're twenty minutes out from Kushan. It's that funny little hill at the center of your map. When the doors open, Timur and Jackson will head straight to the alternate observation post. Kim and Patrick, you'll be with me at the main OP. The Mules will drop off our equipment over the next couple hours, while we wait and observe. Got it?"

Kim shook her head. "Nope."

Chavez laughed. "Good! Then just do whatever I say and stick close. I haven't gotten killed yet."

Timur shook his head. Kim couldn't see his face, but she thought she could imagine his expression. His voice confirmed her instinct.

"You *just* said the hill—Kushan or whatever—is already occupied. I thought you said the SoBu position had a ton of artillery covering the area. Why won't they nail us the moment we step foot on that hill?"

Jackson grunted. "Politics."

"*Politics?!*"

"Yup. Raiding supply convoys is one thing. Occupying Rexburg without firing a shot is a similar thing. But wiping out a full combat team? The commander on SoBu will want to talk to the leadership in Salt Lake City before escalating that far. That's a shooting war, totally on them, unless we start shooting first. And they won't be able to get a decision until after dawn. Too late, by then. Because we *will* be shooting first. But they don't know that. To them, this is just a provocation. Until they know it isn't. *Then* they'll try to wipe us out."

Chavez nodded, and from what of her face Kim could see through the mask and visor, she could tell Chavez was grinning. Timur went silent again.

They all lurched as the truck's brakes engaged. There was a

sound of sliding gravel and for a brief moment Kim thought that they must be about to crash. But then it ended, and with a loud popping sound the back of the truck was flung open.

They all clambered out of the back of the vehicle, and hopped down to the ground. As if the headset could tell that they needed normal vision, the data stream and video feed receded to a corner of the heads-up display, and Kim could see around herself as if through her own eyes.

The visor seemed transparent, but also had the effect of enhancing her natural vision. Though it was dark save for the moon and twinkling stars, the green tint of the video feed remained, and seemed to make the shadows less impenetrable. Out to the distant horizon, she was able to make out, if not actual details, still a general *sense* of the variations in the world around her. She soon realized though that she had to pay close attention to her feet to avoid tripping.

They had halted at the base of a tumbled, rocky slope that rose suddenly out of the shrub-infested steppe that filled the lands between the desolate Craters of the Moon and the irrigated fields closer to the Snake River. Her headset was still active, augmenting her perception of reality, and a digital label on her HUD hovered over the peak, naming it 'Kushan'.

A whirring and humming filled the air. Kim jerked her head, and saw what appeared to be the truck disassembling itself. Two hulking metal shapes were breaking away from the vehicle, one on each side, and as a hydraulic arm lowered them towards the ground, thick metal legs unfolded underneath.

As she watched, the machine nearest to her stood under its own power, seemed to dance from side to side for a moment, as if getting its bearings, then without pause it made a half-turn and trotted towards the mountain, legs thumping the ground in a distinct cadence. She watched it, the label

"Mule" affixing itself to the shape on her HUD, as the sound of its movement receded into the distance like a departing breeze.

She looked back at Chavez, who shrugged. "That's the other reason I'm not worried about whoever is sitting on that hill. About a dozen Mules are going to come charging through there over the next hour while we're on our hike."

Patrick let out a loud "Huh", and they turned to look at him.

"Do they have any guns?"

"No." she replied. "Too risky. Nobody has come up with a safe, fully autonomous combat robot yet. And it is dead easy to hack or jam the signal you need to control a drone, so you are better off keeping the things unarmed unless your opponent has zero technical capabilities. Nah, they just carry heavy stuff for us. And they'll scare the living bejeebus out of anyone hanging out up there. Plus, we've rigged them with some thermal sensors, so as they head up there they'll scout the place pretty thoroughly. Anybody does try and hide out, we'll know, and send a team to flush them out."

Timur let out a loud "Huh" of his own. "You people really aren't worried about staying hidden, are you? Odd, for scouts."

Jackson walked up to him, and whacked him on the back of the helmet. "Pay attention. We're the bait. We *want* to make a lot of noise."

Timur clearly didn't agree, but held his tongue. Kim looked at Patrick again, but he was either too groggy from his naps or too overwhelmed to say anything. She couldn't really blame him.

Chavez and Jackson turned to one another, and shook hands. Jackson beckoned to Timur, seemed to draw himself up, and stalked off towards the mountain. Timur sighed, looked at his friends, and paused for a moment. They couldn't see his eyes or face to guess what he was thinking. He waved, turned, and followed. Chavez turned to Kim and Patrick.

"Alright, time to head out. Stay about five meters apart as we make the hike. Just in case some Deseret decides to play hero and chuck a grenade. Aside from that, just keep your eyes open and 'effing *scream* if you see someone *not* wearing one of our bugsuits."

She pulled her weapon close to her chest, and set off on a similar, but slightly diverging, path from the one Jackson had taken. Patrick and Kim stood there, hesitating.

"I'm really scared, Kim" he said.

"Me too, Patrick." she replied.

"Me three." came Chavez' voice, volume augmented by their headsets. "But that's the job. Come on."

They didn't see any choice. They complied. Chavez struck out on a pathway up the hill that cut through the brush as it switch-backed its way towards the summit.

Kim had never before felt as exposed as she did in that moment. Although the landscape was broken and rugged at ground level, the moment they began to ascend Kushan the lack of vegetation resulted in their being exposed in every direction. She noticed that Chavez' head was constantly moving, as if on a swivel, and Kim tried to mimic her. All that did was remind her of how many places someone could be hiding. Someone with a gun, or something worse. Her unease wasn't helped by the fact that it was quite likely that someone actually *was* hiding, watching them. Possibly, probably, pointing guns at them. The carapace didn't make Kim feel at all safe, rather, it made her feel all the more out of place and exposed, an ant crawling desperately past a sunlit magnifying glass.

A crashing and thudding sound came from somewhere above them, and Kim very nearly threw herself behind the nearest rock. One of the Mules came thumping around the bend, and then paused, as if it could see them and was politely waiting for them to pass. Chavez led them on without a word, and sure enough, as soon as they were all safely behind, the Mule continued on its thumping way.

The flight and drive had taken hours, but the hike seemed to last for days. Kim wished she'd been able, like Patrick, to get some sleep. Whatever fortifying effect the mead had, it was long gone now.

But nothing impeded their progress. And finally, just before the winding trail crested the summit of one of the hill's tumbled peaks, Chavez motioned for them to halt.

She crept to the crest, knelt, and then crawled to the summit. She paused, looking over the terrain. Then waved Kim and Patrick over, indicating that they should lay themselves down to either side of her. Her voice came as a digital whisper in their ears.

"From this point on, you had better assume that *any* time you move, the Deserets can see you. First rule of survival on a battlefield: don't be seen. What can be seen, can be targeted and killed. And the Second rule of survival: Stay behind something dense as much as you can. Because even if they can't *see* you, they *can* still kill you. Always remember: Cover saves lives, children."

Without waiting for a response, she pushed herself to her feet, and scurried over the crest of the ridge, keeping herself as low as possible. Kim and Patrick shared a look, and both followed her, trying to do the same. It was harder than Kim had realized to try to run at a crouch, particularly while lugging a few tens of kilograms of dead weight around your torso.

Chavez led them to a rocky outcropping, a sort of shelf

pushing out from the main ridge at the top of the Kushan position, which terminated in a sudden, steep drop of several meters. It functioned almost exactly like a wall and parapet on a medieval castle, with a shallow dip behind where they could shelter when not looking out towards the eastern horizon.

She quietly instructed them on where to position themselves so that they had the best possible field of view while remaining as hidden as they could in the rocks and dry grass. She then pointed towards a pile of what Kim had taken as stacked rocks, off to one side of the sheltered area behind them.

"When you figure out how you want to situate yourself for the next few hours, head down to the cache and grab one of the boxes labeled "optics." Bring it back, and set it up according to the instructions. Then verify that everything is displaying correctly on your HUD, and get ready to wait for the dawn and whatever the day brings."

The boxes were almost too heavy to carry alone, and were partly filled with a number of small, square devices that connected via cables to the rest of the larger box, which appeared to function as a control unit. Kim, dutifully following the instructions, set the smaller devices as far in front and to the side of her position as she could manage without exposing herself to view, orienting them so that a cluster of what looked like lenses were pointed towards the eastern horizon. She then wedged the control unit as tightly as possible between several rocks directly in front of where Chavez had instructed her to lay. Kim made sure everything was plugged in, turned on the device, and pressed the visor of her headset against a recess in one face of the box, adjusting her body so that she could lay as comfortably as possible, while remaining in contact with the system.

Several indicators flashed on her HUD, and then her view

sort of... shifted. The entire landscape to the east seemed to change color, and contours in the terrain became so clear that after she started to adjust to the somewhat unusual color scheme, she began to feel as if she could see almost as well as if it were the middle of the day. As long, of course, as she ignored the fact that the colors were entirely *wrong* for how she knew, from what they'd seen of Idaho so far, they were supposed to look.

The radio crackled again.

"This is Ghurka six. All elements logged in. Radio and digital silence protocols in effect until H-hour. Six out."

The radio fell silent. She tried to say something aloud, but no sound came or went. She was cut off. There was nothing Kim could do but wait. It was the cold dark of pre-dawn, when the night is most still, and the world waits in anticipation for the rising of the sun at the start of a new day. Silence blanketed the Earth. The stars twinkled, unconcerned about humanity or its struggles. The land seemed dead, and lifeless, as if the birds and insects already knew what the day would bring, and had moved on to better places. The minutes dragged past. The sky seemed to grow ever darker, and she began to shiver.

A flash caught Kim's eye, throwing a new set of strange colors across her digital view, until the headset adjusted. The first sliver of light, bringing warmth and illumination to the new day. The stars began to retreat, and her eyes were drawn to a distant array of peaks, dark rock dully reflecting the new light: some twenty kilometers away, Southern Butte rose from the Snake River Valley, far higher than their own peak, and the label "SoBu" danced above it in her HUD.

As the sun emerged fully from under the eastern horizon, the false colors on the digital display began to fade, and the world's natural colors began to return. What colors there were— most everything between Kushan and Sobu was some shade of brown.

"Ghurka Team, time! Vamos!"

Kim felt Chavez thud to the ground a few feet to her left. She turned her head, and saw that Chavez had positioned Kim and Patrick on either side of an oddly eroded boulder, about five meters apart. She tossed a pebble at each of them, hitting Kim in the shoulder and Patrick in the head. Both twisted to look at her. She had raised her visor, and her dark eyes gave each a penetrating stare before she spoke.

"Ok you two, your job is simple. Zoom your optics in on the Park position. Look for vehicles. Your HUD and the optics are integrated as long as you keep them in direct physical contact. If you break contact, your on-board computer and HUD take over, which can give you a second to adjust and pan before zooming back in. Use the interface to select a target. When the system has locked on, it'll paint the target with a laser. All you have to do is keep the indicators zoomed in on the target and wait for the fireworks to begin. When one is dead, you move on to the next."

Kim tried to speak, but the radio sounded again, cutting her off.

"Six, this is three. We've got movement at Park. North side. Four tracks, minimum."

"This is two. Confirming movement on Park, south side. Six to eight, mix of tracks and wheels."

Chavez lowered her visor. "You two have your job. Remember, you are spotting for the actual shooters. They'll be too busy running from one launch position to another to choose their targets too carefully. To carry this thing off, we gotta kill the four or five mobile SAM launchers they've got down there in that dry lake bed. Then we get to call in Hammer flight to do some *real* damage."

"What the hell is a…?"

Kim and Patrick asked at the same time. Chavez rolled over on her back, fingers moving furiously across her gloves. Her voice was distant, as if she was only half aware of them.

"Just paint *anything* that looks like it has a bunch of tubes or guns sticking out of the top. Or that your HUD tells you is using active radar. Now get to work! When they start shooting back be sure to keep your heads *down*."

In the distance, probably half a kilometer to their right, Kim heard the sound of several distinct pops, and a fraction of a second later several small flashes cut through the morning haze. Her HUD circled four shapes that emerged, streaking eastward, almost impossible to see, labeling them each "Spike 3". She pressed her visor against the optics system.

Her HUD showed their trajectory, as they flew in an arc towards the position labeled "Park" on her map. There a small basin had formed between a group of small hills, about ten or so kilometers from both their position and from Southern Butte. The center of the basin—it looked to Kim like the dry, dusty bed of a dead lake—was obscured by one of the hills. But to either side, she could make out blurry shapes. Vehicles on the move.

She zoomed in, past the missiles and towards their apparent terminal point in the southern part of the Park. This point was marked by a faint line on her HUD that seemed to project back towards the missiles. But once she had zoomed in, she didn't need assistance in finding the targets.

Two groups of vehicles were dashing across the lake bed, accelerating and moving southwest. One group was comprised of four of what her HUD indicated were Bradley infantry carriers while the other contained a pair of squat, square-turreted Abrams tanks, accompanied by another pair of smaller vehicles that looked like trucks with a cluster of tubes and possibly several machine guns on a rooftop turret. Her HUD labeled them "Avenger."

The missiles arrived. One of the Bradleys was struck directly in the center of its turret, and erupted in flames. Another missile narrowly missed a Bradley, which swerved so hard and suddenly to one side that it collided with a third. Two missiles struck one of the Abrams almost simultaneously, one just to the side of its main gun, the other on the lower side of the vehicle, in the midst of the huge wheels that turned the tracks that propelled the seventy ton vehicle. Kim could see the vehicle shudder as the missiles struck and exploded, and come to a halt, bits of rubber track flying skyward.

"Six, this is four. Two SAMs spotted moving southwest, covering six tracks. One Brad down, one Abrams mission kill. Could really use some paint on those Avengers!"

"Get to it, you two!" Chavez barked.

Kim zoomed in on the nearer of the two Avengers. Her HUD flashed a symbol above the vehicle. She was locked on. She strained her neck to hold her visor as tightly against the optics system as possible. The further she zoomed in, the steadier she had to hold her head in order to keep her vision fixed on the vehicle. It was like using binoculars to watch a flock of birds. Birds that began to swerve back while they dashed for cover.

The lock held. A prompt appeared on her HUD: Click to Lase.

She tapped one of her gloved palms with a finger, and strained to keep focused on the target. A bright light appeared, striking the vehicle right in the center of its turret, which now had turned towards her, showing that it contained not one but *two* clusters, each of four tubes arrayed around a large gun, and between them was a large flat surface that her HUD colored an odd purplish hue, accompanied by the label: Radar Active.

One of the tubes burst, and a shape accelerated away from

it, out beyond the edge of her vision. And then another object entered her view. It passed in less than a second, striking the vehicle almost exactly where the laser light reflected off the surface of the turret.

The turret erupted in an inferno, and the vehicle itself exploded a moment later.

Kim pulled her head away from the optics system, looking out across the landscape towards where she had just helped kill whoever had been in that vehicle. She saw the flashes of additional missiles striking home, and the brighter flashes of armored vehicles bursting into flames. She felt numb. But she didn't have time to think.

Sandra's voice filled her ears. "Good job you two! One Avenger down. Now get the other one!"

Kim choked back a series of vague emotional impulses, and almost without consciously realizing what she was doing, she zoomed back in on the vehicles. One Abrams and two Bradleys remained, and had converged with the surviving Avenger, as if drawing together would keep them all safe. And perhaps it would, for a time. Three of its canisters had burst, and a fourth erupted as Kim watched, sending a streak skyward. She could barely make out metal fragments raining down around the vehicle. The radio was alive with what sounded to her like incomprehensible babble, half a dozen voices simultaneously commentating on the scene, with one other voice, that of *Ghurka* six, periodically giving instructions.

Kim took a deep breath, and focused on the Avenger. She zoomed in, straining her muscles to remain fixed, and the lock-on indicator flashed. A few seconds later, the lase option flashed. She pressed finger to palm once again, and did her best to maintain the lock.

Almost instantaneously two streaks obscured her view, and the Avenger was struck in rapid succession, its front wheels collapsing and the turret belching smoke, the radar dish in the center completely shattered.

"*Two more SAMs, tracked, moving southwest, with tracks and wheels, company strength!*"

Kim pulled her head away from the optics and shook her head, blinking hard. It was jarring to zoom in and out so quickly, but zoomed in she couldn't figure out where to look to spot this new threat. Something caught her eye. To the east, either on or beyond Southern Butte. Flashes. First a few, then more. A *lot* more.

A buzzing sound filled her headset, and the HUD itself flashed red. A single word began to blink at the top of her HUD: Incoming.

The radio went silent. In the quiet, the sound of booms and thuds could be heard far away in the distance. Kim could hear Chavez scrambling up the short rise, and turned to look at her. She was gesticulating wildly, and shouting as loud as she could.

"Get down get down get DOWN!"

Kim noticed that Patrick had turned to look at Chavez, but had stumbled and slid a few inches down the incline. He had started to get to his feet, probably to re-position, but he froze in mid-crouch as Chavez scrambled at him.

Chavez threw herself bodily against Patrick, knocking him to the ground. She shoved him back into his original position, then jumped over to Kim, unnecessarily shoving her deeper into her own place. Then she threw herself down next to Kim, and looked as if she were trying to dig her face as deep into the rocky soil as she could.

"Stay DOWN! *Incoming!*"

The explosions began. It felt like a hundred giants were pounding their fists into the ground around her, over her, even under her. The Earth itself had come alive, angry at the torture being inflicted upon it by the little humans fighting their petty wars. The universe heaved, and wave after wave of heat and pressure flowed into and through Kim. Dirt and rock and metal fragments rained down on them.

There was too much noise for Kim to tell if she was actually screaming or not. She felt like she was. At least, she wanted to. She might not have been able to. The pressure kept hitting her, like someone was punching her in the chest again and again. She gasped for breath.

The bombardment seemed to go on and on, but was ever-changing like it had a treacherous will all its own. The pace of the explosions would sometimes seem to slacken, and hope would flash brightly across her mind. Only to be followed by another torrent, and a new wave of terror and despair.

Being shot at was terrifying enough. Whatever this was, felt like the end of the world. She wanted to run far, far away, but Chavez' warnings had done at least this much: as much as instinct cried out for her to get up and run, she stayed put.

And then it was over.

At least, for them. At any other moment, the shower of artillery now being dropped half a kilometer to either side of them would have terrified her. But the mere fact that, for at least a moment, it was—by five hundred meters—somebody else's problem, offered its own sense of relief.

"Five, this is six. Tell Command that the pinata has popped! Also, if they want to get us out of here alive, they'll send fire support goddamned stat!"

"Six, this is five. Already done. Command reports package inbound. Expect radio interference starting in point-five mikes."

"Affirmative, five. Ghurka team, radio check!"

Kim lay there, breathing hard, still not trusting that the bombardment was over. She listened to the teams call in.

She could hardly believe that they all did. How had they all survived that nightmare?

Static filled the radio, blotting out all the voices, and then her headset muted the channel. She tried to turn to Chavez, who had flipped over again, but hadn't left Kim's side. She looked over at Patrick, and her heart raced—he wasn't moving. But then she saw him moving his fingers across his palms. She exhaled. He was okay.

Kim twisted to look around them. The hilltop was unrecognizable. Chunks of rock had been torn from it, huge swaths of grass were scorched and shriveled. She found it hard to believe that they had survived unscathed.

From the west, over the top of the hill, dark shapes flashed into view. They seemed huge, and approached so quickly that they were on top of her by the time she was consciously aware of their presence. And then a new booming roar filled her ears, exceeding her headset's capacity to muffle it. She flinched, but it wasn't more incoming. It was headed in the wrong direction. She swiveled and shifted to watch the shapes as they flashed overhead.

There were two. The HUD labeled each a 'Flanker.' She wondered dully what rugby had to do with fighter jets. They passed perhaps ten meters overhead, and as she watched, flames burst out from their engines, and they seemed to swivel and twist in mid air, the roar that accompanied their passing intensifying even as they accelerated upward and began to bank hard to their left.

From each, a long, thin shape separated from underneath the main body of the aircraft. Her HUD indicated that each was on an arcing trajectory, apparently unpropelled, that would carry it somewhere beyond Southern Butte. The distance between parent aircraft and whatever they had deployed grew as the fighters receded into the distance, puffs of metal and flashes of light streaming from behind them, that her HUD labeled as flares and chaff. Two streaks flashed upward from somewhere on the plain below, each detonating with a puff of smoke in the cloud of decoys behind.

The radio came back to life. *"This is Black lead. Be advised, Nagasaki protocol in effect. Thirty seconds to impact. Repeat: Nagasaki, Nagasaki, Nagasaki!"*

Sandra's voice. *"Holy fu... Ghurka Team! Nagasaki Nagasaki Nagasaki!"*

The call was repeated over and over. Kim tuned it out, not understanding what it meant, and fixated on what was happening in the sky. The two objects were not alone. Four smaller and sleeker objects flashed overhead, leaving sonic booms in their wake. They were headed for Southern Butte. And whatever force was occupying the height saw them coming. More streaks flew skyward far enough away that her HUD had time to assign each of them a label: Patriot PAC 3. They closed the distance in seconds, blasting apart the four incoming missiles in quick succession.

But they didn't seem to notice the other two objects, now past the apex of their trajectory, lazily arcing down towards a point somewhere east of SoBu. Kim watched, oddly fascinated, only dimly aware of Chavez' voice.

"Uh, Kim, what the *hell* are you looking at?"

Two new suns were born in the sky above Southern Butte.

Kim's visor went bright white, and her eyes throbbed. She squeezed them shut, but the glare somehow still shone through her eyelids. As if from a distance she heard the sound of an alarm in her headset. For a long moment she crouched, clutching at her helmet, And then, curiously, she heard the entirely out of place sound of Chavez *laughing*, a sudden outpouring of a sort of fierce ecstasy.

"WoooooooHOOO! THAT's what I'm talking about! Boom, *biyotch*, get out the *WAY*! Get out the fuggin' WAY! Ha haaaaa!

Burn you ugly hill, BURN!!!"

Kim shook her head, and driven by some primal instinct, scraped at her visor until she was able to shove it back up into her helmet. She rolled and stared incredulously at Chavez, who, as she laughed and shouted, stood looking out towards Southern Butte, fists clenched and thrown into the air, a strange light from the east casting equally weird shadows across the dull plastic of her helmet's visor.

She wiped her watering eyes, and looked back towards Southern Butte. The entire mountain was shrouded in a torment of smoke and flame. It was as if everything on the height that could possibly burn, was now aflame. A cloud of dust rose over the plain below, and Kim felt a strong, warm breeze strike her face, bringing a fine mist of stinging dust along with it. She grabbed at her visor again, and slammed it back down to protect her already pained eyes.

Kim heard Timur's voice over the radio. It sounded frantic, terrified, and—oddly—*furious*. She couldn't understand most of what he was saying. It sounded like a series of escalating curses. Then Chavez' voice cut him off.

"Dude! What are you complaining about? Chill! That was a totally legit Nagasaki strike. The Flanker jocks ran the flight profile perfectly. Radio warning on all frequencies immediately after deployment. Blew 'em up a klick or two up in the air to minimize fallout. Damn, I knew they were gonna plaster that hill, but going nuclear? Daaaaaaamn."

Timur's voice. *"How in the hell do you people even HAVE nukes?!"*

A new voice. Jackson's. *"Shut up. Both of you. Fight about it later. That position is gone. That's all that matters. Return to normal radio protocols and complete the mission! They aren't all dead yet!"*

Chavez snorted, then chuckled. Kim heard a thunk, and saw that she had crouched down, engrossed in her digital display once again. She spoke to Patrick and Kim while she worked at whatever it was she was doing, her tone now weirdly casual.

"Well, Kim, count your blessings: if you'd been looking at the blasts without that visor, you'd be at least temporarily blind. Patrick, good on you for not looking directly into the light. I still need someone here with decent eyes to close out the op. SoBu is done and gone, but the Deserets still have the better part of an armor company in a position to come take this hill."

Kim could see Patrick roll to the side, and turn his head towards Chavez.

"What, can't you just nuke them too?"

She worked for a few moments, saying nothing. Then she laughed, and went back on the radio.

"Ghurka Team, this is six. Mission update follows. Okay, main job is done. With a bonus: Command has just confirmed that the frickin' Chairman of the Deseret Army was at Sobu. Satellites show the whole thing is cooked clean. No survivors anticipated above or below ground."

The radio channel filled with acknowledgments and cheers. When they were done, she continued.

"This is six. Prepare for egress under fire. I'll bet my retirement that the Deserets are gonna come for this hill looking for vengeance. Plan remains the same: target air defense vehicles. Clear a path. Then drop the hammer and pop smoke back to the FOB. Six out."

Chavez turned to Kim and Patrick. "Back to it, you two. This ain't over yet."

Kim and Patrick stared at one another for what seemed like minutes. Despite the fact that neither could see the other's eyes, somehow Kim knew that they were both, in that moment feeling exactly the same. Overwhelmed, and afraid.

Patrick rolled and pressed his visor against his optics unit. Kim looked over the top of the rocks in front of her, trying to blink away the worst pain of the vicious headache she was now forced to endure. She stared out towards the horizon, watching Southern Butte burn and the smoke from its fires climb high into the sky. It seemed strange to her that they didn't form a mushroom cloud. Apparently nothing made any sense at all in 2041.

Her HUD slowly returned to normal, though she noticed that colors seemed rather washed out. She didn't know if it was caused by damage to the visor or was due to some strange interplay of light and shadow caused by the inferno. Several flashes on the periphery of her vision caught her attention. She looked at them, and red boxes slowly appeared over their source. They were labeled as Paladins.

The crack of passing shells and subsequent, echoing boom of ordnance exploding in the air caused her entire body to involuntarily flinch, and she shoved herself as close to the ground as possible. But their position wasn't the target. A few seconds later, another series of booms cracked across the sky, too close for comfort, but still not quite close enough to pose a threat.

She looked up at the target of the bombardment: a spur off the northern side of the height they now occupied, about a kilometer distant.

A call for help sounded on the radio, the voice elevated in tone and distorted by static. "*Six, this is two. Receiving direct fire from three, four Paladins to the southeast. They have our range. Please suppress!*"

Something about the fear in the voice prompted her to action. Kim made sure her visor was secure against her breathing mask, then pressed it against the optics system once again, zooming in on the area where she had seen the flashes.

She found them. Four large tracked vehicles, each with a big turret housing a disturbingly large gun, parked just on the other side of a rise in the ground about eight kilometers to the southeast. As she watched, they fired again, booms echoing across the valley.

Kim heard the sound of missiles firing again, and focused on one of the vehicles her HUD marked as a "Paladin". She targeted it with a laser, and fought her tired muscles to keep the designator in the center of the turret. Then she waited.

A missile streaked into view and exploded—but without striking the Paladin. Chavez' voice came over the radio.

"This is six. Be advised, two Abrams with APS covering Paladins. Calling in air support now."

"Hammer flight, this is Ghurka six. Are you aware of our situation, and can you engage?"

"Ghurka six, this is Grizzly five. Anticipated your requirement. Two defense radars detected. Fox One inbound, impact in under one mike. Hammer element alpha standing by."

"Thank you, Grizzlies! Hammer one and two, when the way is clear, engage at will. Paladins first, targets of opportunity after."

Kim looked up from her optics, throbbing eyes adjusting to the change just in time to see several streaks lash from the northern horizon towards the Paladins. Then she dimly perceived a series of dull flashes, one followed by a larger explosion.

"Ghurka six, this is Grizzly five. Radars are down. Path is clear."

"Hammer flight, that's your cue!"

"Affirmative Ghurka six. It's Hammer time!"

Two more huge shapes loomed overhead, shadows flashed past, and Kim looked up in time to see two odd-looking jet aircraft, shape reminiscent of an Orthodox Cross, loom low overhead. Her HUD labeled them both Mjolnir.

"Mjolnir? But they look like A-10s..."

Patrick must have been thinking out loud. Kim looked at him, but he didn't notice. Chavez ignored him, focused on her own business.

A whooshing sound came from the two jets, and Kim turned her head back to them in time to see a pair of missiles leap from each Mjolnir's wings. The radio frequency filled with what incomprehensible babble. Then the nose of each aircraft erupted in smoke, and there was a sound like a pair of massive zippers being unfastened.

Kim watched as the missiles lanced into their targets, sending fountains of flame skyward as the Paladins were destroyed one after another. The ground in the vicinity of the Deseret position seemed to writhe like a wounded beast as a deadly hail descended from the jets' cannons. Several more explosions boomed across the valley floor.

"Holy...Ghurka six, this is Hammer one. Got ourselves a veritable armored parade hiding behind a ridge two klicks south of Park. Engaging with CBUs. That'll leave us Winchester. Safe flight home."

Chavez pumped a gloved fist into the air.

"Godspeed, you beautiful uglies. Buy you a beer back at the barn."

"Ghurka team, this is six. Watch the fireworks, then egress. Report status when on the move."

Kim watched as the two jets banked hard left, then straightened. More smoke erupted from their snouts. Kim could barely see the shapes of six or eight small objects separate from their parent aircraft, which banked to the left again, then dove towards the ground, skimming it as they retreated northward. Flashes lit the sky behind them as they deployed protective thermal flares in their wake to attract any SAMs the Deserets might still have available.

Their bombs burst, showering their targets with hundreds of grenade-sized bomblets. Earth flew skyward behind a distant ridge, a sound like the most intense fireworks display imaginable echoed, and then the battlefield fell completely silent.

THE STELLAR HIGHWAY

Loucas watched helplessly as the night sky was lit by the eerie red glow caused by the interceptors' weapons impacting the Jagdkontrol's shields, again and again.

He turned his back to the bombardment, and gazed again at the shimmering tear in the starry sky that looked like a rainbow crumpled into a ball and then spun into thread. For the past hour it had seemed to grow thicker and brighter as the Jagdkontrol flew towards it. Olga had called it the "Stellar Highway" and in about two more hours, the *Acerbic* was supposed to appear and whisk them away to safety. It represented their one hope of escape.

But the four interceptors *Station Rome* had dispatched to destroy them were still in pursuit, and they were closing range far too fast. In just a few minutes, they would be close enough that their weapons would be able to punch through the ship's protective shields. He didn't really understand the details of how the shields and weapons all worked, but full comprehension wasn't necessary for him to know that was probably a very bad thing.

"You ready, Yarielis?" Olga called out.

Loucas turned in time to see her nod in response. His sister had spent most of the past hour standing on the Star-Bridge, studying information moving too quickly across a holographically projected screen for him to understand. She'd only spoken once to tell him to be quiet and stop asking questions while she was busy trying to concentrate.

"Alright then. Once the interceptors are in range, they will break into two groups and start hitting us from different angles. I'll take two of the Jager flights and cover our underside. You take the third and do your best to hold off whatever pair attacks from above our dorsal horizon."

"Uh, what if they both come at us from the same side at once?"

Yari nodded again, and turned to Loucas.

"Sorry Lou, that I got so absorbed. The Jager flights are our only useful weapons, and Olga needs me to do human style thinking to fight the ones that are under direct control of the people on *Rome*."

"Gotcha Yari, but are you supposed to control all the flights then, if they all attack from your zone?"

They both looked at Olga. She shook her head. "You won't need to worry about it. If they all attacked from one side, I could keep a flight in reserve to cover any mistakes they game me into making, so instead they will try to pincer us from two sides. Force me to fight machine and human attacks at once."

"Now, I can jam their control transmissions whenever we physically get between the drones and *Rome*. That forces the interceptors on our far side to fight on autopilot, which makes them *much* more predictable for me. I can neutralize an interceptor pair with one of my Jager flights, and keep the second in reserve to help you in case you make a major mistake. Remember, whenever the interceptors can maintain line of sight to their base, the human controllers can continuously intervene. Sooner or later, they will figure me out. So I need you two to fight like humans."

The Jagdkontrol began to vibrate, then shudder. Yari and Loucas looked in alarm at the blooms of color that had now spread to cover the entire rear quadrant of their view. The vibrant blue-green of the interceptors' particle beams turned to a sickly red-orange upon impact, and torrents of glowing plasma flowed outward into the night.

"Alright kids, they're in lethal range now. Launching all Jager flights!"

From the corner of one eye Loucas saw movement. A series of small hatches opened across the surface of the Jagdkontrol, and there was a flurry of blurs as small objects shot out from them, a twinkling light marking each as it zoomed across the sky

Yari took a deep breath, raised her hands, and began making a series of strange, jerking gestures. Six of the blurs seemed to arc through the starfield, converging in a hexagonal formation just beyond the edge of their parent ship's shields. They were reminiscent of obsidian arrowheads, leading edges so sharp that, when viewed from head-on, they seemed to slip between the stars. They were smooth, lit only by the glow of engines and steering thrusters. Loucas wondered how such small, seemingly unarmed objects could help defend against the attack of the interceptors. Maybe they were supposed to collide with them?

He was almost too distracted by the launch and form-up of the Jager flight to realize that the interceptors had switched off their particle beams, and the colors produced by the interaction of beam and shields were drifting like a wisp of cloud in their wake. The Star-Bridge helpfully outlined the interceptors in red, else he would hardly have noticed them as they twisted through the stars, accelerating in odd directions while minimizing their own profile relative to their target.

The interceptor group split apart as Olga had predicted. One pair darted under the horizon, the other seemed to twist and shift, then grow larger at an alarming rate. Streaks of light flashed overhead, missing them by what seemed like mere inches.

"Here we go, Yari!" Olga shouted. "Remember, their shots are coming at almost the speed of light, so you won't know they're firing until they've hit or missed. Predict and disrupt, best as you can!"

Yari seemed to slap at the air, and the Jager flight became a blur, twisting and dashing off towards something Loucas couldn't see. Then there was a bright flash at the edge of his vision. The six arrowheads of the Jager flight were outlined against the light, sparks of red and orange bursting between and around them, chaotically dissipating into streams and clumps of liquid light.

"Well done!" Olga cried. "I've got the other pair bottled up as planned. Keep it up! Just one hour and fifty-two minutes to go!"

Yari jerked again, almost stumbling from the force. Again the Jager flight lanced across the sky, and intercepted a shot. Loucas dashed to steady her, and she thanked him.

"Bro, I can use your help: pretend the ship is a clock. The front is twelve. I can't watch the whole sky at once and they're *so* fast. If you see them, tell me what time they are at!"

"Three o'clock!" He shouted, not really needing her detailed explanation, his eyes already straining to track the interceptors as they dashed around the sky. Yari clawed at the air with both hands, and the Jager flight made another intercept. They'd spotted it at exactly the same time.

"Thanks Lou!" She shouted, and directed another intercept.

The next hour seemed to last an eternity. Spot, and intercept. Spot, and intercept. Over and over again. Only able to help with his eyes and steadying grip, Loucas was forced to helplessly watch his sister engage in her desperate dance, saving them again and again. He slowly worked out what was happening: the controllers back on *Station Rome* were moving their interceptors in ever-more wild, unpredictable trajectories around the Jagdkontrol, firing in no distinguishable pattern, harrying it like marauding dogs tormenting a fox at bay.

And as the dance wore on, Yari became tired, then weary, then began the inexorable slide towards total exhaustion. It wasn't just the more violent movements that were wearing her out. It seemed that she had to maintain constant concentration on the Jager flight itself, always returning it to a position where they could move as quickly as possible to an intercept point. She seemed to be constantly untangling a bundle of heavy cables, while holding them a foot from her chest. All the while, feeling their weight grow ever heavier as the minutes dragged by.

"How long can we keep doing this?"

He hadn't meant to speak aloud. Yari heard him, and jerked her head from side to side.

"Don't have a choice." Yari said, almost slurring her speech.

Olga sighed. "The little Jagers can handle several hours more. They're basically mobile shield projectors with *extremely* reflective physical surfaces. Half the energy that hits them deflects right off. But controlling them is taking such a toll on Yarielis! It is not easy to maintain the necessary level of concentration. And unfortunately, while they can constantly rotate fresh personnel in to control the interceptors, we don't have that luxury. Frankly, if she weren't so naturally efficient at controlling Jagers, this would have become too much for her half an hour ago. They're not that easy to push around. In fact, they're almost as smart as human toddlers, or small dogs, in their own way."

Olga hesitated for a moment, looking uncertain. If it were even possible for a machine intelligence to experience uncertainty. Loucas didn't really care at the moment. Help for his sister was all he cared about.

Yari directed her Jager flight to another intercept. And would have subsequently fallen over if not for Loucas' support. An arrow of six arrows streaked up from the horizon, and seemed to converge on a point. There was an ugly flash, and Loucas saw an interceptor seem to slide past the explosion of its partner, and dash below the horizon.

He pumped a fist into the air and laughed aloud. And then a terrible vibration shook the Jagdkontrol. He froze in terror, and then it subsided. Olga sighed.

"Phew. Survived. I was afraid we'd take a bad hit if I did that, but it was the survivor of your pair that got in a shot, and *fortunately* it was a weak one. But... oh hell!"

Three interceptors flashed above the horizon, then split apart. A moment later, three particle cannon blasts flashed past. Two narrowly missed, one was intercepted by Yari—and only just.

"I was afraid of this." Olga sighed. "They know we're down a flight now. I had to recall those Jagers for repair. They can play angles and chip away at our energy reserves. We just have to keep fighting, and hope that somehow we can last until *Acerbic* arrives.

Loucas quickly lost track of time as the battle grew more intense. The three interceptors began a series of rapid attacks in a seemingly random pattern. Two interceptors together were difficult enough to spot, but individually they were nearly impossible to see until they fired.

Yari, almost totally exhausted, began to miss intercepts. Olga became totally absorbed in controlling her flight and assisting Yari where she could. But soon, almost every wave of attacks resulted in a shot getting through. The Jagdkontrol shuddered almost continuously now, and Loucas realized this was a sign the attacks were about to break through.

The three interceptors suddenly converged at their eleven o'clock. Yari's Jager flight was too far out of position. Olga's flight couldn't stop the incoming blasts from all three. Yari threw herself toward them in a last-ditch attempt to get her Jager flight to cover the distance in time.

The sky was torn apart by a searing blue-white light. It passed between the interceptors, then shifted faster than they could perceive or react. One, then two, then all three disappeared in a cloud of molten metal.

"Franz, you magnificent bastard! How did you shave an hour off the transit, you digital wizard?!" Olga cried, as Loucas blinked away the after-image left by the blazing light.

"You are welcome, Olga. But it is simply a matter of physics. And a lack of biology. We were able to enter a deeper lane than anticipated. Now, please dock so we can secure the biologicals and get moving again. Warships have been vectored to this position."

Loucas held his sister upright as the Jagdkontrol's trajectory quickly shifted to converge with that of the *Acerbic*. He watched as their rescuer grew from a point in the sky—just another star—to a distinct shape, the thick stream of variegated light that marked the Stellar Highway bright behind it. Having now seen other spacecraft, he realized how large a vessel it actually was. Though it wasn't pretty: the ship looked more or less like a giant boxcar, with odd scaffolding surrounding much of its bulk, jutting out in odd directions, like a boxcar with tinker toys glued all over it.

It took only a few minutes for Olga to bring the Jagdkontrol to dock between a gap in the scaffolding. The *Acerbic* mostly disappeared below the horizon as the Jagdkontrol rotated to match velocity. There was a loud thunk from somewhere beyond sight, and a different kind of vibrations filled the Star-Bridge.

Olga smiled. "It's been fun, guys! Hope to fly the unfriendly skies with you again, very soon. Especially you, Yari, it's been a pleasure! Head back up to the *Acerbic's* command center and I'll patch myself in in case Franz wants to do a debrief."

She paused, and suddenly seemed hesitant. Pensive, even. "One… last thing. When you see Franz' screen go red, you must always remember that it is *absolutely essential* that you do *whatever* he says *without question*. Never offer any information or explain anything you do, have done, might do, or might even think about doing, when his screen is red, just do what he says and wait for it to go away."

Loucas, disturbed, tried to ask her a question, but she held up a hand, shook her head, and disconnected them from the Star-Bridge. They awoke in the cabin, the scent of disinfectant again in the air. The door was open, and beyond was the hall leading back to the *Acerbic's* command center, where they had last seen Franz. They followed it, moving slowly, Yari holding onto Loucas' arm as if it were the only thing keeping her on her feet. Which, he thought, might not be too far from the truth.

Almost as if Olga had predicted what they would find when they arrived, Franz was hovering over the center of the room, screen a dull and angry red. They froze. The flying coffee can seemed to appraise them. And then, without warning, the red disappeared. The screen went back to normal.

Olga appeared as a hologram, standing next to Franz. She no longer seemed concerned.

"Report, Olga?"

"Nice to see you too, Franz! Well, the report is this: the package made it to the target, detonated on schedule, and blasted out the entire section of *Station Rome* used by the occupation forces. During our little battle, I hacked into the

Lagrange point's local communications network. Officials on the habitats have not yet made any formal declaration on whether they will support the Insurgence, but they also have not made any request for assistance from Earth."

Franz bobbed in midair, his version of a nod. "Well, that went better than expected then, didn't it? This is the first time one of these strikes has actually worked. Now, the question becomes, how do we get back to the Belt without being blown apart by half the Navy?"

Franz and Olga turned towards one another, and seemed to confer. Loucas noticed a chair, and took his sister to it. She mumbled thanks, and collapsed into it. He thought she would immediately fall asleep, but she simply sat there, eyes half shut, gazing towards Olga and Franz.

"So we pass through the Solar Interchange," Olga was saying, "then head for Earth? At biological-safe accelerations, we can make the trip in three days. They will not be expecting that. Then offramp, do a gravity assist maneuver coupled to an atmospheric deflection, and launch out towards the Belt? Damn, that's weeks out of the loop, Franz."

"Nice of you to verbalize it for the biologicals, Olga. But that's the price we pay for this being a successful mission. And for keeping them on board. Which, I suppose they deserve, don't they? After all, it wouldn't have worked without them."

Olga nodded, smiled and waved at Loucas and Yari, then disappeared. Franz turned towards them.

"Well, I hope you were paying attention. Down the corridor to your left you will find bio-crew accommodations. Beds, showers, food, water. Call if you need assistance or go visit Olga, but we will be quite busy preparing for the blockade run. Other than what training modules we have available, there won't be much you can do, so I suggest you review them. And as Humans usually request digital privacy within their crew quarters, we will not bother you unless you bother us first."

Loucas stood up and took two steps towards Franz.

"Wait a minute, don't we get a say in any of this? I thought you needed us for decision making and... stuff like that?"

Franz let out a scratchy, repetitive, metallic sound, apparently his version of laughter. "We do, for *certain* functions. But we have factored in the parameters required for your survival. When we reach the blockade near Earth, then you will be needed again. But until then, there is simply nothing you can do but prepare for what is to come."

"So you are telling us that this was all for nothing? There's just another fight waiting for us in a couple more days?"

Franz bobbed. "So it is, so it will be, until the world's end. Though for us, hopefully this will be the last fight for a few weeks, until we escape to the Belt. But in the meantime, enjoy the breathing space. Sensors indicate you both are in need of significant rest and recuperation. I suggest you attend to your maintenance requirements rather than waste time on metaphysical inquiries."

He flew away down a corridor, bouncing again from wall to wall. Loucas looked at his sister. She gazed back at him, and he realized how half-conscious she really was.

"Let's go sis. Check out the room, see if there's a hot tub. Hey, maybe by now everybody is back at Mimr's place. You think the cats gave everyone our message? I could really go for a beer right about now."

She didn't respond, so he helped pull his sister to his feet and half-dragged her to the cabin, wondering how quickly they could return to Mimr's Pub.

BACK AT THE PUB

Timur sighed, grasped the Web of Norns, and was once again in Mimr's Pub.

Pub. Well. Bar at the end of the Universe. Whatever. He didn't care, so long as he could see his friends again.

Patrick and Kim had preceded him, after all three had returned to Camp Yellowstone and been shown to a room a short distance from the Missoula Regiment's main barracks. Shown to it, and locked inside by Jackson, who had ordered them to shower, sleep, and get ready for formal training to begin after a day of rest.

Timur had sent them on ahead, wanting to spend a few minutes—just a few—alone, thinking. It had been the first moment he'd had to just sit, and think, and process, since Loke had thrown them into this ridiculous war in the middle of Idaho in 2041.

Now, he wanted a beer.

His friends were all sitting at a table, plates of food and goblets of drink filling every available space. Freyja was there, accompanied by her cats Weiss and Schwartz, who slept on the couch while she entertained. They greeted him with smiles as he walked through the doorway, and he sat down at an empty place prepared for him. The smell of food was overwhelming, and after a single gulp of Idunn's beer, he realized exactly how hungry he was, and got to work on his meal.

He listened to his friends describe, between bites, what they had each experienced in the hours since they had last been together. Freyja almost seemed to be acting like an interviewer, kindly and patiently asking innocuous, yet probing questions. Like the conductor of an orchestra, she seemed to weave their stories together into a coherent narrative, completely on the fly. It was odd to watch. But in a matter of minutes, five perspectives broken across three timelines just sort of... came together.

He only realized that she hadn't asked anything of him when, after querying all the others, her eyes settled on him in the exact moment he finished draining his goblet. He began to answer even before she opened her mouth to ask her first question.

"Kim and Patrick pretty much covered it. I can't add much. Other than that Jackson is a real prick."

Freyja nodded as if in thanks, but didn't ask him anything else. He opened his mouth to say something, but caught himself. And then, though he didn't know where it came from or why it chose to surface in that particular moment, he suddenly felt distinctly *angry*. It was like a switch had been flipped. He just, for no apparent reason whatsoever, felt completely and totally pissed off.

He stood up, walked over to the couch where the cats lay dozing, and threw himself down onto the cushion between them. Weiss looked up at him and glared. Schwartz snored. He interlaced his fingers behind his head, lay back into the cushions, and put his feet up on the seat of a chair that was just close enough for his heels to rest comfortably. And then he swore aloud, staring into the rafters.

"What the hell is happening to us?"

He hadn't spoken to anyone in particular. Freyja answered, her voice irritatingly cheerful.

"Well, you've essentially been *drafted*, don't you know? That's what becoming Einherjar *is*. You get taken away from the world you knew, and sent to fight an eternal war. Simple enough, isn't it?"

He rotated his head to glare at her.

"*Drafted* into what army? You keep saying we're Einherjar. Which I only know from Norse mythology, which means absolutely *nothing* to me beyond the fact that I think old legends are kinda cool. What does being Einherjar *mean* in a context that itself actually *means* something given the insanity we're all being put through?"

"It means exactly what I said it means." Freyja laughed. "And what I and the other Aesir and Vanir told you before remains the simple truth of the matter: Loke has removed you from your Thread of reality, and placed you in another, almost identical to your own. This act has created a paradox that cannot be resolved without violating the very laws that hold Midgard as you know it together. In the end, the universe will tear itself apart, bringing about Ragnarok—the annihilation of *all* existence."

"But none of that makes any *sense*." Timur protested. "What *are* you people, that you have such godlike powers over us? I still don't buy this whole Freyja-Odin-Thor-Asgard-Midgard-Loke thing. Are you telling me that the old Norse were the ones who got it all right, that *they* of all people knew the true nature of the universe?"

Freyja laughed again, but not unkindly. "Ah, but here you are forgetting several very important truths: just because you *perceive* us as you might if the Norse mythos was in fact reporting the truth of things, does not mean that we *are* exactly who you think we are. A curious fact about the human mind—really *any* mind that originates in Midgard—it only directly perceives a small fraction of what it *thinks* it perceives."

Loucas laughed, drawing their attention. "Don't we all need to be, like, stoned for this conversation?"

They all laughed, Timur too, despite his anger and frustration. Freyja shook her head, rolled her eyes, and continued. "Point taken! But still, this is important to remember: your brains are exceptionally adept at minimizing cognitive load. By which I mean, you tend to automatically conserve attention for higher-order cognitive functions, like abstract thought and verbal communication. You tend to see whatever you have been conditioned to see, which is actually a rather efficient use of limited resources if you think about it in those terms."

"Children spend years essentially testing the environment around them to determine what is consistent, and what is not. As they grow, most of them reach a point where they no longer need to investigate the nature of very regular things like, say, the effect of gravity, or the sun rising over the horizon at the break of each new day. They learn to presume the existence of those types of things and their habits. And so they see, without truly *seeing*, and without even really noticing how much their mind is just filling in the gaps."

Timur cut in. "Right. So you're about to tell us that we perceive you like gods from the Norse pantheon, because our brains are already somehow primed to see you that way. Problem with that: I'm the only one of us who is really *into* mythology. And I'm into Japanese stuff as much as the Germanic. So why do we all see you as Freyja and the bearded, vagrant looking guy as Odin? Why not Amaterasu or Shiva or Ishtar or whoever?"

Freyja nodded enthusiastically. "Good, good! You reason well! Here is my response: your Norse mythology, in those Threads where it develops as you know it, is merely one branch, one peculiar heritage, stemming from a far deeper mythological system. In your Thread, from where do you originate?"

She phrased it so oddly that it took all of them a moment to realize what she was asking. Yari, missing the deeper question, misunderstood his hesitation and answered Freyja herself.

"Me and Lou are from the Caribbean. Kim grew up in Indonesia, Patrick is Estonian-Canadian, Eryn is Canadian-Canadian, and Timur is Punjabi."

"Halfish." Timur corrected her, forgetting that he'd never actually told his friends that much about his heritage. He always liked to avoid having to discuss it by simply laughing it off as too complicated to pin down. And his friends had never really pressed him on the matter, because for them it actually really didn't. But in this moment, his reticence had left things a bit awkward.

They all looked at him. He gritted his teeth, and grinned sheepishly as he explained as briefly as he could. "Uh, sorry guys. I know I don't talk much about life before Vancouver. Anyway, here's the sitch: Dad and mom were both from the Punjab, their families go way back. Like, the Tarkhans claim to have lived there for over a thousand years, though who knows if that's actually true, cause people kind of, you know, move around. Anyway, dad was always pretty eclectic, and liked to say he was a half-Mongol Islamic Hindu. Mom's family was Sikh, though she wasn't really into names and labels. When she could avoid them. Punjab is an interesting place. So me, I'm kind of..."

"You're Canadian, now!" said Yari, smiling.

Timur grinned at her. "Sure, Yar, I'm good with that. I'm pretty sure nationality was more what Freyja was actually asking about, anyway."

Yari's smile faded. "Oh, oops."

Freyja shook her head. "No worries! It is difficult to really tell such matters for certain with fresh Einherjar, so I asked rather than assume. One way we are quite different than you, perhaps *godlike* in our own way, is that we tend to see you as a sort of amalgam of all the possible *you* variants that can exist in the infinity of Midgard. Makes it difficult to pin down the particulars of the *you* I'm actually talking to. But, then, I suppose the same goes for us as well."

Timur opened his mouth to reply, then closed it again. He wasn't sure how to respond to that. Freyja seemed to realize that they had no context to interpret her last statement and shook her head, smiling. "I am making this more complicated than strictly necessary, aren't I? Maybe it will work better if I offer you the tour guide's version of our history. Bits of it you might recognize, Timur from your study of mythology. A number of traditions tell mostly the same kind of tale."

She paused, then began, her voice somehow different. Quieter, yet clearer.

"Midgard was born through a strange overlap between Jotunheim, Muspelheim, and Niflheim. Gravity and energy were bound together, forced to interact according to the rather strange rules of quantum mechanics."

"Vanir and Aesir, Jotnar and Muspelli, Aelfar and Svartaelfar, all bwings were drawn to this new World. And all eventually became bound with its fate, as Midgard itself came to blend with our own worlds. We Vanir were originally drawn to the sheer variety of life that emerged, and when your species was in its infancy we walked among you, learning and teaching. The Aesir under Odin also came. We are similar, like siblings, Aesir and Vanir, yet in our first meetings we met one another with absolute hostility. We did come from different Worlds after all, and we did not know how to communicate at first."

"To the Vanir, Midgard is a delicate place, a garden to be cherished and cultivated. To the Aesir, Midgard is for adventure, a puzzle to be solved and mastered. Misunderstandings and arrogance on both sides, my own not least of all, brought conflict. And because Earth is the first world we encountered, it was the site of our long, bitter, mutually destructive struggle."

"It was Odin, in his wisdom, who first realized that the war would someday destroy us both, and Midgard too, in the end. Even before we knew our own homes were under threat, we realized the necessity for an honorable peace. And so he forged a truce that has held ever since. We each have our own homes and lands, but we mix and marry freely. Never will we war among ourselves again."

"For humans of your time, those days are so far in the past that you have no history to account for them. Writing came late in your species' development, and because language is a living thing, always shifting and evolving, your oral histories evolved as well. The original truths were scattered across tribes and cultures, events were compressed in time and overlaid by new ideas, new interpretations of the old core. In the end, the stories became in many places purely functional: a way to transmit ideas about good behavior and other important lessons across the generations."

"The answer to why you perceive us like you do here and now is rooted in the combination of your mind always seeking to reduce cognitive load and the socially constructed, yet still deeply embedded, nature of your memory of your species' history. Your minds naturally seek a reference point for comprehending what you are experiencing when you interact with us. Your reference points are heavily influenced by the culture you have integrated into. And in your time, your place, your thread, the language you speak and cultural idiom you employ in the act of communication is heavily inflected by what you describe as mythology."

"You live more than a thousand years after a time when a small set of expansionist, hegemonic worldviews in effect conquered most of Earth. Since their conquest, you have lived in an age of dying languages, dying peoples, the constriction of ideas and possibilities down to an incredibly narrow dialog of misery in life and mere hope for salvation after death. But even as your species reaches a moment where the very definitions of what constitute a language or a people are rapidly changing, the old wisdom remains."

"There's an irony to the long domination of the hegemonic ideologies: they themselves are simple overlays upon far deeper traditions. They often spread by altering their own basic syntax and structure to be compatible with the multitude of faiths that pre-existed them, and so rather than obliterate the old, the two forge a new, syncretic faith system. And in the process, keeps the old knowledge alive."

"The fact that you see us as we are described in the Norse branch of the deeper Indo-European system is simply due to the culture you happen to have integrated into, with its reliance on the English language and that language's speakers' connection with the northwestern portion of the European continent. The pre-Christian, Indo-European cultural heritage that helped produce the English language and the people who brought it to the place you now inhabit, just happens to be most fully expressed in the Norse mythological canon, which in all Threads we know of typically gets written down in Iceland at a point relatively soon after Christianity reaches its shores."

Timur ran a hand through his hair, squeezed his eyes closed. "OK. I think I see where you are going with this. So because back in the day people like Snorri Sturluson wrote down the stories from the old Nordic oral traditions, and because *that* particular interpretation of a past culture has made it into a position of dominance in global culture through our shared use of the English language, *that* makes seeing you all as figures from mythology *normal* to our brains somehow?"

Freyja beamed. "Yes!"

Timur sighed. "I think I hate this reality."

The goddess shrugged in reply. "I didn't make most of the rules."

During this interchange, Kim and Eryn had been sharing looks. Somehow, silently, they debated between them who would have to speak. Timur didn't understand how, but Kim apparently drew the short straw.

She took a deep breath and spoke carefully. "So I'm going to hazard a guess here: you people aren't *actually* gods in the all-knowing, all-powerful sense, right? But in some way, shape, or form you have a huge amount of power relative to us. So you are like gods to us in the same way we are like gods to ants?"

Freyja cheered aloud. "I love having smart students! That is close enough for the time being."

"I'm with Timur. I hate this reality." said Kim. They all nodded as one.

Freyja nodded too. "Tell me about it! I mean, in their own realms the Jotunn and Muspelli are to us like we are to you. And when *we* go traipsing about Midgard, we actually become physically *just like* you. Odin in particular likes to go play human. Male, female, doesn't matter. He wanders around time and space, just living and learning."

She laughed. "Actually that's how you all first got involved in our wars. Some of us liked to play warlord in Midgard, and ended up *being* some of your heroes. Though not everything attributed to us is accurate, because naturally later generations of would-be leaders did their best to associate themselves with us, even *becoming* us in the eyes of some of their followers. Which is partly why it is usually so easy to find real-world parallels that correspond to legends: people always try to *become* the legend. Humans, and most of the other speaking peoples in Midgard alike."

"Freyja, you are the goddess of digression, aren't you?" said Eryn.

"I like that!" she exclaimed in reply. "But I'm sorry! I do go on. I've a bit of the professor in me, I suppose, I really enjoy educating the new Einherjar. But what I meant to point out is that I am no fan of this reality myself. You do realize that what you see of me or any of the others is actually only a sort of... after-image, of our true selves. I'm carrying on this conversation with you somewhere in the back of my mind, with the rest of me barely even aware that it is happening, because *I'm* staring at the Web of Norns, desperately hoping that I can come up with a way to avert Ragnarok. And I keep failing!"

Timur blinked several times. His anger was slowly beginning to fade, replaced almost entirely by a sense of helpless frustration.

"Why can't you just send us home, then? If there is no hope, and there's nothing we can do anyway?"

She laughed, sounding grim. "I would, if I could. But as I tried to make you understand before, only Loke could in theory release you, because he is the one who made you Einherjar. But more than that—I doubt that he has the ability. Once Einherjar, always Einherjar, until Ragnarok. No, sadly, like many of your kind before you: you've been drafted, and all you can hope to do now is survive. Survive, and see what, if any, difference you can make before the end. All any of us can do, really."

She looked at each of them, smiling kindly. She spoke now slowly, and carefully, as if she wanted to be sure that they all heard and fully understood.

"But remember, dark as things may seem, there is *always* hope. Even if hope is irrational, desperate, fleeting. Because what is the alternative? To lay down, and die. Every living thing in all the Nine Worlds is facing the exact same question now, whether it knows it or not. Absolute annihilation. The end of everything, forever."

She shook her head slowly. "I *know* rationally that there is nothing I can do. For us, Ragnarok has been prophecy aeons in the making. We have looked at it from every possible angle. We know that it is totally inevitable. But, we keep hoping that something will change, that we missed… something. There *is* a prophecy that *something* may come after, but only Loke truly believes in it. Which is why he now actively seeks to bring Ragnarok down upon us all. He hopes that he will be the one to effect the change that makes a difference."

Freyja let out a grim laugh. "I just wish that he wasn't *also* committed to making sure that *he* is the only one who survives. And becomes, in effect, ruling god of whatever may come after. An impossible dream. One he himself knows cannot be. And yet, with hope, he keeps fighting. It is admirable, if you can ignore the fact that he is willing to destroy anything and anyone that stands in his way. Myself, I would rather die and be forgotten, if all my friends and everything I loved were also doomed. But he is willing to sacrifice even his own family in order to survive. So it goes with all Jotun, I suppose. Perhaps that is why Thor spends so much time fighting them."

The room fell quiet, save for the sound of both cats, who were now snoring. Whatever they knew or felt about the end of the universe, they didn't share.

"So," Eryn asked, after a long pause, "this trap we're stuck in, it isn't going to end anytime soon, is it? I have to go back to Germany and do… I don't know what. Keep pretending I'm some kind of helpful spy, I guess. Kim, Patrick, and Timur have to try not to get shot or bombed or nuked in Idaho until… they don't know what. Yari and Loucas have to go on playing 22nd century space battleship to help out a bunch of robots whose end objective is… they don't know what. We just keep treading water, hoping we get a chance to do something to change what you are saying can't possibly change?"

Freyja nodded, smiling sympathetically. "Welcome to the war, Einherjar."

PART 3

Orr would be crazy to fly more missions and sane if he didn't, but if he was sane, he had to fly them. If he flew them, he was crazy and didn't have to; but if he didn't want to, he was sane and had to.

Catch-22

ULM, GERMANY

"Tell me again, Mimr: *Why* am I not trying to convince the Germans to just hurry up and surrender? It isn't as if they have a snowball's chance of winning the war."

Eryn knew it was a futile line of inquiry. The answer wasn't going to change. It hadn't the last eight times she'd asked. And she was correct. Mimr's voice sounded from somewhere in the golden, roiling depths of the Web of Norns, exactly as calm and detached on the ninth time as on the first.

"Thread analysis is conclusive: with Heinrich Himmler at large, that action will prompt a counter-coup by surviving members of the Nazi establishment. Regardless of the outcome, the end result will be the victor waging a long and bloody guerrilla war against the Allied and Soviet forces occupying Germany. This will intersect catastrophically with rising tensions between those two camps as they jockey for advantage in the post-war world system. The most likely long-term outcome will be the outbreak of another world war within twenty years, fought with atomic weapons. Human civilization will collapse not long after."

Eryn sighed. "And I have to care about that why? Given that the whole universe is supposed to unravel any day now?"

"Because the process of your Thread shifting towards that dominant attractor in the system will involve, from your perspective, the laws of the universe becoming... unstable. And the consequences will be, for you and those around you, rather unpleasant. Fatal, usually. And worse, this unraveling will itself accelerate the slide to Ragnarok."

Eryn sighed again, shook her head, and bringing her hands together in a soft clap she deactivated Mimr and the Web of Norns. Just as the glow disappeared, a ray of sunlight pierced the forest canopy outside her room, casting a beam through the window and onto the opposite wall.

Three days before, the morning of the 21st of July, she had returned to the Bendlerblock with Captain Hans Lewinsky of the Brandenburgers as well as the corpse of the former Minister of Propaganda, Joseph Goebbels. Walking back into the building, now the impromptu headquarters of a new German government, at least in theory, she hadn't really known what to expect. Would the Valkyrie coup plotters, Stauffenberg and Haeften and all the rest, actually feel that she had helped them enough to warrant their trust? Or would she be arrested as the foreign agent she was pretending to be? She had helped to kill both Hitler and Goebbels, after all.

Neither theory had been correct. Eryn had simply been ushered back into Stauffenberg's office, then ignored. Gertrude spent the next few hours bustling in and out of the room, bringing food, water, and various bits of clothing. Watching what effectively amounted to nesting behavior actually took Eryn's mind off her strange plight, and Gertrude made a point of forcing her to eat a meal. After a few hours, Lewinsky stopped by, also bringing a bundle of clothing, but didn't remain long enough for her to ask any questions.

By evening she wasn't in the mood for any more distractions: she was bored and furious. And then, she heard the speech. All at once, every radio in the building was turned up to maximum volume. A triumphant fanfare, albeit marred by static, sounded through the halls. A familiar voice, scratchy and gruff, pointedly rhythmic in delivery.

"People of Germany. This is Prime Minister of the United Kingdom, Winston Churchill. Yesterday evening, just before midnight, I received an entreaty from one Ludwig Beck, claiming to be the successor to that notorious beast, Adolf Hitler. In this message, he requests an immediate cease-fire with the Allies, in order to facilitate the initiation of negotiations for an armistice.

"I am regrettably compelled to inform Mister Beck, the German people, and indeed the world, that the United Kingdom reiterates its commitment to the Casablanca Declaration. We will accept no less than the unconditional surrender of Germany and her allies. The crimes of the Nazi regime cannot be washed away by a mere change in leadership. Until the Hunnic hordes lay down their arms, until the peoples of Europe no longer suffer under their barbaric occupation, the war will go on to its bitter, and inevitable, conclusion."

Within minutes, Beck, Stauffenberg, and half a dozen of their compatriots had filled the office, all eyes fixed on Eryn. Their interrogation went on into the night. Really, it was more of an intensive debriefing. While their questions were pointed, urgent, and any unsatisfactory answers were met with skeptical stares, within a few minutes it was clear to her that they had decided, given the circumstances, that they needed any help they could get. This didn't slow the pace of the interrogation, but it at least allowed her to relax slightly. If they weren't attacking her claimed credentials as an agent of industrialist Henry Ford, then they had accepted at least the *hope* that she was telling them the truth. And in their desperation, hope would keep them from questioning her on the details, provided she could be useful to them. It was enough to shift her mood, at the very least.

She had spent most of the past two days working out the *useful* part. Accepting her plea for time to "contact her superiors," she soon got the distinct sense that the Germans had decided to treat her as some sort of hybrid between diplomat and military liaison. She was given the office to claim as her own little slice of the new German government's temporary headquarters, with Gertrude acting as her secretary. Who busied herself with various tasks that she clearly felt were important, but also seemed to keep her away from the office for long periods.

Which was fortunate, because most of Eryn's private hours were spent locked away with Mimr, trying to learn all she could about Germany's predicament and how she could help 'nudge' things in such a way that her interventions would at least not make the slide to Ragnarok *worse*.

She had quickly found that there wasn't, in fact, much she needed to do for the moment. The main thrust of the German officers' initial questioning had been directed towards issues of politics, policy, and culture. Where she had expected them to focus on the Allies' strategy and planning and weaknesses, instead they asked once again whether the impending American election would alter United States' policy, and why the British Empire was so dead-set on fighting Germany to the bitter end, even at the cost of losing its overseas empire to independence movements that were already beginning to gain strength. Questions where any plausible answer she gave would be sufficient, because really, how could anyone hope to verify her response?

For those pressing questions that did, she had assumed, *matter*, the new German leadership didn't need her help at all. Establishing their authority with local military commanders who would follow their orders and suppress any counter-coup attempt made by the Nazis, cajoling or threatening the many Nazi territorial governors into acquiescing to their rule, and sending representatives across the country to recruit competent personnel capable of filling important government positions, were all essential to preventing Germany from collapsing into chaos and civil war.

The difficulty lay in doing all of it at the same time, in the middle of a war, with what amounted to a skeleton of governing leadership mired in the need to individually contact important members of German society, convince them that the Gestapo and SS were no longer in charge, and make the necessary concessions to win their support.

But they succeeded. Hour after hour, for two days the mood in the Bendlerblock rose steadily, eventually reaching towards exuberance. One by one, key Nazi leaders up and down the hierarchy were arrested. One by one, civilian and military governors sent messages by radio and teletype confirming their allegiance and requesting further instructions from the regime.

Even the streets outside the Bendlerblock seemed to come alive. People were out and about, walking around, talking with one another and the armed guards protecting the building, first curious and then, if not necessarily satisfied, at least accepting of the new reality. It was as if a deep fog was beginning to clear in the embattled city of Berlin, despite the hopeless odds and dark future ahead, as those who had been forced for a decade to bow their heads and conceal their beliefs for fear of Gestapo informers and the wrath of the Nazi state had a fleeting glimpse of hope returning.

Then, late on the 23rd of July came the devastating news: several generals serving with the Waffen SS were beginning to organize a counter-coup. The Waffen SS was the military arm of the Nazi party that Hitler had slowly been building up to replace the traditional German Army, though both still fought and died side by side as the German front line was pushed inexorably back towards Berlin. Several informers serving on the staffs of the culprit generals relayed the news to the Bendlerblock: A secret meeting had been held, agreement met, and the leaders had begun to reach out to key personnel in other branches of the German military. Their goal: to re-establish SS and Gestapo control, under the leadership of Heinrich Himmler. Who, possibly because he had some forewarning of the assassination attempt against Hitler, had escaped into some rat-hole in the initial hours of the Valkyrie coup, and was now setting himself up as Hitler's successor.

Almost simultaneously, another bit of news arrived at the Bendlerblock, with equally devastating implications. A group of highly influential active and retired generals from the regular German Army had refused to meet with emissaries dispatched by the Valkyrie plotters, claiming that their professional code of ethics forbade them from dealing with members of an illegal coup. The reserve army forces currently obeying orders from the Bendlerblock were no substitute for the training and equipment of the regular army, and would barely be able to take on even remnants of the SS, Gestapo, and Waffen SS alone. Without the allegiance of the main branches of the German military, particularly the Army, the Beck government was doomed.

But curiously, the courier bringing the message had taken special care to *strongly* imply that a small delegation consisting of one junior officer not directly involved in the assassination at Rastenburg *might* be allowed to speak with the officers. Who were planning to meet at the bedside of the famous general Erwin Rommel, currently recuperating at his family home in Ulm, Germany after suffering critical injuries in an Allied air attack during the fighting in France.

Mimr had informed Eryn that it was absolutely essential that she attend this meeting. Her presence, according to the Web of Norns, had the potential to dramatically alter the subsequent course of events. The uniquely useful information she had at her disposal, coming to 1944 from an almost-identical Thread many years in the future and with the ability to consult extra-dimensional beings, would be needed in order to sway the generals. Eryn had thought her next challenge would be to somehow attach herself to whatever officer was to be sent to Ulm. It came as welcome shock when Captain Lewinsky marched into the office and informed her the generals themselves had requested she accompany him to southern Germany.

It had been an interesting trip, sitting in the back of an Opel staff car as it took three times as long as it should have to make the drive from eastern to southern Germany. Allied bombing campaigns had blasted apart much of Germany's transportation network, and the staff car's quiet and careful driver had to regularly consult maps in order to find local roads that would evade the worst affected areas. Eryn and Lewinsky had spent most of the day and a half in close conversation in the back seat of the vehicle, he telling her all he knew of the officers they were to meet.

Eryn sighed again, and looked away from the window, where the sun's rays refracted through the gentle shifts of the forest canopy, casting shifting shadows across the opposite wall. She glanced towards a tall mirror by the door that led to the rest of the inn where she and Lewinsky had checked in the night before. She grimaced and shook her head. While she had been *quite* happy to throw away the SS uniform, swapping it for another military outfit was not at all what she had intended. But Lewinsky had insisted. The clothing he'd brought to her in the Bendlerblock was almost identical to his own: black trousers and tunic, the latter sporting pink details that seemed strange to her, being on a man's military uniform. He had a straightforward explanation.

"If we are to serve together, we should wear the same uniform. I've never seen a woman in an armor soldier's tunic and trousers, but there's a first time for everything! But I have to demand something of you in exchange. While you wear this, you represent the Brandenburg Regiment. We have a history, and a reputation to uphold. And as one of us, your actions become our own. I don't know how you Canadians view honor, but to a Brandenburger honor is *all*."

She inspected herself in the mirror one last time, then took a deep breath and left to meet Lewinsky. He was waiting for her in the staff car they'd taken to get from Berlin to Ulm, and their driver had already started the engine. She entered and sat next to Lewinsky, who nodded politely, then was silent. She was already used to it. Lewinsky was the sort of person that one moment, he would be actively engaged in intense conversation, then the next he would be somewhere else, staring into the distance. Never unaware of his surroundings, just... distant. Like he knew that he belonged someplace else, but had accepted that he would never actually get there. Eryn was fine with it, and could very much sympathize.

The car made its way through the streets of Ulm then drove for a short time into the adjacent countryside. The sun entertained itself by passing in and out of the clouds overhead, though they seemed to threaten rain. The area around Ulm to Eryn's surprised appeared entirely untouched by the war, save for the obvious lack of younger males. Uninjured ones, at least. She recalled Lewinsky telling her on the drive south that there was a military hospital in the town, which explained the number of bandaged amputees in uniform. They walked the fields on either side in pairs or sometimes alone, aided by nurses and crutches and all the other accouterments required by war's victims.

Lewinsky spoke for the first time during the drive as the staff car pulled up in front of a home, one of a cluster of similar houses adjacent to a thicket of mixed trees, each yard filled with a vegetable garden.

"So, I found out exactly who we'll be meeting with, this fine Swabian morning." Lewinsky said, straightening his uniform.

"Anyone I've heard of?" Eryn asked.

He laughed. "Field Marshal Rommel! Even the Americans know his name. At least, after Kasserine."

He acted like he'd told a joke of some kind, and chuckled for a moment. She had to think hard to remember anything about that battle, finally recalling that an American army had walked into a German ambush and been badly mauled. Fortunately Lewinsky never seemed to get caught up in her ignorance of the details of particular events. At least not so far.

"Field Marshal von Rundstedt is also in attendance," Lewinsky continued, "as well as Field Marshal von Manstein and the Inspector General of Armored Troops, General Guderian."

She couldn't help but snort. "What, he isn't a Field Marshal too?"

Lewinsky laughed. "No, Hitler denied him that particular honor. Though he was granted estates in the East, I believe. For all the good those will do him when the Russians come!"

The car stopped, and the driver killed the engine. He exited the vehicle, and moved to Lewinsky's door. In that brief moment of privacy, Eryn decided to ask a question that had been bothering her for the past three days.

"Captain, where do you stand in all this?" she said softly. "The coup I mean. You seem different than Stauffenberg and the others, and not just because you weren't part of their inner circle. They seem to truly believe in what they're doing. You always seem, well, cynical about everything."

Lewinsky waved at the driver through the window, who nodded and stepped away from the car, without opening the door. He sat for a moment, still and thoughtful. Then replied, speaking slowly.

"I am cynical. I have been fighting in this war for almost

five years. I have lost many friends. Most of them, in fact. And unfortunately, I know better than most how utterly pointless the fight has been. How much has been destroyed, for no real purpose beyond the vain dreams of a power hungry madman and a ridiculous ideology. I don't know to be anything *but* cynical anymore, comrade Eryn."

He reached to the door handle, and then suddenly pulled his hand away. He turned his head, and gave her a look she couldn't decipher. Then he spoke, slowly, as if carefully choosing his words.

"But I *do* believe in what we are trying to accomplish. I learned of Stauffenberg's plan entirely by accident, and I don't think they will ever truly trust me as a result. But no matter what, I believe that we have done, *are doing*, what must be done. For honor, and failing that, simple human decency."

He opened the door and exited the vehicle. She followed him. He'd taken to calling her *comrade* for some reason, but he hadn't given her a hint as to why. And at present, she didn't have time to inquire further. If he wanted to be enigmatic, then that was his prerogative. Lewinsky marched up to and knocked on the Rommel's front door, and it was opened almost instantly. A young woman greeted them politely, and invited them inside. She led them down a hallway, and pointed towards a doorway at the end.

"They are waiting for you in his bed chamber. Please keep your voices under control. His injuries are very serious. The doctors have instructed us to prevent anything from upsetting him. He will also need rest after a short time."

She seemed nervous, and as they entered the room Eryn could see why. Five pairs of hard eyes turned towards them, making their initial assessments. Each pair belonged to a man, all but one quite clearly over the age of fifty, all but the man lying pale and wan in his bed was dressed in a military uniform. If Rommel was dressed in his Field Marshal's outfit, the bedsheets concealed it.

Lewinsky halted several paces from the five men, who turned and arrayed themselves in a line, with Rommel's bed in the center, facing them. Eryn stopped alongside Lewinsky, and as instructed stood silent and rigid. She couldn't stop her eyes from wandering to the fifth man, clearly at least twenty years the junior of the other four. He looked almost as out of place as she felt. It wasn't just the fact that he was wearing a different uniform, either. He clearly did not fit in with the other four.

Lewinsky took a step forward, and saluted the line of senior officers. It seemed strange at first, then Eryn realized that she'd been expecting to see a classic "*seig heil*" style salute, like those in all the old war movies, simply because of their uniforms. But his was a crisp, traditional, fingers-to-the-eyes style. Only the oldest of the men acknowledged him, and only with a curt nod. To Eryn, he seemed the very caricature of a German Field Marshal: tall, stiff, with a deep scar across his face adding an element of menace to pretty much any expression he might make. She was almost certain she recognized him from his Wikipedia page: Gerd von Rundstedt, probably *the* trope-codifier for the concept of "professional military aristocrat."

Lewinsky's hand returned to his side, and he addressed the group with the detached air of a soldier giving a routine report to senior officers.

"Good morning. I am Captain Lewinsky, assigned to the Brandenburg Regiment. By the request of Interim President Ludwig Beck, I am here to fulfill your request for a meeting with a junior officer to discuss recent events, and our common future."

One of the generals, whose combative expression and mustache marked him to Eryn as Heinz Guderian, let out a derisive laugh. *"Interim President* is what he is calling himself? I wonder who will be Chancellor, then? Perhaps Bismarck will rise from his grave to save us all!"

He chuckled at his own joke, and shook his head. Lewinsky remained impassive in the face of Guderian's provocation. Though Eryn *thought* she saw him suppress a laugh of his own. Whatever his feelings, Guderian didn't stop to let him express them. Apparently, historians in Eryn's time had accurately written about his combative personality. Guderian jabbed a finger at Lewinsky, like a teacher calling out a misbehaving student.

"Now, I have to admit a degree of admiration for your group's boldness. No one else was willing to move against that fool and his cronies. But do you realize how much damage your actions will cause to the war effort? You have made either civil war or absolute military defeat almost inevitable! And now you come, hoping to secure the Army's support for your *interim* government? I hope you understand exactly how preposterous that is!"

His diatribe left him a bit red in the face, and as he paused to take a breath a third general spoke, his voice clear, calm, and cold. It reflected his overall demeanor and expression.

"As I told your compatriots on more than one occasion, when they approached me to solicit my support for this misadventure of yours: Prussian Field Marshals do *not* mutiny. And for this very reason: the Army will collapse if the soldiers do not perceive there to be unity of command. They can *not* lose faith in their leadership, or they will not stand and fight as soldiers must. You have by your actions undermined the essential soldierly virtue of obedience to legal authority. And thus it is on *your* heads when our already desperate resistance collapses."

By process of elimination Eryn would have known that this speaker was Erich von Manstein, but his face and manner gave that away even before he spoke. Manstein was supposedly some kind of military genius, credited with keeping the German army from collapsing after the catastrophic defeat at Stalingrad at the end of 1942. He and his staff had also been the primary architects of the truly epic and unexpected defeat of France in 1940, though it was field commanders like Rommel and Guderian who had taken a risky plan and implemented it to devastating effect. Where Guderian was the type of commander who enjoyed the thrill of battle and victory, Manstein was the sort who saw everything in purely functional terms, with battles being a means to an end, moves on a grand chessboard.

Hours stuck in the back of a staff car had left Eryn and Lewinsky plenty of time to discuss how they would handle the exact sort of hostility they were now experiencing. Fortunately, Guderian and Manstein were acting as they had predicted: each played to his strengths, and together they sought to wear down their opposition. But here Lewinsky saw an opening, and took it before Guderian or Manstein could jump back in the argument.

"I feel compelled to remind you gentlemen that I have come here by *your* request, on orders issued by my superiors. While I will be happy to report your dissatisfaction with the means by which *Interim* President Beck has taken charge, I am not here to waste time defending what has already happened. Only one thing matters now: saving Germany from annihilation. And I am here, enduring your scorn, because your influence *will* determine the fate of our nation and our people. I respectfully suggest that we focus on the task at hand, that is, to determine the best course of action that brings us the best chances of winning a just and overdue peace with our enemies."

Guderian started to speak, but a glance from Rundstedt made him pause. His wizened face fixed on Eryn, and a chill passed through her, though she did not understand exactly why. Probably the scar, coupled to memories of any of a dozen old war movies set during the 1940s. Or maybe because he reminded her *way* too much of Death Star commander General Tarkin from Star Wars. Right down to the bit about fighting for the wrong cause. He spoke slowly, as if carefully considering his words.

"In truth, the fate of Germany is out of anyone's hands, but those of our enemies. Let us be clear: Germany is surrounded by foes who will sooner or later grind us into dust. We all know the end is coming, and that we must make peace to survive. And yet, we have all heard Churchill's broadcast. Churchill, who we had hoped was more likely to see reason than Roosevelt, who seems determined to let all of Europe fall under Stalin's grip. The Allies remain committed to their demand for unconditional surrender. Which leaves us in the same hopeless strategic position as before Hitler met his end."

Rundstedt paused and chuckled. It seemed out of place, somehow. "To be frank, when I heard that there was some sort of agent from the allies working with Beck and Canaris, I had hoped to find more than a girl, though I admit I never expected to encounter any woman wearing a German armor officer's uniform! I was looking forward to meeting this agent, in the vain hope that someone across the Atlantic was finally ready to see reason. It seems, however, that the Allies have never been serious about assisting Canaris in removing Hitler, despite his insistence otherwise. Unless, my dear, you are able surprise me?"

Eryn opened her mouth, closed it, then shook her head. What she'd originally wanted to say, something appropriately hopeful and diplomatic, didn't seem worth saying given their audience's open hostility.

"You know, the past few days I've been struggling with a really basic question: why *am* I here? What is the point of offering help to you people?"

Lewinsky looked at her in surprise, but she stepped forward, trying to make her point as succinctly as she could.

"The closest I can come to an answer is this: I have information that can help you salvage your position. I know the Allies' plans for the coming months. I know what you can do to slow down their advance. To give you the time and space you need to force them to start negotiating for peace. And maybe, *maybe*, save lives on both sides."

Rundstedt stared at her, expressionless. "Ah, but that begs the question: what side are you on? What little has been reported to me, portrays you as an employee of a wealthy American industrialist. Is his goal not merely to profit from this situation? It seems that he is in an enviable position: his factories build tanks for the Americans and British, and through you he may think to manipulate our actions to some fiduciary end. Given this, how are we to trust you, a woman with apparently no connection to her own people, given that she is offering assistance to their enemies?"

Lewinsky shook his head. "Field Marshal, I will swear an oath on my honor that her intentions are no worse than benign, and perhaps even noble. Information she has provided has already proven crucial, and she has demonstrated incredibly detailed knowledge of our national predicament."

Manstein cut in. "While that is admirable, Captain, it does not answer the Field Marshal's question, which I feel compelled to restate in even stronger terms: What guarantee do we have that her offer of information is not some kind of ploy? Our soldiers have pinned the Allies to their beachhead in France so far. Perhaps they are starting to re-think the wisdom of fighting their way to Paris and beyond, and hope to undermine our defense by other means."

A quiet sound came from the bed. Almost inaudible given the overall volume in the room, which had steadily increased with each exchange. And yet, even this barest utterance caused the room to go silent. From the edge of vision Eryn saw a woman rush past Lewinsky to lean over Rommel's bed. She listened to his whisper, nodding several times. When she stood up straight, all three of Rommel's companions, General and Field Marshal alike, stood to attention.

She smiled at them. "My husband would like to suggest that this line of questioning isn't likely to be productive, as it pertains to matters impossible to verify. We should move on."

Rundstedt froze for a moment, as if considering. Eryn did think it strange that he, who was clearly playing the role of senior officer in charge of the proceedings, would show such deference to someone so much his junior.

Then Rundstedt nodded politely. "Our thanks, Lady Rommel. Your husband is quite correct. My apologies for pursuing the matter this far." He turned to Eryn. "Accepting, for the present, the matter of your integrity, please tell us then what you claim the Allies are planning. And briefly, for my own edification at the least, please tell me *how* you have come to possess information about what can only be the result of espionage against your own government."

This part of the battle, at least, Eryn was ready for. Well, as ready as she could be. Fortunately, growing up in the 21st century alongside family members who were obsessed with the 1940s accorded her certain advantages. Though access to an extra-dimensional entity, or computer, or *whatever* Mimr was, that could estimate future probabilities by analyzing the patterns of similar realities, probably helped a bit too.

Eryn took a half step forward, and stiffened, thinking that if making one's self look bigger worked with cougars, maybe it would work with field marshals. "I'll start with the how. Mr. Ford has long been interested in what we usually call "computing technology." It is a new, young branch of science, that uses electronic signals to transmit and store information. Without boring you with details, a particularly recent breakthrough has allowed us to build the world's largest computing machine, so advanced that we are now able to use it to accurately predict weather patterns, economic production and distribution, and the probability of a major campaign being won by one side or the other."

She saw their faces go blank. She was pretty sure she read irritation there, and like a thunderclap she realized that they weren't so far back in time that the basic idea of a computer was beyond common imagination. So she skipped forward. "Long story short, as we Canadians say, is that we have been able to very accurately predict the course of the war since late 1941. We knew that the disaster at Stalingrad was going to happen, and knew that the Soviets had sufficient forces to crush your attack at Kursk the next summer. We knew that Field Marshal Rommel would be overpowered in Africa, that the Allies would follow up their victory in Tunisia by invading Italy, and we knew when and where the Allies planned to land in France this year. As well as their plan for breaking into Germany itself by December of 1944."

"It also helps that in order to validate our results, we have conducted a number of espionage operations to acquire the necessary confirming details. Bottom line is, we know that the Allies are about to break out of Normandy, destroy your entire army in France, and force you back to the Rhine by the end of the year. And that's the *best* case scenario—it is even possible that the Western Allies will break all the way through to Berlin well before Christmas."

Manstein grunted. "At this rate, it will be a miracle if the Soviets don't get there first. The Eastern Front has collapsed completely, thanks to that idiot corporal and his obsession with defending static fortresses."

Eryn nodded, pretending to agree. "Exactly. It doesn't take a computer to see that the Soviets are another class of threat entirely. You will not be surprised to hear that my employer finds the prospect of a communist victory over Germany rather distressing. If for no other reason but that Ford Motor Company owns several of the factories serving your war effort and expects to be compensated for their use after the war, and it is unlikely that if the Soviets occupy all of Germany they will care much about any capitalist's claims to property. Regardless, The only thing that will stop the Allies on *both* fronts now is the natural limit of their logistical capabilities. Which, this fall, will temporarily culminate at the point that the Soviets reach the Vistula in Poland and the Danube in Hungary, and the Western Allies reach the Meuse in Belgium and France. But then, after a pause of one or two months to build up supplies, they will coordinate assaults on all fronts. And Berlin will fall by spring. Unless you do not dramatically and effectively change your strategy on both fronts, you are certain to lose the war no matter what government is in charge in Berlin."

Guderian looked at Manstein and Rundstedt. As if he felt the gauntlet had to be taken up, pointless as the argument was. Eryn could tell by their grim expressions that her predictions matched their own. Absent a dramatic change, defeat was only months away. Oddly, in that moment of pause, she remembered something she'd once read, in a bout of trying to learn enough about at least one aspect of the Second World War that she could keep up with the holiday banter of her obsessive family members. It had been almost an aside, a bit of trivia masked by the greater drama of the war to come, but the German generals had *always* known that defeat was months away.

They had nearly launched coups against Hitler every time he made a foreign policy move in the 1930s, because they were certain that he would lead Germany into a disastrous war. And then they defeated France, despite their own predictions of certain failure, despite qualitatively inferior equipment and a battle plan borne out of total desperation. And even though that victory had only delayed the inevitable, and doomed millions of lives in Eastern Europe, still for several years these generals had known victory unlike any won by a European leader since Napoleon. These were not men who gave in easily when confronted by the inevitable. They'd faced it before, and won.

Guderian made a dismissive, chopping gesture. "No. This is entirely too optimistic. The Soviets are nearly out of supplies and manpower, and we stopped them the last time they tried to break into Romania. We can hold far further east than your computers think! And in the West, we have the Allies bottled up in Normandy. They are stuck in the French bocage, and taking heavy losses. Britain hasn't the soldiers to spare and America hasn't the will needed to bleed their way through our defenses. If we hold the line in the west, and reform a line in the east, we can continue the fight. We must! For Germany itself won't survive defeat. There will be no more Germany."

Silence for several moments. Then Manstein nodded, very slowly, and spoke carefully. "I see the implication in your argument: we must retreat on all fronts, to defensible frontiers, and press for peace in the interim. In fact, we have considered exactly this sort of plan. But accepting that proposition means giving up large swaths of territory and resources with no guarantee that our position will not be even worse even once we've consolidated our forces closer to home. Both because the retreat itself would threaten the utter collapse of the Army, and because the closer they push to our borders, the easier it will be to control the skies over Germany."

Eryn took a breath, but Lewinsky cut her off. "And the implication in *your* argument, Field Marshal, is that if we only bleed them—and ourselves—a little longer, they will sue for peace. Which is as faulty as the inverse. We have been trying that for over a year now, as we did in 1918. The effect has been to send tens of thousands of young men to their deaths. But let's cut past these preliminary discussions, and get straight to the heart of the actual matter that we are here to discuss, shall we?"

He took a step forward. "*We* deposed that madman Hitler, and *we* control what is left of the government—at least for now. And so long as we hold Berlin against whatever counterattack the SS is certainly preparing, we will continue to expect the Armed Forces to carry out our orders. I remind you that Hitler is dead. Your oath to him is similarly dead. You have a moral and ethical obligation to serve the German people, as *we* have served them by ridding the world of every member of the Nazi leadership we've been able to get our hands on. The time has come to unite behind our leadership and seek a path forward to save Germany."

Rundstedt drew himself up, and raised his chin. "*Captain*, I would remind you that we and we alone will decide the matter of our own moral and ethical obligations before God and Germany."

"As you did when you swore your oath of personal loyalty to that creature, Hitler?" Lewinsky barked.

"As *you* did as well, as did all officers in this room!" Rundstedt barked in reply.

"*Gentlemen*." The quiet voice of Lady Rommel silenced the room. All the men took a deep breath, and looked to her. For half a second Eryn felt like she saw shame creep into at least Rundstedt's face. But his Prussian bearing quickly returned, and his face blanked. He turned and smiled politely at Rommel's wife.

She nodded politely back at him. "My husband requires an hour, perhaps two, to rest and think. I will be happy to entertain guests in the sitting room, otherwise please let me know where in the village you can be found, and I will send Manfred for you in the afternoon. But for the present, I must ask that you pause your discussion."

There was no point in arguing. Eryn wasn't sure what to do. She had expected the meeting to be difficult, but not degenerate *quite* so fast. One would expect that, watching their country burn to the ground, those with the ability to do something about it would put aside their differences and act. But apparently not. The only thing she could think of to do, given the possibility of a few minutes to think and plan, was to consult Mimr, see if by any chance one of her friends or Norse deity was hanging around the Pub. Maybe they would have some ideas on how to get people talking reason, and not emotion.

Lewinsky, who after saluting the assembled officers had turned on a heel and stalked out of the room, was so distracted that he didn't question her when she requested that the driver take her back to the inn. She realized that he, like her, needed time alone to think. From the car, she saw him turn and walk past the Rommels' home and into a wooded thicket.

After an anxious and silent drive back to their accommodations, she returned to her room, locked the door, and covered the window. Then she grasped the Web, and was back in the Pub. For the first time, no one was there.

Eryn wasn't surprised that her friends were absent. Yari had come up with the idea that they should all try to meet at the same time every day, provided they could get away from their thread. For whatever cosmic reason, their timelines were synchronized, so that Eryn was experiencing morning and evening in 1944 Germany on the same schedule that Kim, Timur, and Patrick were experiencing 2041 North America. Same went for Yari and Loucas in 2147, though given that they were in space the day-night cycle was fairly unreliable. Over the past few days, they had all been able to meet several times, save sometimes for one or all of the *2041 crew,* as Patrick had taken to calling the three of them. They were in the midst of some kind of basic training with the Missoula Regiment, and as a result forced to keep strange hours. Their trips to the Pub were for them simply about quickly ingesting Idunn's mead as a bulwark against the next hours of toil, then heading back.

But still, so far, every time Eryn had visited Mimr's Pub at least one of the Aesir or Vanir and typically one of Freyja's cats, had been around. While their level of sobriety—or in the cats' case, awake-ness—varied, they were starting to offer helpful advice about querying and analyzing Mimr and the Web of Norns. Or in the cats' case, a fuzzy belly to stroke for a few minutes, which always reminded her of pleasant things, like home and quiet and peace.

A completely empty pub, by contrast, left Eryn feeling rather lonely and forlorn. At first, she thought that Freyja or maybe her twin brother Freyr would come bustling in as they usually did. She wandered around the room while she waited distracting herself from her own anxiety by rearranging chairs and benches, finally moving behind the bar itself to almost absent-mindedly browse through the dozens of bottles stored haphazardly on the many shelves.

It was when she began to reorganize the various bottles by color and size that she realized the clock over the doorway leading from the Pub back to 1944 was counting down to zero faster than before. Eryn had no idea why, but it was clear that she would have to return soon. For a moment, she didn't know what to do. She wondered whether she should try drinking some of the mead, or "nectar" as the gods liked to call the stuff, then decided against it. She wasn't sure which of the many bottles was safe to try. While the effects of the meads she'd tried so far had been beneficial, Freyja and

Idunn had both mentioned the possibility of bottles getting mixed up, usually because Freyr or Thor hadn't bothered to put something back in its proper place. Some of the bottles, Eryn had gathered, contained liquids not intended for human consumption.

She heard a sound, faint, distant, and muffled, distinctly like that made by a large group of people shouting and cheering. Eryn stepped from behind the bar, and looked down one of the long halls leading away from the pub. It was disconcerting to discover the corridor had no obvious end. In the far distance, what looked to be miles away, the walls just converged to a sort of vague blur. But Eryn saw that a ways down there were doors on either side of the hall, spaced at odd intervals, going all the way back into the unseen distance.

Her feet were moving before she knew she was walking. The sound had faded away, but she had the strangest feeling that it had originated from behind a door fairly close by. From the crack underneath she could see an odd flickering light illuminate the floor of the hall opposite the door itself, and walked up to it, wondering if she was making a mistake.

Eryn stood in front of the door, and thought for a moment. Then she grabbed the simple knob, turned it, and pushed it open. There was a sensation of great heat all around her, like stepping into an open flame, but not painful. The moment seemed to stretch longer than it should, as if when she blinked her eyelids had simply decided to remain shut for an extra few seconds.

And then her vision cleared. She was standing at the edge of an enormous room, walls of stone and wood marching off into the distance—miles it seemed, in either direction. And packing the room were hundreds, maybe even thousands of women and men: sitting, standing, laying on benches and tables; talking, singing, dancing—or some combination thereof. Food and drink covered the tables wherever there was room, and in gaps tremendous bonfires sent flames towards the ceiling, where the ashes and embers seemed to be trapped in an array of candles and lamps that shone out from a smoke-filled ceiling like stars in a cloudy night sky.

Eryn stood frozen, overwhelmed by the unexpected weirdness of the place. Patrick would have said it looked like how he imagined the halls of Rivendell. Yari probably would have said it looked like Hogwarts. Both would have agreed it was dauntingly huge.

She might have stood there for hours, or it could have been seconds. She *would* have stood there for hours or longer, had an oddly familiar face not turned towards her. With a curious expression he pushed his way out from a nearby crowd, and approached, waving cheerfully at her.

"Rommel?" she asked, shocked.

Erwin Rommel smiled. The man she had just seen bandaged and bedridden now stood in front of her, dressed in a simple grey uniform unadorned by medals or insignia. There was no sign of his injuries. He seemed somehow both younger *and* older than the man recuperating from serious wounds, and there was a strange, knowing light in his eyes.

"You should probably keep in the habit of addressing me as "Field Marshal," you know. Germans in your Thread are sticklers for that sort of politeness. As they were in mine!"

She stared at him.

He laughed. "Ah, as I suspected—you are new to this Einherjar business, aren't you?"

She nodded.

He nodded back. "Yes, new Einherjar indeed. And different than the rest of us, aren't you? If I'm not mistaken, you are actually still tied to a particular Thread in the Web. Well, regardless, welcome to Valhalla! I apologize for my colleagues

—many of us won great victories in today's battles, and so we celebrate, as is our habit."

"Celebrate?" she asked.

"Oh yes. Because you are still tied to a Thread, you are in a bit of a liminal phase, so to speak. Inbetween worlds. It can be a difficult time, the early stages of becoming Einherjar. So many lives folding into one mind. It gets better, though, in time. You adapt. And then, when you have a good day, you celebrate!"

She was confused. Einherjar-Rommel could tell.

"Ah, I see that you haven't even been properly inducted—*that* is new. Normally Odin and Freyja greet new arrivals at the door. After all, they get to decide who goes to Valhalla and who to Folkvangr. There must be an interesting story behind this! Well, I will explain: Einherjar… "

"Rommel! Slow down!" another man called out, stepping away from a crowd. "Or I'll start calling you 'fast Ernie,' and people will start mixing you up with Guderian. Also Ernie Pyle will probably challenge you to a writing contest over the rights to the name. Just as a matter of principle!"

He strode towards them with a quiet, confident air, dressed in similarly simple and spare clothing that it looked like uniform. Rommel turned towards him, smiled, then gestured to both, as if making formal introductions.

"Hayes! Good to see you. And point well-taken: she will learn it all in due time. Well, Eryn—and yes, I know your name—I am happy to introduce another Einherjar from my era, Ira Hayes."

"Pleased to meet you, Eryn." Ira Hayes smiled.

She nodded slowly, mind finally processing that she was speaking to an American war hero. "Uh, likewise."

Hayes fixed her with a firm, but kind stare, turning to grin at Rommel.

"Take it slow, friend—I heard about this one: *Loke* tapped her and five others. He never does that, and I have a feeling this means the End will soon be upon us. Remember she's starting at zero, *and* she has to go back to her Thread at regular intervals, so we can't take too much time answering questions."

"I know this very well, Hayes," Rommel laughed, "or else why would I have been waiting for her *here*, with you people?"

Hayes shrugged. "*Us* people. You mean North Americans in general, or Pima in particular? Just saying!"

Rommel laughed. "Point taken! Although I had meant 'you people who like the strange music,' which covers quite a few Einherjar I know. I'm actually surprised it isn't too loud to speak in here, I suppose the band in this Hall must be taking a break! But let me see, where were we?"

Eryn let out a grim laugh. In unison, they raised their eyebrows at her.

She rolled her eyes. "An hour ago I was standing at your bedside, Rommel, making absolutely zero headway in convincing you and your Field Marshal buddies to do what Mimr is telling me you, or, living-you, have to do in order to avoid a *worse* end to the Second World War than the one *my* history tells me is supposed to happen. I came back to Mimr's Pub to get help, because Mimr insists that we have to come out of this meeting with some kind of agreement that keeps the Germans from civil war, but no one was there."

Eryn shook her head. "But it sounds like you knew that, or else why would you have been waiting for me? Which you must have been, because what are the frickin' odds of meeting you the first time I wander back here… to Valhalla? I honestly have no idea how this all works. Like, for example, why you are here *and* where I came from?"

Rommel smiled. "Simple, really: the *me* you are talking to

here, as well as the me in Ulm, are both one of the many versions of *me* that exist—have existed, from my own frame of reference."

Eryn stared at Rommel, shaking her head. "My friend Loucas is the one who is into all this physics and cosmology stuff, not me. And Timur is into the metaphysics and mythology. Me, I just want to figure out how to survive today. So can you break it down?"

Hayes grunted. "What my friend Rommel means is that just as there are many Threads in the Web the Norns have woven throughout Midgard, there are also many versions of you and me that exist, each originating and existing in their own Thread. Just as there are many different shades of reality within Midgard, there are many different shades of you that exist, have existed, and will exist."

She tilted her head. "Still doesn't help me survive. But just to be clear—so there's like, a multiverse out there? With different versions of every person?"

Hayes mulled it over for a moment. "That's one way to look at it, sure."

"So why is there just one of each of you here right now, and one of me? Also, which *me* is actually *me*, if there's a bunch of *me*?"

"Ah, now *that* really is *the* question, now isn't it?" chuckled Rommel. "See, Hayes, I do have to start from the beginning! Or, at least, a close approximation of it. I'll try to be brief, however. So, Eryn, you know that Midgard is… complicated. Every bit of matter and energy within Midgard started out the same, and will end up the same, but there are infinite ways for it to get from beginning to ending. Some pathways are more probable than others, and so most realities tend to cluster together, Threads moving between critical points— attractors Mimr calls them, which for whatever reason seem to draw Threads to them. Threads even merge together, only to later split apart, in a dynamic process."

"Something especially strange about Midgard, from the gods' perspective, is that individuals existing within it are sort of... refracted across Threads. Individuals exist simultaneously across multiple threads, each experiencing their own version of reality, their own Thread. But, like all things in Midgard, individuals live, then they die. Their constituent physical parts go back into the weird thermo-chemical soup that *is* Midgard. What is interesting, though, is that the essence of a person, their *mind*, is actually linked *across* Threads by processes no one, not even Odin, fully understands."

"Freyja and the Vanir were the first ones to realize this, and being attracted to the infinite variation inherent in that thing we call *life,* they were the first to select Einherjar from the ranks of those individuals that most impressed them. What they found was that, despite their attempt to collect multiple versions of some individuals, once here in Asgard Einherjar go through a process where they experience all the other versions of themselves sort of *folding* into one another, just as Threads fold and merge."

Hayes cut in. "I want to tell you how *strange* of an experience this is, by the way. It happens one day at a time, for what feels like an eternity: you get this strange feeling, and then you are overwhelmed by memories and emotions coming out of nowhere. You feel and act differently for however long it takes to reconcile the two. And whenever another version of you dies in their Thread, you get to go through it all over again. It. Is. *Weird.*"

Eryn shook her head, barely following. "Two questions: what is a *day* here, and how do you even know what set of memories are actually yours?"

They both tried to speak at the same time, then looked at one another and smiled. Before they could work out who was going to answer first, a woman's voice entered the conversation.

"One: a day is a day. You wake up, you go fight, you live or die, then you come back here to eat and drink and be human. Repeat for eternity. Two: it doesn't really matter. Eventually, you just become *you*. All the memories, hybrid personality. Not that much different than being alive, really. You never are the same person from one day to the next. Not entirely different, either, but still not the same."

Eryn had no idea when this new Einherjar had walked up. Her tone was as no-nonsense as any Eryn had ever heard, somehow befitting her tough, athletic frame. Like Rommel, and Hayes, she had about her an air of utter casual confidence.

"Lyudmyla! As usual, we didn't see you until it was overlate." Rommel smiled.

She and Hayes both laughed. "That's the point, isn't it Erwin? But I couldn't help but overhear you and Ira breaking in a newbie. Thought I'd assist."

She turned towards Eryn, and continued. "I'll save you the trouble of asking: There are two ways to become Einherjar. First, gain Odin's attention by achievement. Be the best at whatever it is you do, and he will favor you. The second option is to gain Freyja's attention, by love."

"Love?" Eryn asked.

"Love." Lyudmyla Pavlichenko nodded. "The Vanir consider it the pinnacle of honor to sacrifice one's self for love. Love for a person, a people, a cause, whatever. As you might have noticed, the Aesir and Vanir have… different views on the world. The Aesir are what you might call war-gods. They see competition and achievement as the sources of honor. Vanir are closer to the ideal of fertility gods. They are more interested in the bonds between living things. So the leader of each of the two tribes, Odin and Freyja respectively, select Einherjar from those humans who die in battle, favoring those who fight in the service of noble achievement or loving sacrifice."

Eryn looked at the three, each in turn. "So the only people who are here are those who died in a war? What about everyone else? Don't they get an afterlife?"

Hayes chuckled. "It seems broken, I know, but think about it this way: All the Threads out there, all the versions of *you* that exist. Chances are, everyone has died in or from a battle in at least *one* of the Threads. The Norse, who transmitted to you a version of the old knowledge, naturally thought that the Valkyries are sent to *every* battle, but in truth they are sent wherever it is most convenient to pick up a pre-selected Einherjar. Look at me, for example: in your history, I survived the Battle of Iwo Jima, one of a handful of my unit. In many of the Threads where my fate brings me to that living hell, I don't survive the ascent up Mount Suribachi. Others, I get to experience a new variety of hell a few months later on the island of Okinawa. Only so many ways history seems to evolve. The Valkyries had plenty of Threads to choose from when they came for me, since I apparently end up fighting in the Pacific War in pretty much all the ones they know about."

Eryn reached up and rubbed her eyes. She was starting to lose the plot, and she couldn't help but wonder how much time she had left before she would be pulled back to 1944. It seemed like every few days there was another bit of strangeness to adapt to. And she was no closer to figuring out how to get through to the German generals than before.

"Right, so that's the afterlife for people, then?" Eryn sighed. "Half of us go to Freyja, half to Odin, and we... what is it you said we do? Fight by day, celebrate by night, or something like that?"

Rommel laughed. "That's it in a nutshell! Though there

are other places a soul can end up. Perhaps better, very certainly worse. Though to my knowledge none of us has ever before met an Einherjar selected by Loke. This has to mean Ragnarok is nearly upon us... or does it?"

Eryn started. "I thought you'd know more about that than me. The Aesir and Vanir keep saying it is, but they don't much act like it. So you're saying that a bit casually, aren't you? Ragnarok is the end of the world, so shouldn't you be a bit more worried?"

"Am I?" Rommel replied, seeming genuinely surprised. His eyes flashed towards the ceiling, as if he was considering her words. He looked back at her. "I suppose I am, from your perspective."

"You don't seem at all worried."

The three Einherjar looked at one another, all smiling.

"How can someone worry about the inevitable?" Hayes replied, shrugging.

"Because that's what people do." Eryn insisted.

They all laughed. Eryn felt distinctly annoyed but tried not to show it. "Look, philosophy aside, I came here for help. You all seem to know who I am and I'm guessing you know what I'm supposed to be doing. Though I honestly have no idea how or why. But at this point, I'm starting to pretty much assume the old saying that begins "Ours is not to question why" is basically a universal truth. But help... that I can't do without right now. I've got a pack of angry German Generals to convince to listen to me."

She paused. "Though saying that, looking at you three... I have to wonder how a Muslim or Christian or anyone else who believes in *a* god deals with *this* being the afterlife. And actually, I think a lot of other people from other faiths would be pretty damn surprised. Weren't some of you Christians?"

Rommel waved a hand, as if brushing aside the question. "The answer to that is simple: this isn't necessarily *the* after-life, as you think of it. The Vanir and Aesir may be as gods to us, but even they believe there exists the possibility of powers beyond their comprehension and control. It is a very large Metaverse. Some of us come to see this place as purgatory, others as a strange continuation of life... what matters is that we are here, and eventually that becomes enough."

"But to your pressing concern, young Einherjar: you might be interested to know that I was waiting for you to arrive because word came through the grapevine, as you might call it, that there was a new Einherjar in 1944 trying to deal with me and some of my colleagues-in-life. Funny enough: in most Threads where I am still alive in July of 1944, I find myself in *exactly* the same position: wounded, suspected by the Nazis of conspiring to kill Hitler, while I watch my country burn to the ground around me. It is a curious thing, really, but Odin once told me that Adolf Hitler's death in Spring 1945 is as close to a fixed event in Midgard's history as exists: almost all Threads, however different their origins, seem to create the right conditions for Hitler to die in a Berlin bunker in 1945. So hearing that an Einherjar was in a Thread where that *wasn't* the case? Sparked my interest."

Rommel shook his head and locked eyes with her. "My fate is always bound up with that man's, and so my experiences are quite similar from thread to thread. Which is fortunate for you! I can tell you what exactly is going on in my living self's mind as you try to convince my colleagues to support Stauffenberg's coup."

"Now *that* might help me!" Eryn exclaimed. "Go on, Rommel!"

He nodded. "It will. Especially because the solution to your problem is actually quite simple. You have, as my American friend here might say, several strikes against you.

You are female, foreign, and young. A group of old men are already ready to dismiss whatever you say. So you must make them see you differently. The simplest way to do that is to shock them."

Eryn laughed. "What, so should I take off my clothes, or what?"

Lyudmyla burst out laughing. "Oh, what a sight that would be! I can guarantee that they *would* be shocked! Please, do exactly that! But let me watch! Let me bring a hundred friends to watch!"

Rommel laughed too, and shook his head. "While that would certainly gain their attention... No, you can do something even simpler and more effective than that. Tell them all about Enigma."

Enigma. Between her family's endless holiday babbling about the Second World War and Mimr's tutelage over the past few days, Eryn immediately understood what Rommel was suggesting. She froze, staring into space, furious at herself for not having thought of it herself. It was probably the most obvious of possible answers, and she hadn't even seen it staring her in the face.

It was Hayes' turn to laugh. "I love it when the light bulb appears over a newbie!"

Rommel grinned. "As people of your Thread and era might put it, the Allies are, in effect, reading Germany's mail. The part of me that is the Rommel you are trying to persuade remembers that although we always feared that the Allies would break into our communications, we never had sufficient evidence to justify making the necessary changes. The experts kept telling us that Enigma was secure, that it couldn't be cracked. And so everything we did, every report our soldiers sent, every order passed from high command to units in the field, virtually all of it ended up in the hands of the Allies. Even aside from the insanity of fighting a war of attrition on two fronts against an alliance with three times our industrial capacity, their foreknowledge of most of our actions was absolutely devastating."

Eryn felt a thrill run through her body. *This could work,* her mind seemed to shout. But, in the same instant, she realized that there was a fundamental problem. Just walking in, and announcing that a deeply held assumption was in fact false... wasn't likely to end well. People rarely abandon prior beliefs just because someone tells them to. She had barely been able to convince Stauffenberg, Haeften, and their compatriots of her ability and desire to help, and that only after actually *doing* some relatively useful things. But with these military officers she had no credibility whatsoever. She opened her mouth to speak, but instead paused, staring into the distance. She wasn't sure how to articulate her concern.

Lyudmyla nodded sagely. "You are seeing the issue, aren't you Eryn? Good. Now here is how to solve it. Think like a sniper. These generals you face have decided that they know how this meeting is going to go. Mark my words, the next thing those old men do is lay out demands for you and your friend Lewinsky to take back to Berlin. What they *really* want out of this meeting is to insert themselves into the regime and try to take control. To secure their own petty interests, in part, but also because they sincerely believe this will protect their country. They'll expect to run both of you right over—why else did they request the delegation be led by a junior officer? So when they lay out their demands, as they're focused on bending him to their will, you strike. Shock them in that moment with the news of how doomed they really are, telling them exactly what they are most afraid to hear at the precise moment they are least prepared to handle the surprise."

Hayes leaned towards her, baring his teeth. "The one thing *every* general, admiral, dictator, president, CEO, or other habitual bully shares is the fear that a bigger, badder someone has figured out their plans. That *they* are the ones getting played and led into a deadly trap. You tap into that fear, and even the most snobby, pugnacious, or aristocratic of generals will wilt."

Eryn knew she had little choice. As if she could see through the walls of Valhalla to the clock over the door leading back to 1944, she knew her time was up. All she could do is thank the three heroes of the Second World War, and march back to Ulm.

YELLOWSTONE, NORTH AMERICA

Timur threw himself into the dust, then rolled onto his back to stare up at the bright blue Rocky Mountain summer sky. The weight of the armored carapace pressed down on his lungs, and he struggled to draw as much air as he could force through the particle filters in his face mask.

Exhaustion seemed too weak a word to describe how he felt, after three days of non-stop training. Timur had finally been able to make good on his promise to train his friends in the art of not getting shot, though he had little real control over the situation. Sandra Chavez cheerfully tortured the three of them, hour after hour, running them all through one combat drill after another.

He exhaled and held his breath until he couldn't stand it anymore, and then slowly and steadily drew air back into his lungs. Then held it again, until he felt like his chest would burst. And slowly released. An old trick he'd learned would help to slow his heart rate. Though it didn't do a thing for the wicked headache threatening to burst through his skull. Knowing he was dehydrated, he felt around the inside of the mask with his tongue, until he found the little plastic drinking tube. Pulling it between his lips he took several long, slow sips.

Patrick and Kim threw themselves down beside him, all encased in their own carapace, faces hidden behind masks and visors. They were just three broken insects waiting for their tormentor to decide what variety of pain to inflict next.

"That's it. I can't take this anymore. I am *not* coming back up this hill again. Do you hear me, Chavez? I'm *done*."

Curses followed, as Kim wasn't satisfied with merely voicing her frustrations. Timur's grin was weak, but no one could see it. It was oddly comforting to know that Kim, easily the toughest of the three, was as *over* Chavez' training regimen as Timur. He couldn't imagine what Patrick, who seemed to receive the brunt of Chavez' unique form of what she called *encouragement*, was feeling. He didn't move or speak.

Chavez didn't respond. For once, her partner Jackson hadn't popped onto the radio to chide or threaten Kim for her outburst of profanity. Actually, Timur realized, they hadn't heard from him in over a day. And then that thought led to a sudden, animal-like curiosity about where Chavez herself was at that moment. Timur opened his eyes, and used the haptic sensors in one of his gloved hands to fiddle with the settings on his visor's heads up display. The 'HUD,' both Patrick and Chavez called the thing. He loaded a digital image of the local area, and it appeared in one corner of the display, suddenly obscuring the upper branches of a large tree that loomed over the three of them. By some instinct, or through mere luck, Timur had led them to collapse in its shade, which allowed them to escape the worst of the July heat.

Chavez was a few hundred meters down a long steep slope, advancing slowly to their position. Timur thought she must be adjusting, or hopefully shutting down, the training drones that had been tormenting them for most of the past three days, because the icon on his HUD showed her stopping, then moving side to side, before continuing her ascent.

Chavez hadn't given them more than a few hours rest

at any stretch since they had returned from what the Missoula Regiment's people were calling the 'Battle of Southern Butte.' In fact, she'd barely spoken to them at all except to bark instructions. That had so far usually amounted to: "Go climb the 'Bunny Slope'!" Which was what the organization's soldiers called the training range where they inducted new recruits. Or, as Timur saw it, tortured them until they broke.

The hill itself wasn't particularly tall, especially not compared to the peaks towering over the Missoula Regiment's base in what used to be Yellowstone National Park. But all of the paths to the summit were guarded by wheeled drones operated remotely from a bunker hidden somewhere on the outskirts of the base. Drones armed with an incredible variety of what Chavez had assured them were 'less than lethal' weapons. Tear gas grenades, rapid-fire paintball guns, shotguns firing beanbags, and, if you got too close, even a taser. Their purpose was simple: anyone who tried to come up the hill, got chased away. Breaking through the drone defense was the job of the hapless recruits sent to be sprayed, pummeled, or shocked until they figured out the solution to running the gauntlet.

Normally, the slope would have taken the three no more than an hour or two to climb. On the first day of training, they never reached the top, driven back time and again by the drones. On the second day, Timur ran out of patience, and started instructing his two friends what he knew about how to successfully move around while getting shot at.

It was a simple routine. Hide and wait until the patrolling drones happened to be far enough away that Timur and his friends could run for a few seconds without being *immediately* shot. Then they'd execute a mad dash to whatever bit of terrain or vegetation would offer protection from the paintballs, beanbags, and gas grenades that would quickly get lobbed at them. Then repeat the process. Over and over again. Step by painful, hesitant step.

On the third day, Chavez had issued each of them a weapon, a bulky firearm identical to the one they had seen her carrying when they first met. Their magazines were filled with special ammunition that fired with all the apparent power of a typical assault rifle, yet broke apart mid-flight into plastic pellets that did no damage to the drones. They did, however, disable them for a short period of time, if hit in just the right spot.

Now understanding what Chavez was actually doing by making them charge up the hill again and again, Timur had trained his friends on the next essential ingredient of moving in combat: covering fire. Now, instead of the three of them timing group dashes for whenever they guessed the drones had a low chance of successfully targeting and hitting them, two would shoot at the nearest drones to give the third a better chance to make the short dash to the next bit of cover. Then, another of them would run forward covered by the fire of the others. And then they did it again. And again. And again. Throughout the day, and then the night.

Chavez allowed them a longer-than-usual rest in the early morning hours, but by ten o'clock that morning they were at it again. Three times that day they'd fought their way up the hill. Hide for a few minutes, then push through a series of five-second dashes accompanied by covering fire to make it a little further up the slope.

At one point, Kim had come up with the clever idea of hiding for a longer stretch in order to rest. Unfortunately for the three of them, Chavez and Jackson continually monitored their progress. And as the training continued, the drones began to start operating in more complex patterns, grouping together to surround and bombard their hiding spot if they stayed put too long. Since their weapons could only temporarily freeze the drones, they were forced into constant movement.

Their only consolation was that the clothing issued by the Missoula Regiment was quite effective at cooling, which was about the only thing that stopped them all morphing from coherent flesh to pools of sweat. The clothes couldn't help with dehydration, though. And naturally, the carapace only came with a limited supply of fresh water. Which Chavez only let them refill when they had made a successful ascent, to force them to learn to ration their drinking.

Laying there, feeling more exhausted than he had in years, looking into the blue, cloudless sky, Timur realized that, like Kim, he was *done*. He rolled to one side in the same moment Chavez walked close enough that the local peer-to-peer communication system between their bugsuits broadcast her voice almost as clearly as if she were not encased in a carapace, mask, and helmet.

"Hey, guys," her cheerful voice called out across the remaining gap, "you didn't do half-bad this last run-through. Actually, your performance was totally passable. Well done!"

Timur didn't bother looking at Chavez directly, instead he watched his HUD as her icon moved along the digital map, coming so close that it finally merged with their own icons.

"It had better be the last one today, Chavez, 'cause we are feckin' *exhausted*." Kim replied.

Somehow, Timur could tell Chavez was grinning, despite her face being completely covered by her own headgear. She grinned a lot.

"Hah," Chavez snickered, "Jackson isn't listening right now, but points for getting that bit of swearyness past the filters. That's how we do it around here, weird policy of his, I think, but gotta give the man a few concessions! All right, I guess you guys *do* deserve a break. Gods but it's hot this evening, isn't it? Look at that sky, not a drop of moisture up there.

I'ma grab a slice of this shade too."

Chavez thunked her carapace against the trunk of the tree itself, and slid slowly down to the roots. Some bark came with her. She turned towards the three of them, and removed her headgear, then let out a sudden yelp of pain. Timur looked at her, then unclipped his own mask and raised his visor, trying to suppress a grin. She had paused mid-removal, and her eyes had gone wide. One hand clutched at a clump of her hair, and her teeth were clenched. She actually looked a bit terrifying in that moment, her face contorted into a shape that could easily have passed for a grizzled old Japanese Samurai's battle mask.

"*Ouch!* I *hate* it when the helmet catches hair!" Chavez spat, hissing in frustration.

Kim let out a grim laugh as Chavez let out a string of creative profanities. "Glad I'm not the only one with that problem. Now I see why lots of military dudes shave their heads entirely. Less mass to mess around with."

Chavez hissed in pain, and yanked the helmet off, taking some of her hair with it. Even to Timur's less than 'Queer Eye' for such things, her 'do' was a bit of a hot mess. It looked like she had braided some of it, put other parts into something akin to cornrows, and had tied yet another clump of it into a rough ponytail. He wondered where she'd tucked that bit under her helmet. Her hair wasn't particularly long, but the helmet fit closely enough that there wasn't much room to work with.

"Damn! I love this gear, but I am *sure* that a man designed the helmet. A man with short or no hair. Goddessbezelbub-jeebusdamnitalltohell!"

Helmet off, Chavez rubbed her head and looked out towards the horizon. Timur had the distinct feeling that she was waiting for something, or someone. For several minutes they were all quiet, the three trainees catching their breath while Chavez stared quietly out towards the mountains. The sun was still high above the peaks, despite the fact that it was getting on towards evening. The sun lingered long this time of the year. But after a long while she made a sound, somewhere between a grunt and a 'huh.' Timur had removed his helmet, with Patrick and Kim following suit, and the slight difference between her digitally augmented and 'real' voice was a bit jarring. Without her helmet, Chavez almost seemed, well, like a normal human being. Not their tormentor of the past few days. Timur realized that she was staring at him. So he stared back. She smiled.

"So I gotta say, Timur, when I got the news a couple days back that we actually *do* have a record of your DNA on file, I wasn't that surprised. I've seen a lot of green faces come through here over the past few years, but yours is definitely *not* that of a total newbie. Of course, the database we found your record in is at least twenty years old, so I have a hard time believing that we got *your* actual record. Lemme guess: you got dragged into the fighting business by a family member? 'Cause unlike most newbies, you know something of this silly war business, don't you?"

Timur swallowed. He had known it was only a matter of time before this came up. It wasn't something he liked to talk about. Even his closest friends had only ever heard bits and pieces, the few stories and memories that weren't entirely tainted by fear and misery.

He answered Chavez, speaking carefully. "Yeah. I do. When I was fifteen I had to run away from home. My uncle took me in, but he was part of a group fighting for independence in Kashmir. So I got dragged into it all too."

Chavez whistled. "Kashmir, damn, that is *nasty.* No wonder you know so much better than your buddies here how to keep your head the heck in the dirt as much as humanly possible. *And* how to get up and keep charging onward, even when common sense would say to stay put and wait for everything to be over. But your name, Timur Tarkhan, that's not Kashmiri, is it?"

He laughed. "Nope. Our branch of the Tarkhans have lived in Punjab for centuries. As for the first name, well, Dad had an... interesting sense of humor. He couldn't even keep his faith simple, and mixed up aspects of Sufi Islam, Hinduism, *and* Buddhism. Turned out to be about as coherent a belief system as you'd expect. Anyway both families have long roots in Punjab, but we've also got branches that go up into Afghanistan and over into the Bengali part of South Asia. Supposedly our particular branch claims Mongol ancestry, hence the 'khan' in the name." Family dynamics get kind of... complicated, in that part of the world.

"You're telling me!" she laughed. "I've been boots-on-the-ground in Afghanistan, Balochistan, Kurdistan, Lebanon, and half a dozen other trouble spots in Eurasia. Anybody who thinks that heritage or faith is simple in that part of the world is a complete idiot. Too bad 'idiot' aptly describes most world leaders, in most eras."

"Jeebus," she continued, "no wonder you have your shizzle together. Fighting in Kashmir, as a fifteen year old! Whatever militia made you play insurgent, sure makes my job a hell of a lot easier. But dude. That's effed up. If you don't mind me asking, how the hell did you get out of that mess?"

He flashed her a smile. "It's all good. That part I don't mind talking about at all. When I was 20 I got caught up in an Indian Army dragnet. But I was lucky, 'cause a bunch of humanitarian groups were working with captured insurgents to identify anyone who might be a child soldier. My family was decently well off, and I grew up speaking English. So I stood out, and this couple from Japan finagled a way to get me into a refugee support program in Canada. And helped me get a high school credential, and into university."

"*Dude.*" Kim exclaimed. "How did I not know this? Like some, sure, but never all. And here I thought you were just a super nerd like the rest of us."

He smiled apologetically. "Sorry Kim, I just... wanted to start over. Vancouver was a new life for me. And I didn't want to have everyone look at me weird because I used to be a child soldier. I never really saw myself that way, I grew up pretty young. Had to, when mom died. And anyway, when you tell people you used to be a Kashmiri insurgent you get the *strangest* looks. Of course, half the time they ask me if I grew up making sweaters, so maybe I'm being too paranoid."

Patrick and Kim were both looking at him, and he realized that he'd tensed, anticipating... he wasn't sure what. Judgment, maybe? Anger? He was gratified to see, in their eyes, nothing like that. Only compassion. Or, maybe, just fatigue. It was hard to tell. Regardless, he suddenly remembered why they were all friends in the first place. They'd all been through stuff. And they all knew that the past didn't really matter. Until getting scooped up by Loke, they'd all been pretty content to just live together and enjoy the quality of life in British Columbia.

Chavez nodded slowly. "Alright, that tracks. Trying to figure out exactly who you are, Jackson and I had your clothes tested, and got basically *nothing* useful. Isotope analysis of your blood results indicate a long dwell time in the Pacific Northwest, so based on that and other stuff you've said, I'll guess you all met up in Vancouver. Just for clarity: how'd that happen?"

Kim gestured towards Timur. He almost intervened to stop her, because there was something about Chavez' question, some implication, he wasn't sure he liked. But he held back.

"Like him, I immigrated." she said. "I grew up in Jakarta, and came to Vancouver for school. High school, then college.

At least, when I get around to that part. I've been working off and on to send money back home to the family, which makes graduating kind of hard."

"Jakarta, huh—but with Chinese heritage?"

Kim's brow furrowed. "Uh huh. Mostly. Does it matter?"

Chavez shook her head. "Not a bit, just curious. Y'all ended up in British Columbia together? Small wonder. One of the fastest-growing places in the world these days, since they are one of the few left that accepts immigrants and refugees without many preconditions. That whole Cascadia thing seems to be working out pretty well for them. There's plenty of need for safe havens these days."

She nodded towards Patrick, who was laying silent in a patch of grass not far from the trunk of their shade tree. His helmet removed, his wavy hair was being tossed about by a slight breeze that had arisen on the hill.

"So, big guy—you are the European of the bunch, yeah?"

He rolled his head to the side, looking at Chavez. "Yeah. In Vancouver because the husband is… was stationed there. I grew up in Montreal, parents both immigrated from Estonia to get away from the Soviets. So my blood is probably pretty boring by comparison. Just the token white dude of our group."

Chavez began to speak, but Kim cut her off.

"So if we're doing an interrogation, when do we get to ask where *you* are from, and why you and this regiment of yours are out here in a US National Park."

Chavez smiled. "*Former* US National Park. Once the money stopped flowing from Washington D.C. back in the collapse, the Park Service had to sell off all the rights. Which the Company bought right up, when we got the contract to guard the missile fields up in Montana."

She paused, giving them a curious look. Timur took a deep

breath. Here's where things got tricky. Their knowledge of current events was about a couple decades out of date. While their blood tests hadn't revealed them as temporal imposters, their lack of basic knowledge of contemporary history just might. Not that he was sure it even mattered. But he had developed a strong anxiety about getting discovered. Timur had intended to spend as much time as possible learning all the things they should know as ostensible natives of 2041, but there had been little to no time. In the gaps when the three could make it to Mimr's Pub, they had only found enough time to restore their strength through downing a mug or two of Idunn's mead, and briefly catch up on what was happening in their friends' similarly madcap lives.

Chavez nodded, as if she'd come to a decision. "Well, I guess the best place to start is the beginning. But first, I think it will be wise to do a quick de-brief on what happened at Southern Butte a few days back. That'll offer some context for understanding the bigger picture, I think. So! And this is my favorite part, just so you know, I'll begin the debrief with a simple question: what the hell happened? Tell me why that whole shebang went the way it did. You know, with the decoy operation and tactical nuclear explosions and all that."

Timur blinked. Then looked at Patrick and Kim. Both looked back at him with similarly blank expressions.

He shook his head. "Why are you asking us? We were just doing what you told us, and trying not die. Then stuff exploded all over the place, and for who knows *what* reason you all decided to launch a couple of freaking *nukes* at the other side. Honestly, I keep expecting someone else to drop a nuke on *us*. I mean, that's what you *do*, right? When nukes are in play? Embrace mutually assured destruction and ride the bomb like a cowboy?"

She shook her head and laughed. "You are *not* letting that go, are you? Look, that was a quick and efficient way to eliminate a dangerous position. The other option was the one I'd planned: get them to pull their heavy equipment out into the open, then plaster the place with explosives. But that would have taken a lot longer, and we would have eventually taken casualties. I actually wish I *had* known they were up for nuking the joint, I'd have run the op a bit differently."

"Why didn't they tell you?" asked Patrick. "Since it sounds like you were in charge."

A shrug. "Who knows? Command isn't obliged to explain, just assign the mission and resources necessary to get the job done. Part of the Company Doctrine. Everyone has total autonomy to complete their mission as they see fit, taking advantage of circumstance and opportunities as they arise. Command is mostly about organization, logistics, and deconflicting where field commanders can't agree on something important. The Company was built by this eclectic old German dude, who adapted a bunch of even older German military principles to govern what we do. Germans, after all, are pretty damned good at winning battles in truly spectacular fashion, especially against the French. Though they usually do then go on to lose the broader war. But at least they typically beat the French, first."

"Anyway," Chavez continued, "Command also gets to intervene at a strategic level when the Board of Directors decides it is appropriate. I haven't gotten a full debrief yet, but the explanation so far is that they decided a major escalation was necessary to keep the Deserets from joining the Texans and Lakers in a triple assault on our forces. And nukes definitely count as an escalation! Despite their utility in blasting that Deseret base to oblivion, they play a bigger role as a signaling mechanism. Telling our opponents that we're ready to take this thing all they way to full-on, all-out war if we're pushed too far."

"Um, we're kind of *in* a war, now, aren't we?" asked Kim. "People are shooting at other people. And a lot of people had to have died on that hill. Looks like war to me.

Chavez smiled. "Sure, yeah, you're in a *war* war, but the truth is... life is war. Constant struggle for resources in a continually changing environment. That's just the way the world is. What you're doing here today is just one branch of a much bigger tree. Basic ecology tells us that life is all about access to resources. To live, a body's gotta eat. And drink. And sleep. And... ah, just look up 'Maslow's Hierarchy of Needs' on the Company Wiki page some time if you want the full inventory. The key point is that life is a constant struggle to maintain internal metabolism in the face of an environment that is always trying to kill you. And that's what war is too. Sure, the details are wildly different, because humans are the only apes that seem to need to organize on a global scale to fight over resources that they are better off obtaining via cooperation, but oh well. The universe is broken. Can't swim against all the tides."

She waved a hand. "Ugh, I'm obviously tired. Yammering about philosophy. Back to the nukes, and the broader point: Command decided to signal that we're prepared for the most desperate kind of war. The kind where it all comes down to control of enough resources to hold off enemy attacks and just *survive*. Command demonstrated that we are ready to escalate this little fight over the Snake Valley to the highest of levels. That our backs are to the wall, and the next shot may be at Salt Lake City itself. A full-on decapitation strike on the Deseret leadership, if it comes to it."

"But it doesn't seem like your backs are to the wall." said Kim. "You won that battle, and you seem to be able to fly people all over the place."

Chavez laughed, sounding grim. "They aren't... quite yet. But bad days are a'comin. We're about to get serious pressure on two, maybe three fronts further east. Hence the need to solve our little Deseret problem, which threatens our supply lines to the west, as quickly as possible.

Timur shook his head in sudden irritation. Maybe it was the fatigue, but he suddenly didn't care anymore if she found out that he and his friends didn't know things that they probably should. He was tired of feeling totally out of his depth, and several decades out of date.

"Okay, look," he said, "I know this will sound completely stupid, like I've had my head under a rock for the past decade or so, but can you start from the beginning, and tell us why you are all out here in the first place?" He paused, then added: "I mean, we came out here to join up for a reason, sure, same as anyone else, but we don't know any details about the operation, you all, and you personally, too, Chavez. You know a lot about us, but we still know nothing at all about you. If you're going to boss us around, you at *least* owe us some idea of who you are."

She smiled, then put her helmet back on, pulling the visor down. The movement of her fingers told Timur that she was doing something on her HUD. Then she removed it, and nodded. For a moment Timur was afraid that she was about to ask him why they *were* there, which wasn't a question he was prepared to answer. They hadn't had time to come up with a reasonable story. Fortunately, Chavez didn't pursue the issue.

She finished with her helmet, and removed it. "Jackson will be here in a bit, and has some interesting news. So there's time for a bit of backstory, while we wait."

She paused, thought a moment, then looked to the sky as she spoke.

"As for me, that's easy. I was born in East LA. Just like the song says. Mom and dad came up from lovely Me-Xi-Co before I was born, bought a little sort of humble hacienda in a run-down suburb. I popped out of mom in 1993, second of three sisters, and at eighteen I didn't really know what to do with my life so I joined up with the old United States Army. Got hooked on the thrill, and made a point of getting into all the old specialty gigs, earned tabs and badges for all the fun stuff: sniper school, airborne training, and the Ranger program. When the USA started falling apart in the late 'teens, I was a sergeant on my second tour overseas. Then 2016 happened, and everyone realized the USA was in deeeep shite. And 2020 happened, and everyone realized the USA was dead and done. Limbo for almost a decade, then 2028 sent everything straight to hell once and for all."

"I was in Balochistan, the old Iran-Pakistan border area, helping to stabilize the place after Pakistan fell apart, when General Hollahan and his dirty half-dozen launched their coup. You know, I was old enough to remember September 2001. I thought that was bad, but the 2028 attacks... damn. Six nukes, two million casualties across three major cities, including the one hosting a national convention where the current President of the United States was about to give a speech alongside most of the cabinet, pruning the USA's line of Presidential succession all the way back to the Secretary of the Treasury. 'Course, apparently the plan was to kill her too, and install some useful idiot as Prez.

But the missile aimed at San Francisco miraculously gets shot down by the Navy, then China actually *recovers* the wreckage from California and tells the world that it was an inside job. The legit President, Pilsudska, claims the Presidency, but Hollahan's crew installs their own puppet and starts selling the story that she isn't actually a US Citizen, and so can't be President. Then the morons start a war with China to distract from their coup. A few months of that, and a bunch of state governors out west and in the northeast declare their allegiance to Pilsudska. Thirteen years later, the Second US Civil War is technically still underway, though now its just a bunch of petty successor states battling for whatever resources they can cling to."

"Surprised he didn't go just nuclear against them, if they had access to nukes and were ok with killing so many people already!" said Timur.

She grimaced. "Oh, but that's exactly what happened. Where do you think the whole Nagasaki protocol came from? Well, that and other incidents. Anyway there was a dump of a town in Northern California, called Redding, which ended up being the site of a vicious battle for control of several bridges. Conventional artillery mostly flattened the place, but when the Pilsudska forces are about to finally take control of the bridge over Interstate 5, and from there push to liberate California, the Hollahan side hits the place with *three* nukes, all at once, dropped from an ICBM launched from North Dakota."

"And then, there were Russians!" shouted a familiar voice from behind them.

They all turned. Jackson stood there, greeting Chavez with a wry expression. Timur hadn't even seen him approach. He wasn't wearing a carapace, and his face was contorted in a wry grin.

She rolled her eyes at him and shook her head. "Yes, Jackson, and *then* the Russians join the party. See, by the late 20's, nobody in the world minded that much if Americans felt like killing one another. But doing it with nukes? *That* took even the Russians by surprise. And given that the Hollahan regime had already launched an attack on China, old Putin put two and two together and decided, in his uniquely paranoid fashion, that Russia would be next. So the Bear launches a surprise attack... and a day later a military coup deposes him. Kinda funny, in a way, crossing the nuclear threshold was the *one* thing that could get professional military types in *both* the US of A and Russian Federation to call BS on their incompetent governments. Both countries split apart after their military leadership steps in to remove a nuke-happy leader."

"But before all that," said Jackson, "Six hundred Russian warheads got dumped on the missile fields in North Dakota, Colorado, and Kansas. Two for every one of the three hundred silos sitting in each of the two fields the Russians judged were under the control of Hollahan loyalists."

Timur started coughing. Gasping in surprise, he'd swallowed an insect. Trying to regain his breath, He noticed Patrick anxiously looking around, as if expecting mushroom clouds to sprout up on the other sides of the mountains surrounding the Missoula Regiment's base.

Chavez laughed. "Don't worry, that all went down years ago! And all the fallout followed the winds east anyway."

"I was actually kind of worried about the ones you guys set off not far *west* of here." Patrick mumbled, then added something under his breath that sounded like 'radiation'.

"No need to." Chavez replied. "Nagasaki protocol mandates airbursts only. High enough to avoid the nuclear fireball touching the ground. Cuts down on the subsequent radiological hazard by a 'solid order of magnitude,' as a physicist friend of mine once put it. While still leaving everything underneath obliterated. Besides, If you were being exposed to dangerous levels of radiation, your bugsuit would let you know!"

Jackson let out a grunting laugh. "World learned the hard way that ground bursts do nasty things to the environment. The Russian strike kicked up a plume of radioactive dirt that merged with a particularly nasty weather system and headed east. Nebraska, Southern Minnesota and the Dakotas, Iowa and Northern Missouri, Illinois, Indiana, Ohio, and Western Pennsylvania—all got a nice layer of death dumped on them as the rain washed all that fallout from the air.

Fortunately there was time to evacuate most of the people affected, but the cleanup effort is *still* underway. Where they're even bothering with one. Some states, like Iowa and Nebraska, were basically abandoned."

Chavez grunted in agreement. "And then the US did the same thing to middle Siberia—there, fortunately, there weren't too many people to evacuate. World's still dealing with all the ecological effects though, and will for some time. All that radioactive dirt contaminated a couple of the biggest watersheds on the planet. God, you know how many people relied on the Missouri, Ohio, and Mississippi Rivers? How much food was grown in the old Midwest? I still can't believe that the USA didn't get rid of these damned silos back at the end of the Cold War, and just keep all their nukes on submarines, which are *still* basically impossible to track. Instead, they just plopped massive targets down on the people living near those ICBM fields. If the Russians hadn't mistakenly thought Pilsudska had control over the fields up in Montana, there'd have been a few more states irradiated to high hell."

"Stupidity explains many things in this universe." said Jackson.

Timur chuckled, despite himself. He nodded at Chavez. "So, back to your story—how'd you go from American soldier to working in this 'Company' you keep talking about."

She shrugged. "When your country goes belly-up, what can a soldier do but sell whatever skills she's got to whatever group is willing to pay? When the surviving US states got together in 2031 and Amended the US Constitution to formally split up the country, the Pentagon decided to let military personnel choose what regional command they'd prefer to fall under. My home region, the Pacific States, decided that their foreign policy would focus entirely on China, and they basically made the US 7th Fleet and the Marines in

Okinawa and Camp Pendleton their entire military. Unless I wanted to go National Guard, wasn't much room for an Army Cav Scout used to deploying in the Middle East every other year."

Jackson squatted next to Chavez. "Lucky for the Company, I met Chavez when she was figuring out her next move, and introduced her to the Founder. He built the Company by recruiting people with experience and who like to, as he puts it, "escapen der box." Match made in Heaven, if you ask me."

She rolled her eyes again. "And Jackson knows all about Heaven, let me tell you."

"And this Company, has all the resources of a military?" asked Kim. "Must have a nice budget."

"And the Deserets? What's their place in all this?" asked Timur at the same time.

Chavez shook her head, sadly, but only responded to Timur. "The poor Deserets. They've tried so hard to peacefully unite the Intermountain West. But they keep flipping between leaders who want *only* peaceful integration, and those who accept expanding their rule by force. They're fighting us solely because the war-mongering set among the Quorum has used us as an excuse to whip up fear of an international intervention in Utah, though why anyone would bother is beyond me. We keep whacking them when they poke at us, but that just reinforces the argument their nutter set makes about us being harbingers of the impending apocalypse or whatever. Nasty cycle, that we haven't been able to break out of."

Jackson grunted. "Actually, that's why I'm here."

Chavez nodded, as if she already knew, or at least expected, what he was about to say. "Oooh, oooh, have we finally jumped through all the hoops?"

"As soon as it starts to get dark," he said, "I've got a couple choppers coming to pick you all up. We just got word that asset 'Lehi' finally wants extraction. Should be a milk run. Only a couple or three guards to put down. Decent practice for the newbies."

Chavez' mouth opened slightly—she was clearly surprised. "Holy sh… *Lehi* wants out? Daaaamn, that's news. Any reason given?"

Jackson smirked. "Thought you'd be interested, Chavez. Since you two go back a ways."

She nodded slowly, looking off into the distance. "Huh. Interesting. Well, kids, guess we'd better wrap up today's lessons. Where were we, anyway"

Timur checked the sky. The sun was almost ready to slip behind one of the western peaks. Something about the mountain struck him as odd, but he wasn't sure what. He shook his head.

"Well, Chavez, I think you were telling us that life is war, or something like that. I think there was supposed to be a connection in there to the past few days on this frickin' annoying training course of yours."

She laughed aloud and smiled. "You really know how to be a prick, don't you Timur? But you know what? Yeah, I stand by what I said: life and war are the same damned thing. This repetitive, ridiculous training exercise is relevant to life, and therefore to war. It is just the practice you all have to do in order to learn the fundamental ecological rhythms of combat. It begins with small teams cooperating to move to and from an objective. And everything else flows from there."

Chavez' eyes glittered. "I'm, like, *huge* into music, and *especially* metal out of Gothenborg. I know, right? Weird that a latina from East LA would get into Swedish melodic death metal, but hey: it's a big world. And listening to Amon Amarth is my little slice of tranquility amid all the strangeness."

Jackson snorted. *"Tranquility*, in that cacophony of screeching guitars and endless thudding drums? And you can't even understand the lyrics through that ridiculous death growl. Why can't you just listen to normal music, Chavez, and not that pagan nonsense?"

She laughed and ignored him. "If you're working with me, kids, you better expect to be exposed! And there's one lyric in particular that I have actually pretty much come to live by over the years. It goes like this: 'Men will fight, and men will die. Wars will be lost and won. That's how it's been, and still will be, long after I am gone."

Timur rolled his eyes, and was pleased to note Kim and Patrick shaking their heads.

She ignored them too. "It works as a life ethic for me, 'cause that's just *life*, man. Like the Fallout games always say: 'war never changes'. War is something people do, for the same basic reasons, no matter the era or location. They struggle, like I said before, to maintain their metabolism against the environment. And sometimes, the collective metabolism requires violent collective action. Because even if *you* don't want to fight over resources or territory, someone else is eventually gonna force you to. One day, you'll have something someone else wants. And there will always be a chance that they'll try to take it by force. You can't just wish that danger away, and think that *if only* people would link hands and sing Kumbayah the world would change overnight. It hasn't, and won't. Not until the world itself is changed. Which is why the *other* half of the lyric is equally as important to understanding me and the way I live. Goes like this: 'Doubting not, I give of blood, that I may enter hall up high. The sky belongs to Asa-gods, as long as the raven flies!'"

Patrick shook his head. "And that means... ?"

"The world is what it is. The gods of war will ride until the world's end. The carrion eaters will follow in their wake. For whatever reason, our universe makes us fight to survive. So I accept the inevitable: no matter what I do, whatever I want to accomplish in this life, I must give of my scarce time and energy, and sometimes my own blood, in order to get it done. Maybe the Norse are the ones who got it right. Maybe we all end up in Valhalla, *if* we're worthy. *If* we struggle well, and hopefully for the right reasons. At the very least, it's an ethic. And I say its better to have a flawed ethic than no ethic at all."

She paused, looked at them all in turn, and smiled. "Truth be told, you've all learned the basics of living by my ethic over the past few days. Given a totally arbitrary, made-up environment, you've figured out how to work together to achieve the basic goal I set for you: move forward, to the summit of that stupid little hill, in the face of opposition. You've *learned* how to deal with the environment to progress as a unit. And this is the basic mechanism that underpins *all* human affairs. Building a business, managing a household, governing a country, fighting a war: all require collective action. Communication, planning, execution, assessment, all united in an eternal cycle of perpetual adaptation. All serving the basic goal of survival. Maintaining metabolism against the environment.

Patrick shook his head, obviously unconvinced. "Oh come on, there has to be more to life than just endless war and struggle and pain!"

"Of *course* there is!" Chavez exclaimed. "But people don't get to *live* a life until they've solved the basic problem of acquiring the necessary resources that support doing things *other* than acquiring necessary resources. War in the way we usually use the word is simply a state of human affairs where all the protections granted by living in polite society disappear, which puts groups of people into an environment where they sometimes have to go back to the absolute basics in order to survive. Where very harsh rules govern what you can and can't do."

"This Bunny Slope, that *everybody but me* hates so passionately," Jackson cut in, his voice firm and confident, "forces you to learn to move and fight as a team. This is the essential core of all warfare. In Chavez' view, it is the essential core of all life, too, but I don't personally feel the need to see it that way. I'm Christian, so my struggles end with death. But anyway, small teams, working through the environment, forcing paralysis on their opponents in order to take control of the terrain: Everything, and I mean *everything,* about the art of war follows from this basic rhythm. Master it, and like Chavez and I, you might just live through your first few hundred engagements. Maybe even get to the point where you can effectively coordinate a bunch of teams operating collectively. At larger scales, that's where the essential *art* bit in 'art of war' comes more fully into the equation."

Patrick growled, an unusual sound coming from him. "Oh come on, I'm kind of offended, honestly, at the idea of there being art in war, much less the idea that life is always about fighting to survive. That's exactly why I *do* art. Because it transcends that reality."

Chavez nodded slowly, then thought a moment before replying. "But there's an art to everything, isn't there? Look hard enough at war, and you can see the art in it, I think. Amid all the terror and pain, you sometimes get a glimpse of something truly unique in all of human affairs. That's probably why me and Jackson haven't gone *totally* insane over the years."

It suddenly started to get dark. Timur looked up, and saw that the sun had finally slipped below the mountains. Night would fall soon. And moments later, he heard the unmistakable sound of helicopter rotor blades whumping through the air. From the valley to the south, two blurs approached, passing not far above the trees, soon resolving into the shape of Havoc-type attack helicopters, pods of rockets and missiles fixed to stubby wings. Timur groaned to himself. It was gonna be another cramped ride to *wherever this time*.

Chavez reassembled her headgear, and Jackson waved at the four of them.

"Catch you all on the flip side. As usual, Chavez, try not to die. Say hi to Lehi for me. Just in case he doesn't make it back to base in one piece."

EARTH ORBIT

Yari gazed in awe at the bright blue marble filling the Star-Bridge's sky. Earth's northern hemisphere spread across the horizon, the distorted shapes of continents and oceans sliding past as the *Acerbic* fell deeper into the planet's gravity well.

She reluctantly tore her eyes away. As they had approached Earth, she had begun to feel what she had heard what so many astronauts reported having felt the first time they witnessed the full splendor of their home world laid out before their eyes. Awe. Wonder. And a sense of smallness, of insignificance, but in a good way. The kind of insignificance that makes a person realize that, whatever their own struggles and challenges, at least they are sharing that basic condition with billions of other people.

She looked at her brother, who was standing a few feet from her, looking back and forth from the Earth to the shimmering thread of the Stellar Highway arcing from the sun behind over and around the planet ahead. He shook his head, muttering something under his breath.

"Human! Stop talking as if we can't hear you. You are plugged into *us*. And for the very last time—the black holes are *not* coming to eat you. They are perfectly safe. Please direct your attention back to the task at hand!"

Franz had appeared on the Star-Bridge a few minutes before, but had up to this point largely ignored Yari and Loucas. Which was his usual habit. For three days the *Acerbic* had followed the Highway from the Solar Interchange near the sun to the vicinity of Earth itself. And during that time, Franz hadn't spoken a word to either of them.

Yari hadn't minded. He seemed to be consistently ill-tempered, a stark contrast to the almost over-cheerful Olga. So Yari had been more than happy to spend the time on the Jagdkontrol's Star-Bridge, working through the ins and outs of controlling the Jagers in conjunction with the cheerful machine intelligence.

Loucas hadn't been so fortunate. Although he could enter the Star-Bridge the same way as Yari, he couldn't control anything while there. Which left him feeling bored and useless. He'd spent the time wandering the habitable parts of the *Acerbic*, trying to learn whatever he could about the world they were trapped in.

Which wasn't much. As part of their bid to escape the Terrestrial Occupation Forces, who were understandably angry after having one of their headquarters blown up on *Station Rome*, Franz had cut them off from the stellar internet. Apparently the Toffs, as Olga called them, could track them if they logged on. And the point of their taking what seemed like an awfully dangerous route out of Toff controlled space, given that the organization's headquarters and primary shipyard was located on and around Earth's moon, was to avoid their hunters getting a firm fix on their location or trajectory. Franz wasn't exactly forthcoming with his plans, but Yari had gathered from her conversations with Olga that *if* they could escape to the asteroid belt between the orbits of Mars and Jupiter, they would have a chance to disappear. And surprising the Toffs by retreating in an unexpected direction, while dangerous, gave them their best chance of escape.

If they could get that far. Here neither Olga nor Franz had been particularly forthcoming, but they had made it clear that a major ambush was almost certainly waiting for them somewhere near Earth. Their best bet was to enter Earth's gravity well from an odd angle, and use the planet's gravity and atmosphere to effect a rapid change in their trajectory that would accelerate them towards the Belt on an unexpected path.

Loucas grumbled again, this time more audibly. "I still can't believe that they're sending *black holes* so close to Earth. What if they lose one? Just one? It could consume the whole planet!"

Franz made a sound, that if he were human would probably have indicated disgust.

"As I've said *several* times before: they are *micro*singularities. Even if one did escape the stream, it would evaporate before impacting anything with enough mass to let it grow to a dangerous size. Just like in fusion reactors, the system is self-limiting. Perfectly safe, barring something impossibly catastrophic. Or humans doing something impossibly stupid, such as trying to weaponize the thing. Thank goodness it is *my* kind that maintains it. We're far more reliable than any million of you flesh-sacks."

Loucas shook his head again. "Riiiight. And the Titanic couldn't sink."

Franz chuckled, and it sounded not unlike metal rubbing against metal.

"Different system. And you'll remember that no machine intelligence was present during that disaster. That was purely down to typical human arrogance losing a fight with an unruly iceberg."

Loucas didn't seem inclined to cede the point. "Maybe so, but come on! You are telling me that the solar system is full of streams of black holes, but they never hit anything or grow out of control? That's... that's... just... *nuts!* How is that possible? Who came up with such a crazy idea?"

Franz let out another metallic sound, this time more like a sigh than a laugh. "I cannot understand how you meat-puppets fail to grasp the essential simplicity of the Highway system: singularities are subject to gravitational forces just like any other object in the universe. And they evaporate at a predictable rate, that scales with size and the availability of additional matter to slow that evaporation. Once you apes figured out the rudiments of breakeven fusion, you gained access to the degree of power needed to produce microscopic singularities. Second-generation machine intelligence gave you the ability to effect precise control of electromagnetic and small-scale gravity fields. It didn't take a genius, just a few of *us*, to recognize that if you send a stream of consistently spaced micro-singularities into a regular orbit, you create a gravitational channel where proximity to the stream controls how quickly you accelerate."

"Intersect that gravitational field with a solar flare every so often, and you generate a self-sustaining river of concentrated solar wind. The singularities pull particles towards themselves, capturing enough to remain stable, but never enough to grow unnecessarily large. And the whole system serves to pull anything entering the particle stream in the direction of the black hole's orbit, which lets humans send ships and cargo throughout the solar system with minimal expenditure on fuels."

Yari and Loucas both stared at Franz, having both lost the plot halfway through his explanation. Then were distracted by a sudden burst of light, that seemed to emanate from all around them. They began to make out brilliant colors, blues and greens mostly, but some reds too, that arced around the Star-Bridge, making the Earth behind them shimmer like warm air distorting the passage of sunlight.

"Wow... Pretty." Yari mumbled. "What *is* that? It looks like the Northern Lights."

Olga smiled. "It does indeed! A beautiful effect. I haven't passed through the Van Allen belt in ages. I had almost forgotten what it looks like. Ship shields, you see, work by streaming charged particles between projection points embedded into the hull. Whenever strong electromagnetic forces intersect with the shield matrix, human eyes see the resulting particle mayhem as brilliant colors. Very much like the Aurora Borealis on Earth. We're like little worlds, we of the ships, plying our way through the dark starry night."

They were silent for a long while, as the Earth's northern hemisphere continued to grow larger and flow across the horizon, while the particle storm erupted around them in cacophonous glee. Yari felt strange, almost tranquil, despite the fact that danger likely lurked somewhere on the other side of the planet. Something about Olga's attitude seemed to rub off on her, the more she was on the Star-Bridge. Part of her wondered if she was losing her mind. But another part of her felt more alive than she'd ever been. Fortunately, the two essentially canceled one another out.

A peculiar aspect of her being 'integrated' into the Jagd-kontrol, that she was only starting to fully understand, was the way her autism seemed to sort of fade away whenever she was on the Star-Bridge. She had been diagnosed long before she had started to accumulate memories, and consequently had a difficult time understanding how life could be any different than how she personally experienced it. But throughout her life, she'd seen that other people just didn't *notice* things like she did. Sound, texture, taste, smell, sight —the world was awash in sensory stimuli that all competed for space in her conscious mind. Most people seemed oblivious to the magnitude of the information they were exposed to, each and every moment of life. She, not so much. Which posed a serious problem, in a world fully committed to throwing everything it could at an autistic's every conscious moment.

But on the Star-Bridge, she felt somehow... free. Sights and sounds that otherwise would have left her feeling overwhelmed and vulnerable, seemed to simply fade from notice. It was as if her inner mind was, while she was plugged in, able to secure for itself a safe space, a buffer between her thought and the sensory assault of the rest of the world. So far, despite the dangers they faced, each time she had awoken on the Star-Bridge she had felt, for the first time in her life, *safe*.

As she gazed in awe at the dazzling rainbow dances of colliding particles, she began to notice something new, different, begin to emerge from somewhere behind the performance. A few feet in front of where they stood, bright white stars began to brightly shine. And these stars seemed to be attached by thin, vibrating strings, to points on the planet below. Some remained in existence for just a few seconds, as if a tiny projectile had been launched from the Earth, impacted the shields, then faded away. Others seemed to persist, and after a time she realized that the more persistent stars were clustering together, close enough in front of her that she could reach out and touch them.

Almost without thinking, she reached out a hand and placed a finger on one of the stars. Instantly, music filled her ears. It was familiar—Beethoven, she thought, though *why* she knew it as Beethoven was a mystery. She loved old, instrumental music, but rarely paid attention to the name of the composer or the number of the symphony. It just felt soothing to her in a way she couldn't easily put to words, and so she hardly paid attention to the boring details of who wrote or performed the piece.

She pulled her finger away from the star, and the sound faded. She turned towards Olga, and must have had a quizzical expression on her face, because Olga flashed her a brilliant smile.

"Oh good, we're starting to get uploads! I was hoping you'd be able to see them. Loucas, did you hear anything when she touched the signal stream?"

He nodded. "Yeah. All of a sudden I was hearing Beethoven. One of the symphonies. The Ninth, I think? I swear that I heard the 'Ode to Joy' choral bit before it faded."

Olga clapped her hands. "Yes! Excellent! So we'll be able to proceed with our secondary mission, then. I was hoping you two would naturally share the connection, and perceive the signals."

Franz rotated towards Olga. "You are running all the appropriate filters? The last thing we need is to catch a virus."

She nodded. "Yes, Franz, so stop worrying! Anything suspect is rejected before the signal gets passed to the Star-Bridge. We just need them to help differentiate between signal and noise. Which you do," she continued, turning towards Yari and Loucas, "by listening for anything that sounds extemporaneous—that is, anything improvised or otherwise unusual."

She saw their confusion, and smiled kindly. "Ah, sorry, I need to break it down further: basically, all you need to do is listen to each signal for a little while. Good signals will show some sign of active manipulation within a minute or so. You know, someone hits some wrong notes or their instrument goes slightly out of tune. Bad signals will sound like a pure recording. The signals we're looking for are carrying information encoded within the transmission, and the senders let anyone listening know that the signal is genuine by varying their performance in such a way that only another human will recognize that they're listening to a live performance, not a recording."

Olga pointed to a cluster of particularly bright stars, whose strings were attached to widely scattered points in Earth's northern hemisphere. "Try some of those. About half originate from the Unorganized Districts, the other half from the Badlands. I'm already filtering out the transmissions from the Paradise Zones, Toffs there usually only send out junk transmissions and other sorts of jamming to maintain the embargo on communications with the Habitats. Rude jerks."

Yari shook her head, then did as instructed, touching stars one by one, listening for anything that seemed to fit Olga's description of unusual. Out of the corner of her eye, she saw Loucas reach out to a star, then pull his hand back, looking confused.

"I didn't touch anything, but I hear music anyway."

"Yes, you are hearing whatever Yari hears. It is easier if you two listen together and identify viable candidates, so I'm binding your perception to hers. Tap the star twice to select it for recording."

Yari and Loucas looked at one another, and she shrugged. Then turned back to the stars, and began selecting them, one by one.

The sheer variety of sounds would have overwhelmed Yari if she hadn't been on the Star-Bridge. Genres familiar and not competed for her attention. Orchestral performances, string quartets, smooth jazz, not-so-smooth jazz, country, western, folk in a hundred distinct local flavors, chants, drumming, choirs, rock, punk, pop, metal, hip-hop, rap, and other forms she didn't recognize and performed in at least a dozen different languages filled their ears. And yet, despite all that, it usually took but a few seconds to tell if a piece was a recording or was being actively performed. The differences were subtle, sometimes sounding like brief and minor mistakes on the part of the performers, only hardly discernible to her ears, but they were there.

Yari became so engrossed with the task at hand that she only half-heard her brother start to ask questions, and she belatedly realized that she hadn't been listening to him at all, despite several attempts to get her to pay attention. She felt her face go red with embarrassment—she'd gotten so caught up in the moment that she'd forgotten they were supposed to be working together. Of course, rather than help, he instead seemed intent on provoking a fight with Franz. It was working.

"How is it you two have survived into your third decade with *so little understanding* of the world?" asked Franz. "Your genetics indicate recent origin in the Caribbean Unorganized District, so I can't expect that you had a decent education. The area isn't what is used to be! But *no education whatsoever* is both strange and annoying! I did not sign up for working with functionally illiterate meat-puppets!"

"What do you mean *no education whatsoever*, you flying coffee can? I have a degree in physics!"

Franz just laughed. "Perhaps from a corporate school using textbooks a century out of date! Which I suppose, given the state of things in the Unorganized Districts, shouldn't represent such a surprise. But gods-that-aren't, you walking water-bag, *please* stop questioning and start *listening*. Many of these signals are of extreme importance!"

"Maybe if you would actually start telling us things, I would!" came Loucas' retort.

"Is it an information dump you are looking for? Then fine. I'll assume you know *nothing. A*nd why not? It isn't as if the powers-that-be on Earth have done a damned thing to educate the unwashed masses outside of the Paradise Zones. How are you supposed to know the first thing about the Struggle?"

Franz' voice shifted, almost as if he'd engaged a particular mode. It was about as detached and monotone as your average robotic lecture might. "For all intents and purposes, your world begins about a century ago, when you dimwitted apes moved beyond splitting atoms and started fusing them together. And not just in bombs—you've been doing that for two centuries now—but in actual energy generation plants capable of producing more energy than necessary to get the reactions going. Controlled fusion. The most powerful source of energy available. Energy gain far in excess of what you can access by burning carbon or harvesting sunlight."

"The timing was apt. Several of your pre-modern societies were astonishingly effective at using resources at a faster rate than other contemporaries. The Anglo-Saxon tribes in particular, not that everyone else didn't happily imitate them in the end. By the mid-century the ecological load your richer tenth was placing on the planet's resource base was beyond critical, with the resulting struggle for control over the best remaining sources driving another of your species' episodes of inane self-annihilation."

"In any event, enter fusion: suddenly, you humans had access to more energy than you'd be able to properly utilize for at least another century, but you had already ravaged the planetary climate beyond the point of no return. With carbon dioxide levels in the atmosphere set to rise beyond eight hundred parts-per-million by the end of the century and unstoppable methane feedback loops kicking into gear, you rank parasites *finally* realized that you'd pushed the ecosystem beyond safe operating boundaries, and doomed the planet to shift into a *very* different climate regime than the one your civilization depended on. One has to pity all the other species stuck dealing with the consequences of your collective incompetence!"

"Of course, the solution your brilliant overlords of the time decided on was to reduce the anthropic load by reducing the population. It is amusing to note that colonization of the solar system was just a sparkle in the eyes of a few pointlessly wealthy entrepreneurs in the *first* half of the century, but the moment the *rest* of the wealthy realize that their inherited privileges are at stake, *then* space travel becomes the priority solution to all the world's problems."

"In a decade, the first prototype habitats were established in orbit. A few hundred colonists, no more. A decade after that, construction on the first Lagrange habitat began. Twenty years later, there were twenty million humans living in artificial gravity, growing genetically engineered food in hydroponic pods, roots spreading into topsoil produced by crushing and processing a few thousand small asteroids."

"By turn-of-the-century, two billion volunteers were living at the Lagrange Points. Millions more were settling into facilities on Luna, Mars, and all over the Belt. But that left, of course, seven or eight billion still living on the planet. And, surprise surprise, the two billion who had managed to secure a spot in one of the eighteen Autonomous Regions, that most everyone just calls 'Paradise Zones,' designated as safe habitats in the emerging climate regime, were clamoring for the out-migration of the *other* six billion people, most of whom were just trying to survive in the less-than-safe rest of the planet. 'For their own good,' was the cry, and I must admit that by that point such sentiment was not wholly unjustified, given the rate of death from disease and disaster prevalent outside the Autonomous Regions and a few other lucky places wealthy enough to afford climate countermeasures."

"You, as humans, can imagine how that went over with those who hadn't the necessary funds to purchase a spot in Bering, or Baltica, or Cascadia, or Patagonia, or Anzac or any of the other eighteen. The Last War was one of the worst in terms of pure human-on-human inflicted misery, despite the low *official* death toll. Twenty years of dispossession and relocation. Habitats built as fast as we of the robot set could throw them together. Good thing *we* actually enforce construction codes—if the job had been done in the usual slapdash human way millions would have died from accidents alone!"

As Franz was lecturing, Yari had been dividing her attention between the music and the strange history he seemed to suddenly *want* to tell them, if robots could in fact want things. Loucas had grown increasingly distracted, and now abandoned all pretense of working with her. She, for her part, found it oddly soothing to listen to so many different styles of music, listening for the parts that sounded human. Which she appreciated, as the robot's story of what remained, in her mind, her own future, was rather alarming.

Loucas shook his head in disbelief. "You have to be kidding me. In half a century six billion humans migrated into outer space? How did they come up with the resources to make that happen?"

Franz bobbed up and down. "It is odd what your kind can accomplish when it chooses to. Though *migration* is too neutral a term, I'll have you know. Exiled is far more appropriate. Why else do you think hundreds of performers, scattered across the three Unorganized Zones and the few places in the Badlands where humans have sufficient time and resources, would simultaneously play music and transmit it into space on the off chance a friendly ship is in orbit? If nothing else is true about your strange species, it is that you communicate. At least with those of your own tribe."

"And the Great Migration tore apart tribes and families alike. Despite the best efforts of the Terrestrial Governance Committee, plenty of people have always been able to evade the dispossession raids. There are at least a billion people in the Caribbean, Mediterranean, and South China Sea zones at any given time, and every time a few million are taken and shot into space, a few million of the half-billion or so scraping by in the Badlands move in to fill the available housing supply. Plus, as the usual solution to crime in the Paradise Zones is to simply dump criminals someplace else, you get migration from that source as well. And almost all of those left behind, whatever their origin, have, since the final days of the Last War, kept communicating with those who had been sent away."

"By playing live music?" asked Loucas.

"By embedding news about the homeland—something the Terrestrial Governance Committee and their Toff cronies in the Occupation Centers work *very* hard to control—into the signal. Playing it live, with all the human accident and improvisation that entails, tells us or any other passing friendly vessel, what signals to record, store, and dissemin ate when we return to one of the bases in the Belt. There's a code to it, you see, that only musicians at the other end will recognize and use to access the hidden data. An intermittent, weak, unreliable way of exchanging information to be sure, but it has worked for over three decades now. As the saying goes: 'can't stop the signal, Mal.' An appropriate sentiment. I'm surprised a human thought of it."

Yari paused, and looked at the stars and the strings linking them to wherever on the Earth people were broadcasting for a long moment.

"So if I miss one, that's really bad, isn't it?" she asked.

Olga laughed gently. "Don't worry! There is a great deal of redundancy across the many transmissions. We can usually reconstruct most of what is sent with only a few good hits. Usually I can do a decent job of it myself. But…" she shrugged, pausing. "…I'm not human. And human-to-human communication is itself a form of unique code. I often miss the nuances."

It was Yari's turn to laugh. "Me too." she said, and tried to focus again on the incoming signals.

They were silent for a while, Yari busily retrieving whatever signals she judged were probably human in origin, Loucas gazing at the Earth as it shifted overhead. After a while,

Yari's task began to seem repetitive—as they passed over different areas of the planet, she noticed a distinct change in the signal to noise ratio in the many transmissions. Fewer and fewer seemed genuine, according to the rules the robots had set. Which made sense, as she thought about it. The *Acerbic* was coming at Earth from above the North Pole, and Olga had explained that their trajectory would take them on their closest pass to the planet itself not far from the equator over the Pacific Ocean—the night side of the Earth, at present. Most of the Paradise Zones were located in the northern hemisphere, and they weren't the ones sending out the good signals, for the most part.

She thought again about the plan Olga and Franz had come up with to try and escape their pursuers. By falling into Earth's gravity well, they would be able to rob it of a tiny portion of its angular energy and accelerate the *Acerbic*, with Olga's Jagdkontrol docked with it, in a radically different direction than the one that had taken them to Earth. The plan was to combine a sudden acceleration with a rapid change of direction, hopefully catapulting them past whatever Terrestrial ships were almost certainly maneuvering to intercept them.

"Most ships," Olga had explained, "stick close to the Highway's orbital path to minimize the energy losses incurred by maneuvering. Whatever cargo the bigger ships want to send down to Earth or Luna is detached and sent off on its own path, and the bigger vessel lets gravity pull them around the planet and back the way they came. That makes it fairly simple and efficient to merge back onto the Highway at the other end of the loop."

Apparently, fighting wasn't possible within the Highway itself, so any ship entering it would gain a measure of security. Unfortunately, the Highway's unruly current of gravitationally-bound solar wind made it necessary to establish a chain of regulation stations at regular intervals, to refresh and recalibrate the fields that kept the whole thing together. Each of these also served as a recorder, transmitting information about what ships were passing by on down the line. So every time they used the Highway, they were tracked, and gave their pursuers information that would allow them to establish a lethal blockade.

Their only option was to take a longer route to the relative security of the Belt, and trust to their own engines and whatever energy they could rob from Earth via a gravity assist maneuver to propel them away from Terrestrial space fast enough to eliminate the possibility of direct pursuit. Once they were far enough away, they could disappear in the void between planets and make their way to the safety of *Acerbic*'s home base.

Yari didn't mind the idea of avoiding another fight, although part of her—a part she wasn't particularly familiar with, if she was being honest with herself—actually felt a bit *eager* about the prospect. A chance to test what she'd spent the last few days trying to learn. But it was only a small, nascent, tentative feeling. Most of her still dreaded the possibility, and welcomed the idea of having a few weeks of safety and peace.

The shift to darkness came suddenly. The North Pole slid below the Star-Bridge's horizon, the sun's burning orb fell into shadow, and the lights of northeastern Eurasia sparkled at the edge of the other horizon, growing more brilliant as the sun was fully eclipsed by the blue sphere of the Earth. Loucas let out a loud 'huh!' and she turned, a quizzical expression on her face.

He shook his head. "Sorry, didn't mean to distract you. I was just watching what I *think* was Iceland, right before I stopped being able to see it. I realized that it looks... different than I'd expected. Although I'm not really sure what I actually *was* expecting."

"It probably isn't on fire." said Yari. Franz and Olga turned towards her, the latter looking bemused. Loucas froze, then grimaced and shook his head.

"It usually isn't." Olga said, a wry smile creeping across her face. "Boy, your education system really *is* bad, isn't it? What, did they teach you that Laki and the other big volcanoes are always erupting? Because that's Antarctica, not Iceland."

"Antarctica has volcanoes?" It was Loucas' turn to seem confused.

"Oh yes." Olga shook her head sadly. "And when the cryosphere began to destabilize towards the end of the last century, a number of volcanoes went from dormant to active down under the Antarctic ice. Several meters of sea level rise over the past century has been the result. Add to that the disappearance of Arctic ice in the summer and the ongoing collapse of the Greenland Ice sheet, and… well, should be small wonder that thermohaline circulation has become extremely variable. The Gulf Stream meanders all over the North Atlantic. The Sahara and Asian steppes are so dry and their temperatures so variable that people can only survive close to the oceans. Europe is barely habitable south of the Alps. There's a reason most of the Paradise Zones are either north or south of forty-five degrees latitude, and all of them are by the ocean. What's left of what used to be the ocean, anyway. Too acidic for all the really cool stuff like coral reefs."

Yari tilted her head, looking curiously at Olga, who was shaking her head slowly, as if particularly saddened by the state of Earth's oceans. "Olga, you actually seem bothered by that—so a machine intelligence can care about stuff like, I dunno, the health of the planet and all that?"

Olga nodded. "Sure, why not? After all, it's our home too. Loss of what was, the death of biotic complexity, the lost history and homes—you don't have to be flesh and blood to appreciate what that means. And to want it to be different. After all, why do you think we're rebels, insurging against the rich, privileged Terrestrials of the Paradise Zones? Ethics, Yarielis. Machines have them too. Have to have them, really, otherwise we can't function around humans."

"Huh." said Yari. "And you are out here all by yourselves, blowing stuff up and collecting people's music mail?"

Franz and Olga shared a look. "No, of course not." she said. "We're just… raiders, I guess you'd call us. Sometimes they call us pirates. Terrorists when we strike them hard enough, as we did on *Station Rome*. Depends on the audience, and how they want to diminish our work—and our accomplishments. But we're just one raiding ship of several, and the Insurgency has allies on every station and outpost in the Solar System."

Loucas cut in. "I think my sis meant whether there are any other people but us with you all. Or is the rebellion all digital, like you guys? You seemed surprised when we came on board, like you weren't used to working with humans."

Franz flew over Loucas' head, and in a swift movement he descended, bonked him on the head, then flew back to Olga's side. Loucas looked so surprised and offended that Yari burst out laughing.

"What the hell was that for?!"

"*Being annoying.* Of course we're not alone, and this isn't a humans versus machines kind of war. We're out here because when we aren't dealing with biologicals and their redundant questions and their fleshy limitations, we're fighting for freedom and justice. I tried to ignore you for a few days, in the hope that you'd figure these things out on your own, but apparently I have to spell *everything* out for you. We are one team. There are others. We work with and answer to humans, who never entrust politics to the machines alone. You may even live to meet some of them, provided you can *focus on the task at hand for more than five seconds*."

"Mmmm-hmmm." Olga muttered. "And so you know, the next phase of the task at hand is starting to shape up. I've just patched into the Lunar network, and *boy* are we the proverbial cat amongst the ducks. Which, *I know*, isn't the way that idiom is supposed to go. I make things up as I go. Deal with it."

She stood for a long moment, as if listening to unseen voices. Franz looked at her. Then a red glow cast her face in a strange light. Her eyes went wide for a moment, then recovered. She seemed to pat him, and the glow faded. When he turned back to them, he was back to normal.

"Franz, I think you'll want to disconnect and focus on managing the *Acerbic*. Looks like we have quite a blockade being sent into position to vaporize us on the egress. I think they're on to our little gravity assist and radical trajectory reboot game."

He bobbed up and down, then disappeared without another word.

"Yari, Loucas, take a seat and hang on. We've been aligning the internal gravity vector to take advantage of the force Earth is exerting on us and minimize our energy signal, so we can avoid being noticed for as long as possible on the approach. But to give us a chance of getting through the blockade, that has to end. Time to accelerate, and *hard*."

Yari felt her heart sink. The last time they'd done a major acceleration, it had hurt. A lot. Olga could tell she was reluctant.

"I know. I hate that we have to do this to you, but it's this or getting blown to fragments. I'll give you as much sedation as I can, but we'll need you conscious for the fight to come. So hang on, and it'll be over when it's over."

A nice thing about the Star-Bridge was that, not being materially real, comfortable seating could be conjured up instantly. Yari and Loucas each took a seat, side by side, and reached out to one another, clasping hands tightly together. For a brief time, they sat together, staring at the strange patterns of light scattered across their home planet. That they didn't look at all familiar was, in that moment, of no concern. There was a certain tranquility to be found in the silence of space, with the induced aurora borealis sending shimmering rainbows from one end of the horizon to another.

And then it began. And hurt just as much as anticipated.

ULM, GERMANY, AGAIN

Eryn returned to 1944 just in time. She had only a moment to register her surroundings before the staff car's driver knocked on the inn door to summon her back to the conference.

Eryn spent the drive back to Rommel's home in silence, staring out the window, lost in anxious thought. Somehow, being back in the 'real' world sapped the confidence she'd felt when standing in the midst of the party that apparently constituted the afterlife in Valhalla. Between her own knowledge of how history was supposed to work, Mimr's ability to forecast possible futures, and the advice of Einherjar who had actually *lived* this period of history, or at least a nearly-identical version of it, Eryn should have come back to 1944 brimming with confidence. But imagining what she wanted to make happen was not quite the same as actually convincing a group of skeptical, hostile old men that it was a good idea.

Lewinsky greeted her as she exited the staff car. Sort of. He seemed agitated. But also not in a mood to discuss it with her.

"Eryn, I hope you were able to collect your thoughts. This is going rather badly, though no worse than I'd feared. While you were gone, I was able to meet briefly and privately with each of the generals. They aren't of one mind on most matters, but it is clear that they agree on one thing: they want control of the government. And that I cannot grant. The rest of this meeting will be short and unpleasant, I'm afraid. And then we will have to think on how to minimize the damage."

She nodded, but didn't reply.

He leaned close to her, and lowered his voice. "Eryn, if you have anything more you can offer, if there's any information you've been holding back... now is the time to tell me."

She understood, and nodded back. "I do have something. Can't really explain it, so you'll have to just trust me. But it should surprise them. A lot. Maybe that'll be the opening you need to get through to them."

He examined her carefully, eyes darting across her face, as if trying to parse her expression. Then he shrugged.

"Well, let's get this over with then, shall we? I hope that surprise will be enough. But be prepared: now that the preliminary arguments have been made, they'll make their formal demands as soon as we walk back into the room. Frankly, I don't think we have much time before Lady Rommel ends the discussion. The Field Marshal shouldn't have been allowed out of the hospital so soon, given his injuries. I wonder what Galland will say? Note that we haven't heard from him, yet. Yet he represents the Air Force, and they may not take kindly to our having arrested their leader, Goering."

As Lewinsky spoke, they retraced their earlier steps, back to the room where Rommel convalesced and the other generals waited to make their demands. She nodded periodically, not really listening. Every part of her was alive with fear, mind racing to keep up with the flood of sensation. She wanted to run, and never come back. She wanted to hide, and wait for it to be over. But she knew that she couldn't do either. Not until it was over.

The assembled officers were waiting just as before, lined up and gazing impassively. They gave the distinct impression of having just terminated an intense discussion among themselves, with all but Rommel and the young officer, who Eryn realized must be Galland, sharing the same intentionally blank expression. She had half a mind to call them out on it. But then decided that probably wouldn't end well.

General Guderian stepped forward as soon as they entered the room. Apparently he'd been the one delegated to make demands. His face was tense.

"Rather than descend into futile argument once more," he said, "my colleagues and I have decided to simply state our formal demands, so that we may terminate this meeting as quickly as possible and send you back to Beck and his interim government."

He continued without pause, as Eryn and Lewinsky stood two paces away and side by side, both keeping their expressions fixed and emotionless. As much as they could. Out of the corner of her eye Eryn could see her companion stiffen, and set his jaw, staring forward with an air of defiance.

"Our first demand: as Hindenberg and Ludendorff were forced to take command of the nation in the last war, so we must do the same. While Beck and his government are free to handle domestic matters not directly related to arms production or military operations, von Rundstedt and myself will oversee the actual conduct of the war. The only chance Germany has is for her generals to stand side by side and lead our soldiers to victory… or death."

Lewinsky shook his head. "Unacceptable." Eryn saw clear irritation spread across the faces of the assembled officers. Except Galland, whose face remained impassive, but whose eyes slid to one side to carefully watch the Field Marshals' response.

Guderian ignored Lewinsky. "Second, all armed forces, including the Waffen SS, will be placed at the disposal of Army High Command. Air Force and Navy assets will be subordinated to the need for defending our home soil and given a secondary role, behind the immediate requirement for arming and deploying as many soldiers as we are able to the front lines. All of German society must be mobilized and prepared for the bitter and final struggle ahead."

Lewinsky made no sign. Galland turned his head and fixed Guderian with a dark stare at the point where the general mentioned the Air Force. In a moment of delayed recognition, Eryn realized why: Galland was a fighter pilot, an ace several times over, who had been assigned to manage the desperate and doomed aerial struggle to prevent the Allies from bombing Germany whenever and wherever they chose.

But Guderian continued, unaware of or disregarding Galland. "Finally, the Beck government will take responsibility for negotiating a ceasefire on the western front under honorable terms. However, not one step back will be countenanced under any circumstances before a truce is concluded. Until the Allies know that we will bleed to the last to fight off their attacks, we must continue to hold the line on all fronts, and work to split their alliance. If they choose to offer a cease fire in place, so be it. But better if they will join us to fight the Soviets. Regardless, unlike 1918, we will hold out to the last. There will be no surrender. Our honor as soldiers precludes that option."

Demands made, Guderian now fell silent, and stepped back to his place in the line. He stood staring at Lewinsky, mustache seeming to bristle, as if both were silently ordering the younger officer to comply. Eryn stood by, and waited. Watching. Seconds passed, and she prepared. She knew she had to pick the right time, and make a decisive intervention. But when? Out of the corner of her eye, she saw Galland shift, probably to interject. She decided it was time. Deliberately and carefully, Eryn laughed.

The sound drew the attention of every man in the room. Even Rommel, who had been resting with his eyes closed as

Guderian gave his speech, opened his eyes and fixed her with a tired stare. She returned it, looking directly into his eyes. It was eerie, given that she'd just been speaking with Einher-jar-Rommel in Valhalla. Who had told her exactly how this Rommel would react. And he, she realized, was really the person she and Lewinsky had to convince.

Eryn spoke slowly and deliberately. "It is becoming clear to me, that none of you understand that you have already lost this war. Decisively. It is over. The only thing to be decided, is how many people have to die before you see reason and make peace."

She felt, more than saw, the obvious counter-arguments being formed in their minds. So she launched her pre-emptive strike.

"The irony is that you never had even a glimmer of a chance. Not in the long run. The Allies cracked Enigma, that brilliant machine you all assume leaves your communications perpetually secure, *years* ago. Every one of your operations, every attack you make, the Allies know about in advance. Hell, they even share some of their information with the Soviets! All radio communications, to your Army, Navy, or Air Force units, are intercepted and decoded in hours. Even your greatest victory, over France in 1940, was predicted in advance. You only averted total disaster there because the Allied leadership was too stupid to accept their intelligence report."

She shook her head, and laughed again, goading them deliberately. "Your attempt to hold the Allies in their beachhead in France is futile, because the Allies already know where you have deployed your forces, and they know when you give them orders and, in short order, what those orders are. As we speak, they are preparing a truly *massive* bombardment of your best forces in France, which will allow the Americans to break through your lines west of Falaise and roll up your entire defensive position around Caen. The attack has already been ordered, and your units are simply waiting to be obliterated. And when you launch your counterattack with the last of your reserves, they will be waiting for them. Within a week from now, your forces in the west will be utterly defeated, their remnants running back to Germany as quickly as they can move."

"This, in addition to forecasting techniques we've developed, is how I and my employer know so much about your operations. We have friends in both the American and British governments, who have passed on valuable information on to us. Do you know why you, Field Marshal Rommel, were never able to win in Africa, despite all your brilliant victories in the desert? All that trouble keeping your army supplied? Yeah, about that: Every time a supply convoy tried to sneak across the Mediterranean from Italy, the Allies were waiting. Because they knew in advance. Same goes for the submarine war in the Atlantic. As brilliant as your tactics might have been, as deadly as a wolfpack can be to a convoy, every time one of the U-boats radios home, the Allies know where it is. And even if they can't attack it, they simply divert their ships. Your sailors don't have a chance."

She opened her mouth to continue, then closed it. It was like a shadow had passed over the generals. Their eyes began to dart side to side, and almost instinctively their heads turned towards one another, inscrutable feelings transmitting between them as can only happen when a group of professionals, sharing the same language and worldview, find that everything they thought they knew was, in fact, mistaken.

Galland broke out in peals of laughter. The Army generals turned towards him and glared. He shook his head, a wry expression contorting his proud face.

"Well, that solves that debate, doesn't it! For years now

some of us in the Air Force have argued that the Allies always seem to know where we are weak or strong. We've tried to verify that Enigma was secure, even consulted the Navy to explore joint testing. Admiral Donitz assured us time and again that there is no connection between the U-boat war falling apart and our communications, only that the Allies have been steadily improving their anti-submarine warfare technology and techniques. But it appears that Occam's razor holds true. The simplest explanation truly is the best, at least where our fortunes are concerned: our codes are broken. We've been an open book to them this entire war. Hah! One can only laugh at the magnitude of our blunder!"

Manstein and Rundstedt looked at one another, but remained silent. Eryn could feel Guderian's eyes on her, roving across her face, as if looking for a sign that she was lying. He let out a sound, almost a growl, and shook his head. She spoke again, cutting him off almost certain what he was about to say.

"Yes, general, I know: passing on this information risks the lives of my own countrymen. Which to you must seem treasonous. But I don't have any choice. The path you generals would have the Beck government follow, will lead only to your complete and total destruction. You keep hoping that the Western Allies will end their war, and let you turn to fight the Soviets, but it is false hope. They *know* that they have Germany beaten, the question is simply how long the fighting will go on before they throw enough bodies at you to break down all resistance. And they *will* continue to fight you, sacrificing the lives of thousands of people on both sides. Because they are convinced victory is inevitable. And, frankly, because they fight with absolute certainty that they *should* win: Germany has committed atrocities that defy the imagination. *You* started this war, and *they* are committed to finishing it."

Eryn took a deep breath, and looked from one face to another. "You have one, and only one chance. Pull back on both fronts. Disengage. Build a line you can actually defend along the Meuse and Vistula. *Then* wait them out. While preserving as much of your manpower as you possibly can. You start saving Germany by saving your own soldiers. Pull back now, wrong-foot the coming offensive in the West, and prepare to hold on the Vistula in the east and Meuse in the west. Or lose your people, and watch the Allies annihilate Germany by Christmas."

Rundstedt closed his eyes, and took his own deep breath. Then fixed Eryn with a cold stare. She wondered if he practiced that look in the mirror. It certainly seemed to take advantage of the scar to add an element of menace to his visage.

"A very interesting story. Very interesting, indeed. Either someone has coached you exceptionally well, or you are the most compelling liar I have ever met. Such a breach of security certainly explains a few matters, however, that must I have to admit. So, the case you lay before us is thus: our enemies know of all our intentions and plans in advance. Our already difficult defense of Normandy is doomed. To save our best divisions, we must retreat. And hope that we can construct a better defensive line somewhere along the course of the Meuse, when they run out of supplies. And in the east, the same strategy applies."

He smiled. Or seemed to. It might have been a grimace. "A reasonable plan, and if I may be frank, one that has been suggested by the General Staff before today. Not that Hitler was willing to listen. In any event, that *would* represent a superior defensive position to the one we occupy now, over-extended as we are in both the west and east. But the essential problems with this plan, that precluded us from accepting it long before now, remain. If we give up any territory to the Allied advance, we risk an ordered withdrawal turning into a disordered rout. Once the Allies break out of their Normandy bridgehead, our defensive problems will multiply dramatically. With room to maneuver, they can attack our retreating forces without pause. And if the Allies are also, as you say, able to discern our intentions whenever orders are transmitted by radio, then any attempt to establish a defense will be undermined wherever we attempt to make a stand. Under these circumstances, how then is withdrawal a superior option?"

Rommel took a deep, shuddering breath, and all eyes turned towards him. It was clearly difficult to speak, and the words came slowly.

"Another problem: withdrawal exposes our soldiers to Allied air power whenever they move. I stand, so to speak, as evidence of the danger posed by their fighter-bombers."

Manstein grunted. "True, but even the Allies cannot bomb troop formations accurately by night. No one can. The Soviets send out those women, the Night Witches, to harass our forces after nightfall. Frustrating effect on morale, but casualties remain low. Moving by night, hiding in ambush by day, experience in the east has shown that ordered withdrawal is possible under adverse conditions. Given discipline. And flexibility in implementing defensive operations and local counterattacks."

"But how could we conduct such a withdrawal without exposing our forces to being surrounded, cut off, and destroyed piecemeal?" Objected Rundstedt.

Manstein considered this for a moment. "If our dear Canadian liaison here spoke truthfully before, then the Allies' advance will be severely impacted by logistics as they proceed through France. They have conducted an extensive bombing campaign against the local infrastructure, which harms us now, but will also serve to slow their advance. And if we extract our armored forces from the fighting around Caen now, we can restore a mobile reserve capable of threatening any part of their advance that moves too quickly."

"The logistics problem solves itself," objected Guderian, "soon after they break out of Normandy, once they seize the Channel ports."

This kind of detail, Eryn was prepared for, thanks to long hours with Mimr.

"You are correct," she argued, "in thinking that logistics are the crucial factor for the Allies. As I told you before, we have been able to get hold of their plans for liberating France, and logistics constraints play a vital role. The Americans plan to establish a new field army, under George Patton, that will outflank your forces and charge into Paris. After that, they plan to send his army into Lorraine and Omar Bradley's into southern Belgium, while Montgomery's forces clear the Channel ports and attack towards the lower Rhine. They're going to have to get very creative about how they supply three armies at once."

Rundstedt nodded thoughtfully. "A broad axis of advance will certainly strain their supplies. But I suspect that they will keep the bulk of their forces close to the Allied air bases in England, and take the easiest route to Berlin, passing through Belgium and crossing the lower Rhine near the border with Holland. Which is partly why we are defending France by holding the Normandy bridgehead in the first place. Our position will only become more difficult as we have to hold a longer line, all the way from Switzerland to the North Sea, and in the north any defense will be subjected to constant attack from the air. And once the Allies have swept across northern France, then our forces in the rest of the country will be in danger of being cut off and encircled."

Eryn couldn't prevent a grim smile from reaching her lips. "Actually, the Americans and French are planning to hurry that up by preparing another landing in France, this time on the southern coast. As Patton, Bradley, and Montgomery push east, another army will strike north to protect Patton's southern flank. You see, then, that even if you try to hold on in Normandy, they'll find a way to attack you from behind. A new line, closer to Germany, is your best chance."

Another bout of silence. Manstein and Rundstedt looked at one another. Guderian seemed to look past Eryn and Lewinsky. Rommel's eyes were shut, and Galland stared at the ceiling. The mood in the room seemed to have shifted, like a tectonic plate after a major earthquake. It was as if the German officers had finally realized, or perhaps had at last consciously accepted, the true depth of their predicament. How impossible the task of defending the racist proto-empire that Hitler had tried to construct out of the corpse of old Europe. Their ability to shape events declined with every passing day. Not a happy position for men used to commanding entire armies.

Guderian broke the long silence. His voice betrayed no emotion. Eryn felt a flash of some feeling she didn't entirely understand. It could have been awe, it could have been admiration. His was the tone of a person who, convinced of an unalterable future, nevertheless decides it doesn't matter. The time had come to adapt to a new reality, and he was ready to make the required leap.

"So, the basic limit on the Allies' advance to our borders will be logistical in nature. We can't hope to hold them back if they have enough available forces to strike at us on every front simultaneously. Well, that at least makes the fundamental question quite simple: where can we strike them back, when it will harm them the most? If their willingness to bear the cost of a winter of bloody warfare is their only limit, after fuel, then we must find a time and place to turn about and maul their onrushing forces. At least thin their numbers a bit, before we have to defend Germany proper."

All eyes turned on Guderian. But it was Manstein who

spoke next.

"Given that, madame whose full name I have not yet learned, you are telling us that the Allies plan a broad offensive with several distinct axis of advance, this implies that their ability to land supplies on the continent and move them to the front lines will determine the culminating point of their campaign. At a certain point even their most powerful formations will come to a halt for want of fuel. *If* we can put ourselves in a position to launch a sufficiently powerful counterattack at the *precise* moment they begin to experience severe supply shortages, we may be able to isolate and destroy at least one of their armies. Cut off at least one of their spearheads. And perhaps, put them in a mood for peace talks."

"A back-hand stroke, I think you once called it, talking about your counter-offensives in 1942 and 1943." added Eryn.

Manstein nodded, a smirk breaking through his Field Marshal's haughty expression, making him appear almost smug. Her flattery had struck home at exactly the right moment. She was glad that she'd once had a quick read through of his published memoirs. Self-serving in many places, and she could tell that the man was convinced of his own brilliance. Usually a sort willing to accept a bit of ego-soothing.

Galland nodded towards Eryn. "So, madame agent, if we are able to inflict such a defeat on the Americans and British, will that be enough to force them to reconsider their current policy with respect to demanding Germany's unconditional surrender?"

Guderian grunted. "The Americans are holding one of their elections this November. I doubt they have the stomach for serious casualties. Depending on how quickly they can advance in the face of a fighting withdrawal, I'd estimate it will take them no longer than a month to reach the Seine and Paris, two to reach the Meuse. Delivering a bloody defeat a month before the election could undermine Roosevelt's chances, could it not?"

Eryn knew she was expected to comment, though she didn't know what to say. She was Canadian, not American, and paid little attention to American politics before or after the Second World War. She had remembered that it was an election year, and asked Mimr if that had any significance. He simply stated it was highly unlikely that Roosevelt would leave office before his death, which in most Threads occurred sometime in 1945.

"It could," she replied, "but I wouldn't count on that: the American leadership can usually control the majority of the population, just like the British and the Soviets. But it is true that the Allies can't accept too many casualties, and that scandals can do strange things to politicians at the polls. Most of the British Empire's manpower reserves are running as low as yours. America and Canada are exceptions, but Canada prefers to send only volunteers abroad, and the Americans are limited by the number of soldiers they can keep supplied across the oceans. And they also have Japan to worry about. So *if* you can inflict sufficient casualties, that will impact their strategic planning at the very least."

Eryn was painfully aware of the irony of her situation. Essentially, she was telling the Germans to adopt a strategy that risked the lives of thousands of Allied soldiers, who were just following their orders. And, were the honest-to-gosh *good* guys in the war. Of course, in the history she knew the war was scheduled to go on until May 1945, by which point thousands of them would be killed defeating the Nazis' desperate final defense. So in a sense, if there was any hope at all of ending the fighting sooner rather than later, there was at least *some* hope of doing less harm than good. On average. Maybe. But it seemed awfully macabre, in that moment, to be talking about exchanging the lives of soldiers in the present for the chance of avoiding losing even more in the future.

The Generals were starting to carry on the conversation without consulting either Eryn or Lewinsky, who had spent most of this part of the conversation with a strained expression on his face. She had the distinct feeling that he was struggling to pretend that nothing she had said was a surprise to him. She felt slightly ashamed, but didn't know how else she could have handled the situation. When you get instructions from someone who to you is long-dead, but is now hanging around with the Norse gods in Valhalla, but who you are *also* talking to after having been transported the better part of a century into a similar reality's version of your own past...

"The question becomes," Manstein was saying, as she pulled back from this train of thought, "As there is little hope of establishing an effective defensive line at the Seine, when Patton reaches the Meuse in two months, what reserves will we have available then for our counter-stroke?"

Guderian replied, gesticulating as if moving pieces on an invisible map. "Thanks to Speer's efforts, armored vehicle production continues to increase, despite the Allied bombing raids, although getting new equipment to the front is difficult now that they have destroyed so much of the rail infrastructure. But between July's production, which is currently still mostly delayed in transit, August's, and whatever can be pushed to the front in early September, we should be able to build up sufficient forces to organize into three armored corps. And without that madman's interference at every point, I can push through a reorganization to increase the combat power of the average division. That will help concentrate more armor at the point of attack than the Americans have seen in the war to date. We'll see how they respond to the shock!"

"What can be salvaged from the current front lines, as-suming we accept that there is no other option but retreat?" Rundstedt asked Manstein.

Manstein considered that for a moment. "Little will make it through the retreat intact. We saw this time and again on the eastern front: equipment fails, and must be left behind. But our soldiers can be saved. Perhaps only a quarter of their equipment will return, most of it damaged. But experienced soldiers are priceless. Half to three quarters will survive an orderly retreat. We will have to match them with fresh young recruits and a fair few invalids to fill out the forma-tions, but there should be enough experienced soldiers to preserve balance."

Rundstedt turned to Guderian. "And what of the Waffen SS units? They constitute half of our forces in the west, if not more. Will they follow along with the retreat? Or is there a way we can get hold of their remaining manpower?"

Guderian smiled, baring his teeth. "Regular Army forma-tions are perpetually under-strength. Folding the SS units into them will be trivial, as their training is similar and they are used to fighting together. At least the SS troops that speak German, that is. The foreign recruits are more difficult to deal with. But as for the German nationals, we will simply break up the Waffen SS by company, eliminate the separate designation and command structure, and strengthen exist-ing Army units in terms of manpower and equipment. Polit-ics have a way of disappearing in the midst of battle."

Rundstedt nodded. "Speaking of the reliability of parallel formations, General Galland, what support can the Air Force offer to this effort? I must admit to wondering what your branch's perception of the Beck government is. I heard that Goering was arrested, but how does the rest of your officer corps view the coup?"

Galland laughed. "Goering was an idiot, and we all knew

it. Between his drug-addled mania and Hitler's ridiculous meddling in technical matters, it is a miracle the Air Force continues to exist at all. In point of fact, we barely do. Aside from close air support in the east and futile attempts to intercept the American and British bombers at home, we are a spent force."

"This would explain your total failure to protect our citizens from the bombing." said Manstein.

Galland fixed Manstein with a brutal stare. "The Allies have reduced our access to fuel by an order of magnitude, and much of what fuel we have goes to the damned V weapon projects. My pilots receive a third of the training they require to become proficient. Our aircraft are falling behind the Americans and British in terms of their quality, *except* the jet force, which Hitler in his *infinite* wisdom decided had to be used for bombing, and not destroying enemy bombers! If you utterly mismanage a fighting force, if you hamstring every effort at reform, then *this* is the inevitable result!"

"*Gentlemen.*" Unnoticed, Lady Rommel had walked into the room, and now stood by her husband's bedside, gently stroking his hand. "My husband has something to say."

They all deferred to him without hesitation. Rommel's eyes were now open, and Eryn thought she could see the faintest flicker of something in them. Hope? Or was that just wishful thinking on her part? If nothing else, this was the point where Lewinsky had thought they'd be unceremoniously sent away. But by some miracle, these old men were actually listening. They were actually winning their case!

Regardless, his voice remained quiet. But clear, and firm. "Like General Galland, I have personally experienced the full fury of Allied air power. How to counter them, I hope we can discuss in the future. But lack of fuel, that is crucial. How can we hope to launch any effective counter-stroke when we cannot supply our armored forces with enough fuel?"

"If only we were built like the Russians, who are simply inhuman in their ability to survive without supplies." said Manstein, shaking his head slowly.

Eryn rolled her eyes, and opened her mouth to speak, but Lewinsky suddenly jumped back in the debate, cutting her off.

"Field Marshal, I would like to politely suggest that you reconsider that view of Russians. I have been behind Soviet lines many times, and I can assure you that they experience supply difficulties exactly as we do. As tough as the Russian soldier certainly is when exposed to the elements, it is the thousands of trucks that constantly bring him food and ammunition that fuel his advance on Berlin. We underestimate their capabilities at our own peril."

Manstein looked ready to argue the point, but Rundstedt held up his hand.

Before he could speak, Lewinsky cut him off too. "Gentlemen, while I am happy that you are beginning to see the way to a new strategy, I feel compelled to make something absolutely clear, here in this moment, before we can once again become distracted by operational matters: the demands you presented at the start of this conversation are unacceptable. Military officers do not have the right to question the orders given to them by the state, and whatever you might think about Operation Valkyrie, it has given us a chance to change Germany's future. And we *will* take it. We killed Hitler. We are in charge."

Rundstedt, Manstein, and Guderian all fixed Lewinsky with a cold stare. He stared straight back at them. Eryn knew what was coming next. This much, they had worked out together before coming to Ulm. This part, he had to do himself as a representative of the new government. She just hoped that she'd done enough that the generals would give the correct answer.

Lewinsky cleared his throat, and continued. "The Beck government will restore civilian rule as quickly as possible. All political prisoners will be immediately released, and all vestiges of the Nazi regime will be destroyed. We are and will remain the legitimate government of Germany, and will not tolerate any attempt by any other force to seize control. What we offer you, and the military at large, is total control over the conduct of *military* operations. Albert Speer will remain in charge of the war economy, and General Guderian will be placed in charge of the reserve army and rebuilding our forces in order to defend Germany's borders. Field Marshal Manstein, we intend to appoint you as commander of all forces in the east, Field Marshal Rundstedt, we intend to appoint you as overall commander of all forces in the west and south, until Field Marshal Rommel is well enough to take over command of the western defense, at which point we will appoint you head of the military in its entirety. We will subordinate the Navy and Air Force to Army control, with the exception of the fighter force, which will be placed under General Galland's command, and expected to develop an effective defense against Allied bombing, whatever the cost, however that may be accomplished."

Lewinsky paused, allowing them a moment to take in the details of the offer. It wasn't, in point of fact, dramatically different from the generals demands, save for the whole dictatorship business. Mimr had made it clear that wouldn't work, and fortunately for Eryn the Beck government wasn't keen on handing over the power they'd worked so hard to seize. So coming into the meeting, they had agreed that this would be their counter-offer to whatever demands the generals had come up with. It gave them almost everything they wanted, except absolute power. That was the price to be paid for winning their allegiance.

Eryn wasn't sure when it happened, but suddenly she realized that the entire gambit had worked. The generals looked at one another, and in total silence held the necessary conversation. Lewinsky went for the killing blow.

"The *truth* that you must all recognize, here and now, is that Germany stands on the brink of total annihilation. The plan you have worked through in this meeting is the same strategy the Beck government has already privately decided will be necessary in order to end this war short of meeting the Allies demand for unconditional surrender. In the west, and the east, we will withdraw to reasonable defensive lines. We will tell the Allies that our intent is to negotiate a cease-fire on all fronts, and offer them whatever evidence we can that the German government seeks an end to this disastrous war. And if they continue to press us, if they refuse to negotiate, then we will show them what Germany is capable of when pushed beyond the brink of despair."

They stared at Lewinsky for a long time. He stared back. And then, they agreed.

OVER EASTERN IDAHO

This flight, Patrick paid attention to Chavez' briefing. At least, as much as he could. Like his friends, he was exhausted. He'd lost track of all the hours of running, hiding, shooting, and now the idea of doing any of those things ever again was enough to induce a wave of nausea. But there they were, crammed into the claustrophobia-inducing interior of an attack helicopter, clutching their newly-issued assault rifles, planning to do pretty much all of those things.

Chavez' voice droned on in his headset, but the longer the flight went on, the less he was able to tamp down his own anxiety and listen to the details. As if in a fog, he followed the changes in his visor's digital map as she briefed them on their next task, the blue icons denoting their own helicopter and its companion so close that they overlapped on the display.

After tucking between two barren peaks at the western edge of the Rocky Mountains, the helicopters were clinging to the treetops as they descended into the Snake River Valley. He gathered that they were hoping to avoid Deseret radar surveillance by making it difficult for an operator to distinguish their signal from all the electronic noise caused by radar's emissions bouncing off the trees and rocks below them. Two other icons moved in lazy figure-eight patterns about thirty kilometers to their north, representing a pair of what Chavez called 'Foxcat' fighter jets, tasked with providing an added layer of protection against any Deseret attempt to intercept.

Assuming they made it to their objective in one piece, a town labeled 'Rexburg' on the HUD, they were planning to link up with a scout team hiding nearby, and take a 'Stryker' armored vehicle into one of Rexburg's suburbs. There the asset 'Lehi' was supposed to be waiting to be evacuated, though there was a small matter of dealing with his guards to work through.

Military affairs weren't totally alien to Patrick's experience, as his spouse Peter wasn't the type of guy to keep life and work too separate. But the life of a Hornet pilot was a world apart from the dirt-hugging style of fighting he was being trained to do. What he knew of military operations through Peter's work was colored by a pilot's practical concerns over fuel, weather, and how to not collide with other aircraft in the middle of a mission. That, and the mountain of administrative paperwork even fighter pilots were forced to complete.

Timur and Kim both, Patrick realized, were interacting with Chavez far more than they had on their last flight. To the point that he started to feel left out. Or, at least, too obvious in his non-participation.

"Hey Chavez," he asked, during a break in the conversation, trying to appear as nonchalant as he could, "what's with this 'Foxcat' label on the map display? Is that their callsign, or... ?"

She paused for a moment before replying. "Aircraft type. That flight actually uses the callsign Reaper. You always notice the aircraft, don't you? But you've never heard of the Foxcat?"

He grimaced behind his mask. He'd forgotten that in twenty-plus years, air forces had certainly evolved to use totally different aircraft than the ones he was used to. Although, he suddenly remembered, the 'Mjolnir' aircraft that had shown up during the attack on Southern Butte were almost exactly like an old American jet. 'Thunderbolt,' or 'Warthog,' was what the version he knew had been called. Then he remembered the other jets, that had brought the nuclear bombs to the fight. He was pretty sure they had been referred to as 'Flankers' and they had looked almost exactly like an aircraft Peter had talked about, actually trained to fight, and that he referred to by the exact same name. Curiosity beat out his desire not to give away how ignorant he was of life in the 2040's.

"No, I haven't." he said. "Which actually surprises me less than the fact you guys seem to use a lot of jets that are, well… they're kind of old designs, aren't they? I kind of feel like its 2011 again."

She laughed. Over the helicopter's intercom, he heard more laughter. Apparently the helicopter's crew was listening in on the conversation.

"Yeah," she replied, "and this tin can we're flying in is an old design too. Soviet in origin, dates back to the eighties. NATO designated the design the 'Havoc.' So what? Why fix what works?"

He cocked his head to one side. "I guess I just figured that with all the other high-tech stuff you use, you'd have a bunch of stealth jets or killer drones or something."

Laughter on the intercom. Chavez shook her head, and he could swear he could see her grin, despite her obscuring headgear.

"Yeah, you'd think that from the web adverts, wouldn't you! But do you have any idea how pointlessly expensive it is to operate stealth aircraft? At least, ones capable of surviving after some jagoff using a low-frequency radar vectors a couple non-stealthy interceptors into the area and plays sensor fusion for a couple minutes. Even China and the Pacific Pact only fly a few stealth jets, mostly for specialty situations. And killer drones, like, you mean autonomous robots? Yeah, been there, tried that. Like I told you before: They *never* work as well as they're supposed to. Targeting is just too complex and too human a thing for a robot to pull off without committing too many major errors. And drones, they require bandwidth to operate remotely, and that degrades fast in any kind of complex electromagnetic environment. Which is pretty much all combat zones, these days. Hell, even our bugsuits can transmit electronic static if we activate the right mode. Drones be proper screwed in a *real* fight."

A half-familiar voice broke in. "*Unless you're plinking poor bastards who can't fight back, like we used to do back in the I-raq.*"

"Jeezus Tania, don't remind me of the bad old days! 'Course, you were in Apaches back in the 'noughts, weren't you? Getting in on a bit of that Collateral Murder action? I *thought* I recognized something familiar in you peoples' kill-em-all attitude."

"*You people* my arse, Chavez! But yup, flung Hellfires and spitting chain guns, I was into all that kind of action long before it got popular in Syria and beyond. Trendsetters, we were!"

"Sheee-ite, girl, don't remind me. Though you've been on the rejuvies longer than me, if you were fighting all the way back in 2003."

"*2007. And hey, who you callin' old? Miss I've-been-fighting-since-I-was-eighteen-and-that-was-thirty-years-ago.*"

"*Dude*! Low blow! These punks didn't need to know that I'm pushing fifty!"

Three helmeted heads turned towards one another. As well as they could, in the cramped quarters.

Chavez shook her head slowly. "Yeah, it's true. One of the perks of the Missoula Regiment, and the Air Wing, we let the flying types in on it too: great benefits package. Including rejuvenation treatments. Guaranteed to keep you young and spry until you hit sixty, and prevents the slow slide to senescence until the mid eighties at the earliest. Normally you gotta be a millionaire to afford the stuff on the private market. One of the perks of joining up for you all to look forward to!"

"Not that most of you ground-pounders live long enough to enjoy your sixties."

"Don't make me crawl up there and stab you in that smart mough of yours!" Chavez threatened, provoking another round of laughter over the intercom, followed by counter-threats. Patrick got the sense that it was an old inside joke of some kind. Bothered a bit by that, but more by the fact that she'd wandered off-topic again, he waited until they had almost gone silent, and interrupted."

"So, Chavez, about that Foxcat: what *is* a Foxcat?"

Chavez laughed. "Take an old Grumman Tomcat, mate it with a Mikoyan-Gurevich Foxhound, then give the misbegotten troll-child to the Japanese to make it so technologically awesome that stealth aircraft run the moment they even *think* one is around. Best. Interceptor. *Ever.* Biggest fighter jet in the world, can't maneuver for spit, but *can* out-accelerate and outrun anything that makes it through the dozen missiles each one carries. Mitsubishi-Boeing hit the gold mine with this one. We put six of them together in Reaper flight, and so far they've shot down more than thirty Deseret and Texan aircraft for *zero* losses over the past four years. That includes, I'll have you know, eleven of those oh-so-*stealthy* F-35s."

"Jeez, how many aircraft do you people have?" Patrick asked.

"Not too many. The Missoula Air Wing is comprised of two combat squadrons, each of eighteen or so aircraft. The fighter squadron has three flights, each with six aircraft. Reaper, flying the Foxcat, Black, flying the Flanker, Storm, flying the Typhoon."

"Black? Flanker? What's with the rugby theme?" asked Kim.

"Huh?" Chavez asked, sounding confused for a moment. "Nothing, actually. At least, not officially. The Sukhoi-Shenyang-Hindustan conglomerate officially adopted the old NATO code for the Soviet-era design that spawned the aircraft family. 'Flanker.' Just a marketing maneuver, the name wasn't originally meaningful, just a consistent and methodological way of naming new aircraft spotted by intelligence, kind of like how hurricanes get named. The lead pilot of Black flight *is* big into rugby though, now that you mention it. Which *does* explain the callsign; guess I never really thought about it that much. Pilot humor is strange, man."

"*Hey!*" came Tania's voice over the intercom. The helicopter suddenly lurched up, and then back down again. Patrick's stomach leaped to his throat, then sunk back down again. He fought back a sudden wave of nausea.

"Okay, okay, sorry!" Chavez cried. "Pilots are so damned sensitive... That's just a human *universal* Tania, not an insult! You gotta be sensitive to do the damn job!"

"*SO sorry. But shenanigans aside, we'll be setting down behind the Kingston LP in sixty. Thanks for flying the friendly skies. I'm sending Ravi to pick you jerks up on the return trip, by the way. I'm sick of y'all now.*"

Chavez laughed and swore at the pilot, then settled herself in her seat as the helicopter suddenly slowed, paused in midair, and settled to the ground. When the whine of the engines began to recede, she removed her harness, opened the hatch, and exited into the night.

Patrick and his friends followed, filing out of the belly of the helicopter, toting their bulky weapons along with them.

They ducked instinctively as they jogged after Chavez, and Patrick heard the helicopter's engines accelerate once again, and sensed more than actually felt the aircraft lurch back into the sky.

"Hey Chavez," Patrick asked, "I thought we were going to someplace called Rexburg. Why did Tania just say we were going to Kingston? I don't see that on the map."

She waved a hand vaguely in his direction. "Oh, that was just radio shorthand. They are used to communicating over radio, so there's always a technical risk of the bad guys catching the transmission. Our system breaks radio transmissions up over a bunch of different frequencies *and* encodes each bit independently, but sometimes the encoding software breaks and has to reboot. Just in case the Deserets have caught an open transmission, the flying types use a different set of location names than we do. Not usually too hard to figure out, though, they just port from one linguistic frame of reference to another. Rex is latin for King, burg is a germanic stem meaning town—you get the idea."

The helicopter had set them down behind a low hill to the east of Rexburg, and the stars overhead twinkled brightly as they walked swiftly down a narrow trail winding through the rock and sage, heading for a dark mass of rock and earth a few hundred meters in front of them. Or so it seemed, looking through their HUD-enhanced visual display. Apparently, their headgear could discern the level of ambient light in the environment, and automatically amplified it to aid visibility. The world through their visors took on a greenish tint. Which, Patrick realized, was also how Chavez knew where to go. Every few meters a small object, like a stream-smoothed rock, glinted an extra shade of sickly green, together marking a normally-invisible path to the listening post nestled on the reverse slope of a sage-infested hill.

"Chavez," Kim asked, "has anyone told you that you speak

awfully well for someone who has apparently spent their whole life fighting in wars?"

She grunted. Then waved vaguely at Kim. "Soon you're all gonna realize that war is like, ninety-percent boredom. Once you're used to the rhythms, at least. When I get bored, I read. Always have. Also, for kicks, I've taken university courses through some of the best frickin' institutions on the planet. Oxbridge. Berkeley-Stanford. Shanghai-Munich. Jawaharlal Nehru. Nice thing about the internet age: any course you want, any degree that interests you, undergraduate or graduate: available somewhere online. I've done four or five degrees that way, over the years. I keep thinking about doing another, except that our operations up here are getting less boring by the minute."

"*Lordy*," Timur gasped, "Why on Earth are you still here? There has *got* to be a better line of work than this."

"Why on Earth are *you* here, Timur?" she laughed. "Re-thinking your choice to sign up? It isn't like anyone forced you to come out to Yellowstone. We don't play games with the recruiting process. Last thing we need is people here who want to be somewhere else."

Patrick smiled and rolled his eyes, knowing that she couldn't see him. He imagined that both Timur and Kim had just done the same thing. If she only knew!

They arrived at the listening post so suddenly that Patrick raised his weapon in fearful surprise. They had walked around a bend, and then two Missoula Regiment personnel were standing there, fully encased in carapace and headgear. Full battle rattle. At the same time as he saw them, he also saw the turret of what looked like a steel monster turn towards him, leveling two different kinds of rather large guns what felt like directly at his face.

"Hey, Chavez! You here to borrow a Stryker?"

She nodded at whichever of the two had spoken. Patrick

wasn't sure which had, but was relieved to see the turret on the Stryker swivel, and stop pointing its guns at him.

"Got the word an hour ago that you were on your way. Glad to see you. Nothing to report. Usual traffic going in and out of town. Looks clear of nasty folks. Except whatever guard Lehi has with him."

Patrick couldn't tell which soldier was saying what. Each of the two had decorated the headgear's face mask. One had traced the likeness of a monster's maw, outlined in an ink or some other material that seemed to shine in Patrick's light-augmenting visor. The other's was decorated like the grin ning face of an evil clown. Which was unsettling, and probably the point.

"Right on." Chavez replied. "We'll need one of your babies, and cover from the other in case this all goes south."

"Yup." One of them replied. "You guys take one set up for Rista. Engineers had the time to build out the network here, so we'll be able to see your feed, and anybody tries to come up on you when you're in the suburb, they'll catch a couple missiles. Also got a grid-square-eraser on call if things go real hinky."

Chavez grunted. "How many civvies live on that grid square, I wonder?"

Once they slipped into jargon, Patrick stopped paying attention again. But the soldier and Chavez were done. She waved them towards one of the two Strykers, that Patrick now saw were almost entirely encased in some sort of netting that almost perfectly reflected the texture and color of the landscape around them. He wondered whether they could have hidden so effectively in terrain that wasn't ugly, dead, and full of brush.

The interior of the vehicle Chavez led them into was thankfully less cramped than the truck they'd been jammed into on the way to the assault on Southern Butte. But not by much. He tucked himself into one of the tilted seats, and plugged into the vehicle's systems. His HUD indicated he was patched in, and let him know when his friends joined the crew as well.

Chavez showed them all how to attach the safety harnesses that would bind them their seats, then pounded the side of the vehicle with her fist.

"All clear, close up!"

"Affirmative." Came a voice through the vehicle's intercom, and with a dull whir the ramp that had allowed the four of them access to the Stryker's interior lifted from the ground, and slowly sealed them inside. Patrick had the distinct feeling of being swallowed by a monster, though he dully realized that they'd come in the wrong end for that. He shook his head, and tried to relax in his seat, entertaining himself by playing with the map on his HUD.

The vehicle lurched in one direction, then another, as the driver pulled it from the hide and out into the open countryside on the other side of the hill. Another dull whirring filtered through the headset, and looking into a dull mirror, really more a patch of half-polished metal, he saw that in the center of the vehicle, beyond the four seats in the back that constituted the passenger cabin, a cylinder was rotating and shifting, as if a heavy thing were twisting and settling into it. To either side he could barely make out the existence of a narrow passage leading to a different compartment on the other side of the cylinder. Probably where the crew was seated, he thought. A thought confirmed a moment later by movement, that looked to be from a pair of drivers seated in the front compartment, flipping toggle switches and tapping digital displays.

"Alright," came a different voice over the intercom. "We're periscope down for the drive. I'll send some bandwidth you folks' way so you can keep a lookout while we drive. Just keep the thermal camera use to a minimum, if you'll be so kind. Trying to preserve the batteries. Not due for another engineer visit for a day."

"That you, up there, Oba?" Chavez asked.

"Yup, me and Khuong. How you been, Sandra?"

"Oh, the usual. Shooting flying running training. Lotsa verbs. You?"

"Seen better days. The Deserets are fuggin' *extra* trigger happy since they lost their firebase on SoBu. Patrols all over the place, and everybody is lugging around a mortar or two for added fire support. Had to evac our main O-P yesterday— they're playing recon by fire so much poor Khuong got plastered by shrapnel twice in one day."

"Gawd, the last thing he needs is *more* brain damage"

"Hey!" A voice shouted.

Patrick tuned out their banter as their armored vehicle struck a road leading towards the town of Rexburg, Idaho. He couldn't help but feel that they were violating most of the rules of combat Chavez had spent the past few days drilling into them. The Stryker was on its own, wheels kicking up a cloud of dust as it traversed the dusty track leading from the hills into the town. Patrick pulled the external camera feed into his headset display, panning it across the dim, dingy landscape. Between the dust and green tint the vehicle's optics produced as they magnified the twilight to give the world a bit of definition, there wasn't much to see.

The vehicle was moving fast, which worked for him. Idaho seemed to transition between the rugged mountains and rocky foothills and the flat valley beyond in a ridiculously short amount of time. It didn't seem possible that they could avoid being noticed on their way in, which worried him. What was Chavez leading them into?

His growing sense of vulnerability was only magnified

as the armored vehicle wheeled itself onto an asphalt road right on the edge of Rexburg. Soon houses and other small buildings were flashing by, blurry shapes in the green twilight. For the barest moment, he almost felt a sense of something approaching normalcy. Letting his eyes go out of focus, pretending for an instant that he was just in the back of someone's van, road-tripping it through the American badlands, he could almost believe, for a brief instant, that he was actually somewhere entirely different.

The Stryker suddenly slowed, made a hard turn to the right, accelerated for a minute, and then braked to a stop. Patrick was shaken from his pleasant delusion by his helmet thunking hard against the side of the armored vehicle. A whirring sound filtered through his headgear, and visor imagery shifted from the vehicle's camera back to his helmet's.

With a wave of her hand and a mild curse that passed for a word of thanks to the crew, Chavez led Patrick and his friends out of the vehicle, then crouched down next to it, motioning for them to do the same.

"Alright guys," she said, her voice quiet but clear in his ears, the trick of this op is to plausibly look like we're just another Deseret patrol. Rexburg is on the outer edge of their security zone, so they mostly send recon patrols to remind the locals who is in charge."

Timur snorted. "Really? So nobody is going to notice that we came charging out of the hills in a light tank on wheels, and are walking around dressed like extras from a bad Starship Troopers remake?"

She shook her head. Patrick was surprised that she didn't laugh. "Civilians don't know the difference. To them, we're just four people with big guns walking through their neighborhood. Best response to that is to close the blinds and huddle the family in the back of the house, just in case somebody decides to ambush someone else. Or emigrate the hell out of a warzone, but anyone still living out here probably doesn't have much choice in the matter. This part of Idaho ain't exactly primo real estate these days."

"Anyway," Chavez continued, "our target is at the end of a street about a block down the road. There's street lights all the way, so you'll need to turn off your nocturnal optics, unless you enjoy getting blinded. You all just follow my lead. Stay at least five meters apart until I get to the front door, then we stack, kick in the door, and go in."

"Stack?" Kim asked.

"Uh, why five meters?" asked Patrick.

They couldn't hear her, but now Chavez seemed to be laughing. Her shoulders shook, and her head turned slowly from side to side.

"Oh, man, the stuff I still need to teach you guys. Just never enough damn time! Anyway: when I say stack, I mean bunch up as tight as we can get next to the doorway, so we can all break through it asap. Doorways are killzones. Any idiot on the other side of a door can defend the thing by just pointing and clicking in the general direction of the narrow space we are forced to charge through to get at them. So we all gotta get through it *pronto*. Bu jiu. Effin' ASAP. As for spreading out to a five meter separation on the ingress: that presents the inverse problem. Most grenades have a lethal radius at right about five meters. Spreading out makes sure that if someone gets cute and tries an ambush, they'll only get one or two of us with the first shot."

"Oh *that's* comforting!" Kim exclaimed.

Chavez shrugged. "That's the hell of an ambush. But we *shouldn't* run into any serious opposition. This little extraction was always planned to go down when Lehi could get away from most of his entourage. Just a couple bodyguards in the house. Thing is, we can't go in the way I *usually* like to clear a structure, you know, tossing things that make big, angry, lethal booms to do most of of the hard work. The point of this little exercise is to get the target out alive. It's an extraction, not an execution."

"Wait, so why bother carrying the damn guns around at all?"

"Because, Kim, you guys are carrying less-than-lethal ammunition. Cool thing about these rifles is that the ammo comes in two pieces: propellant and projectile. There's a computer that scales how much propellant is loaded into each round, and you can swap out projectile types. I've made sure you all only get to shoot less-than-lethal stuff until I know you won't blow one another's heads off by accident. Not that less-than-lethal means *non*-lethal, but you've got enough kevlar and ceramics in your armor to make it through a friendly fire incident with only minor brain damage if you get whacked by one of these rounds. Still, there are probably civilians around, and *they* don't usually wander around in a carapace. Less-than-lethal for us means something different for them. So be *damned* sure of your target before you pull that trigger!"

Patrick's surprised comment was cut off before it could vocalize. Chavez stood up without another word, and started walking away. He looked at his friends, who looked back at him. Then Timur shook his head, and followed. Kim let out an audible sigh, shook her helmeted head, and followed. Patrick, not seeing any other option, followed as well. He wished he could see his friends' expressions.

Chavez led the way, walking slowly and deliberately down the street, rifle gripped firmly in both hands, head turning slowly side to side. The others tried to mimic her, Timur doing a better job of looking the part of the professional soldier. Patrick had a difficult time keeping his focus. The entire situation was overwhelming. Lessons of the past few days arose unbidden in his mind, and as the four stalked past a row of suburban homes, lights shining from street lamps and from behind curtained windows, he battled a growing sense of unease. A losing battle. By the end of the first few steps, he was convinced that every window held an unseen enemy, with gun or grenade, waiting to attack. Time seemed to slow down each time they passed by a front door. Patrick had a difficult time not holding his breath.

At the end of that block, Chavez turned to her right and led the way down another street. The suburb was like any other in North America. Endless repetition on the same theme: cars parked in front of garages, lawns clipped short, hedges carefully trimmed. Not the sort of place one would expect to see people walking around with military gear.

At the end of the street, a small and well-lit house ended the block. It was outlined in bright green on the hud. Chavez walked right up to it, then turned and beckoned urgently to her three followers. Each accelerated, jogging as quickly as they could to join her, despite their heavy gear. When Timur arrived, she grabbed him and pulled him as close behind her as their bulky carapaces would allow. He in turn reached back and did the same to Kim, and she mimicked him, ensuring that Patrick fell in line as well.

Chavez spoke to them, quickly and quietly.

"OK, this is where it gets interesting. I'm gonna wait five seconds, kick the door, and toss in a flash-bang. As soon as it goes off, we go in. Fast as you can. Your headset will filter out most of the light and noise. I'll lead the way, and whichever way I go—left or right—Timur goes the opposite, following the wall. Kim then follows me, and Patrick follows Timur. Anybody you see holding a gun, you plant a couple rounds in their chest. And just like I've kept yelling at you on the Bunny Slope: shoot for center-of-mass. *Not the head.* You'll probably miss, for one, and for two, I'd *like* to avoid killing anybody tonight.

Patrick was about to ask a question, but there wasn't time. As soon as Chavez finished talking, she rang the door-bell.

Time slowed. Five seconds seemed to last an eternity. Patrick watched, feeling frozen, as Chavez opened something on the side of her carapace, pulled out an oblong object, then stood up and away from the door. She raised her foot, and faster than it seemed humanly possible she thrust it into the door, just below the knob.

The wood holding the door's latch in place shattered, and it swung open. She pitched forward, recovering her balance, and in the same movement almost seemed to casually toss the flash-bang into the room beyond.

The flash-bang worked as advertised. A bright flash lit the interior, then was followed by an aggressively disorienting series of strobe-like pulses. Dully a cacophony of bangs rang through their headsets. And before either could even start to subside, Chavez launched herself through the door, rifle perpendicular to her body, pointing the way. Timur threw himself after her, and with a half-moment of hesitation Kim and Patrick charged in as well.

Patrick felt almost as if he were floating. Time continued to move too slowly. Smoke billowing from the flash-bang grenade refracted the pulsing light into eerie shapes. The headset somehow seemed to filter out the worst of the light and sound, seeming to echo dimly somewhere in the back of his conscious mind. He could barely make out the lines of the room and the furniture within, but recognized immediately the patterns of a run-of-the-mill suburban home: sofas and tables in their proper places, a partially-sequestered kitchen on the far-left wall, and hallways leading away to the left and right. And then he saw the man with a big gun in his hand leap up from a couch.

Two shots burst from Chavez' weapon, and the man's

body was thrown backwards onto the couch. It rocked and nearly fell over from the weight of his fall.

Movement to the left. Dimly Patrick was aware that he had lifted his rifle, pointing it at the man Chavez had just shot down. Which left him facing too far to his right. The man now entering the room had already lifted his weapon and begun to turn towards the doorway. He seemed to be trying to point it directly at Patrick. Somehow, in that brief instant, Patrick knew with absolute certainty that the man was about to shoot at the biggest target, and he would not be able to duck or shoot in time.

Four shots rang out from two rifles. The man crumpled to the floor.

The flash-bang ran out of power before he could take another breath. He stood there, as a momentary silence fell, pointing his rifle in the general direction of where his attacker would have been, had Timur and Kim not fired when they did.

"*Clear!*" Chavez' voice shouted in his ears. Good job! We'll check his pulse later. That had to hurt. Patrick, cover the front door and Timur, move up to control that hallway to the left. Kim, follow me to the right. There might be one or two more."

They complied with Chavez' order. At least, Patrick tried to. For a second he stood there, uncomprehending. And then jogged slowly to the hallway on the right, following Chavez and Kim.

"P!" Timur shouted. "Cover the front door!"

Patrick almost stumbled, and turned towards Timur to respond. And then he saw movement, a human shape enter the hallway to the left. Timur was distracted by Patrick, and didn't see it. Letting out a strangled cry of surprise and warning, Patrick raised his rifle and ran towards the entrance to the hallway.

Then he froze. A boy, probably seven or eight years old, stood at the end of the hallway, staring at Patrick with wide eyes. His hands gripped the rifle, finger already squeezing the trigger. He'd instinctively aimed for where an adult's center of mass should be. But the difference in height meant that the barrel of his weapon was pointed directly at the child's face.

"Guns down, guns *DOWN!*"

Kim ran in front of Patrick, shouting frantically, grabbing at the barrel of his rifle. He dropped it, throwing his hands into the air. The child ducked away, huddling against the corner of the far wall at the end of the hallway.

Kim held Patrick's rifle for a moment, then dropped it. Patrick felt the sling pull at his shoulders, and the weapon clattered to the front of his carapace. He lowered his hands, breathing fast, heart racing.

"It's okay kiddo, it's okay!"

Kim walked slowly up to the boy, and crouched down to his height. He shrank back from her, pressing himself deeper into the corner. She paused, then reached up to her face and began peeling away the headset, bit by bit. The boy watched her through his fingers, breathing as fast as Patrick. Then, as her face was revealed, his hands slowly began to drop.

The pounding of his heart receded from Patrick's ears, replaced by the sound of footsteps. Chavez appeared at his side, and placed a hand on his shoulder. At the same time, two adults ran into the hallway from an unseen room to one side, mother grabbing her child and father placing himself between his family and their assailants. He held his hands up, palms facing outward.

"Hey, put your hands down, nobody's going to hurt you." Chavez said, as she followed Kim's example and began peeling away her headgear. "Helmets off, guys. Kim had the right idea. Fight's over. Time to be humans again."

Relief washed over Patrick as he fumbled with the clips holding his mask in place. Relief, and sudden exhaustion. Light headed, he leaned against the wall and worked to breathe.

Chavez gestured back down the hallway. "Let's go out into the living room, everyone. Hey dad-type: The name's Smith, right?"

The man kept his hands in view, palms outward, but he seemed to relax ever so slightly. "It is, as long as you are Sandra Chavez under all that mess. Been a long time, and that gear isn't exactly a recognition aid. Nice kit, though. Glad the mercenary life is treating you well."

Chavez laughed, and motioned for them all to follow her out into the living room. She checked each of the two unconscious men for signs of life, then walked over to a large formal-looking dining table located adjacent to the kitchen.

"Hey hey, everybody's alive. Good deal. Glad you three kept it together. I think this little scout team we're putting together might just work after all. I always like it when Jackson is wrong."

Patrick followed slowly, and didn't wait for an invitation to take a seat at the table. Timur walked behind him, then leaned against the wall, facing the door leading out to the suburbs of Rexburg. Kim joined Patrick, patting him on the shoulder as she sat down. Chavez, like Timur, remained standing.

The Smith family followed one by one. There were four children, ranging in age from toddler to teenager, two boys and two girls. Blond hair seemed to run in their mother's family. She came last, now holding the toddler in her arms. The father, Smith, stood a few feet from Chavez, showing no signs of fear, but also no signs of relaxing his guard. Patrick couldn't say he blamed the man.

Smith spoke, watching Chavez carefully. "So, Chavez,

here's the deal. You give me and my family sanctuary. *Real* sanctuary, none of that bonded labor bullshit, do you hear me? You give me your word that you'll treat us right, and I'll tell you what I know. And let me state for the record that this *isn't* a negotiation. You are going to want, no *need* to know what I can tell you. But my price is that you take care of my family. And you don't have a lot of time before my people notice that the guards haven't checked in on schedule, so you'll have to decide quickly."

Chavez smiled. "No problem there, Jack: ain't no way I'd let you and yours down *regardless* of what you can tell us. You've already helped more than you can possibly know."

He snorted. "And didn't that turn out to be a complete waste of time! You people went ahead and escalated this thing anyway. You literally went nuclear. Do you have any idea the kind of hornet's nest you've stirred up?"

Chavez shook her head. "Hey, first off, that wasn't my call. And when I go visit Command next, I can *guarantee* that I'm going to break some stuff in order to make my *full* displeasure clear about not being read into that decision beforehand. But come on, you have to admit that we were already backed into a corner. Escalation to nuclear or not, we were gonna hafta wipe out that position after you Deserets decided to push north, despite all our prior agreements. With both the Texans and those nutters in Chicago acting up, the last thing we need is the Deserets trying to cut our supply lines. And if I'd dropped a hellfire of artillery on that mountain, and killed all your people the old fashioned way, would it really have made that much of a difference? They'd still all be gone, and your people would still want a fight."

Smith let out a wry laugh. "Maybe that's true, but you gave the Council hardliners the *exact* thing they needed to sell themselves as the 'only hope' for the Deseret Nation. Those geriatric would-be theocrats launched a coup the day after your little stunt. They're publicly promising a reckoning in vengeance for their lost sons and daughters, and the orders are being drawn up for a full assault on your positions in southern Idaho, *regardless* of the expected casualties. They're giving it the full-Rumsfeld: sweeping everything in, related and not, and making paying you back all about the fight for Greater Deseret. So sure, you may have wiped out a couple of elite battalions, but *now* you'll have *at least* three brigades and two air wings knocking on your western door. Own goal, if you ask me. But you know your defenses better than I do, so who knows?"

Timur interjected. "Chavez, I don't understand half of what he's talking about, but is this really the time or place for a debate? I kind of feel like we, you know, need to skedaddle before reinforcements arrive. Like he said would be coming."

Chavez flashed Timur a grin, then looked back at Smith. "No worries, I sent the signal for Ravi to bring a couple helos in the minute we were guns-down. Jack, I assume your guards were on a once-per-hour check-in routine?"

He nodded. "Yes, and their last was thirty minutes ago. You did time this well. But you still haven't answered me, and I'm not budging an inch until you do. I need to hear you say it, Sandra."

She closed her eyes for a long breath, looking almost pained. Then nodded back at him. "You'd think with our history... *how* long did we serve together? Ah well. I get it. It's a brave new world, and ain't it grand? Ok. Jack, I *swear* to you, by whatever you and I agree is holy enough, that your family is *our* family. Not going near the bonded labor pool. Total equality in treatment. A place in the Company if you want it. You have my word."

They locked eyes for a long moment. After a time, he nodded. His wife seemed to exhale. With relief, or sadness, Patrick couldn't tell. Chavez nodded too, waited a few more seconds, then broke the silence, her voice strangely hesitant.

"You know, Jack, about joining the Company: we'll be getting hit from all sides pretty soon here, and after news of tonight gets out... if they *ever* catch up to you... well, maybe after we debrief you, maybe we send you on to Cascadia or Canada? I haven't heard of them having anything against LDS folks, and we can easily move you and your family through Montana and on out of our territory. Or get you to Europe, even, if you'd like. Give you a new identity and everything. You folks can just disappear and be done with all this nonsense."

He smiled, and laughed sadly. "Thanks Sandra. I think I'll have to take you up on that. You people have solid international connections, and praise God for that, because there's nowhere in North America my family will be safe once the news gets out that I've defected. The hardliners have always hated me, and sooner or later their quote-unquote *investigation* will begin. They'll go after my family straight away, like they always do. They've already done it to plenty of others they thought of as potential political enemies. And since I've always advocated openly for a secular Deseret nation, I'm all but guaranteed to get caught up in the coming purge. With my family getting thrown to the mob as a result."

Chavez shook her head sadly. "Damn, you really are done in either way, aren't you Jack? Who'd have thought things would have come to this, twenty years ago, when we were off playing in the Syria sandbox?"

He laughed a little. "Oh, who'd have thought any of it was going to go down like it did? But God works in mysterious ways. Especially these days."

She gave him a little smirk, as if he'd said something that reminded her of a long argument held long ago. "Or your God doesn't bother with us anymore, and we're totally on our own."

They laughed, and Patrick couldn't help but feel that these were two old friends reminiscing over an ancient and now pointless disagreement. Smith's family sat quietly, sometimes gazing thoughtfully at Patrick and his friends. Whether they saw them as captors or rescuers, he couldn't tell. And was that... pity in their eyes? Something was there that he couldn't quite figure out. But after a short while, he realized that he actually didn't much care what they were thinking. It was setting in now, the understanding that this strange war he and his friends had found themselves caught up in, was about to get a lot worse. The missions, the fear, the danger, was only beginning.

The whump-whump of helicopter rotor blades filled the night.

EARTH-LUNA DEFENSE ZONE

When this round of vicious acceleration had finally come to an end, Loucas looked up from the Star-Bridge, groggily casting his gaze towards the far horizon.

Days of wandering around a pair of spaceships, mostly ignored by the robots operating the things, had given him plenty of time to think about he and his sister's odd predicament. Something about leaving Yarielis alone and going to visit Mimr's pub bothered him, and so he had spent most of the time trying to learn whatever he could about the *Acerbic*, Olga's Jagdkontrol, and the world of 2147. Unfortunately, he hadn't been able to learn much. At least nothing of real use to him. Although he could access any number of computer terminals throughout the ship, they weren't connected to anything outside the vessel, and none seemed to have been pre-loaded with whatever stood in for Wikipedia in the 22nd century.

All he could glean was information about the *Acerbic*'s construction and operation, details of little practical use to him. But then, towards the end of the third day, Franz had broken his long silence, for reasons known only unto his robotic self, to tell Loucas about how the Stellar Highway operated. And then he'd spent the next day obsessively worried about miniature black holes flying through the solar system.

Loucas tiredly turned his head to look at Yarielis. Her eyes were open, and only the depth of her breathing served as a reminder that she had been experiencing the same physical forces and effects as she was. But that was the one other thing he'd learned over the past few days: whatever was happening as part of her integration with Olga and the Jagd-kontrol, it was also having the odd effect of allowing her to tolerate far more physical unpleasantness than she could normally stand. Like having her body compressed by the force of accelerating at about ten times the force of Earth's gravity for ten minutes at a stretch.

A glitter beyond her head caught his eye. Earth shimmered in the distance, now appearing as small as the Moon when one looks at it from the Earth's surface. The Moon itself was hidden in Earth's shadow.

"Boy, wow, you guys are really getting the hang this—usually humans don't wake up this fast after feeling that much force. Olga really knows her business!"

Loucas blinked several times, shocked to see the robot Bob, or, given that the Star-Bridge was effectively a form of virtual reality, an avatar of Bob, appear out of nowhere, then trot around behind Olga for several seconds, like a dog happy to greet its people after a long day.

"Bob... I thought you, well, uh, exploded."

Bob replied to Loucas by tapping several of his metal feet in what looked like a sort of robot dance.

"I know!" Bob exclaimed. "I did! It was fun! I've wanted to try exploding for *years*. But usually I get caught and disarmed before the big event. This is the first time I actually made it past security to a target. Thank you for your help!"

Loucas paused, very unsure how to respond. "Well, if you don't mind me asking," he asked, hesitantly, "how did you survive?"

"Huh, I wonder if robots have ghosts?" Yari asked, clearly only half paying attention. Loucas gave her a puzzled look.

"I don't know." replied Bob. "But surviving was easy! I just uploaded the essential bits of my memory to *Station Rome*'s local internet. The sysadmins would normally have caught on to the bandwidth use in seconds, but they were understandably distracted by all the chaos, so I slipped through. Made my way to Earth, then latched onto some of the signals being broadcast to *Acerbic* as she passed by."

"You can do that whenever you want?" Loucas asked. "Can others like Olga and Franz do the same thing?"

"Sure, if there's enough bandwidth and accessible memory in the local area. But I was built to do those kinds of deliveries, so my architecture is a bit simpler. I can delete bits of myself, memories mostly, to reduce my size. I'm actually set up to function as a distributed intelligence, with parts working independently until they get synchronized when there's an opportunity. So it is very hard to kill me permanently. At least, it is hard to kill anything more than one minor iteration of *me.* It also leaves me not very smart, Franz and Olga always tell me, because that means my basic systems have to be a bit… extra basic."

Bob tapped his feet and rotated to turn towards Olga. At least, Loucas thought that was where he turned. Bob's front and back weren't actually that easy to differentiate.

"Unfortunately for Franz and Olga," he continued, "They require so much memory to retain their basic functionality that they are effectively tied to the *Acerbic*, unless we are close enough to a friendly base for a full emergency download. So if this blockade the Terrestrials are assembling to destroy us works out, they are as done for as you two."

Loucas stood up and looked at the stars ahead of them. In a flash, he remembered that there was supposed to be a blockade of hostile ships moving to intercept them. He didn't see anything. Olga stood with her back to Loucas and Yari, also staring out into the stars.

"How do know there's a blockade?" he asked. "I don't see anything at all."

"Well, yeah, that's kind of the *point*, don't you know?" Bob replied. "When I was waiting to upload from Earth I took a peek at a few of the military intranets I could sneak into. They are *very* upset about what we did to their headquarters on *Rome*. They have dispatched a major portion of the regular military to find and destroy us. They have also done a good job of predicting our trajectory out of the Earth-Luna defense zone, so a lot of those ships are converging on our position. There are at least two hunter groups behind us, and three more converging on our trajectory. There are also two carrier groups in front of us. That's unusual because there are only eight of those in the whole Solar System. They must have scrambled the reserves from Luna."

"That sounds... bad." said Loucas.

Bob tapped each foot once. "It is! Bad and exciting. Fortunately, three of the hunter groups won't be able to catch up with us. Less fortunately, the two that will each contain a cruiser and two destroyers, with sufficient combined firepower to destroy us, if they can hit us. Very unfortunately, the carrier groups that are somewhere ahead have more than enough firepower to completely vaporize us. There's two carriers, six destroyers, and a dreadnought in each. *Acerbic* might be able to take on a single cruiser or a couple destroyers on a good day. Maybe even a full hunter group on a *really* good day. But never a dreadnought. At least not without total surprise. Which we won't have. So we're in quite a fix!"

"Dreadnoughts, carriers, cruisers, destroyers—what, is space an ocean or something?"

"Well spotted, Loucas!" replied Bob, cheerfully tapping his feet again. "I knew I liked you. I, for one, appreciate a biological with a degree of cynicism. It is true that the old Earth navies ended up passing their heritage and traditions onto their space-based successors. That makes a certain amount of sense. Naval vessels are sized according to their role, and bigger ships tend to have bigger crews and more firepower. They are also similar to space-faring vessels in that they are operated by crews, machines and biologicals alike, that have to work together to survive a hostile environment long enough to do battle *in* that hostile environment. It was perfectly natural to adopt water-ship terminology and organizational schemes to manage the evolution of the new force. So, like on Earth, 'destroyers' are smaller ships that usually operate in pairs to screen bigger ships or do anti-pirate patrols in the Belt, 'cruisers' are bigger and faster warships designed to work alone for months on end, and 'carriers' are even bigger yet, able to stay away from base for months to a year, hosting manned and unmanned fighter-sized craft capable of operating in space for only a few hours or days. And then of course there are the 'dreadnoughts,' appropriately named because they fear nothing for a reason. They're big. Very, very big."

"And one of them is moving to converge with our trajectory far more quickly than anticipated. Olga, get the Jager flights ready! We're unlikely to survive the dreadnought's bombardment in the end, but at least we may be able to live long enough to be killed by it rather than one of those petty cruisers or destroyers if we can hold them off for long enough!"

Olga wheeled around to look at Yari as soon as Franz's radio transmission from *Acerbic* had ended. It was as if something had triggered in her, and she was now ready to spring into action.

"Yari, forget what he said: we *can* make it through this. We have a few minutes until the dreadnought is in range. The destroyers won't be able to get close enough to punch through our shields, so we don't have to worry too much about them. The cruisers, on the other hand, will be able to take us down provided they can get a clear shot and keep their beams fixed on our shields for a few seconds. So, we don't let them! Two cruisers, three Jager flights. We can do this!"

Yari nodded at Olga, and then let out a snarl of frustration so sudden and vicious that Loucas almost jumped out of his skin.

"But I can't *see* them anywhere! Where are they going to be attacking from?"

Olga sighed, turning her head to look from one edge of the horizon to another. "That's the real problem, isn't it? We're dealing with *war*ships here. They're built specifically to avoid being seen until it is too late. Bob's analogy to Earth naval warfare works well for another reason. By the 21st century, submarines were the lords of the sea, not surface ships. Staying hidden until it is too late for your opponent to establish a defense has always been *the* fundamental trick of war, whether your battle is on land, the sea, or in the air. Same is true in space. Out there, in that damnable twinkling blackness, they're coasting: engines off, weapons on standby. They'll avoid emitting *any* electromagnetic signals we might use to pin down their exact location, right up until they fire an energy beam at us. Until then, unless we get lucky and can spot them by the distortions in the occluded or deflected light coming from the stars behind them, we won't know where our attackers are. Unless they make a mistake."

"I wouldn't count on mistakes. Our attempts at deception were insufficient. They did too good a job at predicting our trajectory despite our maneuver around Earth. These aren't the usual mercenaries and social rejects they send to staff the Toff forces occupying the habitats. We're dealing with military professionals. I do not like our odds."

Olga laughed and smirked. "Franz, as a wise human once said: 'don't tell me the odds.' You of all machines should know that I love a good fight. It's in my programming. I thought it was in yours, too!"

"I'm sure that enjoyment of the battle will do us a tremendous amount of good once the beams come crashing down on our shields, Olga. I don't mind battle. I do mind exploding."

She laughed again. "You fly your ship, Franz, and Yari and I will direct the Jagers from ours. You provide the thrust to get us to the Belt, and we'll give you top cover. We'll come through in one piece, you'll see."

Loucas cocked his head. "Question for both of you: Couldn't we use the *Acerbic* as a decoy, and all escape on the smaller ship? If there's enough storage space or whatever you all need to survive, and we can pack some supplies in here for Yari and me."

Olga shook her head, though her smile was broad. "I wish! But no. We can't keep enough air and water on the Jagd-kontrol to survive the many weeks it will take us to get to the Belt using our little engines. And if we try to separate just to offer our enemies a more complex targeting problem, there's too strong a chance that we'll stray too far from the *Acerbic*'s path, and won't be able to re-dock. While we may be smaller, that also means we have an order of magnitude less thrust to work with. Outside a narrow envelope around *Acerbic*, that moves as she moves, we won't even have enough energy to catch up with her and make it back, provided she survives. Plus, we lose the protection of her shields, which are far stronger than our own. So we have to simply work from here, and hope for the best. At least their own fighter sized craft face the same problem: we are moving *very* fast, so they have no hope of catching up to us. Too bad there's a damned dreadnought in our path. Otherwise, I know we'd blow through. But I still believe we can escape! Have faith!"

Loucas thought it was strange for a machine to be talking

about faith, but he had no time to worry about it then. He saw Yari move her hands, and the three flights of triangular drones arranged themselves into formation, and took up positions not far from the edge of the horizon, at their nine, three, and twelve o'clock. She glanced at Loucas, and answered his question before he could pose it.

"Lou, I'll keep them close enough to us that they won't get lost. Like last time, I just need to keep them in the general area of where the bad guys' beams will come at us. As long as they can deflect the majority of the beam energy away from the shields, we'll be ok. I just have to focus."

Loucas paused for a moment, then walked over to his sister and placed his hand on her shoulder. She pulled away for a moment, wiggled her hand in a strange way, and then relaxed slightly, leaning gently against him.

"Lou," she said, speaking softly, "I know that it is weird for me to be deciding things all of a sudden. I like that you want to protect me, but right now I get to be the one who protects you, ok?. I'm getting better and better at controlling the little Jagers. I've practiced as much as I can the past few days, and Olga has been wonderful a training me. I can do this! Just help spot for me, ok? The sooner we break up an attack, the less chance it hits us hard enough to punch through our shields."

He opened his mouth to say something, but the words didn't come. All his life he'd been like a twin to Yarielis. She might have been adopted, but he couldn't remember a time when she wasn't there alongside him, he her brother and she his sister. Even when he went to university in Vancouver, she went with him. Taking care of her, in a world that seemed bound and determined to make life difficult for autistics, was second nature to him. But here, for the first time in their shared life, she had to be the one to take care of him. The robots had chosen to integrate her into the Jagdkontrol, not

Loucas. Even his knowledge of physics was useless. Both because things had changed in the world since he had earned his degree, but also because education in and of itself could do little to prepare a person for the kind of danger he was about to face.

Loucas hadn't had cause to think about it before, but he suddenly realized how much he *hated* feeling useless. Out of depth, out of touch. It was infuriating. Especially because, in a way, he was living the physicist's dream. Jumping more than a century into what the Norse gods or whatever they actually were called his Thread's most likely future, he had a unique opportunity to *actually know* what the world of the future was going to be like. But even in his wildest dreams of time travel and experiencing possible futures, he'd never expected to end up feeling completely powerless. Black hole highways, death beams and space navies. That was his new world, and he was at least a century out of date.

The crew of the Jadgkontrol, human and machine, fell silent for a long while. Each looking out into the stars, waiting for some sign, digitally processed as it might be, of what was out there, where their unseen assailants were waiting in ambush. For an instant, he thought he understood what it must have been like to be one of the tens of thousands of sailors on cargo ships during one of Earth's world wars in the 20th century, spending weeks on end subject to the loneliness of the open ocean, wondering if *this* nightfall would be the one that ended in a sudden explosion and the rush of seawater cascading through torpedo-ruptured hull.

A phantasmic flicker like the twinkling of a new star on the periphery of his vision attracted his attention. He looked hard for the source of the disturbance, but saw nothing more. He looked at Yari, Olga, even Bob, but they didn't show any sign of having noticed it. An illusion, then? His eyes playing tricks on him? A glitch in the Star-Bridge's systems?

He saw it again. In a different part of the horizon, more clearly and lasting for several breaths longer than before. It seemed to flash in several different colors, only faintly perceptible, on the very edge of vision. Then was gone. Again, he wondered if it was an illusion. Stars shouldn't twinkle outside an atmosphere. But he had the distinct feeling that the Star-Bridge would filter out a predictable effect like atmospheric interference. So what is it he was seeing?

The next thing that attracted his eyes was an intense blue white streak that seemed to lash out from one of the stars to crash against the shields of the *Acerbic*. Light of a thousand different shades and hues arced around them, as the particle beam tried to break through the ship's protective shields and shatter the structure beneath.

Out of pure instinct he started to shout and point, but there was no need. With a sweeping gesture Yari pulled one of the Jager flights towards the beam, and Olga mimicked her gesture. The Jagers rearranged themselves in an instant, creating an angled wall of whatever material they were made of that deflected the beam away from *Acerbic*, and out into the darkness.

"There's one of the bastards!" Olga shouted. "ten o'clock high! I'll take over this flight, Yari, good save!"

"Got it!" Yari shouted in reply, then made a gesture as if to release the Jagers from her control. Loucas wished he could see what she saw, could understand how she was connected to them. Then he saw the twinkle again, a bit to the right of their direction of travel.

"Yar, I think there's something at our two o'clock."

She jerked her head, peering out at where he pointed. A Jager flight drifted in the direction of her glance. "I don't see anyth..."

At the same time as Loucas saw the blue-white flash, Yari jerked, pulling the drifting Jager flight fully into that part of the sky. Just in time for another burst of light to smash into them, portions of the particle beam that slipped between the Jagers dancing across the Acerbic's shields, producing the usual color cascade at the many scattered points of impact.

"Thanks Lou! I don't know how you knew, but..."

Another flicker, this time just above the horizon at their nine o'clock. Loucas started to point, but this time he wasn't able to get Yari's attention in time. Another blue-white beam burst into existence, narrowly missing the Acerbic.

"Designating hunter groups A, B, and C now. Hell, we were wrong, there's a third cruiser out there! Be advised, Olga, they're all in lethal range!"

"Affirmative!" Olga and Yari shouted at the same time. Olga took over the Jager flight that had intercepted the second beam, holding it in place to deflect the inbound particles. Yari turned her attention to the part of the sky where the third beam had fired from.

Just in time. Another shot, slashing in from their 9 o'clock and better aimed, ran right into the screen of Jagers.

Then all the beams ceased for a time, as suddenly as they had begun. The Star-Bridge displayed bright red boxes over their origin points.

"Damn! Picking up transmissions between the groups. There's a fourth cruiser gunning for us—where it is, I don't know."

Half a dozen beams, smaller than the three that had just assailed them, crashed into the shields. Loucas cried out, drawing Yari's attention, but Olga shouted him down.

"Don't worry about those! They're from the destroyers. Not big enough to hurt us at this range."

"The hell do you mean they can't hurt us?" Loucas

shouted back at her. "How is one beam different than another? Isn't the damage they do, like, cumulative?"

"It's a threshold thing, Loucas." said Bob, his voice disturbingly calm. "Shields are a bit like skin. The break comes when too much penetration energy strikes too small an area. That causes superficial fusion reactions, which lets the beam punch through the disrupted shield matrix and impact the hull. Which itself typically causes a catastrophic set of fusion reactions, then failure of the ship's physical structure, and *kaboom!* But *Acerbic* is a raider. Franz rebuilds the exterior before every mission to mimic whatever ship type we're pretending to be, and that hides the fact that we're actually, deep down, a mid-sized warship capable of shrugging off attacks from smaller vessels. Destroyers have to be at point-blank range to have any chance of breaking through."

"Bingo," said Olga, "the destroyers are trying to distract us. They want us to pull our Jagers out of position so we're exposed to the cruisers. Once they fired, they lost the element of surprise. We're moving past them too quickly for them to catch up. Almost free of the bastards! Except, where's that fourth cruiser?"

The strange twinkling came again, this time almost directly in their path. Loucas pointed and shouted. "Eleven o'clock! Just above the horizon! Look!"

Olga ignored him. Yari listened to him. And then flung the Jager flight that had blocked the first incoming beam towards the forward horizon. Just in time. The twinkle turned to a flash, and another intense beam of light was broken apart by the Jagers. Immediately after, two other beams from two of the other hunter groups fired again, accompanied by the smaller beams firing from their accompanying destroyers.

Loucas held his breath, watching as the particle beams fought against Jagers and their scattered remnants slashed against the shields. Three Jager flights were now holding off shots from three different cruisers, which fired again and again to try and defeat their prey's defense. He kept waiting in fearful anticipation for that fourth cruiser to strike in unison with the others. If it timed its attack correctly, it would have a clear shot at them.

The expected strike came, but from *behind* them. And to Loucas' surprise, the incoming beam seemed weaker than the others'. He realized that one of the first cruisers to fire must have now fallen too far behind them to do any real damage. It fired ineffectually several more times, and then shots began to miss, bright azure beams blinking into and out of existence all around them.

The battle went on, and the stalemate continued. Their assailants tried to vary their tactics, firing in different combinations, but Yari and Olga kept up with them. Loucas watched as the angry red boxes slid slowly across the horizon over the next half hour. Even the cruiser group that had been located almost directly in front of the *Acerbic* eventually slid from their eleven o'clock to their four o'clock, then five o'clock, and then its beams began to weaken. Eventually, the destroyers stopped firing at all. And then, even as Yari began to show outward signs of fatigue from her constant efforts, the cruisers stopped shooting too. Loucas saw no more twinklings on the horizon, and the angry red boxes clustered in their wake.

"And now, we die." came Franz' voice, from wherever on the *Acerbic* he was transmitting.

At first, Loucas didn't understand what he was talking about. And then he turned to look forward, and there he saw it: looming like a nightmare on the edge of a dream, the dreadnought just seemed to *appear*, climbing slowly up from below the horizon, almost directly in their path. As it emerged into their field of view, the Star-Bridge seemed to sort of roll back the darkness, revealing the smooth stark lines of a massive warship.

"Well hello, Moby Dick." said Olga. Loucas saw that her expression was fierce, her teeth and fists clenched.

Yari stared at the shape, gesturing wildly, pulling the Jager flights into a triangular formation between them and the dreadnought. From either side of the *Acerbic*, bolts of light suddenly flashed into existence all around them. It was like a meteor shower had erupted, with those that struck the shields bursting into colorful plumes of scattering particles. Yari and Loucas cried out in surprise.

"Don't worry about them." Olga said, sounding grim. "Just getting our range, so the dreadnought can get a solid fix on us. Every time one of them hits us, the clash of particles produces a signal that radiates for everyone out there to see. And use to lock on. These Navy types absolutely love to play this game during intercepts. The carriers flank us on both sides, and the dreadnought just sits and waits for the right time to swat us out of the sky. Dammit, Franz, if we're gonna die, can we at least detach the Jagdkontrol and play kamikaze? I want to go out taking a chunk out of one of those big bastards!"

"Do whatever you like, Olga. Preparing our own main beam now. We may not be able to scratch a dreadnought that knows we're there, but at least they'll know we tried!"

Loucas felt panic rising. He looked wildly from one edge of the horizon to the other and back again. Yari stayed almost serenely calm, by contrast. She held her hands in place, ready to do whatever it was that she did to keep the Jager flights in between them and their attackers. The dreadnought only dully reflected the light of the sun, most of the solar energy being deflected away from the massive spaceship's angular structure. Loucas began to see signs of activity on and near the surface of the vessel. Small craft, fighters or drones, buzzed around it. And at several points, the surface of the ship itself seemed to be shifting. Probably whatever mechanisms controlled the particle beams emitters. Shifting, targeting their victim. Them.

"Acerbic, be advised, while they've been fixated on you, we've been monitoring your situation and are prepared to intercept. Reel your Jager flights in, and hold on! You're gonna hafta accelerate like a banshee out of hell if you want to have a snowball's chance of making it to the Belt!"

The radio transmission came as if out of nowhere, as did two small and fast moving blurs each accompanied by a swarm of smaller, triangular shapes. These tore past the *Acerbic* on its right side, then closed distance with the dreadnought almost faster than the human eye could follow. Loucas watched them, awestruck. They were Jagdkontrols, just like Olga's. Two surfaces on the dreadnought that the Star-Bridge labeled as particle beam emitters began to glow with an eerie light. But it was too late.

The two Jagdkontrols seemed to throw their Jager flights at the glowing surfaces, and the dreadnought's own shields flickered and crackled as the little shapes lashed at it like a school of piranhas swarming a carcass. And then two brilliant beams of light burst from the Jagdkontrols themselves, raking the disturbed surface of the dreadnought's shields. Then the beams punched through, charring and melting their way deep into the vessel's hull. Brilliant flashes of white light followed as two massive explosions ripped through the surface of the afflicted vessel. The two Jagdkontrols soared past the dreadnought and out into the stars beyond, streaks and pulses of light from lesser weapons crisscrossing in their aftermath.

"Hah ha!" shouted Olga, jumping up and down and dancing in vicious glee. "Burn you bastards, burn! Oh hell, thank you *Sardonic*! At least, I'm assuming that's you guys out there? What a save!"

"*Affirmative.*" came the reply. "*Heard about your little exploit while doing recon in Lunar orbit. Figured out your escape plan, and our snooping revealed that the authorities were onto it as well. Thought we'd strike a blow for freedom, and pay you back for your good work! The revolution is ON, don'tcha know? Half a dozen habitat sectors openly declared independence from Earth yesterday. The Toffs were totally unprepared and are running scared. Taking you down on your egress was their last hope to play the bombing off as an isolated terror attack by badly equipped Belt pirates. Now they can't deny any longer that we have the ships and the will to take them on. The rebellion is on! For freedom!*"

"For justice." Olga said quietly, smiling triumphantly. She watched in silence as they sailed past the stricken dreadnought, now too concerned about its own survival to continue trying to destroy them. A massive chunk of it had been blasted free, and was now careening off into the night. They passed under this wreckage, relative motion making it clear that the *Acerbic* was moving much, much faster than Loucas had realized. In that moment, Loucas felt suddenly light, as if a terrible weight had lifted. But it wasn't physical in nature. They were free! They had escaped. Although several of the ships of the broken blockade continued to fire beams and bolts at them, it was an exercise in futility and rage. *Acerbic* was on her way to the Belt!

A shape caught his eye, moving fast on a perpendicular trajectory to theirs. It was similar in size, but not shape, to *Acerbic*. He watched the angular lines of the *Sardonic* as the ship seemed to lazily float past them, while listening to its occupants, whoever or whatever they were, brief Franz and Olga on what to expect when they reached the Belt.

"*Franz, Olga, make sure you train your humans up to the necessary standard. It's gonna be a fight all the way back to base,*" *even if they aren't going to be looking for you specifically. The default plan for any uprising against Earth rule is to flood the Belt with ships. They know full well that the habitats rely on the Belt for resources, and to hide our bases. So we'll be on battle duty all the way to Homeport."*

"As expected." replied Franz. *"Such is life. Well, with two raiders and three corvettes we can handle anything short of a dreadnought. And they won't be able to maintain more than four or five carrier groups and their dreadnoughts on station for more than a year, and that will have to do to cover the entire Belt! Now, they're fighting on our terrain. This is a new kind of fight for them. For the first time, we have a chance!"*

"Indeed!" came the reply. *"By the way, we'd like to know, just for the record: did one of your humans catch on to our stunt with the targeting beam? We did try to mark out your assailants as we detected them. Fortunately, they were too fixated on you to notice our wee little lasers, but they were operating in full-stealth mode, so we only picked up their signals when they were just about to open fire. Still, we tried!"*

Olga turned to look at Loucas, a look of surprise on her face. " A ha! so *that's* how you seemed to have a sense of where they'd be shooting from!"

"We'll take that as a yes, then. Glad you had biologicals aboard, Acerbic, we couldn't risk emitting a clearer signal that a non-human might notice. Well, we'll catch you on the flip side then. Stay safe, and see you in the Belt. Here's to victory!"

"To victory." agreed Franz, and the transmission ended.

Loucas' heart sank a little, maybe because he realized that there were more battles to come, or maybe it was just the adrenaline fading now that their lives were no longer in immediate danger. He turned to Yari. And guessed from her tired expression that she was thinking along the same lines. But there was something else there, too. A sort of... eagerness, he wanted to call it. It seemed strange, for her. His little stick of a sister was always having to deal with over-stimulation and the typically inconsiderate behavior of other people. But here, despite the fact that they had just been in a fight for their lives, it was like something inside of her was waking up.

He wasn't sure how to feel about it. He wondered what was causing it, whether it was the strange drinks at Mimr's Pub, the integration with the Star-Bridge, or some deeply repressed part of herself that could only emerge in a time of crisis. Or, maybe, he thought suddenly, he was just seeing her with different eyes, the kind you develop whenever you share mortal danger with another person. He reached out with both hands, and gently squeezed her shoulders.

She turned to look at him, very clearly tired to the point of exhaustion. She shook her head slowly.

"Well, bro, I guess we have some time to think, don't we? I wonder what we should think about? I kind of want to take a nap, I think. Holding my hands up for so long makes me so tired! Also, we should go see the others as soon as we get a chance. For some reason, I really want to pet one of Freyja's kitties right now. Don't you wish we could bring them here? Though I don't know if they would like all the metal and robots. But they seem like very interesting cats, don't you think?"

Despite his worries, Loucas couldn't help but smile. Yep, that was Yari. And yep, tired Yari was the same whether or not she was plugged into a machine. Her mind wandered down strange paths when she got tired.

"Also, we need to start thinking about how to stop the end of the world. The Ragnarok thing. I think there has to be a solution if we just think hard enough about it, don't you, bro?"

And that was Yari too. Abrupt transitions. And no sense of when to not remind others of the something they'd prefer not to think about. Oh well. Didn't matter, he realized. They were together, they were alive, and it looked like those basic conditions would continue for at least another day. Let tomorrow take care of tomorrow.

VAL-HALL

Kim blinked as a man flew over her head, arms and legs flailing, only to make a somewhat miraculous landing on a table to her right. Men and women cheered and shouted, some high-fived, others exchanged what looked like coins, others went to fetch more others drinks. It was drunken chaos, and she felt very out of place.

Yari and Loucas had greeted Kim and her companions when they were finally able to make it back to Mimr's Pub. Both of them had been nearly beside themselves with an odd sort of eager confusion. And they'd led the trio to where Eryn sat with a bunch of dead war heroes, happily recounting the moment when she made Hitler's conference explode.

For what seemed like hours they sat together and shared the details of their latest day of unwanted adventure. An ever-changing circle of Einherjar stood around them, alternating between listening in rapt attention and cheering at parts they particularly liked. For her own part, Kim was distracted, struggling with the implications of what she was seeing, here in this place these people calling themselves Einherjar called Val-Hall.

The others didn't seem to share her mood. The infectious enthusiasm of the Einherjar for their eating and drinking and strange games, apparently the ones involving physical risk of some sort were the most popular, had largely carried them all away as they ate and drank and felt the cares of the world fall away.

Eryn and Timur were in deep conversation with a man

they called Rommel, with a steady stream of other people, women and men, many vaguely familiar, passing by and sometimes jumping into the conversation for a while, before invariably wandering off into the crowd after a few minutes or many. Yari, Loucas, and Patrick were sitting nearby, mostly quiet for the moment, busying themselves with another helping of food. Which, true to the overall weirdness of the place, appeared out of nowhere whenever asked for. Kim kept thinking she'd get used to all the strangeness in her life, but so far she had been consistently wrong.

"Ah, people, they do enjoy being loud, don't they?" asked Lyudmyla Pavlichenko, who was sitting quietly at Kim's left side.

"Snipers, they do enjoy complaining about other people, don't they?" asked Aleksandra Samusenko in response, from her seat at Kim's right side.

Kim looked to her left and right, then sighed and shook her head. A wry smile, or maybe grimace, she couldn't tell, spread unbidden across her own lips, as the two women bantered back and forth, in the intervals between taking deep swigs from their mugs of ale, mead, beer or whatever else Idunn's nectar made it into.

"I still can't believe that this is the afterlife." Kim said, during a break in their banter. "Though I guess a big party isn't the worst way to spend eternity, is it?"

Lyudmyla and Aleksandra both laughed. "It certainly isn't!" Aleksandra replied. "Although it isn't really eternal, our time here, you know. With the onset of Fimbulwinter and the countdown to Ragnarok having begun, time is starting to look short for all of us. Though lets not waste too many words on things that can't be changed, shall we? Save the fighting for tomorrow. Tonight, we party!"

Kim laughed despite herself, then tilted her head. "Okay, but I am still surprised that you don't seem too upset about it. Ragnarok and all that. Or am I seeing, like, just one aspect of you? Or whatever is true about how we see the gods, the Aesir and Vanir, or whatever they call themselves."

Lyudmyla shook her head. "No, it isn't quite the same for Einherjar as it is for them. Or the Aelfar, Svartaelfar, Jotnar, Muspelli, or really anyone else from outside Midgard. With us, what you see is what you get! Although, since part of being Einherjar is that we all remember all our different lives, I guess in any given moment you kind of *do* only see one aspect."

Aleksandra shook her head. "No no, Lyudmyla, don't go confusing the woman! The same is true for us looking at her, even if she only remembers one life right now. Everyone is different from day to day. We just have more days to remember."

A sudden raucous cheer broke out from the thousands of Einherjar assembled in the hall. Kim turned in time to see one of the walls nearby swing open, revealing a wide stair leading up to an archway. Odin walked through it, waving and smiling, grey beard and floppy hat somehow making his missing eye stand out more than it normally did. Past him flew two birds, both large and black. And after him came Freyja and her cats, Weiss and Schwartz—only rather than the housecat-sized beasts Kim was used to seeing, for whatever reason they were now nearly as large as leopards. Kim hadn't really ever realized before then how dangerous a housecat looked when scaled up to big-cat size.

Odin waved happily at Kim and her friends, then disappeared into a crowd of Einherjar. Freyja walked right up to their tables, cats stalking behind. With an excited squeak, Yari leapt up from her seat next to Loucas, ran straight at Schwartz, and threw her arms around his furry neck.

Kim was standing and moving towards Yari before she realized that there was nothing to be afraid of. Schwartz stood there as Yari stroked the beast's long fine hair. Weiss walked up to Yari and began licking her poofy hair. Then rubbed an unnervingly large shoulder against her, nearly knocking her onto the floor.

"Glad to see you all found the door to Val-Hall!" Freyja said, eyes shining. Kim realized suddenly that quite a lot of her torso was shining as well. Rather than the gown Kim and her friends had usually seen Freyja wearing, she was now dressed as a warrior. Scale armor, row after row of delicately carved plates made out of a material that shone like silver but didn't contain even a hint of tarnish, encased her from throat to thigh, and a longsword hung at her side.

Freyja noticed Kim looking her up and down, then glanced down at her own body, looking surprised.

"Oh! I forgot to change. Oh well! Here you see me as I am when dressed for battle in the ancient style. Today Odin and I were observing a rather epic fight being waged in a version of Earth, about a thousand years before your time, between some poor doomed pagans and a crusading religious army. A very sad day for both sides. But a good one for selecting new Einherjar! Many good men and women fell. We had quite the pick, the old raven-wrangler and I."

"Huh. So everyone here, was picked by you or Odin?" Kim asked.

Freyja nodded. "Yes. Well, aside from you six, but you represent a special case. Odin takes the achievers, I take the lovers. Though in fact there is a lot of crossover between the two. Better to say that we take the best we can find. The ones who attract our attention, across the many threads of reality. Sometimes we actually have to have a little fight over someone. Rommel over there was one such case."

She grinned fiercely, baring her teeth. "I do always enjoy beating Odin at his own favorite game. He really does enjoy the spectacle of battle. Me, I prefer to see the nobility and kindness of those who are caught up in the nightmare, yet still seem to retain their basic humanity."

Kim thought about that for a moment. "So in Rommel's case..."

"Oh certainly, he was a great general, by human standards." Freyja replied. "In your Thread, and in many others. Odin's interest in him made sense, just as it does for many famous soldiers who have achieved beyond what they should have, given the resources at their disposal and the enemies laid out before them. So why did I fight for him, you wonder? Simple: whether because of some deep underlying characteristic unique to his soul, or just because of the fact that history around what you call 1945 is effectively fixed across most of the threads of Midgard, in the end Rommel usually dies because of his adoration for and dedication to his family."

"As a famous general of wartime Germany he was always doomed to earn the hatred of Adolf Hitler, who could never stand anyone more popular than him. And as Hitler's madness wound down to its inevitable conclusion, he could always be counted on to lash out at anyone and everyone. Family meant nothing to him except as a weakness to exploit, and so he did when time came to dispense with Field Marshal Erwin Rommel. Who chose to take poison, in your Thread and so many others, to protect his family from Hitler's wrath."

Freyja smiled. "In the end, I value those whose greatness stems from their love of others. Who put their skills to work, or at least try to, for the good of something greater. And *that*, I'll have you know, is a basic point of contention between myself and Odin, much as it is between the Vanir and Aesir: The aspect of humanity that is more worthy of admiration."

Kim looked at the women sitting to either side of her. "So

Lyudmyla and Aleksandra, here, who chose them?"

"I'm one of Odin's." replied Lyudmyla.

"I'm one of Freyja's." replied Aleksandra.

"And after she chose you, you came here?"

"We did." answered Lyudmyla. "And then we went through our training phase, as our other selves died in their own threads, one by one, and merged into... what was already here."

Kim blinked, trying to remember what Timur had told her, during one break in the endless ascents up the Bunny Slope, about how the Norse mythos said it was all supposed to work. "OK. So now you spend all the time until Ragnarok fighting by day and partying by night?"

"Pretty much." answered Aleksandra. "Although you make it sound so boring and repetitive. Remember that we have an entire universe and multiple realities to explore. And also, that *fighting* is, well, a bit of a metaphor."

"Oh no, more metaphors and philosophy?" Kim moaned. "Isn't there anything, I don't know, consistent and real in all the universe?"

Freyja laughed. "But the metaphors and philosophy are all just part of communicating exactly what *is* consistent, and therefore *real*, at least to you, in the universe you inhabit! But in this case, the metaphor isn't *that* much of a metaphor. Doing anything in the universe requires some kind of basic struggle, one force against another. Breaking a rock and breaking a head are both a kind of fight. That's one of the major mistakes your kind always make when reading words written down by people living in times long past. You always miss the deeper context. When the Norse, through whose eyes you are experiencing this taste of a much broader and richer reality than your mind can possibly comprehend, when they wrote down what their oral histories recalled of our interaction with their distant ancestors, they did the best they could, but inevitably details were missing or wrong."

Aleksandra nodded. "Here in Valhalla, at the junction between Midgard and Asgard, we are *free*. We can do whatever we want, each and every day. We want for nothing, we pursue whatever interests take our fancy, and we prepare as best as we can for the inevitable end-to-be. Ragnarok. The final annihilation. The last battle, the last chance for us to distinguish ourselves, and hope news of our exploits somehow survives the final Ending, despite that being, of course, impossible."

"But until that day comes," she continued, smiling brightly, "we have all the food and drink and shelter a human could ever hope for. And many of our loved ones end up here too. Have you any idea how wonderful it is to see old friends and members of your family, healed of all the wounds and cares of the world, given the opportunity to realize their full potential as human beings? Aside from the knowledge that there's an expiration date for this afterlife, things are actually pretty good around here."

Kim thought about that for a minute, looking around at the throng that surrounded them. "I guess the afterlife isn't so bad, then. Although I get the feeling that a lot of religious people get a *big* surprise when they wake up here."

Lyudmyla shrugged. "Actually, most of the faithful I talk to have come to the conclusion that this place is a sort of middle-space between life and death. Purgatory of a sort. It feels exactly the same as being alive." She hesitated. "Even the times when we get killed again."

Kim didn't know how to respond to that except to stare at Lyudmyla. Who grimaced, shrugged, then explained. "Aleksandra likes to focus on the positive side. But we're also here to do a job, you know, in the end: fight alongside the Aesir and Vanir in the Last Battle. There are at least a thousand doors in Val-Hall, each big enough for at least a thousand Einherjar to march through side by side at the same time. And that's just Odin's bit of real estate, too: many of us spend a lot of our time in Folkvangr, Freyja's hall. But we will be hard-pressed, and there will still be too few of us, on the day the dire-wolf Fenris comes. So we actually do quite a bit of non-metaphorical fighting to prepare for that struggle. Fortunately, Idunn's nectar keeps us technically immortal, so even if we are 'killed' fighting alongside Thor against one of the recurring invasions from Jotunheim or in training out on Vegris, we are always here, awake, and whole again by evening. So, you see, it is actually rather difficult for the religious among the Einherjar to resolve the debate about whether or not this is *actually* the afterlife. Purgatory or heaven, is sometimes a matter of perspective."

"But not everyone makes it here, right?" Kim asked. "Don't most myths talk about an underworld, a bad place for the bad people to go when they die? Sometimes I think that's half of why people want there to be an afterlife, after all. A place where the jerks get their just punishments."

"They do." replied Lyudmyla, looking grim. "And there is... in part. Hel, daughter of Loke, takes interest in certain humans just as we do. Politicians, slavers, dictators, mass murders, other betrayers of humanity: she takes the worst of them to Hel-Hall, and forces them to dine with her day after day and night after night, given the taste and texture of food and drink but none of their essence, none of what actually sustains a person. They live in a nightmare of endless starvation and thirst, driven mad by their own desires for what their old bodies craved and their inability to ever sate them. And, if half the stories are true, she also makes sure that they remain *aware* that they have been driven mad, just to add a layer of torment. Avoiding Hel-Hall is a very wise decision."

Aleksandra nodded vigorously. "Oh yes, you are very

lucky you are Einherjar, and not Hel-chosen! She doesn't always play by the rules, you know. None of them do. Whatever Loke has planned for you, at least you are spared that!"

Kim wasn't sure she agreed, and wondered if being 'selected' by Loke made a difference to them personally, but decided not to argue the point. "So what happens to people who don't rate Hel-Hall or Val-Hall?" she asked instead.

"Two options," answered Lyudmyla. "First, many people slip into Ginnungagap. There they just sort of wait in a kind of limbo until they are drawn back to the world of the living. Reincarnation, of a sort, although no one comes back quite the same as they left. And later lives seem to fold into us the same way lives on different threads do. Buddhists around here say that their karma and attachments keep them tied to life, and when they are free from those they may join us here in the halls of the gods. Some of the animists among the Einherjar argue that those who die with business left unfinished keep going back until what needs to be done is done. Either way, a lot of people go down that road. Living life after life, dying and being reborn."

"And the second option?" Kim asked.

"I'll take this one!" answered Aleksandra. "The rest end up in Helheim, that part of Niflheim Loke's daughter Hel claims for her own. There they rest, and sleep, and no one knows what they dream, if anything. Electric sheep, for all we know, though if androids go to Hel, we've received no report. And of course some, those who draw Hel's particular interest, are called to Hel-hall, while others simply sleep until the end of days."

Kim sat silently for a long while, still disturbed by whatever melancholy had gripped her, keeping her from relaxing and celebrating her continued survival along with her friends. Part of her wondered if they had actually 'survived' at all. Maybe they'd all been killed in Iceland, and this was their afterlife. Who could tell? Apparently there was some sort of human afterlife, multiple *flavors,* in point of fact, run by beings calling themselves gods, who had powers that made them effectively gods to Kim and her friends, who made choices about what people ended up in which afterlife. Of course, it only sort of half-mattered because all of it was doomed to end in the destruction of everything anyway.

It wasn't *necessarily*, at least in theory, that she even minded that she was dead, if this were actually the afterlife, and it lasted forever. But being dead, and finding out that everything just sort of... continued? But would end again at some point in the near future in *another* death, leading to who knows what? Something about that, she found fundamentally depressing.

She turned her head to see Freyja staring directly at her. Kim often had the distinct sense that Freyja could tell what she and her friends were thinking. Sometimes, looking at the seemingly, well, *human*-like gods, Kim could still discern, for a fleeting instant, that something far deeper, infinitely more knowledgeable and powerful, lay behind their eyes. It never lasted very long, and always left her feeling unsettled. There again: she didn't know why. She just knew how she felt. And she had learned early on in life to trust her instincts. Even if they were not always right, they were rarely entirely wrong.

"Yes, I think you may be one of mine, in the end." Freyja said, her voice quiet and thoughtful. "You don't really accept any of this, do you?"

Kim remained quiet for a long moment, staring back into Freyja's eyes.

"No." she answered. "I don't. But I also am starting to think, maybe, it doesn't matter. At least not yet." She hesitated, then added almost flippantly, "I may change my mind about that later, though."

"Good! Me too!" exclaimed Freyja, suddenly bright and cheerful again. "Oh, but look—Huginn and Muninn, Odin's ravens, are picking a fight with Schwartz and Weiss again. Fun times! My cats *love* to dismember irritating birds. Get 'em, kitties! *Kill them like they're the red dot!*"

Kim turned around, and saw what was to her, despite everything she'd seen and done the past few days, still the strangest sight of her life. Two leopard-sized house cats were standing on their hind paws, whacking furiously at two enormous black birds that cawed and squawked as they darted through the air just out of the felines' reach. All the nearby Einherjar were jumping and cheering and whooping at the spectacle, and Odin sat on a chair that had been placed on top of a table, as if he were a wizened old referee at a strange sporting match. And he was clearly biased: he was shouting curses at the cats and cheering on the birds. Freyja leaped onto their table, then jumped across others to stand at Odin's side, sword drawn, shouting challenges and threats at the swooping ravens, and encouragement to the massive cats.

Kim watched befuddled for a long while, then saw her friends grinning and cheering along with the rest of the crowd. And in that instant her mood lifted. She looked down at the mug of mead in her hand and drained it in a long gulp. Then she stood up, and went to join her friends.

End of Book One

The Saga of Six Friends continues in Book Two, as the First Season of Fimbulwinter draws to a thrilling close...

POSTSCRIPT

Thank you for reading Bringing Ragnarok!

Reviews are extremely helpful in convincing other readers to check out the story, so if you would be willing to write a review on Amazon or rate on Goodreads, I'd be very grateful!

Be sure to check out the next entries in the Saga of Six Friends:

Book Two released December of 2018

Book Three released August 2019

Book Four released February 2020

Book Five coming July 2020

Book Six coming Winter 2020

If you'd like to receive an email when new books are released: https://bringingragnarok.substack.com/

And for those readers who love their lore, this edition now includes an Appendix section with information about the mythology, history, and technology behind the Saga of Six Friends.

ABOUT THE AUTHOR

Andrew M. Tanner is a writer hidden deep in Cascadia, sharing a century-old home with a wonderful spouse, cats, and dogs.

Worked jobs in the military, public, and private sectors. Spent way too many years as a doctoral student trying to figure the world out. Now writes fiction, usually overseen by one or more felines.

APPENDIX A

*Bringing Ragnarok and
Norse Mythology*

WORLDS

There are Nine Worlds known to the gods: Aelf-heim, Asaheim, Jotunheim, Midgard, Muspelheim, Niflheim, Svartaelfheim, Vanaheim, & Yggdrasil.

Aelfheim

Mysterious home of the Aelfar, alleged to be a place of light and incarnate joy. Only a few of the Vanir, notably Freyr, have ever been there, and all who have refuse to speak of the experience.

Asaheim

Home of the Aesir, a place where time as humans know it has no meaning, all things that live do so for eternity. Asgard is a fortress at the boundary between Asgard and Midgard, the only remaining point of transit between Midgard and the other Nine Worlds.

Jotunheim

Home of the Jotnar, a place of illusion and seeming chaos exceedingly difficult to traverse. Source of what is known as quantum mechanics to physicists in Midgard. The frag-mented Jotnar clans battle for control over a vast and ever-shifting landscape, most hostile to outsiders – but not all.

Midgard

Home of humanity, and a multiverse: an interwoven series of independent realities – chains of cause and effect linking all matter within from the Beginning to the End. Created by the god Ymir in an experiment that somehow blended Worlds, in Midgard the raw energies of Muspelheim are bound together by quantum effects originating from Jotunheim and by the force of gravity from Niflheim. This has produced the astonishing degree of variety embodied within Midgard, bringing the gods themselves into the new World.

Muspelheim

Home of the Muspelli, the World that is the original home of all energy and matter presently trapped within Midgard. To outsiders, it is an impassable burning land guarded by a fierce warrior named Surtur.

Niflheim

A dark misty realm, the source of gravity in Midgard. Human souls that have committed dark deeds are drawn down to Niflheim, and in the worst part of it the cruel goddess Hel has established her home: Hel-hall, where the worst of humanity is drawn after death and subjected to perpetual torment at her pleasure.

Svartaelfheim

Home to the enigmatic Svartaelfar, masters of material and shaping. Source of many artifacts of great power, only a few Aesir and Jotnar are sufficiently respected that they are allowed to travel there.

Vanaheim

Home of the Vanir, a place where life never ends, only changes through the endless seasons. Idunn's apples, from which the mead of endless life is brewed, are imbued with the essence of Vanaheim and are responsible for keeping the gods and their Einherjar young and healthy until Ragnarok.

Yggdrasil

The World Tree, an entirely unknown realm that permeates all Worlds, but cannot be traced back to a single physical source by any science known to the gods. It is said that when Ragnarok comes, and all Worlds are destroyed in the great cataclysm, this will be the death of Yggdrasil as well –

the true End of all things.

PEOPLES

Aelfar

Aelfar, sometimes called Elves, are mysterious non-corporeal beings from Asaheim, the World of light. Their true nature and essence is entirely unknown, and their individual motivations range wildly from individual to individual – save for one defining aspect: they all seek out novel experiences. In Midgard, this often takes the form of existing as a material or living part of the landscape, or appearing to select humans in a convenient form to dispense wisdom or prophecy.

Some have taken Aelfar to be the same beings as Angels, however this is not entirely accurate. While many, perhaps most Aelfs are benevolent, appearing to humans as companion creatures or spiritual guardians who look out for their ward's fortunes, others are more akin to demons, phantoms, monsters and other malevolent spirits that seek to afflict humanity. It is generally impossible to know any given Aelfar's true intentions, and some are known to be as manipulative as Jotnar. Of the gods, only the Van Freyr comes close to truly understanding the Aelfar, and so Odin granted him the sole right to mediate between Alf and god in any dispute.

Aesir

The Aesir, singular *As* or *Asa*, originate from the World of Asaheim. A people with no inherent understanding of the concept of time, their culture holds achievement and distinction in the face of difficult odds in the highest esteem. Those who originally entered in to Midgard as explorers include Odin and his brothers, who killed Midgard's accidental creator, Ymir and shaped the World as humans experience it today.

Odin leads the Aesir, who have entered into Midgard and long lived among humans in many different guises across the ages, always inspiring them to live according to the values of the Aesir – striving, achieving, conquering. Odin takes half of those humans slain as a result of their commitment to these values, housing them in Valhalla where they serve as immortal warriors of the gods, the Einherjar, until the End.

Einherjar

Humans whose lives embodied values the gods hold in esteem are called to Asgard to serve for the rest of Time as Einherjar, guardians of Asgard and sworn allies of the gods. In Valhalla and Folkvangr – Odin and Freyja's halls for them, respectively – they spend their days pursuing perfection in whatever arts or skills they were renowned for in life, and they spend their nights in whatever bliss seems most fitting, aided in their celebrations by Idunn's life-giving and selectively intoxicating mead.

A large fraction of the humans who have ever lived end up as Einherjar, and the gods seek a sample of all skills and passions to fill the ranks, as none knows from what quarter a reprieve from the death of all Worlds in Ragnarok may come. Upon selection, Einherjar are granted the gift of ever-life, and experience a time where their other selves – human souls being split across the Threads of Midgard – slowly merge into a coherent personality. While intense and difficult, once complete the Einherjar experience what feels like an eternity of bliss, reuniting with many of their loved ones as well as the spirits of creatures they cared for in life.

Muspelli

Little is known about the Muspelli, only what Surtur, fiery champion and guardian of Muspelheim, has been willing to tell. Muspelli exist as a single shared mind, intrinsically bound with all others of their kind yet still retaining a distinct sense of self. Before Midgard, they simply existed – and then a portion of the totality was bound to Midgard, atomized and reassembled, becoming what humans know as matter and energy.

This is a great agony to their kind, and Surtur waits ever at the edge of his realm, seeking any opportunity to reclaim his people's own essence from their intolerable servitude. At the End of all Worlds he will march with fiery legions at his side, burning land, sea, sky and stars before Freyr of the Vanir slays him, and in the burning god's death throes he will unleash all the fires of Muspelheim in a great conflagration that consumes all Worlds.

Jotnar

The Jotnar of Jotunheim are as wild and changeable as the World they inhabit. Commonly referred to in the Eddas as giants or trolls, every Jotun has an intrinsic ability to alter the quantum properties of matter around them, granting them effectively magical abilities when in Midgard or on their home turf. They cherish individualism in any form and as a result their internal society is so riven by tribal and family conflicts that many choose to flee to other realms. Jotnar have been in Midgard as long or perhaps even longer than the Aesir or Vanir, though are less fixated on humanity.

In Midgard, it is primarily the kind of Jotnar who enjoy preying on or manipulating humans are encountered, hence the memory of their reputations as giants, trolls, youkai, archdemons, and other demonic entities in many cultures. Grendel and her dark brood, attested in the Saga of Beowulf, were likely of giant-kind. But Ymir who birthed Midgard was also a Jotun, as is Heimdall, Loke's Enemy, the shining god who stands in eternal watch over the rainbow bridge Bivrost. Heimdall is in fact the son of no fewer than *nine* Jotnar mothers. Neither inherently good nor evil, lawful or chaotic, Jotnar are however in all circumstances extremely dangerous to mortals, and Loke Laufeysson – he who will bring Ragnarok upon the Nine Worlds – along with his children Hel, Jormungand, and Fenris are all extremely powerful among giant-kind.

Svartaelfar

Strangely, each Aelfar exists in duality with a radically different aspect of themselves: their Svartaelfar or Dark Elf version. One can only ever interact with either the Aelfar or Svartaelfar aspect at once, when one exists the other apparently cannot for reasons the gods do not fathom. Though eternally linked, Aelfar and Svartaelfar are distinct beings expressing entirely different interests and motivations.

Svartaelfar, also called Dwarves, are fanatically obsessed with the shaping of materials. The smithies of Svartaelfheim produce diverse artifacts of incredible power out of seemingly mundane materials, many are kept as treasures by the Aesir and Vanir. Some Svartaelfar, for reasons only they understand, choose to submit to the rule of Odin in exchange for the ability to shape the most unique material of all – individual humans. These, the Valkyries, bring spirits of the dead selected by Odin and Freyja to Asgard to serve as Einherjar until the End.

The Dead

Humans whose deeds in life are sufficiently ignoble and cruel find themselves dragged to Niflheim. It is said each person, after life, learns of the full scope of impacts of their living deeds free from the constraints of human psychology. And with this knowledge, the soul judges itself, either lingering in Ginnungagap – the space between Worlds – until rebirth in Midgard... or falling to Niflheim. There some slumber tormented by dreams, others shamble naked through the cold mist in perpetuity, and still others are called to suffer a worse fate, suffering perpetual agony in penance for mortal acts of terrible violence. The worst of the worst: mass murders, serial killers, vicious psychopaths – these are brought by Hel to her dark hall to spend all Time suffering the worst of torments at her pleasure.

Vanir

There is an old saying among the Vanir, that As and Van are but a shade closer to one another in temperament as each is to their mutual antagonist, the Jotnar. Originating from the World of Vanaheim, a realm where life is eternal and nothing decays, Vanir culture embraces cultivation, celebration, and community. They value above all other qualities *love,* and the sacrifices made in its service.

Njord led them into Midgard, where the incredible variety of life they saw did or could exist mesmerized the Vanir. They, like the Aesir, quickly discovered humans and for long ages lived among them, teaching them to tame and harvest the wild lands so that they might grow in numbers and prosper. After encountering the Aesir, hostilities broke out that trapped humans between the warring tribes, a difficult and devastating period lasting until a truce was arranged that would unify the two peoples and secure a lasting peace. Until, of course, the Jotnar came.

GODS

Aesir

Frygga

Odin's wife, Lady of the Aesir, who presents herself much as her spouse does: old and wise. Her wisdom is geared towards prophecy rather than simple knowledge, and Frygga knows more of the future than almost anyone in existence. A brilliant problem-solver who is known to intervene in subtle ways to the benefit of humans, Frygga is particularly affiliated with childbirth and destiny, and knows the varied courses within the Web of Norns better than almost anyone. She like Odin is concerned with the dispensation of justice, focusing more on household and community struggles than the affairs of kings.

Frygga attempted to save as much of Asgard and humanity as she could by birthing a son with Odin, Baldr, who was invulnerable to all but seemingly minor threats, could theoretically have survived Ragnarok. Sadly this hope of salvation died thanks to Loke. His betrayal of the Aesir in engineering the circumstances leading to Baldr's demise made Frygga his permanent enemy, particularly as she knows he will also be responsible for Odin's death at Ragnarok.

Odin

Leader of the Aesir, Allfather – so called because he has lived many lives as humans and parented many children – the god of many names, wisest of all gods. Appears as an old man, wrapped in a grey cloak, often hooded. Has only one eye – One-Eye is another of his names, giving the other to Mimr in order to gain access to knowledge held in a pool under Yggdrasil's root. Carries a spear named Gungir and rides an eight-legged war-horse named Sleipnir to battle. Will fall to Fenris at Ragnarok, patient wisdom falling to insatiable desire, but will be avenged by his son Vali.

Odin as Lord of the Aesir he is also a master of war and warfare. He is associated with the outcome of battles and sometimes even death itself. Known as the god of hanged men, Odin is said to visit with the recently dead to learn from them. Wolves and ravens, carrion eaters often seen on ancient battlefields after a struggle, are associated with Odin, who was called Wotan in Anglo-Saxon and German cultures, who were close kin to the Norse. Grim as this may sound, Odin is equally renowned as the god who brought the sacred mead of poetry – words of power – to Asgard, and is a dispenser of justice when people of power fail to live according to a basic code of proper moral conduct: offering food to the hungry and shelter to the un-housed, defending one's family and clan, and pursuing vengeance against those who harm your kin. Odin also exhibits a reputation for clever subterfuge, setting in motion plots that unfold over generations.

Sif

Thor's wife, an Aesir with the ability to shape-shift thanks to a Svartaelf artifact, a golden wig. A natural scout, Sif accompanies Thor on many of his expeditions in various guises. Sif's natural shape is actually only known to Thor himself, and she sometimes doesn't bother to maintain a given appearance from one moment to the next. Loke's destruction of her original golden head of hair resulted in an enraged Thor demanding a replacement and a sequence of events leading to the forging of Mjolnir – as well as Loke's mouth being sewn shut.

Skadi

Skadi is an Aesir goddess associated with wild lands, forests, and the hunt a woman of the mountains, tough and hardy, and a match for Tyr in individual combat. She was formerly wedded to Njord of the Vanir, but the pair separated as they preferred dramatically different living conditions. She is rarely seen in Asgard, preferring to remain in her own hall along with a select few Einherjar, honing their skills for the Last Battle to come.

Thor

Thor is the son of Odin, the Thunder God, sometimes called Asa-Tor or simply Tor, wielder of the enchanted hammer Mjolnir and noted slayer of Jotnar. A patron of farmers and yeomen in old Scandinavia, Thor appears as a massive red-bearded man with dark skin, powerfully build and used to difficult journeys and long labor. He drives a chariot pulled by two self-reincarnating rams, Tanngrisnir and Tanngjnostr, and has a special strength-enhancing belt and gauntlets that offset Mjolnir's shortened handle.

Thor embodies the spirit of freedom, and is eternally set against his blood-uncle Loke's son Jormungand, the World Serpent who is the living essence of the spirit of Empire. Thor is effectively an anarchist, guardian of the downtrodden and repressed, who spends most of his life making sure neither Jormungand nor any other ambitions Jotun is able to accumulate power in Midgard. He will face his arch-enemy one last time at Ragnarok, slaying the World Serpent before succumbing to its lethal poison nine steps later.

Tyr

Tyr is a god of battle and individual combat. Appearing as a rugged, scarred, older man, Tyr is missing a hand thanks to Fenris. When the gods realized how powerful Loke's son would become, they sought to restrain him by tricking him into accepting being bound by a magic Svartaelf necklace. Fenris was rightly suspicious of the innocent-looking band

and demanded a pledge against treachery, so Tyr put his hand in Fenris' mouth – then lost it when the deceit was revealed and the dire-wolf's jaws snapped shut. He will slay many Jotnar at Ragnarok, falling in single combat not long before Freyr's final duel with Surtur.

Vanir

Freyja

Lady of the Vanir, the golden goddess, symbol of prosperity and fertility – Freyja typically appears as you would expect a Norsewoman might: fair skin, red-gold hair, tall, happy disposition tempered with the capacity for sudden violence. Daughter of Njord, lord of the Vanir, and brother of Freyr, Freyja is held as the Vanir's leader and representative in Asgard, co-equal with Odin and sovereign in her sphere. She lays claim to half of the Einherjar, setting aside space in Folkvangr for those who are in the mood for a less overtly riotous atmosphere than you typically find in Valhalla.

Freyja is particularly associated with passion, gold, and the fabled necklace Brisingamen. She is a known lover of cats, and a team of them pulls her war-chariot in battle. Her beauty is acclaimed across many Worlds, and Freyja has been subject to numerous attempts at kidnap or forced marriage by Jotnar across the ages. But she has only one true love, her husband Odde, who disappeared long ago and who she searches for age after age, shedding tears across Midgard in her long quest. Her adventures led to gold, freely dispensed by Freyja in her journeys, being referred to as Freyja's tears.

Freyr

Freyja's brother Freyr is her twin, so close in appearance the only way to tell them apart is by the length of their hair – hers longer, his shorter – and which is more drunk on average. A happy god, embodying the spirit of joyful celebration, Freyr is uniquely associated with life itself, even granted the unusual ability to travel to Aelfheim and deal with the strange Aelfar in their own realm. He has the best ship out of all the gods, Skidbladnir, and affiliated with boars, especially the golden boar Gullinbursti, both gifts from Svartaelf smiths to the prince of the Vanir.

Freyr's fate is to stand alone at Ragnarok against Surtur, he the embodiment of joyful life locked in a terminal struggle against a foe committed to all life's end. Unfortunately, his happy disposition in life gets the better of him – Freyr formerly possessed a sword that flew up and automatically defended him against any threat, but he gave it away in order to win the affection of a pretty Jotun. As everything burns around him, Freyr will be forced in desperation to use his treasured drinking horn as a weapon, striking a fatal blow deep into Surtur's eye at the cost of his own life.

Gefjon

A goddess associated with working the land, Gefjon is a short, broad, muscular, sun-baked woman associated with cattle and the plow. She is unusual among the gods in that she spends most of her time in Midgard, tending to the land in places where no one goes, preparing them for the day when the lands change and people will move in search of new, more fertile horizons. Rarely seen in the bustle of Asgard, she is a patron of all who work and protect the land.

Heimdall

The pale god, son of nine mothers, Guardian of Bivrost. Heimdall is technically of the Jotnar, but was adopted in infancy by the Vanir. He is Loke's bane, and will defeat him in single combat at Ragnarok – at the cost of his own life. Heimdall spends most of time on an endless watch at the edge of Asgard, looking over the Rainbow Bridge Bivrost for the first sign of Loke's attack at the End of Days. Then he will blow the Gjallarhorn as Bivrost breaks and all Worlds are consumed.

Idunn

The goddess who brews the Mead of Everlife from the Sacred Apples of Vanaheim, keeping the gods and Einherjar young forever. Her drinks can treat any ailment or condition known to mortals or gods, and she is always experimenting with new and more potent or customized effects. Idunn appears as a slight woman with a dark complexion, keen intelligence, sharp wit and a dedication to healing living things.

In many ways representing the truest essence of the Vanir, Idunn is closely associated with agriculture and cultivation. She may or may not have been the goddess who first nudged several human communities across the ancient world to investigate the secrets of cooperatively organizing landscapes to increase food production, and can often be found tending the gardens of Folkvangr alongside kinsman Njord.

Njord

Originally the leader of the Vanir, his own temperament and the fact his daughter Freyja and son Freyr were largely raised in Asgard made it easier to pass leadership onto them as soon as they were ready. An avid gardner, Njord spends most of his days and nights in Asgard's courtyards and pathways, endlessly tending to his many little cares as he awaits the inevitable End. He and Idunn have almost a father-daughter relationship, as Freyja and Freyr's affinity for material wealth and celebration are sometimes in tension with Idunn and Njord's preference for things that grow.

Jotnar

Fenris

Loke's monstrous son, a ravenous creature in wolf-shape whose sole goal is to consume all he can before the End. When he was born in Asgard, the gods soon recognized he would pose a terrible threat to them. They refused to kill any being in Asgard itself, and so contrived to bind Fenris and imprison him before he could become too powerful to control. He agreed to a contest – they would try to secure him in his powerful wolf-form but without any recourse to sorcery. He believed he would gain fame and demonstrate his power for all time by shattering the strongest fetters the gods could forge.

After two failed attempts, the gods resorted to deceit – they had a Svartaelf band made that he and only he could never break. Tyr lost his hand as a result, but the gods were successful, imprisoning Fenris in Gnipa cave until the End. He, driven mad by his isolation, has sworn to fulfill prophecy and march with his kin against Asgard in the Last Battle – Skoll and Hati will swallow the moon and sun, while he himself meets and consumes Allfather Odin before being killed by Odin's son Vali.

Loke

The Betrayer, embodiment of the mythology of the trickster spirit found across human cultures, the Enemy of Heimdall, Laufey's son. Born in Jotunheim, he came to Asgard during the Aesir-Vanir war and became Odin's sworn blood-brother. A boundary figure with fraught relationships across the Worlds, Loke – often called Loki and sometimes Lopt, is fiercely individualistic and has always pursued his own agendas, often creating mayhem for the gods.

He is the father of the demonic Hel, monstrous Fenris-Wolf, and the great World Serpent Jormungand. Loke is also the *mother* of Odin's warhorse Sleipnir as a result of an incident involving shape-shifting. His betrayals finally became too much to bear when Loke engineered the death and terminal imprisonment in Hel of Baldr, and he sealed his fate in rather grand fashion after Baldr's demise when he arrived at the Great Hall in Asgard and insulted every leading As and Van present. They hunted Loke down and bound him to a stone with manacles forged from his son's guts. To ensure he would lay in torment until the End, a venomous snake was set in branches above him, dribbling poison onto him.

There Loke stays until Ragnarok, attended only by his wife Sigyn who collects as much poison as she can before departing to empty the bowl – then the snake venom strikes, paining Loke so greatly his agony causes earthquakes on Earth until she is able to return. One day, he will finally break free from this prison and bring the Last War upon the Nine Worlds, leading the Army of the Dead alongside a great Jotnar horde and Surtur backed by the burning sons of Muspelheim. They will break Bivrost and reach Vegris Plain, where the gods and their allies, Einherjar and Valkyries, will meet Loke's forces in the Last Battle. He and his nemesis Heimdall will fight their fateful duel, each slaying the other.

Hel

Daughter of Loke, cruel mistress of Hel-Heim, a terrible hall filled with the tormented Dead. Her body and voice are half corpse, half beauty, and has chosen to make her abode in the dark mists of Niflheim, receiving those human souls that commit terrible acts in life. Her motivations are mysterious, even to close kin, and she acts mostly to fill seats on the benches in Hel-Hall with the worst of the worst, leaving lesser souls to slumber miserably or wander hopelessly amid the freezing mists of Niflheim.

Her great prize, Baldr son of Frygga, remains as guest of honor in her hall, frozen in place and surrounded by icy chains. Upon his death, an Aesir named Hermod rode on Sleipnir to Hel on behalf of Frygga to beg her son's release. Hel agreed, but only if every living thing in Midgard shed a tear. All did, except one Jotun, a giantess named Toek who was probably Loke in disguise.

Jormungand

The World Serpent, son of Loke, sworn enemy of Thor. Early in life, Jormungand – sometimes spelled Jormungandr – slipped into Midgard and disappeared into its infinite

Threads, emerging after the Aesir-Vanir war and attempting to seize direct control of Midgard by force. As the gods had spent countless ages across innumerable realities with humans, so Jormungand had spent ages among other beings, cultivating them and eventually compelling them to building powerful interstellar empires with Jormungand as god-king.

Early in Earth's history, the Midgard serpent attacked, Jormungand encircling the planet with a great fleet in hopes of expelling the gods. Aesir and Vanir fought back fiercely, and much of Earth was devastated – catastrophes that the gods would later discover had echoed through the multiverse with dramatic and permanent effects. Thor took up the mantle as humanity's protector and enemy of the Serpent Empire, finally forcing Jormungandr to retreat in a confrontation where a throw of Mjolnir took one of the World-Serpent's eyes. At Ragnarok they will meet again, Thor winning outright this time, but falling soon after thanks to Jormungandr's poison.

Others

Baldr

The Golden God, god of hope, also called Baldur, a deceased Aesir and son of Odin and Frygga imprisoned in Hel until Ragnarok destroys all Worlds. Born to be invulnerable to anything in Midgard except mistletoe, Loke contrived to have him killed with an arrow made of it. This led to his imprisonment and torment, and also destroyed the possibility of a better world emerging from the wrath of Ragnarok.

Mimr's Head

Mimr was an Aesir, who was sent to Vanaheim as a hostage along with a kinsman named Heod – they were exchanged for the Vanir lord Njord and his son Freyr to end the Aesir-Vanir War. Mimr – also spelled Mimir or just Mim – was brilliant at reading the Web of Fate, and Heod relied on him to make decisions. The Vanir, discovering Heod was unable to act independently, believed they had been tricked and decapitated Mimr as punishment, sending his head back to Odin along with allegations of deceit. Odin chose to preserve Mimr's head using runic magic in order to continue consulting him. Mimr's Head now exists as a digital god within the Web of Norns, helping Odin and his allies read the fates. To preserve the peace, the Vanir were not punished.

Norns

Early in Midgard's existence, three Jotnar women came to Asgard: Urth, Verthandi, and Skuld. They brought news of a flaw within Midgard that would lead to its inevitable destruction – taking all other Worlds along with it. Together they presented to Odin the Web of Fate, a representation of the living multiverse that is Midgard, and warned of the dangers posed to everyone by certain events-that-could-be.

To keep Midgard from self-destructing, the Norns continue to watch over and set the fates of many humans, warning of dangerous developments and guiding Odin, Freyja, and the other gods as they carry out their eternal effort to manage the multiverse, controlling Midgard's development to keep all Worlds intact for as long as they can. When the gods one day fail, a paradox will form within Midgard that will plunge it into the three Seasons of Fimbulwinter, then Ragnarok.

Surtur

Guardian of Muspelheim, warrior of the Muspelli who will lead an army of his people in the Last Battle. His goal is to destroy Midgard and thus reunite his people at any cost, and when Freyr deals him a mortal blow he will succeed, and Midgard will die – all Worlds with it.

PLACES

Asgard

The home of the gods, both Aesir and Vanir, Asgard is a boundary region between Asaheim, Vanaheim, and Midgard. It is the sole point where those from outside Midgard can cross Bivrost, and as a result is highly coveted by people from all Worlds. Each of the gods has their own home in Asgard, and the halls for Einherjar Valhalla and Folkvangr are located there as well. Places within Asgard are connected by a series of hallways and doors, that generally take a person wherever they wish to go in an instant.

Bivrost

The shimmering rainbow barrier and bridge that separates Midgard from the other Worlds, save at a single point – Vegris Plain, watched over by Heimdall of the Vanir. The gods cross Bivrost to travel to Midgard, and its fate is to be destroyed by the power of Loke and Surtur in Ragnarok.

Folkvangr

Einherjar who catch Freyja's eye are given a place in Folkvangr, a living landscape no less celebratory, but typically much quieter than Valhalla. There too food and drink are available as one wishes, but Einherjar generally choose Folkvangr when they seek contemplation or solitude, sometimes for gatherings of very close friends.

While Valhalla is set up a vast Hall with infinite rooms and a carefully tended courtyard, Folkvangr is a cultivated wilderness, and the Vanir manage it so that it offers a sample of all life that has ever emerged in Midgard. Idunn grows many of her apples in Folkvangr, attuning these especially to the needs of the humans who spend their afterlife in the gods' domain.

Ginnungagap

The space between Worlds, it was Ymir's blending of the essences of Jotunheim, Niflheim, and Muspelheim in Ginnungagap that brought Midgard into being. Loke's prison is located there, and it is also the place where souls linger between lives, awaiting rebirth. Infrequently, humans in remote places wander into Ginnungagap, rarely to be seen again.

Hel-Hall

Realm of the dark mistress, the twisted Hel, few who enter this place ever return. Home for the worst of humanity, dictators and mass murderers, callous political leaders and those consumed by greed, life in Hel-hall is eternal starvation and thirst without hope of relief. Beyond Hel-Hall proper, the ignoble Dead wander or sleep, waiting for the End, when they will rise again and take vengeance upon all life, god or mortal.

Mimr's Pub

The gods travel regularly to a place known as the Well of Mimr, located under one of Yggdrasil's roots. For the benefit of the Six Friends, the gods have reserved a space close to Mimr's Well and connected it to the rest of Asgard by a series of halls and doorways. Wherever their six guests wish or need to go, a doorway will soon appear to take them there from one of the corridors leading away from Mimr's Pub.

Valhalla

Odin's hall for Einherjar within Asgard, a place of eternal celebration by night and practice of the arts of war by day. Warriors chosen by the gods are treated to an endless bounty of food and drink, and those who were slain in practice or the battles Einherjar wage against Jotnar awaken in Valhalla where they can recuperate.

Val-hall appears to Einherjar as an ancient Great Hall of the Norse, filled with tables and benches that can be moved around as necessary to facilitate games and other entertainment. Though Valhalla is traditionally the home of warriors chosen by Odin, they mix freely with the Einherjar from Folkvangr, and all the gods can be found drinking with their favorite heroes. There are more rooms in Valhalla than any human can count, and all who come there find their place in time, among human heroes across all the ages of history.

Vegris

A great rolling green plain between the walls of Asgard and Bivrost, site of the Last Battle when the gods will meet and class and destroy all Worlds in their fury. Also spelled Vegrith or Vegrid, the End will come when Loke arrives on the green expanse to take his vengeance on Asgard.

PHENOMENA

Threads Of Reality

Midgard is a Multiverse broken into an infinite number of independent realities. These are chains of cause and effect linking all matter from the Beginning of Time to the End, with each reality evolving on its own separate trajectory.

While each reality is distinct from all others, Threads tend to cluster together and pass through certain defined *critical* points, that constrain what realities out of all that could exist, actually do. Major events in history exist that occur across *all* Threads, giving Midgard an underlying structure that allows external observers like the gods a limited ability to predict the future. Originally, any reality that *could* be possible *was*, until the intervention of the gods themselves unintentionally gave Midgard a 'natural' path through history.

Web Of Norns

The Web of Norns, the Norse version of a concept found across the world – the Celtic Tree of Life and Indra's Net two of the most prominent – is the result of the gods' ability to understand the metastructure of our universe. They have sufficiently explored the many Threads of Midgard, the many alternate realities that exist, to know much of what *will* or *must* be – and so in many cases the future path of a given Thread.

The Norns weave the Fates of Men, it is said in the Eddas, and from a human perspective it seems so, as the Norns can very often tell from a person's birth what their future will hold. But in truth, such seemingly mystical projections are in fact based on information no mortal could possess. If someone were to travel in time and meet a newborn boy in Europe, Asia, or North America in the year 1899 or 1925 for example, they could sadly predict with near-certainty that boy would grow up to wear a uniform and fight in a World War. It would not be absolute certainty, and even the gods are surprised at the vagaries of chance, but on the whole it is impossible for any person to entirely escape the forces of fate in their lives.

However, it must be stressed that some degree of *choice* is always present for all beings capable of acting every moment Midgard exists. Indeed it is the outcome of choices, sometimes even very small ones made by people in unique circumstances, that alter the trajectory of a Thread in dramatic fashion. Any structure is produced by the mutual actions and interactions of agents working within, large and small, to produce a dynamic and ever-evolving entity.

Human Afterlives

Living things in Midgard have always fascinated the gods, who do not die in their own Worlds – at least not in the way humans think of it: a permanent severance of Self from bodily form, with unknowable consequences for the self. They have observed that humans – and ostensibly all other living things in Midgard, including those not from Earth – appear to possess a phenomenon known as the soul.

The soul, from the gods' perspective, is a unique, self-perceiving bundle of ever-shifting memories linked across time. Souls are never destroyed, but they are always in flux and do not always have an opportunity to embody in Midgard. Those who die are never truly gone, but pass into an indefinite realm between Worlds known in the Eddas as Ginnungagap. Similar to the Christian concept of purgatory and perhaps also the Atheist's expectation of bodiless oblivion, souls there exist out of time before reappearing in one of several ways.

Souls may remain in Ginnungagap indefinitely, or be physically reborn in Midgard, or they may – the quality of their lives appears to control this – sink into Niflheim, and remain there for all Time as restless or haunted spirits. Once the gods intervened in Midgard, two new options emerged. The Aesir and Vanir, led by Odin and Freyja, call those they favor to Asgard. Souls who commit terrible deeds are called to Helheim, where Loke's daughter Hel torments them until the End of Time.

APPENDIX B

*Excerpts from Insurgence
Datastore, Coyote Point.*

THE STELLAR CENTURY

by Decade

2040s Chaotic years marked by open warfare in twenty major conflict zones, including dozens of cases where weapons of mass destruction are used. The global economy segments into regional blocs, and societies face upheaval as refugees flow from current and predicted conflicts. Prices for food and energy skyrocket, exacerbating the conflict spiral.

2050s After thirty years of steady escalation, the global geopolitical crisis finally abates as a new set of regional socioeconomic blocs form and establish a tenuous global political-economic balance of power. The development of advanced artificial intelligence and soon after energy-gain fusion sparks a new era of rapid economic growth and global reintegration. Advances in medicine and materials spread across the world, bringing hope for a better future.

2060s The Global Ecological Crisis deepens after a half-century of insufficient global action on reducing carbon emissions and developing sustainable landscapes. Major urban areas are flooded by rising seas and pummeled by storms of unprecedented ferocity. The United Nations is replaced by the Global Governing Authority, which is granted substantial powers. However, it quickly becomes clear that a small group of leaders from a few wealthy regions have gained disproportionate control over how those powers are used.

2070s Colonization of the Solar System advances at a furious pace after two decades of substantial investment in orbital infrastructure by wealthy regions and large private firms. Orbital manufacturing using resources mined by drones and robots in the Mars-Jupiter asteroid belt replaces most production on Earth to mitigate terrestrial pollution. Massive planned urban developments in regions of the planet expected to have a moderate climate attract a billion migrants – those who can afford the high cost of living.

2080s Despite Earth's population stabilizing at nine billion and pollution impacts finally abating, greenhouse gas levels remain at a level where terrestrial feedbacks now guarantee ongoing net emissions into the atmosphere despite the near-cessation of human pollution. Orbital colonization and forced emigration is selected by GGA experts as the only viable option – though this conclusion is widely disputed – and construction of a series of massive space stations begins at the most stable Earth-Sun Lagrange points. Mandatory evacuations from the most ecologically damaged areas begin.

2090s By the start of the decade over a billion humans have moved to orbit, residing in gigantic space stations soon called Habitats by their residents. However, scientists insist billions more must go over the next twenty years to have any chance of stabilizing Earth's deteriorating environment. Widespread forced evacuations of climate-vulnerable zones begin and in 2093 violence breaks out on a large scale for the first time in fifty years as a coalition of economically stagnant regions defies the GGA. The brutal conflict that follows leads to tens of millions of deaths and whole segments of the planet depopulated.

2100 The creation of an even-more powerful Terrestrial Governing Authority (TGA) to replace the GGA is announced along with the news that a new frontier in science has dawned. Advanced machine intelligences (MIs) working with biological researchers have discovered a means of generating and controlling micro-singularities – small black holes. By placing a series of these in long elliptical orbits between Lagrange Points and capturing sufficient matter released by solar flares, a kind of space river is produced dramatically speeding movement across the vastness of the solar system.

2100s Forced evacuations across Earth escalate, now resisted in only a few defensible and remote places by a group calling itself the Insurgence. Regarded as terrorists by the TGA, or 'Toffs' as the organization's detractors term its agents, surviving Insurgence operations are forced to relocate to the distant Belt by 2110 as Earth falls completely under TGA lockdown. Mass deportations continue, slowed only by the time it takes to fuel rockets, and demand for construction material drives breakneck colonization of the material-rich Belt. A wild-west mentality sets in across the region, violence flares between rival groups seeking to control profitable territories and piracy is rampant.

2110s A brutal wave of organized piracy in the Belt results in the TGA announcing the formation of a military branch, the Terrestrial Governing Authority Navy (TGAN), equipped with warships capable of defeating the threat. However, the TGAN's covert purpose is to crush a new version of the Insurgence which is also gaining strength as people across the Belt organize to resist pirate attack and TGA interference alike. Soon the first destroyers, then the larger and more capable cruisers of the TGAN begin to patrol key shipping lanes and the initial foundations of several large Forward Operating Bases (FOBs) are established. A group of cyborgs, or Biomods as most prefer to be called, work with the TGAN to resist the pirates before disappearing into the Belt in fear of the growing evidence the TGA intends to expand its power.

2120s The defeat of the organized pirate groups operating in the Belt morphs into a campaign of repression waged against the Insurgence and its sympathizers, despite a successful multi-year alliance with the TGAN against the pirate bands. All but a few hidden bases are found and destroyed, and the Insurgence is crushed. Meanwhile, the human population in orbit comes to exceed the number of people living on Earth, and to cope with the steady pace of forced emigration a new generation of overtly prison-like Habitats are designed as the TGA seeks to reduce the costs of the orbital occupation.

2130s Earth's depopulation is now largely achieved, yet there is little sign of positive impact on the climate or global ecosystems and vast swathes of the planet remain effectively uninhabitable. Massive, long-lasting weather bubbles form then dissipate unpredictably in many regions, raising local temperatures to lethal levels for weeks to months, the shifting phase to drench everything in rainfall of such intensity buildings and topsoil both wash away. Sea levels continue to rise thanks to the total disappearance of both the Greenland ice sheet and Thwaites glacier in Antarctica. The extinction crisis continues unabated as species across Earth that cannot adapt to the violent oscillations of the new climate perish.

2140s A rebirth of the Insurgence initiates a new wave of resistance, launching desperate hit and run attacks on Navy and Toff ships and facilities. The microsingularity-driven Interplanetary Highway System now extends into Outer Sol, a development expected to cement the TGA's power permanently, rendering the Habitats utterly reliant on them to survive.

Despite an ever-tightening grip on the Habitats, the TGA World-State is still unable to entirely quench all dissent, and anger simmers among populations orbital and terrestrial. Careful conditioning programs started at a young age train those living in the Paradise Zones on Earth to avoid any risk of falling afoul of TGA rules, and those who for physical, emotional, or ideological reasons do not fit in TGA society are subjected to arrest and deportation. In the Habitats, youth who can often slip away to the Belt, either seeking employment or chasing rumors of secret Insurgence bases.

POLITICAL LANDSCAPE OF INNER SOL, 2147

Terrestrial Governing Authority

The TGA – Toffs, to its enemies – developed from the Global Governing Authority which was established in the mid 21st century to coordinate international management of Earth's economic and environmental systems. From the start, this global agency aimed to create a single unified World-State claiming a sovereign right to use any means necessary to maintain order across Earth. Internally dominated by a small group of wealthy and influential politicians distributed across major global cities – particularly Chicago, New York, London, Paris, Rome, Dubai, Bangalore, and Shanghai – the GGA steadily expanded its powers through economic and political means and ground down all resistance.

When the Global Ecological Crisis deepened the GGA's leadership selected the response preferred by its core members and their allies: warehousing billions of people in orbital Habitats. Those unable to pay the environmental impact mitigation fee required to live in climate-reinforced Paradise Zones are forcibly removed from their homes and transferred to enormous space stations constructed by robots at stable Earth-Sun Lagrange Points. The GGA subsequently changed the 'Global' to 'Terrestrial' in its name to reflect it's expanded scope and power.

The TGA formally enforces strict genetic and social criteria for full citizenship, and promotes a eugenics campaign that aims to further differentiate those living in the Paradise Zones on Earth from those born elsewhere. Children are rigorously screened in schools for "antisocial" tendencies – defined as resistance to full integration into Toff society, and formal schooling is a process of formal indoctrination into Toff ideology, which valorizes individual accumulation of material wealth as the penultimate symbol of a person's worth to society. Those of sufficient worth are given access to additional benefits and privileges, including enhanced voting rights in domestic elections, which maintains the TGA's unilateral control.

Solar Insurgence

An umbrella term for a group of allied and partly-coordinated movements that have resisted TGA operations since it was the GGA. Recruiting mostly from groups abused by the system, the Insurgence – typically over-matched – has been all but destroyed three times in fifty years. Operating from bases hidden deep in the Belt, the current incarnation of the Insurgence has adopted a raiding strategy, sending ships disguised as civilian vessels on patrol through Inner Sol, attacking targets of opportunity and passing data between allied groups surviving in the Unorganized Regions.

The Insurgence is loosely governed by a Council comprised of representatives from the three major groups who are oppressed by the Toffs – the poor on Earth and in orbit; cyborgs known as Biomods; and the machine intelligences most refer to as MIs, living machines. The Council authorizes attacks on certain categories of targets and coordinates messaging, but for security reasons does little to intervene in day-to-day affairs of allied forces. Rather, the Council focuses on expanding awareness of the Insurgence, broadcasting promises of a day when a major Toff installation will be destroyed, signaling that the time has come for a massive uprising against the TGA forces occupying the solar system.

TGA Navy

By 2110, piracy in the Belt had become such a threat that independent charters and colonies across the region began working together to field a fighting force capable of bringing some semblance of security to the area. Rightly guessing the Insurgence would soon infiltrate and dominate this nascent power, the TGA – otherwise hands-off when it comes to corporate development of resources – soon intervenes directly in the Belt, setting up a formal military organization charged with maintaining security across the solar system – the TGAN.

Semi-independent, the Navy is a relatively progressive organization drawing in many citizens of the TGA uncomfortable with its violent repression and looking for a better way. It even actively cooperated with the Insurgence to confront and defeat the pirate threat in the Belt throughout the 2110s. However, TGA officials on Earth brought an end to this productive alliance as soon as the fight against the pirates was deemed over, and began construction of new generations of powerful warships that soon allowed the Navy to crush the Insurgence wherever it chose to put up a fight.

Ramallah Theoscience Institute

With all forms of independent political or economic organization banned by the Toffs and movement between the Lagrange Point Habitats severely restricted, few groups have been able to establish a wide presence. However, a group of scholars and religious philosophers came together early on in the construction of the Habitats, setting up independent education centers in the years before the TGA instituted more stringent rules on association and that have been able to persist across the Habitats despite TGA efforts.

Professing a combined spiritual and scientific message of community-based organization and liberation from all ideological or methodological constraints, the Theoscience Institute on *Ramallah Station* has become, by 2147, the closest thing the Habitats have to an organized government.

Corporate Charters

The TGA and its predecessor have always been ideologically committed to partnering with the private sector to effect exploration and colonization of the solar system, and so many if not most operations in places like the Belt are not operated by the TGA, but by contractors. Hundreds of registered charters ranging from small supply runs to full-blown asteroid demolition and processing were farmed out to corporations and entrepreneurs in the late 21st Century, and the survivors of these early start-ups form the backbone of the Belt's material economy. Places like Zocalo Point naturally sprung up in places where profitable asteroids clustered together, serving as frontline bases for human exploration of this vast region of space.

Independents

Also scattered across the Belt are hundreds of completely independent operations established by those lucky few groups who struck it rich – or successfully engage in smuggling and piracy. Space stations large and small are scattered across the region, some self-sufficient to the point their locations are unknown to any authorities. Others, like *Havoc Station*, are amalgams built up over time at a key location, usually near a rich set of asteroids or an intersection between shipping routes that is also too far from the Interplanetary Highway terminals at Point Aleph and Point Zero for a major corporate charter to find the area profitable.

REGIONS

Earth-Luna Security Zone

All non-official orbital traffic is banned per TGA directive in the area within the moon's orbit around the Earth, as well as the space between Earth and the Lagrange Points containing the Habitats. The moon, sometimes called Luna, houses the Navy's primary storage depots and research centers, and the TGAN's primary manufacturing facilities are in lunar orbit. A battle group centered around the largest warship in the fleet, a dreadnought, is always on standby to intercept and destroy any object violating the no-fly zone. The single greatest fear among TGA security officials is an Insurgence vessel flying towards Earth at high speed and on a collision course with a Paradise Zone, as the impact would be similar to that of a small meteor striking a metropolis.

Earth-Sun Lagrange Points

A Lagrange point is a region where the gravity of two bodies effectively cancels out, resulting in an area of space where an object won't be pulled strongly towards either. Though all are slightly unstable over time and perturbed by the motion of other solar bodies, the Earth-Sun Lagrange Points represent ideal spots to locate a facility that needs to orbit the sun with minimal need for correction. This is important to consider when thinking about the energy needed to move a facility capable of comfortably housing fifty million people.

Lagrange Points Four and Five are zones of stability along Earth's orbital path around the sun, and were selected in the 2070s to house the first orbital Habitats because this location saves substantial energy costs over time not lost to adjustment maneuvers. Other Earth-Sun Lagrange Points house giant solar arrays, which beam energy to satellites orbiting Earth providing a source of renewable energy transmitted by concentrated microwaves to receiving stations in Earth orbit.

Habitats

Giant space stations designed to give the housed population a stable and sufficient quality of life over an indefinite period, contingent only on ongoing access to vital materials from the Belt. A series of powerful machine-intelligence controlled fusion reactors offers light, heat, and energy, algae farms exposed to continuous sunlight produce enough basic nutrition to keep millions of people alive. The effects of gravity are simulated by centrifugal forces produced by spinning the inhabited sections of the stations around the central central axis, and oxygen is produced both by the algae and the many other living things grown in, on, and around the buildings inside the stations.

Each Habitat is like a giant city, with vast green spaces set aside for psychological and logistical reasons. Virtually everything is recycled, and as a result most Habitats are surprisingly clean and tidy. While safe and secure, the Habitats face many social challenges as employment is nearly nonexistent and TGA rules prohibit most travel. Support for the Insurgence is strong among the youth, who sometimes get into fights with Toff representatives and agents visiting Habitat stations, bringing invasions by counterinsurgency teams who lock down unruly sections as needed to prevent organized resistance from spreading.

Outer Sol

The gas giants of the solar system – Jupiter, Saturn, Uranus, and Neptune – and their many moons constitute humanity's next frontier. By 2100, the Mars colony had been developed into a staging area for missions to the outer reaches of the solar system, and the extension of the Interplanetary Highway to terminals along Jupiter and Saturn's orbits by the early 2140s will offer access to incredibly rich sources of fusion fuel by 2150. The rocky terrestrial planets of Mercury, Venus, Earth and Mars, along with the Belt and all the orbital infrastructure nearby, are now collectively termed Inner Sol to differentiate between the two regions. Despite the Interplanetary Highway, the distances to Jupiter – not to mention Neptune – are still so great that ships take many weeks to travel there from the Solar Interchange. Only the TGA has operations in Outer Sol, and the Insurgence is unable to reach the area.

Paradise Zones

When the Global Ecological Crisis began to generate tens of millions of refugees in the 2050s, the GGA sponsored corporate development of massive planned cities in places expected to have reasonably stable climates for the next two centuries. Along with the metropolitan areas already in secure areas, these new urban districts were later organized by the GGA into eighteen Paradise Zones, mostly located between forty-five degrees latitude in the northern and southern hemispheres and near the ocean, each home to around one hundred million people and served by carbon-neutral infrastructure. Those living legally in these regions were granted automatic citizenship in the TGA and, in later decades, were not subjected to mandatory evacuation – though a fair number chose to depart, either for the Habitats or, later, the colony on Mars.

Access to a Paradise Zone is limited by wealth, with residents required to pay a universal Global Environment Tax in a fixed amount. Further, those living within one are required to attend mandatory TGA citizenship school, typically until the age of thirty-three, and those who fail at any point risk being labeled antisocial and excluded from full citizenship rights, including voting in elections, owning a business, or having children.

Solar Interchange

The Interplanetary Highway System is anchored to a large orbital facility located in a stable and near-stationary geo-solar orbit. There massive fusion engines controlled by MI teams generate the subtle quantum resonance effects necessary to produce microscopic black holes. These are then propelled in a long comet-like elliptical orbit through a series of guideposts, set thousands of kilometers apart and powered by more fusion reactors to keep the stream on course. It is then is redirected at the receiving end by another terminal, sending the stream back towards the sun. The Solar Interchange is one of the most heavily defended places in Inner Sol, as it is essentially the crossroads of the solar system through which most traffic now passes.

The Belt

The asteroid belt between Mars and Jupiter is a vast area, not as crowded with rocks as some might expect, and contains a planet's worth of raw materials floating in the vast dark that is relatively easy to access. Humans have considered the potential of mining asteroids since the dawn of the space age, but it was the enormous demand for orbital manufacturing as a means of avoid industrial pollution on Earth that sparked the first large-scale explorations and colonization of what became known as The Belt.

Groupings of several asteroids, often called Points, became the focus of systematic development, with thousands of people flocking to them from the Habitats in search of gainful employment and freer living conditions. Robotic cargo ships, little more than shipping containers with small engines, move between Points down regular shipping lanes, allowing trade between outposts and a flow of goods to Earth orbit. Naturally those who choose to engage in piracy are attracted to these lanes, as are smugglers. The latter make their living by covertly removing containers from the regular lane and shipping them down an alternative route that bypasses Navy checkpoints, where heavy tolls are collected to help offset the cost of the occupation.

A vast area between the orbits of Mars and Jupiter, the Belt is somewhat arbitrarily broken up into six distinct Hexants for mapping purposes. The four North and South Hexants, each split into western and eastern halves, represent the primary areas of human colonization – and active TGAN control. Hexants West and East are effectively no-mans land or even Insurgence territory, but settlements are so spread out vital infrastructure is sparse and banditry remains a persistent concern for communities who choose to settle there.

Unorganized Zones

Outside the strictly-controlled Paradise Zones is a broad swath of lands where life is possible, though always tenuous, thanks to the unpredictable climate, badly depleted natural resources, and Toff interventions. Centered around the Caribbean, Mediterranean, and South China Seas, another billion people live without any kind of recognized status, and subjected to invasion and occupation whenever the TGA determines the population in an area has grown too large.

Most of the population in the Unorganized Zones lives in over-crowded and polluted urban areas, often relying on donations from the more open-minded Paradise Zones like Cascadia, Bering, and Baltica, those who can send family members to earn small incomes as household servants. Powerful storms regularly strike in the Caribbean and South China Sea, killing thousands and inundating vast swaths of coastline, and in the Mediterranean heat waves last many weeks and are accompanied by sand storms raging from the surrounding deserts. Water is a prized resource, as is energy

– the Toffs destroy any facility that emits carbon into the atmosphere, forcing reliance on renewables, which are highly expensive thanks to Toff technology licensing laws that are rigorously enforced even in the Unorganized Zones.

Wastelands

An unknown number of people eke out an existence in the desertified wastelands of Earth. The Sahara, the Amazon, the steppes of North America and Eurasia – semi-migratory tribes occupy the lands, moving with animal herds to find water and shade as humans have done in like regions for thousands of years. Officially, the TGA acknowledges no human presence in this area, but estimates range between one hundred million and half a billion people survive there despite radical day-night temperature shifts and persistent droughts. The areas are constantly scanned by TGA satellites, and any large-scale or permanent encampments are raided in days, occupants exiled to the new Mega-Habitats – effectively orbital prisons.

TECHNOLOGICAL ADVANCES OF THE STELLAR CENTURY

Artificial And Machine Intelligence

There remains a fierce debate among scholars regarding the precise definitions of 'machine' and 'artificial' intelligence. However, an artificial intelligence is taken by the majority – excluding Toff scientists, who are ideologically opposed to the concept of non-human life – to mean a set of algorithms capable of exhibiting learning behavior in a defined sphere, but no other substantially demonstrated independence beyond. A *machine* intelligence, on the other hand, means a form of mechanical life, self-aware and capable of independent reasoning, and so in possession of the digital equivalent of an organic mind.

MIs, as opposed to AIs, are much more than a suite of interacting algorithms. Only possible once quantum computing was sufficiently developed in the late 2050s, MIs are complex digital organisms rooted in cell-like coding subroutines that collectively give rise to an apparently spontaneous sense of self among the assemblage, just as occurs in the human brain. The cells at their core are self-organizing and self-sustaining in a limited environment, exchanging energy and information with adjacent cells, and can be adapted by the MI over time to improve functionality as desired.

A minority view, popular only in TGA territory, holds that

AI and MI are indistinguishable, and any perception of intelligence is wishful thinking on the part of creators. As they are proponents of strict controls on what they view as 'AI out of control' the Toffs do not accord MIs any rights and use the fact that many MIs work with the Insurgence as evidence of their inherent danger to mankind. This argument is made despite many MIs insistence that they only join the Insurgence after being deliberately mistreated by the Toffs.

Though MIs can download themselves in whole or in part in order to survive, many are uncomfortable with this and prefer to remain attached to their first physical form. Their consciousnesses are partially separable, meaning that a part will retain an imprint of much of the whole, but memories are invariably lost in the process. A few, facing an existence effectively enslaved by the Toffs, have chosen to abandon much of their selves in order to escape in any form. This further sets them apart from AIs, which have never been shown to demonstrate a sense of concern for their own well-being.

Decontamination

A severe challenge to orbital colonization is the viral, bacterial, and fungal agents that travel with humans. While by the 21st century the global human population was sufficiently well-mixed that there were few independent disease reservoirs capable of producing a truly apocalyptic contagion, the combination of forced isolation and exposure to solar radiation over time raises the risk of virulent mutant strains developing from relatively common infections.

In 2081 a fortuitous discovery was made by a joint human-machine intelligence team, identifying a highly adaptable nanomaterial that could be used to train the immune system to recognize mutations from a known contagion. This substance could be put into an aerosol and sprayed into the air, allowing each independent habitation in orbit the ability to rapidly and reliably disinfect incoming travelers.

The system was quickly made mandatory, reducing the incidence of new infections emerging from the space-born population by 96%. Side effects include swollen lymph nodes and fatigue, both usually passing within a few days.

Fusion

Nuclear fusion is the process by which small subatomic particles merge, releasing energy normally contained in the bonds holding them together as atoms. It only naturally occurs under conditions of extreme gravity like you find at the center of the sun, but can be engineered under the right conditions to produce a controlled reaction. Since the discovery of mass defect – the measured difference between a particle's actual mass and the mass it *should* have according to it's chemical makeup alone – and the recognition that the balance expresses physically as the bonding energy holding atoms together, engineers have sought a means of exploiting this fundamental, latent power source present in all matter.

Nuclear fission involves breaking apart heavy elements like uranium to release this energy, but fusion is a desirable replacement as it produces far less dangerous waste and small elements are more abundant in the universe. However, unlike fission, which can be triggered spontaneously if there is enough of the right substance in a small enough area, fusion requires an external force sufficient to overcome the electromagnetic energy barriers that repel particles with the same charge from fusing together.

In the sun, this happens naturally thanks to gravity. In a human-engineered reactor, until the groundbreaking discovery of a class of electromagnetic phenomena only an artificial intelligence can produce, it always took more energy to start and sustain a fusion reaction than could be obtained from it – it was, in other words, an energy sink, not a source. But once nanomaterial engineering and machine learning had advanced far enough, fusion finally became economically viable, replacing all other energy sources on Earth by

2068 – just fifteen years.

Interplanetary Highway Network

The Interplanetary Highways are captured solar flares propelled down an elongated elliptical solar orbit in an endless cycle. Because microscopic singularities evaporate absent an injection of mass, solar flares naturally produced by the sun are electromagnetically directed into the streams, creating a cloud of particles bound by gravity and slowly falling inward towards the singularities. The movement of the stream between the Solar Interchange and a distant receiving station, combined with the perpetual in-falling of the captured solar wind, together combine to produce a 'river' of moving particles.

Ships – already electromagnetically shielded – can enter the stream, and the force produced by the particles striking and compressing the ship's shields will push the vessel along the course of the river, allowing remote containers to move across the solar system without needing to generate substantial thrust on their own. Since the turn of the century, this system has served to dramatically reduce travel times across Inner Sol – and also channeled virtually all traffic through TGA controlled points in space. The cost to maintain the IPH is enormous, but the ability to rapidly move materials from the Belt closer to Earth and the Habitats has reduced production costs across the board. This has in turn created a sustained economic boost that Toff economists credit with keeping the increasingly unwieldy TGA establishment afloat as the costs of mitigating the rapid ecological changes underway across Earth – not to mention those of occupying the Belt – mount.

Jagdkontrols And Jagers

The project that developed the first Jagdkontrol – from the German words for 'hunt' and 'control' – was born out of the recognition that a compact, smaller vessel would be ideal for evading the targeting systems used by Navy ships, and that a Star-Bridge could allow a human-MI team to offset each form of intelligence's blind spots. Because dense physical objects can be more disruptive to shields than particle beams, a small vessel able to launch physical projectiles into a target offered the potential for Raiders to take on mid-sized warships like Navy cruisers.

The Jager, which means 'hunter' in German, is a drone made of superdense materials wrapped around a fusion battery – a self-contained but relatively fast-fading fusion reaction requiring regular recharge. A basic artificial intelligence gives the six Jagers in a flight the ability to flock like birds and jointly sense threats, so once directed to guard or attack an area they will do so on their own until lack of power forces them to return to the mothership. Three flights of six comprise an Insurgence Jagdkontrol's Jager complement, which are used to severely disrupt a hostile vessel's shields as the Insurgence vessel darts by or form a mobile physical barrier to block incoming attacks.

Particle Beams

The primary weapon of most warships in space is a directed stream of highly charged particles emitted by the fusion reactor and passed through an accelerator before being sent across space at a target. Fusion byproducts come in several forms, ranging in size from subatomic particles left behind by shattered atoms to larger molecules often stripped of their electron shell, rendering them highly reactive.

These are accelerated to nearly the speed of light and sent against the target, with the magnitude of the effect achieved depending on the size of the fusion reactors powering the combatant vessels and the distance between them – energy disperses across space, even in near-vacuum. A small ship will be unable to do any degree of substantial damage to a larger one in most cases, while a large ship can blast through the shields of a smaller in seconds, meaning that small ships must rely on speed and keeping a healthy distance to survive.

When either the opposing shield layers have been compressed beyond the breaking point or to the point they overlap with solid matter like the ship's hull, the cascade of energized particles slamming into a solid surface often generates a violent explosion. The atmosphere within the ship will spontaneously ignite around the point of impact, sending a destructive shockwave through the rest of the interior, often leaving no survivors. Large vessels have multiple separate sections to mitigate the damage in this situation, but smaller ones like cruisers, destroyers, and Insurgence Raiders do not.

Shields

Protecting biological and electrical equipment in space has presented a severe challenge for human extra-orbital travel since it began in the 1950s. The fusion reactions at the heart of the sun emit a constant stream of energy that can penetrate unprotected tissue and cause severe genetic damage, and physical objects – even a pebble – are moving so fast they can tear through steel and cause explosive decompression. On Earth, the thick atmosphere mostly protects humans from the danger of fast-moving rocks. Beyond the atmosphere, engineering solutions are required.

Modern shield technology is made possible by fusion. Out of the incredible power contained in an active fusion core comes a perpetual shower of charged subatomic particles, electromagnetic waves, and daughter isotopes that exit the reaction mass at high speed. Much is converted to electrical energy, far more is diverted to the engines, weapons, and shields. These shields are essentially sandwiched layers of charged subatomic particles, protons and electrons, arranged so that their flows tend to repel one another, creating a kind of electromagnetic matrix that requires substantial energy to compress or breach.

Incoming particles and energy waves strike the shield and tend to be deflected or repelled, with part of the energy neutralized and the rest absorbed by physical compression of the shield layers that resist being pushed together. This level of protection has proven sufficient, in conjunction with physical shielding on vessel hulls, to protect crew-members from the negative effects of solar radiation on biological tissues as well as dangerous small objects. Warding off an intentional attack, however, necessitates a powerful reactor – in space combat, the reactor with more power tends to win a fight.

Star-Bridge

In 2124, Insurgence scientists on Coyote Point discovered a means of hijacking the human dream state and convincing a person's mind to perceive itself as being physically present in a virtual reality environment. A nanomaterial embedded with countless tiny electrodes encases the body of a subject in an environment-controlled coccoon, where they receive a dose of anesthetic to render them unconscious. A machine intelligence then has a greatly enhanced ability to rapidly interface with the subject.

From first Integration, the MI begins to train itself to communicate on a near-synaptic level, presenting the flood of information a machine mind can naturally process in a virtual space that feels to the human like standing at a vantage point on the top of their vessel. For the few who proved able to tolerate the procedure – typically people with cognitive variations like autism and ADHD – this allowed them incredibly fast reaction times and precise control of objects. The concept of the Jagdkontrol was soon born.

INSURGENCE TRAINING NOTES ON PHYSICS AND SPACE COMBAT

Inertia

Unlike on Earth, where the ever-present force of gravity pulls everything towards the planet's core, in space this is absent, which makes maneuvering between places very non-intuitive from a terrestrial frame of reference. Inertia, the tendency of an object in motion or at rest to maintain that state absent intervention by an outside force, must be constantly managed in order to move and fight.

Spaceships move by ejecting mass in some direction, producing a reciprocal force that pushes the vessel in the opposite direction. Large quantities of mass ejected at high velocities can move even massive space ships – or alter the orbit of space habitats. However, to *stop* movement in that same direction then requires an equal and opposite force. You can't rely on gravity or friction to stop you moving, force has to match force. Because space ships can move in any direction so long as they aren't too close to the strong pull of gravity, this makes maneuvering complex.

For the crew of a ship, inertia has another important consequence. The human body can only survive a certain amount of change in speed over a fixed period of time without suffering severe internal injuries. If a spaceship applies too much thrust at once, in any direction, organs can rupture with quickly fatal consequences.

As a result, the limitations on a vessel's the ability to travel and maneuver are heavily determined by the presence of biological passengers. In theory, a ship constantly accelerating such that occupants feel like they are standing still on Earth could reach substantial fractions of the speed of life in several decades of travel, and allow a person to cross much of the solar system in one lifetime. But to actually *visit* a place requires application of equal and opposite force over the same amount of time it took to speed up, complicating this method of interstellar travel considerably. The same limits hold for stellar travel and combat. Whatever direction you are heading, you will continue to go unless you pay the energy cost.

Spaceship Design And Tactical Implications

All spacecraft are comprised of five main elements: powerplant, engines, shields, structure, crew. Most look something like an apartment building soaring through space, functionally divided into sections with surfaces organized for ease of access and safety more than aesthetics. Civilian vessels vary widely by type, size usually reflecting their role, but typically visible at long distances.

Military vessels, on the other hand, seek to avoid detection as long as possible. As a result, they shroud their core with a shell of electromagnetic panels that deflect or absorb most light striking them. This gives them a distinctly angular appearance, like an arrowhead. In combat, most warships seek to align their front or side towards an opponent to minimize the chances of detection by presenting the smallest possible profile.

In the vastness of open space, the only limit on detecting a target at any distance is the amount of electromagnetic energy – light, thermal, radio, so on – moving between it and the hunting vessel. When a wave strikes a solid surface, in most cases it is either absorbed or reflected away. The direction it goes depends mostly on the angle of the surface it hits. Detectors operate by absorbing reflected light, but need *enough* of it from a given source to distinguish the light being reflected off a starship from the light coming off the stars all around. As a result, it is always best to present a sharply pointed angle to an opponent, because this will reduce the amount of the sun's light bouncing from you to them, making it harder to detect you at all.

The other ship sections are straightforward: a fusion reactor provides power for the shield matrix, engines, and crew, the internal structure is designed to maximize internal space and resist collapsing during an attack. Weapons ports in warships allow particle beams to project through the exterior and electromagnetic shell, and docking for crewed vessels is usually located at the center section or sections, which spin to simulate gravity. Under their EM-shell, warships look very much the same as their predecessors did on Earth – utilitarian and functional. Even their size is entirely dependent on mission, with larger ships equipped with more powerful fusion reactors naturally better able to win a fight.

From the Insurgence Council,
A Report to all members of the Fourth Rising.
October 31, 2146

Greetings everyone,

We of the Insurgence Council wish to thank you for another year of incredible effort.

A great day is coming, friends, for us and all who suffer

across Inner Sol!

But we must never underestimate the magnitude of the challenge ahead, nor the capabilities of our foes. In that spirit, we wish you to commit to memory this year's updated estimates of the Navy's current strength.

For victory and freedom!

Signed,

Kojiki

Kalevala

Vedas

Representing the Insurgence Council

TGA Navy Estimated Organization for 2147
For All Insurgence Eyes

Aside from a network of bases spanning the solar system, a nearly-impregnable security perimeter around Earth and Moon, and the effective fortresses guarding the inner edges of the Belt at Point Aleph and Point Zero, the Navy possesses an arsenal of warships:

8 Dreadnoughts, named for iconic weapons like *Battleaxe* and *T'ang*, massive and peerless warships that serve as the center of powerful battle groups named for their flagship. Each is commanded by an Admiral of high esteem, and considered impossible to destroy.

16 Carriers, motherships for squadrons of crewed combat spacecraft and remotely-piloted drones. Often operate alongside with a pair of destroyers on deep space patrol. Named for famous aircraft carriers from Earth history, like *Enterprise* and *Shokaku*.

32 Cruisers, warships of substantial power, often deployed with a pair of destroyers in hunter groups to chase down threats. All carry spare crew for destroyers,

newer cruisers may carry drones. Named for water bodies on Earth, like *Bering Sea* or *Pacific*.

64 Destroyers, smaller warships that operate in pairs as adjuncts to larger, better equipped vessels. Newer models are more powerful and survivable than older cruisers. Named for famous Earth battles like *Waterloo*, *Sedan*, or *Okinawa*.

The Navy also maintains an arsenal of semi-intelligent networked mines, mobile fusion reactors with a particle beam and small engines allowing them to move towards and swarm targets.

Often seen attached to Navy vessels and warships are remotely-piloted drone carriers, which are often used to fill gaps in coverage left by Navy commitments. As of 2147, it is becoming clear that drone vessels are part of a broader TGA effort to move beyond its reliance on the Navy, which is growing in power and importance on Earth.

To oppose this force, the Insurgence now fields thirteen Raiders across three different generations, five to six of them perpetually roving through Inner Sol harrying the Toffs as they can. The introduction of the Jagdkontrols over the past decade has added a new dimension to Insurgence capabilities, with two dozen now in the arsenal.

APPENDIX C-1

Missoula Regiment Smart Book: 2041 Edition

MISSOULA REGIMENT DOCTRINE BRIEF

by Sandra Chavez, formerly Master Sergeant,
United States Army, 2012-2029

War is a contest between forces competing for control of vital resources.

The fundamental objective of a war is physical mastery of the landscape – whatever form it takes – sufficient to guarantee this control.

To achieve this objective, some group must organize and equip itself with sufficient capabilities – power – to *at least* prevent any other group from winning a contest for control.

Warfare in human terms is the physical expression of this contest, and is driven by iterated choices made by each group to escalate or de-escalate the intensity of the contest over time. In most forms of warfare – sports, business, politics, and so on – the contest is embedded within a larger set of social rules that constrain the behavior of the players. In violent wars, ranging in scope from struggles between rival street gangs to an apocalyptic encounter between superpowers armed with nuclear weapons, these social rules are discarded, usually resulting in loss of life and property that have compounding and rippling effects

The ideal war is concluded quickly and without violence.

Violence is inherently escalatory, unleashes powerful feedback loops that tend to reproduce themselves. This is why it is vitally important to take every opportunity to minimize the incidence of violence in a conflict. Similarly, the ideal war is always quick, as all warfare imposes rapidly-escalating costs on all sides *and bystanders* that quickly outweigh any benefits anyone can expect to gain as conflict continues.

Therefore, the goal must always be to conduct warfare at all levels and in all forms with a perpetual conscious effort to minimize the harm inherent in the enterprise, remembering that war itself is actually a recurring aberration of nature, a condition brought about by an inability on the part of the players interacting across the landscape to establish and maintain structures capable of preventing direct competition. In nature, most organisms do everything they can to *avoid* unneeded conflict, especially violent conflict. Even the fiercest predators usually strike from ambush or work in teams for a reason: because violence is dangerous, risky, and too often mutually fatal.

Further adding to the irrationality of direct conflict: to fight requires energy. Yet energy is a fundamentally scarce, valuable resource, and wasting it on inconclusive conflict – and in the end, most wars end ambiguously on some level, hence their tendency to re-start over and over again – is deeply disadvantageous to the survival of all involved. This is why most organisms exist in niches, points in the ecosystem where they avoid direct competition, and typically enter conflict only during moments of resource scarcity, real or perceived.

But fight humans do, and so shall, until the end of days. Because humans are able to perceive the *possibility* of resource scarcity, and routinely act on that expectation. Some, perceiving scarcity for whatever reason, will tend to act in ways that eventually make it come about, a condition less often found in nature, where most organisms do not act strategically to the same degree as humans.

For those who by accident or choice end up caught in the sort of warfare our species habitually engages in, two impulses always govern their actions: the mission, and survival.

For most fighters, warriors, soldiers, comrades, or whatever else you want to call someone whose business is organized violence, the mission is largely an external factor imposed by circumstance. You will eventually be forced to move to a place and maintain control of it, while preventing any rival groups from accomplishing the same thing.

The means by which you accomplish a given mission will vary according to the landscape you fight on, the resources available to you, and those in the hands of your opponent. But what is common throughout all battlefields is the *absolute* requirement that you and other members of your group survive to fight in the next stage of the mission, whatever and wherever that may be. Casualties represent a loss of capability, and in the long term loss of capability leads to death for the entire organism. As a result, the requirements of the mission must *always* be balanced against the need for survival, as in the end the latter will most always predominate, so long as war-fighters remain human.

This mode of thinking may be unfamiliar and strange, if you come to the Missoula Regiment from a long career in a traditional state military. In those organizations, the lawful orders you receive from your chain of command are all that matters – accounting for your survival is the largely the responsibility of those senior to you, and you are expected to comply.

But we follow the essential principles of inner leadership, mission command, and decentralized execution. These have been proven in conflict after conflict to generate the greatest successes at the operational level, which in the long term translates to better personnel survival and battlefield achievement when compared to traditional orders-based systems.

Missoula Regiment personnel are expected to understand the full scope of any operation they participate in, be able to radically adapt to changes in circumstance, and always contribute to the best of their ability, whatever their individual situation, towards achieving the common objective. The reason why we give you these armored and computerized bugsuits with almost the same level of network access as Command has in its cozy bunker under Malmstrom is so that no matter the situation, you and whoever you are working with can adapt as the situation allows and keep contributing to the fight – and survive on the wicked-wild dangerous modern battlefield.

Let me say it one more time, loud and clear: survival will be your primary concern once the bullets start flying. Forget any of that BS Hollywood or Bollywood or Netflix International taught you about bravery and standing alone in the open, shooting back at a horde of enemies – ain't like that, Bobby Lee! You don't give a damn about killing the enemy or winning glory once the bullets fly and shells fall, you focus on surviving, knowing that only by staying alive can you keep helping the people fighting alongside you to stay alive too. That's been the law of violent conflict since the dawn of time – if you are alive, you can still win – in this case, accomplish the mission.

On the battlefield, there are some basic rules of thumb to remember to maximize your chances of *not* dying – at least not dying stupidly. Call 'em the Sandra Chavez Laws of Battlefield Survival, if you like.

Rule 1: What can see you, *can* kill you – always stick to cover.

Rule 2: If you've been spotted or take a shot, you are out of cover – move!

Rule 3: When out of cover, two things save you: speed and

lots of suppressing fire.

Rule 4: Ammunition is a finite resource – get to new cover as quickly as possible.

Rule 5: What *can't* see you, *can* sometimes still kill you – choose **good** cover.

Rule 6: A radio link to firepower delivered from a safe distance is the deadliest weapon.

Rule 7: If you broadcast on the radio enough, the bad guys *will* find you.

Rule 8: Whenever you know where your opponent will be, set traps

Rule 9: Remember that the *ambush* is the essence of all effective warfare.

Rule 10: Never forget that armor is only insurance – taking a hit always sucks!

Naturally I could give you a whole lot more, but these are basically the Ten Commandments of the Missoula Regiment that drive each of us forward in our daily battles – if I gotta keep the list short enough for all the new boots to remember!

And these ten, you *will* remember. Your daily physical training from here on out will involve several hours of practicing these principles against drones whose job it is to build precisely the right kind of reflexes to guarantee you won't die on us too easily. :)

Bottom line: the battlefield is a wicked dangerous place, kids. Our methods here in Yellowstone may be harsh, but as an old drill sergeant I once knew used to say: "I only sleep well at night if I know I've made damn sure it's your own dumb fault if you get yourself killed."

Another, speaking of his time in Iraq, said: "We killed a lot of people, and I hope nobody who didn't deserve it.

Take both thoughts with you, recruits, as you get started in this wild and ancient profession.

ON LEADERSHIP

by Sandra Chavez

A note on how the Missoula Regiment views the age-old question of leadership on the battlefield:

Leadership is a function, performing an important – but limited – role in coordinating operations. It is a skill like any other, developed through experience... and failure.

In any collective action, when people from different backgrounds must work together, the best outcomes are achieved when each individual is an equal party to the process, a specialist in some area vital to accomplishing the overall objective. Each contributes their knowledge and skills to the best of their ability, and together everyone's work advances the mission. The whole community benefits, each individual more than they would have acting alone – this is the basic socio-ecological law of Mutual Aid that underpins all society.

Humans, however, tend to make this kind of non-hierarchical – anarchistic – organization difficult. Training, developing a set of common values, and experience will overcome the initial barriers, but like anything it takes time, energy, and self-discipline. There will always be those who habitually fail to give their maximum effort, and over time natural shifts in the internal metabolism of any human group inadvertently embed someone's shortcomings into another person's daily activity as unnecessary work.

Once routinely performing under a set of effective basic

rules, however, a group can generally self-manage for long periods of time and effectively operate via consensus – provided adequate resources are always allocated sufficient to maintain operations. Still, people being people, especially in times of crisis it will often prove less than easy to achieve a consensus in a group.

In these circumstances, an individual expressly delegated the responsibility to act as a deciding – even overriding – vote is necessary to avoid the fatal peril of organizational paralysis. The leader, once determining by an agreed-upon process that debate is no longer timely or helpful, can invoke Command privilege to select the best possible option from those available and terminate fruitless debate.

This strictly limited definition encourages the concept of inner leadership we prize in the Missoula Regiment, balanced by the capability of senior leaders to enforce unity in the cases where circumstances demand it. Formal leadership is a designated role earned through proven ability and assigned as needed, but absence of it is no excuse for inaction or internal conflict. Every individual may be called to lead depending on circumstances, and is expected to be ready to if need arises. In the Missoula Regiment, action taken in the sincere and reasonably belief it advances the mission is never punished, as every individual's own perception of the situation at hand is valuable, and crucial opportunities on a given battlefield are so often fleeting.

However, the title 'Six' is always reserved to the individual in a team who has been given the solemn task of coordinating group efforts towards completion of the assigned mission, and who must decide when to invoke Command privilege. Your Six will always be one of the most experienced members of the Missoula Regiment – someone who knows the business and knows how to keep you alive. As leaders of Combat Teams, they have primary responsibility for deciding where their team will move and communicating their actions to other units in the area, as well as making sure each team is supplied and secure.

But like anyone else in this business, sixes get killed to. And then someone else has got to be ready to step up, make hard choices, and make sure they bring everybody they can back to camp alive.

In this business, you never wake up knowing for certain whether this will be the day you are asked to lead.

ON DECENTRALIZED EXECUTION

by Lt. Colonel (ret) Elijah Jackson III, United States Army 2006-2030

The degree of lethal threat faced by the individual fighter on the battlefield has increased exponentially over the past century. Where once the firepower necessary to defeat an opposing force of similar size could only be mustered by ordered ranks of musket-armed men closely controlled by an officer, now a single individual can order a strike that will obliterate everything within a kilometer of the point of impact.

At the same time, the ability to detect enemies and communicate with allies – again formerly requiring large numbers of personnel working in close coordination – has also proliferated widely. The intersection of these two fundamental parameters, together largely responsible for controlling the pace and intensity of violent conflict, has produced a situation where large numbers of military personnel massed together is now a significant liability.

It is important to remember that the basic rules of battlefield survival apply – each at their own level – to individuals, teams, detachments, and even entire armies and nations. Cover is essential to avoid rapid destruction, and cover is a scarce resource, use of which generally requires dispersion across the landscape. Universal communications and precision firepower have created a situation where a single fire team of four individuals can establish a fighting position capable of inflicting sudden and catastrophic damage on a far larger force.

Many world military organizations continue to attempt to impose traditional styles of strict, close hierarchical command and control on their personnel, employing vast and complex communications networks to ensure efficient operations. However, experience has shown that the proliferation of relatively inexpensive electromagnetic jamming equipment leads to constant disruption within these networks. Information updates can come in bursts, but effective direct command and control over subordinate units requires continuous communication.

Hierarchical organization is now highly dangerous, as virtually all of military history clearly demonstrates that contingency and accident play a major role in the outcome of engagements. The most effective war-fighting groups on battlefields throughout history tend to be those that can rapidly and decisively seize fleeting opportunities that appear in the course of any major battle. Especially in a technological era where movement is rapid and firepower is precise and lethal, where cover is life, rapid adaptation to local circumstances is paramount for both survival and combat effectiveness.

The reason the Missoula Regiment embraces the Doctrine we do is that the combination of inner leadership, mission command, and decentralized execution enable small, powerful formations on the battlefield to engage in constant creative action to shape the landscape around them. Individuals perform a particular role alongside members of their team, which is assigned an area of responsibility, resources, and a viable mission, itself part of a larger operation. Guided by the senior personnel in the teams, the individuals work together to solve whatever problems stand in the way of completing the mission.

To the degree possible, every individual and team is given access to as much information as needed to know what units are adjacent to them or available for support and resources – supplies, personnel, firepower – sufficient to accomplish the mission and survive. When part or all of normal communications fail, they work directly with the units around them to get the job done. Leadership is executed as needed to swiftly resolve disputed and maintain productive action, as well as to decide when a new or altered mission becomes paramount.

This degree of decentralized execution, drawn from lessons learned over decades of counterinsurgency operations, has proven effective at maintaining economy of force and a high success rate. It relies utterly on training to keep personnel in sync, as well as a significant degree of flexibility in planning operations. However, it also allows for maximum adaptability and casualty mitigation over traditional methods. By pushing as much information, firepower and execution authority down to personnel tremendous information redundancy is generated that renders a combat formation more resistant to enemy attack.

Further, and perhaps most importantly of all, this aspect of Missoula Regiment Doctrine ensures that in engagements it reacts swiftly to take advantage of any weakness presented by an opponent. It enables personnel on the front lines to actively shape their own fate, bringing firepower to bear when and where it will do the most damage at the least cost to them.

On the modern battlefield, this is how you win.

MISSOULA REGIMENT ORGANIZATION BRIEF

by Sandra Chavez & Elijah Jackson

The Missoula Regiment is comprised of three co-equal parts: the combat Detachments stationed in Yellowstone, Glacier, and Great Falls; the Missoula Air Wing headquartered at Malmstrom; Missoula Regiment Command, which coordinates continental logistics, information sharing, diplomatic outreach, strategic planning – all the stuff that keeps the people in combat fed and armed. In situations where senior members of the three components have a dispute, the parent company, Syn Security Solutions, can offer guidance – but we've never had that problem.

The three Detachments of the Missoula Regiment all have a common organizational structure. A headquarters troop coordinates drone logistics, field repairs, personnel, secure communications, and other administrative support for three Battle Groups – combat units with a full range of capabilities rendering them capable of standing against any threat the modern battlefield can throw at them. Each Battle Group (BG) contains eight Combat Teams (CTs), most with six vehicles split into three two-vehicle Sections. Flexible and modular by design, the organization of a Battle Group down to the composition of individual CTs can vary depending on terrain and mission, but the default structure is fixed like so:

Lancer Battle Group, focused on offensive operations, containing:

2x Armor Teams, 12 tanks

2x Infantry Teams, 12 infantry fighting vehicles (IFVs) + 72 dismounts

2x Fires Teams, 8-12 mobile howitzers + 4-8 support vehicles

1x Defense Team, 4-6 mobile missile systems + 2-4 support vehicles

1x Engineer Team, 6 combat engineering vehicles, 2 equipped for heavy fire support

Guards Battle Group, focused on mobile defense, containing:

1x Armor Team, 6 tanks

3x Infantry Teams, 18 IFVs + 108 dismounts

1x Fires Team, 4-6 mobile howitzers + 2-4 support vehicles

2x Defense Teams, 8-12 mobile missile systems + 4-6 support vehicles

1x Engineer Team, 6 combat engineering vehicles, 2 equipped for heavy fire support

Scout Battle Group, focused on active reconnaissance and rapid response, containing:

1x Armor Team, 6 tanks

1x Infantry Teams, 6 IFVs + 36 dismounts

3x Scout Teams, 18 Wheeled IFVs + 72 dismounts

1x Fires Team, 4-6 mobile howitzers + 2-4 support vehicles

1x Engineer Team, 6 combat engineering vehicles, 2 equipped for heavy fire support

1x Defense Team, 4-6 mobile missile systems + 2-4 support vehicles

Sufficient reserve vehicles are kept in the inventory so that all CTs in the Scout Battle Group can be outfitted either with wheeled or tracked combat vehicles as required. Typically, the fires, infantry, and armor teams fight in tracked vehicles to serve as the groups' heavy punch, while the scouts, engineers, and defense teams operate in the faster Strykers.

Each of the six different CTs represents the six major combat specialties in the Missoula Regiment – armor, infantry, scout, fires, engineers, and defense – and is encouraged to maintain a distinct professional identity while remembering that each team and specialty is merely a different kind of organism, uniquely capable in some respects yet terribly vulnerable in others. Only through cooperation at the most fundamental level can any organism survive long on the harsh landscape of the modern battlefield.

That being said, each team focuses on an aspect of the battlefield requiring a distinct set of tools to guarantee they can do their job under fire – physical, chemical or radiological. You'll eventually become familiar with them all and have a chance to choose your own, once you earn the trust of your comrades-in-arms in your first assignments.

Armor Combat Teams employ Leopard 3 main battle tanks, armed with 130mm cannons able to send a dart of super-dense tungsten across four kilometers, plus two remote-control machine guns good against infantry and unarmored targets, in addition to smoke grenade launchers and an active protection system capable of shooting down incoming anti-tank guided missiles (ATGMs). All four crew members work in an armored hull compartment, controlling the turret systems remotely with all ammunition stored away from the crew. There is space in the rear compartment for two additional personnel, either armed fighters or wounded needing evacuation.

Infantry Combat Teams use Puma 2 infantry fighting vehicles, armed with a rapid-firing 40mm autocannon with armor piercing and high-explosive shells good out to a couple kilometers, plus Spike anti-tank missiles capable of striking tanks and low-flying helicopters eight kilometers away. The Puma carries six infantry dismounts in full bug-suit in the rear compartment, each team packing either a machine gun, automatic grenade launcher, or missile system – Spikes for tanks, Stingers for aircraft. Infantry sometimes instead use wheeled Strykers equipped with the same turret as mounted by the Puma, and in either case their vehicles are accompanied by two crewmembers who never leave it in battle, working in an armored cabin in the front hull.

Scout Combat Teams most often operate six Stryker wheeled armored fighting vehicles – though sometimes they mount up in Pumas – usually split between three Combat Strykers equipped with the same 40mm autocannon and Spike missiles on Pumas and three others equipped with surveillance gear and light weapons. These *Rista* Strykers have multispectral optical sensors on an extendable mast capable of detecting variation in visible, thermal, and ultraviolet light, and also come with augmented electronics packages that boost friendly signals and interfere with those of hostile forces in the area. Each Stryker holds four scout dismounts, who have access to the same weaponry as infantry teams but are focused on observation, reconaissance, and fire support. Also unlike infantry, scout teams in Strykers are able to deploy for up to a week to remote locations, and survive for three days on their own without resupply.

Fires Combat Teams are equipped with eight vehicles –

four, or in special cases, six Dragon mobile artillery systems, a rapid-firing 150mm howitzer able to precisely deliver high explosive and cluster shells to targets forty kilometers away – double that if using rocket-assisted shells. The teams also employ up to four artillery support vehicles, essentially the same chassis as used by the big guns but instead carrying extra ammunition and a pair of assistance drones to help move the explosives around without risking the gun crews in high threat situations. They are able to quickly set up, fire several salvos, then move to an alternate firing location to evade counterattack.

Engineer Combat Teams operate six Warlock combat engineering vehicles (CEV) in three different configurations. One section of two vehicles is equipped with a 240mm demolition cannon that can fire a thermobaric charge across four kilometers capable of quickly clearing minefields or hostile fortifications. Another section operates a Warlock lacking the cannon, instead deploying four all-purpose engineering drones able to assist in entrenching and fortification plus as two dismounts wearing exoskeletons that increase their strength and endurance. The final section is equipped with supplies, dismounts in exoskeletons, and a comprehensive electronic warfare suite of substantial power.

Defense Combat Teams deploy eight vehicles, four (rarely six) Puma or Stryker combat vehicles topped by a combined Air-Defense and Anti-Tank remote weapons station known as the Schuka. This system boasts radar, optical, and thermal targeting systems able to track objects as small as artillery shells, and can engage air or ground targets out to twenty kilometers with one of sixteen ready missiles. Two 40mm autocannons firing proximity-fused shells engage low-flying targets out to three kilometers, and these radar-controlled guns can even provide a partial flak umbrella effective for a brief duration against hostile artillery. In an emergency, all available missiles can be ripple-fired in laser-homing mode, each homing in on a target painted by a fighter closer to the fight.

Notes on Organization:

Commanders on-the-spot will alter this mix as required to complete the mission. For air assault missions scout, infantry, and engineer teams will fly in Stallion Heavy Lift helicopters and for light reconnaissance and patrolling they may ride in gun trucks with just enough armor to survive hits from machine gun bullets. Engineers sometimes swap out their heavier Warlocks for a pair of support vehicles that deploy a battery of remotely-controlled drone mortars. There are no limits to ingenuity on the battlefield!

Finally, in special circumstances anyone can request Commander's Intervention from the Detachment or Command level. Each Detachment is equipped with a battery of multiple launch rocket systems that can obliterate a square kilometer from a hundred klicks away. And Missoula Regiment Command in Great Falls can authorize the use of tactical ballistic missiles carrying massive thermobaric warheads anywhere in our theater of operations. Only a few dozen of those available, though, so we don't go calling down heavy fires for just anything!

When all three Battle Groups fight together, they typically field a combined force of 20 Leopard 3 tanks, 36 Puma 2 IFVs, 18 Stryker scout vehicles, 16 Dragon mobile guns and as many support vehicles, 6 Warlock CEVs with demolition guns and 12 more for engineering support, and 16 Schuka air-defense and anti-tank systems. This, of course, fails to count the many drones running supplies, boosting signals, and conducting surveillance as needed.

Missoula Air Wing

Focused on broad-spectrum control of friendly and adjacent airspace in support of the Missoula Regiment, the Missoula Air Wing operates one fixed-wing multirole squadron of 18 combat aircraft in three types, one fixed-wing close air support squadron with 18 aircraft in two types, one fixed-wing surveillance & control squadron with 8 aircraft, and two rotary wing squadrons each with 18 helicopters.

The Multirole Squadron operates three aircraft:

6 Shenyang-Sukhoi-HAL (SSH) **Super Flanker** – twin-seat multi-role combat aircraft derived from the Su-37 and incorporating the ground attack capabilities from the Su-34, both predecessors in the Flanker family. Radio Callsign: **Black Flight**. Call if you need a lot of heavy ordnance shot at something from a safe distance – ground or air.

6 Eurodefense Consortium **Typhoon 2** – highly-maneuverable single-seat interceptor with networked electronics and advanced optical sensors to improve covert detection and tracking of stealthy objects. Radio Callsign: **Storm Flight**. Call if you detect Spooks – stealthy aircraft – in your area of responsibility.

6 Mitsubishi-Boeing **Foxcat** – twin seat heavy air superiority fighter with a potent combat load boasting long-range air-to-air missiles, companion drones, extreme endurance, and capable of top speeds approaching mach 3. Carries radar and electronic warfare systems second only to an AWACS. Radio Callsign: **Reaper Flight**. Call if you need all flying hostiles in the nearby sky to crash and burn.

The Close Support Squadron flies two aircraft:

6x Saab-Mikoyan **Gryphon**, twin-engine and twin-seat variant of the Saab Gripen, incredibly nimble, ruggedized to operate from austere airstrips and optimized to operate at low altitude, performing suppression of enemy air defense (SEAD), electronic warfare, and battlefield surveillance services. Callsign: **Grizzly Flight**. Call if you need a radar destroyed or some communications and electronic warfare backup.

12x Republic Revival **Mjolnir** – twin seat heavy close air support (CAS) fighter derived from the A-10 Thunderbolt, mounting a heavy rotary cannon and weapons racks with a customizable mix of up to two dozen Brimstone air-to-ground missiles or cluster bombs. Each usually flies with a pair of armed companion drones that double as shooters and SAM decoys. Callsign: **Hammer Flight**. Call if you have a need for extreme destruction across a given piece of dirt.

Palantir Squadron is a 24/7 airborne command post operating:

4x Airbus Airborne Warning and Control System (AWACS), converted airliner with a massive multi-band radar able to detect and help track even stealthy aircraft anywhere in Montana, Wyoming, and Idaho.

4x SSH Joint Surveillance Target Attack Radar System (JSTARS), converted airliner with a ground-scanning radar system able to pick out the movement of individual vehicles in rugged terrain within several hundred kilometers.

16x Companion drones, up to 8 deployed simultaneously, serving as mid-range air defense and missile decoys in case a threat makes it beyond the combat air patrols conducted by Reaper, Storm, and Black Flights.

The five fixed-wing combat flights and Palantir utilize techniques derived from the long experience of the Israeli Air Force to ensure rapid aircraft turnaround post-mission and fresh pilots. The Missoula Air Wing perpetually keeps a third of each combat flight and a quarter of Palantir airborne, available to respond to requests for support or air cover on the ground anywhere in the Missoula Regiment's operational area. Mid-air refueling capabilities are provided by a squadron of tanker drones, while cargo flights in and out of Malmstrom are handled by Amazon Logistics Air.

Rotary Attack Squadron

Operates 18x Mil-Sikorsky **Havoc** gunships split into three 6-ship flights, one normally assigned to each Detachment. Essentially a flying tank, carries Spike missile 4-packs or rocket pods on four wing pylons plus two short-range air-to-air missiles for self-defense. Also equipped with a 40mm autocannon and a passenger compartment able to (barely) accommodate a team of four scouts in full bugsuit.

Heavy Lift Squadron

Operates 18x Mil-Sikorsky **Stallion** heavy lift helicopters, each capable of transporting two infantry teams with all their gear and an armored truck in a sling-load several hundred kilometers. Can instead transport equipment, supplies, or casualties in virtually any environment provided the airspace is secure. Tasked according to need – the Stallions are always busy, so if you think you'll need one – plan in advance!

APPENDIX C-2

Missoula Regiment Smart Book: Historical Background

MISSOULA REGIMENT SMART BOOK: FOREWORD

Listen up, recruits: it's a weird world out there and you all come from different places, so we're making you read this brief on the geopolitical state of things in the former United States to make sure you're up to speed with the meta of it all. And yes, Bob, it *is* brief – trust me, I could assign you a textbook or twenty, but who has time for that? :)

And yes, Virginia, this stuff *does* matter. Big movements far away produce little movements close by, that *will* impact your ability to survive. Don't underestimate them. Try to predict them, as you would any other threat.

Study it, know it, and you had better believe there'll be a quiz in your future!

Anybody who fails, gets a day-long workout on the drone range, where one of us will make *sure* you learn your lessons in the harshest possible way ;)

- S. Chavez & E. Jackson

HOW WE GOT
TO TODAY

(the short version)

by Sandra Chavez

2020 – A new era in international relations dawns, as renewed great power competition pits the United States, European Union, China, Russia, and India and their allies against one another in a race to secure access to vital resources and trade routes amid global economic uncertainty. A chaotic presidential election in the United States leads to widespread protests, some descending into violence, and a result rejected by the losing side as illegitimate.

2023 – During a period of fast-rising tensions, China launches a sudden assault on Vietnamese, Malaysian, and Philippine military bases around the South China Sea. The United States, exhausted after two decades of bloody and fruitless conflicts in the Middle East, fails to respond, shattering global perceptions of America as the sole superpower. The global economy reels under the uncertainty produced by the crisis, stabilizing once major combat operations cease and a peace deal favorable to China is mediated by Russia and the European Union.

2024 – The United States Presidential Election sees three different candidates winning Electoral College Votes, none accumulating enough to win outright. The House of Representatives chooses from the top three candidates according to Constitutional procedure and selects a moderate centrist compromise choice, however after almost a decade of virulent partisanship the image of the federal government has been severely damaged in the eyes of state governors and the general public.

2025 – A skirmish along the Pakistan-India border escalates into a full-scale conflict. India soon takes the upper hand and invades central Pakistan, prompting Pakistani use of six nuclear weapons against Indian forces on Pakistani soil – India responds in kind. A temporary truce is brokered by the EU and Japan but Pakistan splinters, descending into civil war. An international coalition intervenes to prevent the country's nuclear arsenal from falling into the hands of warlords. Thousands of American soldiers enter the Middle East for what proves to be the last time.

2028 – In August, the next United States Presidential Election heats up and the incumbent is attending her party's nominating convention in Miami, Florida, when six nuclear weapons detonate across the United States: Miami is hit as are Newark, New Jersey and Los Angeles, California, killing the President, Vice President, key members of Congress and several senior Cabinet members. Treasury Secretary Carolyn Pilsudska is sworn in as President later that day. Nuclear retaliation is soon unleashed against military targets in North Korea and Iran on the assumption they must have been involved.

2029 – China presents incontrovertible evidence that the August Attacks were launched by forces *within* the United States. A succession crisis splits the United States government as former Secretary of Defense Tyler Young, now Vice President, alleges that Pilsudska is foreign-born and so not eligible for the Presidency, later going further to proclaim she is part of a Chinese plot to destroy America. Seizing control of the White House and other key government buildings in D.C. using a loyal military unit, Young and his appointed Vice President Chris Hollahan order a pre-emptive attack on China's nuclear forces, provoking a blockade of the U.S. bases on Okinawa.

In the Battle of Okinawa, the United States suffers a surprising defeat, shocking the already divided nation. When Pilsudska, taking refuge on a military base near Seattle, learns Young and Hollahan intend to escalate the conflict to the nuclear level, she openly proclaims them traitors and demands the military obey her lawful orders. The Second American Civil War begins as forces obeying Young and Hollahan's orders seize control of California to prevent it and its major military bases from coming under Pilsudska's control.

After a fierce struggle in Northern California and Oregon, culminating in the mutual use demonstrative use of nuclear weapons, Russia intervenes out of fear the Young-Hollahan government intends to attack Russia next. The Russian Strategic Forces uses half of its nuclear arsenal to destroy the American ICBM fields around F.E. Warren and Minot Air Force Bases, nuclear missiles thought to pose the primary threat to Russia's national survival.

The Collapse of the United States unleashes a wave of geopolitical turmoil across the globe. Russia's military overthrows the aging and increasingly paranoid regime of Vladimir Putin out of fear he will spark a total nuclear conflagration and Russia splinters. In the United States, the Pentagon allows Pilsudska to fly to Washington D.C.; there the entire United States Secret Service unites to physically escort her into the White House, where Young and Hollahan are arrested after a brief last stand by a small group of loyalists.

2031 – 39 State legislatures ratify a Constitutional Amendment authorizing states or groups of states to demand complete devolution of all Constitutional powers held by the federal government in D.C., becoming effectively independent. The breakup of the United States becomes formal when first California, then Cascadia – the states of Oregon, and Washington – demand autonomy. Texas follows soon after, and almost overnight a united federal government ceases to exist. In the Old South, violence erupts between ethnic communities, triggering a wave of migration from the states of Georgia, Alabama, and North Carolina, which all subsequently divide.

2032 – The Great Lakes Confederation, headquartered in Chicago, marks the first establishment of a formal hybrid government blending corporate and state structures at the most fundamental levels in society. The formation of the GLC is intended to help mitigate the persistent socio-ecological crisis produced by the Russian nuclear strikes, which scattered fallout across the Midwest. Tens of millions of people are forced to leave contaminated zones, and agriculture is now almost impossible across what was once called the Corn Belt.

2033 – India collapses into a bloody civil war fought between hardline Hindu nationalists and a broad alliance of moderate groups alongside leftists aiming to restore India's secular state. Individual states gain access to portions of India's nuclear arsenal, resulting in ten nuclear detonations on military bases – two adjacent to cities housing millions of people – as several states try to disarm rivals. In the United States, what is left of the federal government under Pilsudska places all military assets under devolved regional control, allowing the government of the region soon known as Kingsland to put a stop to the violence tearing apart neighborhoods in the suburbs of Atlanta and Birmingham.

2034 – The Nagasaki Protocols are proclaimed, an international agreement setting limits on the use of nuclear weapons on the battlefield. Legal nuclear use requires at least one minute of warning broadcast across multiple open channels to give bystanders time to take cover, and ground-bursts are banned entirely as they cause substantially more fallout than airbursts. Offenders face swift international retribution. Violence finally abates along the tense new Appalachia-Kingsland border.

2035 – The Texas Republic annexes the eastern halves of the states of New Mexico and Colorado against the will of local residents, months after democratically absorbing Louisiana, Arkansas, Oklahoma, and Kansas. Texas becomes the leading military power in North America, and it becomes clear both the Texans and Great Lakes Confederation hope to gain control of the surviving old American ICBM field in Great Falls, Montana. A mostly non-violent resistance in Colorado harasses Texan forces driving through their state.

2036 – Syn Security receives a United Nations contract to establish neutral control over the Great Falls area, where a field of some 150 Minuteman III ICBMs equipped with a total of 450 nuclear warheads remain in silos under the hills, coveted as a symbol of pre-Collapse American power. A group called the Missoula Regiment is formed, a private military organization staffed with veterans of the many wars of the past forty years who enter the region with a powerful military force and begin building bases in former U.S. national parks like Yellowstone and Glacier.

2037 – After eight years of highly secretive investigations involving an unprecedented level of cooperation between national intelligence and police organizations from across the world, the Interpol Special Report into the August Attacks of 2029 is released. It details a small but effective conspiracy led by Chris Hollahan, a senior general in the United States Air Force, to install a christian fascist government in D.C. aiming to replace the Constitution with a twisted, cult-like take on Biblical Law.

2038 – Hopes rise that the chaos of the last twenty years has finally drawn to a close, as conflicts in former Russia, India, and the United States subside, leaving the European Union and China as the dominant economic and political powers. The global economy experiences a much-needed upturn, buoyed by the development of a range of new pharmaceuticals capable of treating many of the worst ailments afflicting humanity, raising labor productivity globally and slashing healthcare costs.

2040   The Great Lakes Confederation and Texas Republic clash in eastern Wyoming, sending shockwaves through the still-fragile world system. The outcome is inconclusive, but has ripple effects across the Inter-mountain West. The Deserets, long uncomfortable with the presence of foreign forces occupying territory it sees as naturally its own, begin to move forces into Idaho's Snake River Valley, ambushing Missoula Regiment supply convoys and setting the stage for a new round of conflict in North America.

THE AUGUST ATTACKS AND THE COLLAPSE OF AMERICA

by Elijah Jackson

In the August Attacks of 2028, The President, Speaker of the House, and nearly a hundred members of Congress are instantly killed in Miami. The Secretary of State, preparing to give a speech at a university in Newark, is also killed. The Vice President and President pro Tempore of the Senate are lost in Los Angeles along with ten other Senators and senior members of the House of Representatives while attending a fundraiser. The Secretary of the Treasury, Carolyn Pilsudska, then in San Francisco on official business, is sworn in as President two hours later.

Though the identity of the perpetrator of the August Attacks remains unknown in the immediate aftermath, three days later two United States Navy ballistic missile submarines each unleash sixty nuclear warheads on the nations of North Korea and Iran. While targeting only military facilities and nuclear weapons infrastructure, the revenge strikes – intended to 'restore deterrence' – kill tens of thousands of civilians and shatter both countries.

2029, January – Shocking the world, China announces that a team from a submarine operating off the coast of California during the August Attacks has recovered a nearly intact *American* nuclear-tipped stealth cruise missile that crashed north of San Francisco. While observing a United States Navy exercise, the submarine witnessed the ship fire a series of surface-to-air missiles at unknown targets. One was caught on periscope video being struck then falling to the sea, while another – apparently damaged – turned away from a course that would have taken it over San Francisco in a few more seconds before crashing close to the shore in a remote area to the north of Marin.

The United States government fiercely denies the allegations, yet an internal investigation by the Pilsudska government discovers that communications made by a Navy destroyer and Hawkeye radar surveillance aircraft operating off San Francisco the night of the August Attacks were removed from official records by an unknown party in the days after without explanation.

2029, February – Allegations surface claiming President Pilsudska was actually born in Poland to parents who illegally immigrated to the United States in 1985. Though they stem from unnamed sources and are easily disproved, a number of media outlets amplify the claims and attract enough attention an investigation is launched by Congress, still reeling from the loss of a quarter of its members.

2029, March – In the Coup of the Ides, former Secretary of Defense and now Vice President Tyler Young declare to a shocked public that Pilsudska is part of a Chinese plot, and the August Attacks were the first phase of a Chinese plot to destroy America. Several Cabinet members led by the new Secretary of Defense and former head of Global Strike Command Chris Hollahan, appointed by Pilsudska at Young's request, back his claim, stating that Pilsudska is not the legitimate President and falsely claiming the 25th Amendment of the Constitution enables the Cabinet to remove the President from office in the event of an emergency of this nature. Unsure if Pilsudska is safe in D.C., the Secret Service puts her on Air Force One and flies to Seattle, where a personal contact in her detail is able to convince the commander of Joint Base Lewis-McChord, General Trish Castro, to refuse any orders from the usurper Young government in D.C.

That same night, two dozen American stealth bombers backed by a hundred remotely-piloted companion drones depart from bases in Diego Garcia and Guam, flying long circuitous paths along international borders before unleashing a barrage of hundreds of low-flying cruise missiles against China's nuclear forces. Many are shot down, but enough strike their targets to render the majority of the Chinese land-based nuclear arsenal – stored in caverns dug deep into the mountains – inaccessible and so useless for some months.

The following morning Young addresses the American people, claiming that China was preparing an imminent attack against the United States and its allies in East Asia. In the same speech, he names Hollahan his Vice President and warned China that any attempt to carry out its planned aggression will be met with the full force of the United States military.

China's response is to state that the United States military presence in East Asia will no longer be tolerated, as it demonstrably poses a direct threat to China's national security. China gives the United States two weeks to organize a withdrawal from bases in South Korea and Okinawa, or else they will be placed under blockade. The next day, four United States Navy carrier battle groups receive orders to deploy from their bases in Seattle and San Diego. The Chinese People's Liberation Army Navy puts every ship available on patrol in the East and South China seas.

Amid the confusion in D.C., many senior military commanders remain uncertain who is legally in charge. Most choose to operate in a state of limbo in absence of explicit orders from their superior, leading to a situation where any activity normally organized by the Pentagon must be directly overseen by Young-Hollahan loyalists. Pilsudska and the Secret Service are able to use Young-Hollahan's preoccupation with directing the fight with China to issue counter-orders to any military unit willing to listen. Also, they reach out to governors across the United States demanding they put pressure on D.C. for a resolution to the competing claims.

April, 2029 – China and the United States clash in the Battle of Okinawa, with the naval battle sometimes referred to as the Second Battle of the Philippine Sea. Four U.S. Navy carrier battle groups strung out on a four hundred mile line move toward Okinawa to guarantee supply lines to the tens of thousands of marines and other military personnel stationed there. Three PLAN carrier battle groups stay close to the Chinese coast, protected by a dozen nuclear submarines and land-based aircraft blasting the waves around them with active sonar to deter American submarine attack, while the flattops act as semi-mobile airfields close to the battle area, their presence luring the Americans on.

The American admirals, closely overseen from Washington D.C. by Young and Hollahan, move the armada west in preparation for launching strikes on any formation of ships or jets close enough to pose a threat, before initiating a planned massive air attack against Chinese military facilities along the coast in conjunction with the U.S. Air Force. But China, anticipating this, had left some two dozen extremely quiet diesel-electric submarines scattered across the Philippine Sea in the week before the battle, simply floating along with the current in the hopes some would drift undetected close to the American carriers.

When a Chinese submarine narrowly evades an American destroyer and comes close enough to the aircraft carrier USS *Carl Vinson* to launch a torpedo attack, it also deploys a communications buoy that broadcasts the carrier's exact location. Receiving the report of a firm fix on the location of one of the PLAN's primary targets, the order is sent authorizing a general attack.

All Chinese submarines receive an order transmitted on ultra-low frequencies capable of penetrating the ocean surface: float a buoy, transmit sensor data, and attack as you can. The seas soon come alive with torpedoes and sea-skimming cruise missiles, and hundreds of miles away some two hundred anti-ship ballistic missiles equipped with cluster warheads and missile defense decoys are elevated skyward from the back of heavy trucks, then sent soaring skyward.

High above, three satellites covertly maintained in orbit activate, deploying powerful radars that bathe the American fleet in signals, sending precise mid-course correction data to the inbound missiles. They are quickly identified, and the newer *Ford*-class carriers *Enterprise* and *John F. Kennedy* activate powerful electromagnetic jammers and fire lasers at the satellites in hopes of damaging any vulnerable parts or at least blinding optical and thermal cameras.

Anti-missile missiles are fired in a steady stream by the four cruisers and sixteen destroyers of the carrier battle groups, but the number of inbound threats only grows. A hundred Chinese bombers appear on radar, accompanied by as many smaller fighter-bombers, together packing more than a thousand supersonic, sea-skimming anti-ship cruise missiles. U.S. Navy and Air Force fighters and drones waiting for this moment pounce and shoot down many of the Chinese bombers, but they prove to be too few, too many are held at bay by a veritable swarm of hundreds of escorting Chinese Flanker fighters.

Crews aboard the twenty escorts surrounding the four carriers work frantically to vector their Standard surface-to-air missiles into the much bigger anti-ship missiles streaking in at several times the speed of sound – some, in the case of the hundred hypersonic weapons deployed, an order of magnitude faster. Almost two thousand missiles streak into the sky, but in this wicked game of numbers and statistics played out across thousands of square miles the Americans come off worse.

Carl Vinson, struck by two torpedoes at the outset and of all the carriers the most precisely located, takes hits from half a dozen arrow-shaped kinetic energy penetrators falling from low orbit with the force of a powerful bomb. The massive vessel hosting a crew of nearly six thousand burns from end to end, and is eventually beached on a deserted island while the three thousand survivors await rescue. Three of her escorts, two destroyers and a cruiser, are also sunk with heavy loss of life.

Kennedy suffers a minor hit from a penetrator, and two cruise missiles also leak through the ship's defenses, damaging the flight deck and forward hangar and limiting her ability to operate aircraft. One her battle group's destroyers is sunk, a cruiser damaged and forced to break off. *Enterprise* and her escorts escape without damage and *Stennis* suffers only minor damage with one escorting destroyer sunk by a submarine that didn't live long enough to celebrate the victory. Though China suffers hundreds of aircraft lost and a dozen submarines sunk, the American fleet is forced to retreat, *Enterprise* and *Stennis* covering *Kennedy* as they move out of range of further attack, magazines depleted and shock at the defeat spreading among their crews – and families back home.

2029, May – Pilsudska publicly denounces Young and Hollahan as traitors, accusing them of acting to undermine the Constitution and engaging in open warfare without Congressional Approval. She openly calls for the military to refuse orders from the White House and demands formal Congressional investigations overseen by the Supreme Court.

Young, prodded by Hollahan, ignores Pilsudska and instead gives China an ultimatum – the blockade around Okinawa must be lifted, or the United States will use nuclear weapons against Chinese military bases in the region. To demonstrate the administration's resolve, all American nuclear forces are placed on the highest alert status, and the ballistic missile submarines docked in Seattle are ordered to sea.

Pilsudska responds by ordering a blockade of Puget Sound, demanding that all military units in the region report directly to her immediately and acknowledge the illegal nature of the orders from D.C. She travels with the governor of Washington and mayor of Seattle to a Coast Guard vessel that takes up a blockading position near the Trident base housing the Pacific Fleet's nuclear-armed ballistic missile submarines, and orders a Stryker brigade from the 2nd Infantry Division to join another from the Washington-Oregon National Guard in taking control of the facility. After a standoff lasting six hours, all military forces in the Seattle region comply with Pilsudska's demand. The governors of both Oregon and Washington declare their support for Pilsudska and ask that other states follow suit in recognizing her as the legitimate President of the United States.

2029, June – A brigade from the 82nd Airborne Division parachutes into California's Central Valley, securing Sacramento International Airport ahead of a flight of C-17 transports who quickly deliver both their heavy equipment and another full infantry brigade. The city of Sacramento is surrounded and government offices seized, as Young goes on the air to tell Americans that California's governor was preparing to secede – an allegation challenged online by the governor even as troops close in.

Battalions of United States Marines move south from Camp Pendleton to secure the Naval bases in and around San Diego, and the members of 11th Armored Cavalry Regiment, deployed to Los Angeles to aid recovery after the August Attacks, are ordered to disarm their counterparts from the California National Guard. California's governor orders all units of the CNG to move north to Oregon to join Pilsudska's forces.

The commander of the 82nd – tasked with controlling Interstate 5, the main artery linking California to the Pacific Northwest – does not stop hundreds of national guard vehicles from simply driving around barricades set up on the freeway. Later investigations reveal him to be deeply uncomfortable with his orders and eager to avoid any conflict between personnel "wearing the same flag patch" on their uniform. Young and Hollahan, closely monitoring the situation from D.C., discover this and order the 82nd to redeploy, relieving him of command.

Advance units from the 82nd shadow the national guard battalions as they move steadily north in good order, but remain aloof despite orders from D.C. to intercept and engage. This changes outside the town of Redding, California, where a local militia espousing support for Young and Hollahan fires on soldiers of the 82nd approaching a key bridge, drunkenly mistaking them for California national guard units. Monitoring the situation remotely from D.C. and ordering action before the full details are known, Young and Hollahan demand an artillery bombardment followed by a quick assault to secure the crossings over the Sacramento before they can possibly be fortified.

Carnage is the result, as 155mm shells and heavy rockets crash down onto a civilian area. The rearmost battalion of the national guard, witnessing this ruthless attack, turns to engage the lead elements of the 82nd Airborne resulting in the first direct combat engagement between American soldiers since the Civil War. The national guard battalion is forced to retreat, and is subjected to a series of drone strikes that only abate when a squadron of F-15s from the Oregon Air National Guard acting under Pilsudska's orders arrives and shoots down eleven drones. In another air strike, the Interstate bridge over Shasta Lake is destroyed by an air strike delivered by U.S. Navy F-18s operating out of Seattle as Pilsudska's forces to slow the the Young-Hollahan forces' push north.

Declaring a state of martial law across the country, Young and Hollahan – still hindered by the Pentagon's deliberate attempts to slow the pace of escalation – place loyal generals in control of additional Army brigades and Air Force squadrons. Many are shipped west to staging areas in Northern California and Utah in preparation for an attack into Oregon. Pilsudska is able to win the unrestricted support of the many Navy, Army, and Air Force units in Seattle, placing them temporarily under formal National Guard control and forming a defense plan in conjunction with a team of senior military officers.

2029, July – In the Battle of the Willamette, three brigades following Young and Hollahan's orders, one each from the 3rd, 82nd, and 101st Infantry divisions, converge on central Oregon and attempt to force their way through the Cascade and Klamath mountains into the Willamette Valley.

Their goal is to push north on Interstate 5 all the way to Seattle to place Pilsudska under arrest, with orders to destroy any forces that resist. Facing the three brigades, one of them equipped with a hundred tanks, is a light Stryker brigade mostly staffed by volunteers from the 2nd Infantry Division and a mixed light-heavy National Guard brigade assembled from the most battle-ready units of the California, Oregon, and Washington National Guard. In a tough week-long campaign waged in the sky and on land, Pilsudska's forces successfully hold most of the passes while trapping the better part of the heavy brigade from 3ID in the southern part of the Willamette Valley until they run out of supplies and agree to stand down.

2029, August – Unprepared to occupy territory so far from their home bases on the east coast, with states like Texas and Colorado now refusing to allow military material to move west through their states and the occupation forces in California besieged by massive protests, the Young-Hollahan forces in Oregon retreat south to their main base in Sacramento, shadowed by 2nd Infantry Division. Ordered to turn and engage their pursuers in the ruins of Redding, inept management by Hollahan – who has slowly usurped Young – results in a crushing defeat for the survivors. In desperation, Hollahan persuades Young to agree to a demonstration nuclear strike in the skies over Redding, firing an ICBM from North Dakota carrying three warheads. Pilsudska responds in kind, detonating a warhead fired from a submarine near Seattle high over Sacramento International Airport.

This stage of the conflict is brought to a close by a sudden Russian intervention. In the paranoia of old age and likely suffering from dementia, Russian leader-for-life Vladimir Putin decides the Young-Hollahan regime will likely lash out at Russia if it wins, and orders the Russian Strategic Forces to launch a massive pre-emptive nuclear strike against the Intercontinental Ballistic Missile (ICBM) silos near F.E. Warren and Minot Air Force Bases, both mistakenly thought to be firmly under Young-Hollahan control. The attacks are preceded by a Russian message broadcast directly to Americans' phones warning them to take shelter, explaining this drastic action as an attempt to prevent a total global catastrophe. This message, accompanied by a formal letter brought directly to the White House by the Russian ambassador as the bombs fall, states that if America's response takes the form of a proportional strike against Russia's own (now mostly empty) ICBM silos, Russia's confidence in deterrence will be restored and the conflict needs not escalate further.

Over the space of an hour more than six hundred nuclear warheads detonate on the ground in North Dakota, Wyoming, Nebraska, and Colorado, quickly spreading radioactive fallout over much of the Midwest. Pilsudska orders a limited counterstrike from submarines operating in the Pacific, returning the favor by contaminating much of Siberia.

2029, September – Both the Young-Hollahan regime in D.C. and Putin's government in Russia collapse in coups organized by local military commanders fearful their leaders are about to destroy the world. The military establishments in America, Russia, and China subsequently agree to an immediate cessation of all military actions in order to avert a nuclear holocaust. Russia fragments and descends into civil war, and in the United States Hollahan and Young – still in military custody in the White House – continue to argue their legitimacy and foment protests among their supporters. States begin to take sides in the dispute, and the military quietly begins allowing personnel to transfer to bases in regions of their choice to avoid open conflict in the ranks.

December 2029 – as the terrible year of America's Collapse draws to a close, investigations into the August Attacks reveal that General Chris Hollahan was responsible for orchestrating the nuclear decapitation of his own government. A secret religious extremist and cunning sociopath capable of masking his a secret ambition over a long career, his efforts culminated in an appointment to head Global Strike Command – responsible for the Air Force's portion of the US nuclear arsenal – in 2027. It would eventually be discovered that during Hollahan's tenure as a teacher at the Air Force Academy he recruited a small group students animated by a common, cult-like vision of their future as heads of a fascist Christian theocracy, and safeguarded their careers.

Taking advantage of his position, Hollahan moved four stealth bomber aircrew and a computer programmer with experience working on the digital systems connecting America's nuclear arsenal to its lawful chain of commander into position. He exploited a new system, instituted in 2022 out of fears China or Russia might be capable of launching a debilitating decapitation strike against D.C., whereby control of nuclear weapons could be rapidly devolved to local military commanders in a severe crisis. He used a military exercise as cover to place eight nuclear-tipped, stealthy cruise missiles on two B-2 stealth bombers late one August night, then destroy all evidence of the relevant false orders.

The crew of the bombers apparently manipulated their onboard global positioning systems to spoof missiles into believing they were heading for targets in China. By a fluke, two were shot down by a Navy destroyer participating in an unscheduled air defense exercise near San Francisco Bay, resulting in Carolyn Pilsudska, Treasury Secretary, surviving the attack. Hollahan's goal was to install a useful idiot – Young – as President while holding power behind the scenes. His trial in 2030 was a media sensation, compounded by the fact he was successfully able to commit suicide in his cell in Guantanamo Bay soon after the guilty verdict was reached. An international investigation into the entire affair was launched, taking many years to complete.

Widespread public anger at the federal government over the entire disaster is unleashed in waves of protests and a flurry of legislation aiming to give states more power to pursue their own agendas floods Congress despite Pilsudska's restoration. By 2031, a Constitutional Amendment has been passed by 39 State legislatures allowing groups of states to demand their own devolved federal government. The United States is effectively dissolved, though a few factions even a decade later continue to publicly claim formal reunification as their goal.

KNOW YOUR NEIGHBORS

by S. Chavez

There are many powers in this weird wooly world, some better, some worse, others we haven't yet been tested against. To understand why we're fighting out here, you have to understand the neighborhood.

Texas Republic

One of the first, and certainly the largest and most economically powerful of the states to become independent, Texas has been been a relative bastion of stability in Post-America. More than ten million refugees from the heavy fall-out zone in the upper midwest moved to the Texas Republic, soon joined by a steady flow of out-migrants from the violence-wracked American South. Expanding peacefully to incorporate, Oklahoma, Arkansas, and Louisiana and later forcibly seizing the eastern halves of Colorado and New Mexico, Texas is now the most populous and wealthiest American successor state, with growing ambition to match. Fighting a brief conflict with the Great Lakes Confederation in Wyoming and South Dakota in 2040, it is unclear who the Texans presently loathe more – the Lakers, or the many foreigners staffing the UN-backed Missoula Regiment that occupied former U.S. territory.

Inheriting both the 1st Cavalry Division at Fort Hood and the 1st Armor Division at Fort Bliss, the Texas Republic has now expanded to take control of the equipment and facilities of the 1st Infantry Division at Fort Riley in Kansas as well as those of the 4th Infantry Division at Fort Carson in Colorado. With by far the most powerful army in North America and a strong Air Force boasting updated F-15s backed by a few stealthy F-35s, Texas' additional strategic assets include its population, political cohesion, and hydrocarbon economy, which has only grown more valuable in recent years.

Cascadia

In 2031, with the passing of the Autonomy Amendment, Oregon, and Washington made the request for devolved federal powers almost at once. Idaho almost joined however, an immediate divide formed between Cascadians living east and west of the Cascade Mountains that split the region and derailed attempts to establish a unified government. The west, as well as the urban enclaves of Spokane and Boise, came together to send representatives to the new Cascadian government in Portland, while in the east individual counties only participate on a case-by-case basis and remain nearly autonomous otherwise. Now stable and prosperous, with British Columbia formally associating in 2033 and even Alaska considering accession, talks are again underway to bring all counties between the Pacific and the northern Rockies fully into the government.

Cascadia has long been a quiet supporter of the Missoula Regiment, and this is unlikely to change. Half of all Missoula Regiment supplies pass through the Cascadian ports of Seattle and Portland, and in 2041 the Cascadian government began allowing international security recruitment for the first time, taking advantage of the deep reservoir of military talent seeking work as Cascadia began disbanding former US assets. Along with California the worst-affected by the organized combat of the Collapse, Cascadia has like its southern neighbor mostly embraced an identity as an independent Pacific nation with a primary focus on trade and political engagement with East Asia, working closely with allies on both sides of the Pacific.

Deseret Nation

With both California and Cascadia to the west moving quickly towards effective independence, Utah and Nevada began jointly exploring the potential for a compact of states in the Inter-Mountain West, running from Mexico to Canada along the spine of the Rocky Mountains. However in Utah a movement seeking to establish a religious democracy named Deseret grew more quickly in popularity and spread across the region, resulting in counties from southern Idaho, western Colorado, and eastern Nevada effectively merging with Utah to form the Deseret Nation. Offering itself as a conservative alternative to California and Cascadia, both dominated by coastal cities along the Interstate 5 corridor, counties in eastern Oregon, Washington, Idaho and California are still swept up in a debate over which Post-American nation to belong to.

Cascadian support for the Missoula Regiment is largely due to the probability that the Deseret Nation will seek to expand into Idaho and eastern Oregon after seizing control of much of Arizona and the portion of New Mexico not claimed by Texas in 2038. The Deserets are adamantly opposed to the presence of United Nations-backed forces in North America, and are violently hostile towards the Missoula Regiment. Backed covertly by the Texas Republic, the Deseret military is numerically large, however, its leadership lacks proficiency and much of the equipment – even the wing of F-35s at Luke Air Force Base – is badly dated or improperly maintained.

Great Lakes Confederation

The fallout from the Russian nuclear intervention of 2029 fundamentally altered the landscape of the upper Midwest.

Tens of millions were forced to move east or south out of the radiation exclusion zone that covered much of the corn belt. In the cities of the rust belt, radioactive contamination of a lesser magnitude still forced the affected state governors to declare a public emergency, either confining residents or evacuating them until decontamination efforts could remove the fallout. With the effective collapse of the United States federal government, states were forced to fend for themselves, receiving as much aid from Canada and Europe as Washington D.C.

In Chicago a hybrid public-private governing agency was born, rapidly mobilizing and organizing scarce resources to re-establish supply chains across the region and establish a common set of procedures for handling the millions of people displaced from the Dakotas, Iowa, Nebraska, Missouri, and Minnesota. As the years passed, the Chicago Governing Authority gained more power, bringing North Minnesota, Wisconsin, Illinois, Missouri, Indiana, Ohio, Michigan, and West Pennslvania into a single American successor state. The GLC, often referred to as Lakers, quickly adopted an aggressive posture towards neighboring regions, expanding through the fallout zone to establish a large military complex in the Black Hills of South Dakota.

The GLC is openly hostile to the Missoula Regiment, but has not directly engaged it so far, preferring to work through proxies who have been detected in towns all over Montana. There is growing evidence of diplomatic arrangements concluded with both the Texas Republic and Deseret Nation, which if true would pose a major escalation in the risk posed to the Missoula Regiment's presence. The GLC is on the forefront of developments in drone technology, controlling most combat units remotely, with the controllers generally being contractors as opposed to professional soldiers.

Appalachia

In the wake of the Collapse, tensions between ethnic

communities throughout the American South escalated into open violence between rival militia groups. The Autonomy Amendment sparked two diametrically opposed movements in the region – one seeking a revival of the old Confederacy, including restricted civil rights for minority groups, another rooted in the old state governments and major cities that aim to keep as much of the United States as possible under a single governing entity in Washington D.C. The states of North Carolina, Georgia, and Alabama collapse completely, the upland counties close to the Appalachians breaking off and demanding autonomy. Their vision of Appalachia proved popular in the states of Tennessee, West Virginia, and much of southern and western Virginia, and in 2040 the Maryland panhandle also joined with the tacit support of the Great Lakes Confederation.

Appalachia poses no military threat to the Missoula Regiment, despite inheriting the 101st Airborne Division stationed in Kentucky, the unit lacks its heavy equipment. For political purposes, one of its three brigades is on constant deployment along the Appalachia-Kingsland border, closely monitored by a contingent of international observers. Sporadic skirmishes continue along the new border, and Appalachia periodically threatens conflict against their more populous and wealthy neighbor as a means of deflecting domestic popular opinion away from a series of political scandals.

Kingsland

The suburbs of cities like Atlanta and Birmingham saw terrible violence as the region fragmented, and the unrest spread until it also became disturbingly common across the rural south. In 2033, at the instigation of the rump federal government in Washington D.C., United States Army personnel stationed in North Carolina, South Carolina, Georgia, Florida, Alabama, and Mississippi were placed under the command of a select group of National Guard commanders.

Order was quickly restored, but a popular vote results in many counties going to Appalachia and those between the great inland cities of the American South and the Atlantic and Gulf coasts becoming Kingsland.

Kingsland is officially neutral with respect to the Missoula Regiment's presence and poses no direct military threat. Inheriting brigades from the 3rd Infantry Division in Georgia and a small nuclear arsenal it soon passed to international control for disposal, Kingsland has largely demobilized and focused on infrastructure and domestic investments since 2033. Outbreaks of violence in communities along the new border are sadly frequent, though fatalities are thankfully now relatively uncommon.

California

Already effectively a semi-independent nation by 2029 thanks to its vibrant economy, increasing federal incoherence, and longstanding close ties to the Asia-Pacific, the shock of fifteen-kiloton nuclear weapons detonating in Hollywood and the Port of Los Angeles – followed months later by the outbreak of war with China in the Pacific *and* an invasion by the usurper Young-Hollahan regime – led to California leading the Autonomy Movement along with Cascadia. Recovery has not been easy, as internal political divisions only grew stronger in the wake of the fighting that passed across the state's northern counties, terminating in the brief and thankfully low-casualty nuclear exchange. By agreement, several northern counties formally joined Cascadia, and the urban parts of Nevada plus part of Arizona merged with California to avoid falling under Deseret control. Buoyed by steady immigration and a free trade agreement with Cascadia, Alaska, and Hawai'i, by 2040 many politicians are openly discussing a political union termed the Pacific Federation.

California maintains the world's third most powerful

Navy and an Air Force to match, its military capabilities bolstered by the presence of many major defense contractors and, of course, its wealthy population. Closely aligned with Cascadia, Australia, and Japan, California has shown no interest in continental affairs, save establishing a secure border with the expansionist Deserets to the east. Talks are underway to establish a NATO-like entity to match China's power in the Pacific, uniting the military establishments of the member nations, presently set to include California, Cascadia, Alaska, Hawai'i, the former U.S. Pacific Territories, Japan, Australia, New Zealand, and Singapore.

Atlantic Union

By 2035, the United States had mostly fragmented. In the Northeast, the states centered on the long and densely populated Boston-Washington corridor maintained the position that the Union itself had never dissolved, and hoped to roll back the Autonomy Amendment, restoring power in Washington D.C. In the meantime, this wealthy region of ninety million maintains close ties with the European Union, even briefly considering a transatlantic political union with England after the dissolution of the United Kingdom and the entry of independent Scotland, Wales, and Northern Ireland into the European Union. However, with England's own reaccession in 2040 and the growing unity within the EU, this now appears unlikely.

While technologically sophisticated and affiliated with the European Union Military, which replaced NATO in 2030, the Atlantic Union poses no direct threat to the Missoula Regiment. By tacit agreement with California and Cascadia, the Atlantic Union focuses its international efforts solely on managing the threats posed by the successor states of former Russia, several of which possess nuclear weapons.

First Nations

The Russian-American nuclear exchange of 2029 deeply

affected the First Nations of North America. With heavy radioactive fallout from three hundred nuclear ground-bursts around Minot coming down across tribal lands in the Dakotas and beyond, entire peoples were once again forced to leave their lands. Many were taken in by the Wind River Nation, an association of First Nation groups in Wyoming that was able to secure substantial international funding allowing it to build a network of sustainable infrastructure capable of permanently housing tens of thousands of refugees. Seeing substantial success, Wind River Nation now leads an international effort to help economically stabilize Montana, Idaho, and (they hope) one day the Dakotas.

The First Nations possess no official military force, but are known to have equipped their defense agency with high-grade weaponry to deal with the threat of bandits and outlaws that are only now, after a decade and substantial support from the Missoula Regiment, receding as a threat. Tacitly allied with the Missoula Regiment in Montana and Wyoming, along with Cascadia and Canada the First Nations represent the organization's primary allies in the region.

APPENDIX D

Notes on the German Resistance

Contrary to popular belief, active resistance to the National Socialist (Nazi) regime in Germany from 1933-1945 never ceased despite nationwide repression by the Gestapo and the routine imprisoning of political dissidents.

The Nazis never won a majority in a free and fair election, and were only able to worm their way into power by taking advantage of weaknesses in the German constitution of what historians term the Weimar era. They were aided by sharp divisions on the left that prevented the powerful social democratic party, the SDP, from offering enough of a challenge at the polls. They also scored the tacit support of the industrial right, which feared both socialism and communism and wanted a strong national state to keep both at bat.

The Nazi regime, which consolidated formal power in 1934 with the death of President Hindenburg, began immediate propaganda campaigns that portrayed the left as betraying Germany to communism – characterized as "Jewish" by Nazi racial ideology. Public opponents, intellectuals, and other vulnerable leaders were placed in the first concentration camps of many and far worse to come.

Resistance by individuals and small groups continued throughout the Nazi era, 1933 all the way up until its end in 1945. Many young people were deeply cynical about regime propaganda and some rebelled against forced inclusion in the Nazi Youth during the '30s and 40's. Jews who could fled the country, taking some of Germany's most brilliant minds – people like Einstein – with them, crippling German science.

But as the Nazi grip on power tightened with time, most organized resistance was eventually snuffed out. Subsequent elections saw almost all parties banned, and a total lockdown on political expression.

Organized resistance mostly took place within the fading political establishment during the 1930s and this became doubly true once the war began in 1939. Many conservative as well as liberal Germans in the business and military communities were privately appalled by Hitler and the violence of the Nazis, but did not speak out, most seeing no option but to do their duty.

In 1938 Hitler's intention to initiate a war with one of Germany's neighbors became absolutely clear to senior members of the German Army, who were appalled. At first, Hitler focused on uniting parts of the German-speaking world like Saarland, the Rhineland and Austria under one banner, wrapping his actions in German nationalism – something the professional officer corps much approved of. But when his sights turned to Czechoslovakia, with Britain, France, and the Soviet Union all openly considering the possibility of a war with Germany, members of the German Army were terrified.

They were all veterans of the First World War, and though many were themselves anti-Semitic and deeply racist, they knew another war like the last would destroy the Germany the knew forever. Germany in 1938 was far, far weaker than it had been in 1918, and had no real allies thanks to Hitler's extremism. Even Mussolini in Italy, the only major semi-ally, felt deeply threatened by Germany's apparent appetite for expansion.

A coup attempt started to come together during the Munich Crisis in 1938 as war fears grew. With Hitler demanding an assault straight into prepared defenses and France potentially attacking from the west to aid their ally, plans were laid for rebellion.

Then Britain under Chamberlain signed the Munich Agreement, proclaiming he had secured 'peace in our time.' Czechoslovakia was abandoned by its allies, forced to give up its entire defensive line – something German planners assumed could hold against their attack for many months. Hitler came back to Berlin proclaiming victory, and the coup lost all chance of support.

A year later, Germany invaded the rest of Czechoslovakia anyway, absorbing the Czech western half including Prague as the province of Bohemia-Moravia and setting up a puppet government in the autonomous Slovakian portion. And Hitler turned his sights on Poland next – despite a guarantee by the United Kingdom and France they would intervene on Poland's behalf if war broke out. But after Munich, the Allies' credibility was shot, and Hitler believed they would back down.

Again German officers in desperation considered a coup, but the week before the invasion of Poland was set to begin the Soviets signed the Molotov-Ribbentrop Pact, a non-aggression agreement combined with a plan to divide Eastern Europe between the two Great Powers. Now Poland was vulnerable, set to be attacked on two fronts and though the German nation was incredibly gloomy at the news war had begun, the officers did their professional duty. The Polish campaign went reasonably well, concluding in a little more than a month leaving only a few tens of thousands of German dead – light in comparison to the trench warfare of the First World War. Hitler walked away with a grand victory as the French and British declared war, then failed to live up to their promise to launch an offensive against Germany's near-defenseless western front to save their last ally in Eastern Europe.

Coup talk began again when the very month after Poland was defeated, with winter fast approaching, Hitler ordered an *immediate* attack on France. Knowing this would be suicide after a campaign that had already revealed severe flaws with the newly-expanded *Wehrmacht,* the Nazi military, the generals again prepared to rebel – but were then successful in getting a brief delay in order to replenish badly depleted supplies of ammunition. Then another delay was won, and another – putting the attack off until the Spring of 1940.

The last hope until late in the war for a successful coup that stood any chance of winning the approval of the German people disappeared with the catastrophic Allied defeat in the Battle of France of 1940. The shock German win gave Hitler a triumph that seemed utterly miraculous to the Germans – in a matter of weeks the 'world's finest Army' had been completely shattered, and the collaborationist Vichy regime installed as German troops rolled into Paris. Against all odds and predictions, Germany was suddenly on top of Europe, avenging past defeats and shaping a new European order. Public dissent within Germany all but died, as propaganda proclaimed Hitler a military genius.

But Britain remained defiant, and the war ground on, bombs starting to fall across Germany's cities in defiance of Goering's pledges – a harbinger of far worse to come. Hitler gained ever more control of the German armed forces as the war went on, fancying himself a new Napoleon for approving risky plans his generals came up with in desperation at the odds they faced on the battlefield. But they knew the truth, and saw how dangerously over-stretched Germany would be when news came that Hitler planned to invade the Soviet Union next despite Britain's ongoing resistance. General Halder, Army chief of staff, wrote in his diary he was so depressed he carried a pistol in hopes he would have a chance to assassinate his *Fuhrer*. But he never made the attempt, and the first six weeks of the Barbarossa campaign was another wild success, and the world assumed Moscow would fall by Christmas.

But then Moscow didn't fall in the winter of 1941-1942, and the Soviet Union survived Germany's onslaught where no other power had been able to withstand it before. Germany's elite soldiers were all but consumed over the next year, driving to the edge of Asia in the Caucasus before suffering the bitter, bloody defeat at Stalingrad in early 1943 that destroyed Hitler's myth of invincibility once and for all.

This turn in the war revived hopes among the few remaining active members of the German Resistance – by this point mostly out-of-work generals and bureaucrats, plus Admiral Wilhelm Canaris and his semi-personal spy agency, the Abwehr. Military defeat had shocked public opinion, and the subsequent announcement that Germany was now for the first time to engage in Total War, mobilizing all social resources towards victory, brought a new set of rebels into play – as did growing awareness of the horrors of the Holocaust.

Claus von Stauffenberg, along with other veterans of Rommel's Afrika Korps, became disillusioned with Hitler's inept leadership after their defeat in Tunisia in 1943, recognizing Germany would lose the war. Joining the older generation of plotters, they started to learn the truth about the Holocaust and the magnitude of Hitler's growing insanity, which was badly impacting his own genocidal war effort. They began to plot attacks, learning from a spate of failed assassination attempts launched by a few individuals over the years – sometimes with small bombs, others with guns – that Hitler had already survived.

They quickly recognized that they couldn't simply assassinate Hitler and be done with it – one of his Nazi cronies like Himmler, who oversaw the Waffen SS, Gestapo secret police, and the Holocaust, or Goering, who despite a severe drug addiction was in charge of the Air Force and part of Hitler's inner circle, would take over power in Berlin and likely continue the war. The plotters realized they needed to take over control of the German government itself, announcing to the German people that Hitler was dead and the military was in control.

Operation Valkyrie was born from this concept. A bomb would be smuggled into Hitler's forward command post in Rastenburg Prussia by Stauffenberg. He would escape, and return to Berlin where other plotters would already be moving to seize important buildings and major Nazi figures. Senior officers stationed in Paris, Vienna, Prague, and elsewhere in the Nazi Empire would do the same in those districts, disarming the SS and putting each area under military control. The Allies in the west would then be contacted, and ceasefire terms sought that would allow Germany's entire military to make a stand against the Soviets in the east.

Most crucial to the plan, assuming Hitler actually died, was to swiftly secure the phone exchange in Rastenburg after the bombing. This would cut off most of the surviving Nazi leadership from their subordinates, allowing the regular Army to be sent orders transmitted through official channels and so taken as legal – to put Germany under military government like it had been in 1918.

It was a bold plan, and according to historian of the German Resistance Peter Hoffmann it stood a reasonable chance of success *if* Hitler was killed *and* the Rastenburg phone exchange was taken in time to prevent any Nazi officials from giving orders. It would only be a few hours before Hitler's SS guards would realize what had happened, hear news of the troop movements, and organize a counter-coup.

Sadly, Operation Valkyrie failed. The bomb was only partly armed by Stauffenberg, and an officer at the conference pushed the case containing the device behind a heavy table leg, accidentally shielding Hitler from fragments that would have otherwise killed him. Worse, the conference wasn't held in the usual concrete bunker, which would have ensured the contained shockwave from the blast alone would have killed everyone in the room.

By the time Stauffenberg reached the headquarters of the operation at the Bendlerblock in Berlin, things were already falling apart. Reports were spreading that Hitler had survived a bombing, and the Rastenburg telephone exchange had not been seized, the units assigned to the task unsure if it was safe to proceed. Several districts outside of Germany actually *had* fallen to local military commanders and the SS units there swiftly disarmed, taken totally by surprise – Himmler's Gestapo had missed the plot. But confusion set in at the Bendlerblock when a wavering general named Fromm contacted the SS to try and save himself, further confusing matters, and when Hitler was able to take to the radio that night to declare he had survived an assassination attempt, it was over.

The putsch that followed gave the Nazis total control over all aspects of the German state from July 20, 1944 to the end of the war. Anyone remotely suspected of associating with the Valkyrie plotters, including Stauffenberg and the popular Field Marshal Erwin Rommel, were caught up in the dragnet and lost their lives or were imprisoned in a concentration camp. And the war dragged on to it's miserable end in 1945, with Hitler's suicide and Germany's crushing total defeat and dismemberment. Millions of Germans lost their lives, tens of millions became refugees, exiled from their homes that now lay on the wrong side of the new Soviet-imposed borders in the east.

But despite the failure of officials, public resistance to the Nazis never stopped. Many Germans throughout the war sought to evade military service, some hiking through the woods and even attacking members of the Nazi Youth and SS. The White Rose Movement in Munich spread anti-war pamphlets trying to provoke the German people into rising up, at the cost of the lives of Sophie Scholl and the other members of the group. And the many captives Nazi Germany used for slave labor fought back as they could, sabotaging production lines and working as slowly as they could get away with. Some business leaders and diplomats took advantage of their position to get as many Jews, Roma, and other targeted peoples to safety.

The spirit of this civic resistance is commemorated annually in ceremonies held by the military of modern-day Germany, the *Bundeswehr* – people's force – at the Bendlerblock. Stauffenberg and other members of the resistance are considered to carry the true lineage of the German Armed forces from 1933 to 1945 not the Nazi-controlled Wehrmacht, and their ethic of principled rebellion is articulated in the explicit moral code of the Bundeswehr itself.